P9-DHC-226

WITHDRAWN

Cinnamon and Gunpowder

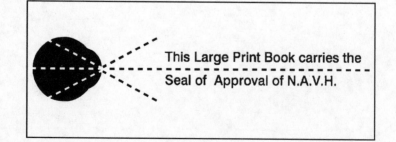

This Large Print Book carries the
Seal of Approval of N.A.V.H.

CINNAMON AND GUNPOWDER

ELI BROWN

THORNDIKE PRESS
A part of Gale, Cengage Learning

GALE
CENGAGE Learning®

Detroit • New York • San Francisco • New Haven, Conn • Waterville, Maine • London

GALE
CENGAGE Learning

LIBRARY OF CONGRESS CATALOGING-IN-PUBLICATION DATA

Brown, Eli, 1975–
  Cinnamon and gunpowder / by Eli Brown. — Large print edition.
    pages ; cm. — (Thorndike Press large print historical fiction)
  ISBN 978-1-4104-6316-6 (hardcover) — ISBN 1-4104-6316-8 (hardcover)
  1. Kidnapping—Fiction. 2. Women pirates—Fiction. 3. Large type books.
  I. Title.
PS3602.R697C56 2013b
  813'.6—dc23   2013024468

Published in 2013 by arrangement with Farrar, Straus and Giroux, LLC

Printed in the United States of America
1 2 3 4 5 6 7 17 16 15 14 13

FOR DAVON,
who picked me up and dusted me off

"I'd strike the sun if it insulted me."
— CAPTAIN AHAB,
Herman Melville, *Moby-Dick*

CONTENTS

1. Dinner Guests 13
   *In Which I Am Kidnapped by
   Pirates*

2. The *Flying Rose* 26
   *In Which I Am Bent to New
   Employment*

3. Use of a Spoon 41
   *In Which I Receive Valuable
   Advice from a Mysterious Friend
   and Witness an Execution*

4. Fiat Leaven 69
   *In Which I Make Contact with a
   Fellow Prisoner*

5. Jeroboam's Plan 96
   In Which I Vow to Stop Mabbot

6. Dining with the Devil 115
   In Which I Earn a Pillow

7. Fragile Vessel 141
   *In Which I Am Rescued by an
   Unlikely Ship*

9

8. The Dreamer 155
   *In Which I Am Entertained by
   the King of Thieves*

9. The *Patience* 176
   In Which Many Are Punished

10. Sauerkraut and Theater 202
    *In Which Cabbages and History
    Are Mistreated as We Cross
    the Equator*

11. One Woman's War 232
    In Which Mabbot Reveals Herself

12. The *Diastema*. 255
    *In Which We Are Bitten by the
    Fox*

13. *La Colette* 270
    *In Which Justice Catches Up
    with Us*

14. Etiquette for Close Combat . . . 281
    In Which I Lose Much

15. Dead Man's Stove 294
    *In Which We Lick Our Wounds
    and Joshua Tells His Story*

16. Teaching a Dog 319
    *In Which Mabbot Surprises Me
    and I Receive a Gift*

17. Sabotage. 339
    In Which We Visit a Witch

18. Lost Treasures 358
    In Which I Am Misunderstood

19. The Culinary Uses of a
    Cannonball 376
    In Which Trust Is Betrayed

20. Killing the Messenger 400
    In Which I See My Error

21. Wolves and Sheep 413
    In Which I Attempt a Final Escape

22. The Brass Fox Found 431
    In Which Mabbot's Hunt Ends

23. Broken Bread. 457
    In Which a Sacrifice Is Accepted

24. Gold for Cornmeal 468
    In Which I Discover the Saboteur

25. The Barbarian House. 494
    In Which the Sea Boils

26. The Last Supper 524
    In Which I Fight for Mabbot

    EPILOGUE 541
    ACKNOWLEDGMENTS 547

1
DINNER GUESTS
IN WHICH I AM KIDNAPPED BY PIRATES

Wednesday, August 18, 1819
This body is not brave. Bespeckled with blood, surrounded by enemies, and bound on a dark course whose ultimate destination I cannot fathom — I am not brave.

The nub of a candle casts quaking light on my damp chamber. I have been afforded a quill and a logbook only after insisting that measurement and notation are crucial to the task before me.

I have no intention of cooperating for long; indeed, I hope to have a plan of escape soon. Meanwhile, I am taking refuge in these blank pages, to make note of my captors' physiognomy and to list their atrocities that they might be brought properly to justice, but most of all to clear my head, for it is by God's mercy alone that I have not been driven mad by what I have seen and endured.

Sleep is impossible; the swells churn my

stomach, and my heart scrambles to free itself from my throat. My anxiety provokes a terrible need to relieve myself, but my chamber pot threatens to spill with every lurch of this damned craft. I use a soiled towel for my ablutions, the very towel that was on my person when I was cruelly kidnapped just days ago.

To see my employer, as true and honest a gentleman as England ever sired, so brutally murdered, without the opportunity to defend himself, by the very criminals he had striven so ardently to rid the world of, was a shock I can hardly bear. Even now my hand, which can lift a cauldron with ease, trembles at the memory.

But I must record while my recollections are fresh, for I cannot be sure that any of the other witnesses were spared. My own survival is due not to mercy but to the twisted whimsy of the beast they call Captain Mabbot.

It transpired thus.

I had accompanied Lord Ramsey, God rest his soul, to Eastbourne, the quaint seaside summer home of his friend and colleague Mr. Percy. There we rendezvoused with Lord Maraday, Mr. Kindell, and their wives. It was not a trivial trip, as the four men represented the most influential interests in the Pendleton Trading Company.

I had been in his lordship's employ for eight years, and it was his habit to bring me along on journeys, saying, as he did, "Why should I suffer the indignities of baser victuals in my autumn years when I have you?" Indeed, it had been my honor to meet and cook for gentlemen and ladies of the highest stature, and to have seen the finest estates of the countryside. My reputation grew in his service, and I have been toasted by generals and duchesses throughout England. Happily for me, his lordship rarely went overseas, and even on those occasions he left me in London, respecting my considerable aversion to the rolling of ships.

This particular trip had me at my most vigilant, not only due to the prominence of the guests but because the Percy seat was reportedly rustic, of unknown appointment, and sporting a historic oven without proper bellows or ventilation. Try as I did, I could not acquire reliable information as to the status of the pantry prior to arrival. For this reason I provisioned myself with a menagerie of ducks, quail, and a small but vociferous lamb, as well as boxed herbs and spices, columns of cheeses, and my best whisks and knives. Lord Ramsey teased that I had packed the entire kitchen. But I could see in his face satisfaction at my diligence. His faith in me was a poultice for my nerves. As usual, I had worried myself sleepless over the event. The modest size of the house prevented me from bringing my able assistants — a stroke of luck for them, as they are safe now in London. Rather, I relied wholly on the staff brought by the other guests.

Eastbourne was as lovely as I had heard, with foals cavorting in the pasture and the woods promising moss-cushioned idylls. The house itself commanded stunning views of the channel, an azure scarf embroidered with sails and triumphal clouds. As it happened, both pantry and scullery maids were more than adequate. While I always prefer my kitchen at his lordship's seat in London — every inch of which I have organized, from the height of the pastry table to the library of spices catalogued both by frequency of use and alphabetically — I nevertheless took pleasure in anointing a new kitchen with aromas.

With great energy I oversaw the unpacking of my provisions and set a scullery maid to heating the oven in preparation for a four-course meal. Despite my anxiety, I was looking forward to this short week away from the noise and bustle of London and had planned to take an early-morning stroll the following day to savor the wildflowers and sylvan air.

What ignorance. Even as Ramsey lifted his glass for a toast, unwelcome guests were moving through the garden.

Basil-beef broth had been served, with its rainbow sheen of delicate oils trembling on the surface and a flavor that turned the tongue into the very sunlit hill where the bulls snorted and swung their heavy heads. The broth was met with appreciation (the kitchen was close enough to the dining room, just a door away, that I could hear every chuckle and whisper of praise). I had just arranged the duck. The brick oven had surpassed my expectations; the cherry glaze flowed like molten bronze over the fowl and pooled in crucibles of grilled pear. The servants were carrying the platter to the table when a frightful noise at the front vestibule brought all levity to a halt.

I opened the kitchen door just far enough to poke my head into the dining area. The other staff crowded around me to see. We made a comical sight, no doubt, so many heads peering through one door like the finale of a puppet show.

From there we could see what was left of the entrance. A petard had left a smoking hole where the lock had been. A second later the door was kicked in by a mountain of a man I would come to know as Mr. Apples.

My shock at the sight of this breach cannot be expressed, and so I will content myself with descriptions of a visual nature.

Mr. Apples might have been drawn by a particularly violent child. His torso is massive, but his head is tiny and covered by a woolen hat with earflaps. His shoulders are easily four feet in span. His arms are those of a great ape's and end in hands large enough to hide a skillet.

He surveyed the room and, seeing no immediate resistance, stood aside to allow the others in. He was followed by not one but two short Chinamen in black silk, twins in face and dress; they entered with their hands clasped behind their backs, swords swinging from their hips. One of them wore his queue wrapped around his neck like a scarf. They took their positions flanking the hall.

The three made a curious group, the hulk of Mr. Apples and these two child-sized Orientals. If not for the mutilation of the door, I would have thought we were about to enjoy a mummer's theater.

Then entered a pillar of menace, a woman

in an olive long-coat. Her red hair hung loose over her shoulders. She sauntered to the middle of the room, her coat opening to reveal jade-handled pistols. Using a chair as a stepping stool, she walked upon the dining table to Lord Ramsey's plate and stood there looking down, as if she had just conquered Kilimanjaro. Her boots added inches to her already long frame. No one dared tell her, apparently, that tall women confuse the eye.

Even I, who know only what I read in the dailies, recognized her at once. There, not twenty feet from me, was the Shark of the Indian Ocean, Mad Hannah Mabbot, Back-from-the-Dead Red, who had been seen by a dozen credible witnesses to perish by gunshot and drowning, and yet had continued to haunt the Pendleton Trading Company routes, leaving the waters bloody in her wake.

Lord Ramsey leaped from his chair and fled toward the back steps (never had I seen him move with such urgency), but he was intercepted by one of the twins, who must have given him a blow, for he crumpled to the floor gasping. Mr. Percy, finally realizing his obligation to protect his guests, made a valiant attempt to retrieve an heirloom sword from the mantel, but the massive Mr.

Apples brought down his fist and ruined Mr. Percy's face as a child ruins a pie.

A terrible silence filled the house, interrupted only by the wet whimpering of Mr. Percy and the equine clopping of Mad Mabbot's boots as she descended and approached Lord Ramsey's supine figure. There, with pleasure plain on her face, Mabbot drew her pistols and leveled both barrels.

Posterity will reprimand me for not making an attempt to protect him, and well it should. Despite my girth, I am a sorry pugilist. As a child, I was bullied by children much smaller than myself. Mr. Percy, whose fate I had just witnessed, had fought against Napoleon's cavalry. I had no hope of faring any better. I should like to have a better excuse, but I was simply frozen under my white toque.

Mabbot was only paces from me, and I could hear as she spoke to Lord Ramsey in the cheery tone a milkmaid may use to soothe a cow.

"No, don't get up — we can't stay long. Once I learned you were in the neighborhood, I simply couldn't miss the opportunity to drop in and see you in person. Did you know your clever corsair is using red-hot cannonballs now? Those were a treat!

You can imagine the excitement."

Ramsey cleared his throat twice before speaking, and still his voice quavered as he said, "Mabbot . . . Hannah, let me propose that we —"

"But the world is glutted with your proposals," Mabbot interrupted. "Mr. Apples, would you like to hear a proposal from Ramsey?"

"Rather eat my trousers," the giant said from across the room.

"You haven't aged well," Mabbot said, lifting Ramsey's chin with the tip of her boot. "Are you really so surprised? Did you think I'd be content to be hunted the rest of my days and not find a way to return the favor?" Leaning close, she murmured, "But between you and me, it's going after the Brass Fox that really irks me. I can't let you win that race, can I?"

At this point Lord Ramsey said something more. I didn't hear it. Most likely he was taking the opportunity to mumble a prayer.

Mabbot bit her lip, frowned, and said, "Tell the devil to keep my tea hot. I'm running late." Then she fired point-blank, without mercy or provocation, into his defenseless body.

One of her guns did not go off, apparently, for as Ramsey writhed, she examined the trigger with irritation. She knocked the faulty flintlock with the butt of the other gun, aimed it again, and discharged it directly into his poor heart. He lay still at last.

Even as I write this, my body starts at the memory of that merciless retort, the smoke and spatter.

Satisfied, the red-haired rogue sat in Ramsey's seat at the table and forked a glistening cherry into her mouth while her thugs threw the other guests to the floor.

The desire to live moved me, and, remembering the small door beside the pantry I had seen the servants use, I made for my escape. I tumbled down dark steps into a subterranean brick tunnel, through which I groped as quickly as I could, sure it would lead to the staffs' quarters behind the house. When the tunnel branched, I veered left and came upon another set of steps and a door. I burst through, prepared to run, but I had misjudged the direction, for I found myself in the library with Mr. Apples's hand on my shoulder. He tossed me like a sack of laundry back into the dining room, where I was obliged to sit on the floor with the others. I took my position next to his lordship's body and held his still-warm hand while the fiends ransacked the house.

I confess that my mind was not prepared for these events. It failed under the pressure and became that of an idiot, lingering on the lace of the tablecloth and bringing to light the oldest and most obscure memories quite randomly: being taught to swim in the freezing lake behind the orphanage with the other boys by Father Keenly, who bade us fetch coins he threw into the water; kneading my first loaf of bread and wondering at the magic of its rising. Father Sonora's voice, so long ago I was sure I had lost it, now came back, as vividly as if he were just behind me, saying, "Hush, child, God despises whimpering."

Fear, for the moment, left me and was replaced with a readiness to meet my wife, Elizabeth, in heaven. I saw her then as I had last seen her, holding the newborn child curled upon her breast, both of them serene in the coffin. Then my sight fixed on Lord Ramsey's torn chest, where grew, slowly, a scarlet bubble. I cannot say whether it was two minutes or two hours I stared at that gory dome before I came to my senses.

The staff had gathered before the mantel, and the rest of the party remained on the floor near the table in various states of distress. One maid wept where she sat and inched her way across the floor to avoid the puddle of blood spreading toward her. This was the young woman I had just yelled at an hour earlier for washing a copper-bottomed pot with strong vinegar. She had held her composure then, but now — who could blame her — the tears darkened her smock. When she discovered blood upon her apron and began to scream, I crawled to her, worried she might bring the pirates' wrath upon us. I blotted the stain with my towel, saying, "There, see? It is only a splash of wine. They'll be gone soon. Just hold on." I put my arm around her and hushed her, but I was too late; Mr. Apples was headed our way.

As he reached down, I beat at him with the towel. "Don't touch her," I wheezed. "She's done nothing to you!"

But the giant was after me, not the maid. He yanked me rudely to my feet and held me by the arms while Hannah Mabbot examined me.

"Is this spirited man the cook?" she shouted. "Are you responsible for this delightful feast? What a piece of luck! . . . What is it you say, Mr. Apples?"

"Like shittin' with the pope."

"No, the other thing, less vulgar."

"Whistlin' donkey."

"Quite! A surprise and a delight like a

whistling . . . How is it that these phrases make sense when you say them? Anyway, bring him along."

2

THE *FLYING ROSE*

IN WHICH I AM BENT TO NEW EMPLOYMENT

Thus was I bound with hemp and shoved along to a boat hidden under the willows in the cove. As Mr. Apples rowed, I sat pressed against the lacquered side by one of the twins. Mabbot, at the prow, rested her feet on a large sack full of house silver and jewelry taken from the guests. She carried a leg of the duck wrapped in a damask napkin and gnawed at it with pleasure. She lounged against the stern, savoring her coup.

Below us, the water was crystalline, and the fish darted among the tangles of seaweed. Sped along by Mr. Apples's powerful arms, the boat charged out of the cove, and I thought, *These fish neither know nor care that I am being so savagely ripped from my life.* The idea of sardines coming to my aid brought from me a burst of crazed giggles that, just as involuntarily, devolved into whimpers. Mr. Apples raised an eyebrow at me as he rowed. I considered toppling over

26

into the brine to make my escape but, bound as I was, hand and foot, I would surely have drowned. There was nothing for me to do but be pulled in lurches across the surf, toward my fate.

I break now to rest, for the rocking has gotten worse.

Wednesday, Later

As sleep eludes me, I have retrieved this log from under my sack of sawdust and continue by the light of the rancid tallow taper.

Our boat rounded a craggy outcropping, and we were suddenly in the shadow of the *Flying Rose,* the four-masted barque whose voluptuous ornamentation has been related in *The Times* by those rare souls who had seen her firsthand and lived.

She was lurid and terrible to see, the fallen Lucifer on the water, blind to the pelicans moving like gnats across her bow. I was still in shock — my mind had none of its native tone — and I quailed, as we approached, at the crimson curve of her hull, the countless bundles of rigging, and the sails clustered like clouds above me. Since my journey to France as a young man, I had not returned to sea, and boats had been, to me, merely quaint objects moving sleepily against the horizon. Even in my fear, I marveled at the ingenuity of man, at the countless arrangements of ropes threading into the sky. The men moving about the deck could play this massive instrument; they knew which lines to pluck to achieve a subtle shift of course and power.

I had once seen a fox trot up to a picnic on the grounds of Asford Manor and, despite the crowd of revelers, make off, more or less unnoticed, with a string of sausage. Such are the rewards of brazenness. With the sentinels of the Royal Navy searching for the *Flying Rose* in the Indian Ocean, here she was, quietly anchored not a mile from English grass.

Befuddled, I found myself climbing obediently up a rope ladder, crossing, as I went, the strata of barnacle, stout wales, moldings shimmering with gold leaf, and rubicund bulkheads. I had no idea what was in store for me save for the certainty that I would be shortly murdered. At this unhappy thought, I began to tremble. Cracked by the strain, I heard myself mumble as they led me to my cell, "There, there, Wedgwood. You'll wake up soon enough . . . Wake! Wake, man!"

During the two days I spent locked in this narrow cell, my fear and horror bloomed fully in the dark, and I became again the child stifling the sounds of his weeping through the night. Periodically, to soothe myself, I opened the locket around my neck and sniffed its contents.

When they let me out to wander the deck, whose rails and fixtures had been carved into gargoyles by a deft and perverse hand, the land was already gone. Around us was a glittering wonder of water. The air and light helped quell my vomiting. I return to the cell at night and, locked in, sleep here on a sack of sawdust. By day this ship is my prison; I stumble about the rolling deck, not speaking, not spoken to, and avoiding as best I can the sweaty men who go to and fro with hammers or marlinspikes, bellowing songs and obscenities.

Never have I seen such a motley assemblage of characters. Except that we are at sea, I would believe that I had been abducted by a traveling circus. There are men here of every hue and size, also men whose race cannot be determined due to the indigo tattoos that cover their faces and arms. There are men with bullrings through their noses, with turbans large enough to hide a samovar, with gold thread braided into their hair, with scimitars lashed to their hips; some with teeth sharpened to points, some with no teeth at all. Many of the men have lost fingers, one has no ears, and not a few of them sport blistered patches upon their faces, necks, and forearms. These scars look very much like the effects I have seen after inept assistants burned themselves with hot oil. Mr. Apples, Joshua the cabin boy, the cooper, and Conrad the cook all bear these marks. I do not know whether it was plague or punishment, and I pray not to be present for a recurrence of either.

I'll say here that I do hate ships. What I know about sails, I learned as a young man, when it was necessary for me to hide under a heap of them in the hold of an olive barge for three days. I have never wanted to learn more. When conversations occasionally turn nautical, I have found that there are always herbs that need drying or cheeses to press.

Three days aboard and I have not seen the captain again save for her silhouette one sunset on the deck above her cabin.

I eat gruel — swill, really — oats or some other bloated grain seasoned with lard and flaccid onions. There is a king's ransom of black pepper aboard, which, even with profligate use, helps not at all. I eat little. I have learned to relieve myself, in view of God and all, through a hole in a plank suspended out over the water. I have learned to walk a straight line on the bucking wood. I have learned by exposure the names of the myriad corners of the ship.

Then, this morning, Mr. Apples unlocked my door and handed me a letter, folded and sealed with the *Flying Rose* emblem. I opened it and read:

Dear Mr. Wedgwood,

Welcome to the *Flying Rose.* I hope you have settled to sea comfortably. Your lot may improve in direct proportion to your willingness. I do look forward to more of your fare. Let me lay out my proposal: You will, of a Sunday, cook for me, and me alone, the finest supper. You will neither repeat a dish nor serve foods that are in the slightest degree mundane. In return I will continue to keep you alive and well, and we may discuss an improvement of your quarters after a time. Should you balk in any fashion you will find yourself swimming home, whole or in pieces, depending upon the severity of my disappointment.

How does this strike you?

In anticipation,
Capt. Hannah Mabbot

For the second time since this horrible trial began, I laughed. What else could be done? She was as mad as the legends warned. Upon hearing my laughter, Mr. Apples stated that he would show me the galley.

Mr. Apples, as I have described, seems to have been built for hand-to-hand combat and serves as Mabbot's first lieutenant and commander. He, like many here, goes barefoot most of the time. He seems sensitive to drafts, as he always wears knit caps and sometimes a long scarf that he knots thickly about his throat. Hanging from a chain around his neck are a pair of smoked-glass goggles, so thick and dark I'm sure nothing can be seen through them. Perhaps he won them as a trophy in some desert where the sun never sets.

My smile quite disappeared when we entered the grim, wet-walled box they called the galley. The hearth was just a pile of bricks and not venting properly. The narrow porthole near the ceiling brought no fresh air to cut the smoke. Hanging from an iron bar above the hearth was a great cauldron full of the awful gruel I had been eating. It was being stirred dejectedly by a man with open sores on his face — a man they call Conrad.

I laughed again. "Impossible," I said. "Tell her it's impossible."

Clearing his throat before he spoke, as was

his tendency, Mr. Apples said, "Mistakin' me for a message monkey. Tell 'er yourself."

Taking my courage between my teeth, I marched in the direction he pointed me, straight to the stern where the captain's quarters sat hidden under the poop deck, all the way whispering to myself, "Be a man, Wedgwood. A man!" I let my boots clatter upon the deck and found the small door that was decorated with a tiger's pelt. I had just turned the latch when I was struck in the face and flew back upon the deck. When I caught my breath, I saw Captain Mabbot looking down on me, flanked by the twins, Bai and Feng.

Mabbot herself is like something from Shakespeare's imagination. While those around her knot their beards and blow their noses into their vests, she appears to be cleanly prepared, at all times, to greet nobility. Her boots, long-coat, and belt are of supple leather and creak as she moves about. Her hat is wide and stylish. She was now wearing, instead of her olive coat, a cloak made from another tiger pelt. She has, it seems, a need for fashion, yet out here among heathens and savages, her taste has become fevered. If one could ignore for a moment her monstrosity, he would note that she is indeed as lovely as they say. She appears to me to be mulatto of some thin percentage. Her hair is thick and eddying. Up close, as I have had the misfortune to be, one sees her face is misted with freckles, as if she had walked through a miasma of blood. Her lips are full. Her eyes are flecked with the unholy green of fox fire.

She was laughing. "Did you receive my correspondence, then? Was my handwriting legible? I haven't used the post for quite some time." Her hair moved in the wind like the flame of a guttering torch.

I rose, brushed myself off, and stated as bravely as I could, "You're insane."

No sooner had I uttered the truth than Feng flew to my side and folded me in half like a clean towel. So swiftly did it happen that I could not tell if I had been hit with a foot or a fist.

Mabbot asked, "Are you quite all right? Another bout of seasickness? It will get better with time."

From the ground, where I had resigned myself, I said, "I won't play your game." A blow rolled me over. Vomit pooled under my cheek before I recognized it as mine.

Mabbot said, "A terrible misunderstanding, but I'm sure it's nothing. Do tell me you're all right."

"Impossible in that dank box. No utensils,

no ingredients —"

Another kick made me quiet. I became fascinated with and strangely grateful for the cool grain of the deck where my forehead rested.

Then Mabbot was crouching next to me. "A terrible misunderstanding," she whispered in my ear. "But I'm so glad we've sorted it out."

The Chinaman looked to give me another beating, but Mabbot calmed him with a few words in his own tongue. The pyre of indignation within me had been reduced to wet ash. I wanted only to be allowed to crawl back to my sack of sawdust and lie still until the aching stopped.

"Sundays . . ." I groaned.

"Yes?"

"I cook for you only on Sundays?"

"I am a human being; I eat every day. Mostly I eat what my crew eats — it's good for morale. But there are certain expectations of a leader." She was close enough for me to feel her breath on my cheek, and behind the leather and sweat, I smelled tea and lilac. "Occasional extravagance demonstrates authority," she continued. "If I were just another deckhand, they couldn't take orders from me — their pride would not allow it. So I sleep on down and silk. I

35

drink the rarest Barolo and Médoc. And now, once a week, I will dine as well as any emperor. Don't think you're on vacation; if you enjoy this side of the water, you'll work hard. Some of the crew have heard of you. The Caesar of Sauces — did you invent that title? You will spend your entire week preparing for these meals: simmering, sharpening your knives, whatever it is you do."

"I have no knife —"

"Yes, a knife. I'll arrange it. Shall we start, then, next week? That should give you plenty of time to settle in."

"And fresh meat, eggs, butter —"

"Yes, yes." She was bored now, and I listened to her boots clop back to her quarters.

With care, I picked myself up and saw that our encounter had been watched, from a distance, by much of the crew. Mabbot flicked her wrist and the cabin boy, a twelve-year-old with lively black eyes, took me by the elbow and helped me gently below deck, studying my face as we went.

Before I could retire, though, Mr. Apples was demanding again that I follow him. He led me to a room full of sacks and barrels, littered with what I hoped were currants but turned out to be rat droppings.

"The provisions," Mr. Apples said. Strands

36

of yarn hung from his pocket.

"Sir," I said, "there are things I need, paper for notes, a proper stove and oven . . ."

"Conrad manages."

"Mr. Apples, this request from the captain, it is something altogether different from what Conrad does." I felt blood trickling from my split lip and wiped it away. "You've had Conrad's cooking. It tastes like, well —"

"Like a fart boiled in a shoe," he volunteered.

"That is it. The very thing. You're a poet."

Mr. Apples fiddled distractedly with the yarn, then said, "I'll find you some paper."

That is how I came to be writing these pages. It is, if I'm not mistaken, Wednesday, and I am looking forward to the week as eagerly as one looks into the gullet of a bear. I do not know how I will manage, but I suppose I must try. My head, I've been assured, remains attached to my neck only as long as I do not bore the fiend. I will feed her until I can devise a way to liberate myself. My first task will be to take a true inventory of the pantry. This I will do as soon as my aches recede enough for me to rise.

The cabin boy, Joshua, appears occasionally to refill my jug with "panch," a foul mixture of wine, tea, lime juice, ground cloves, and water. The word itself means "five," owing to the number of its ingredients, and panch serves here as clean water serves on dry land. I've had, in the course of my life, occasion to imbibe the most eccentric juices and cordials and have never parted my lips for such a treasonous potion. True temperance is impossible on this ship, but, I'm sure, the heavens will forgive me inasmuch as I am not enjoying the spirits and have, anyway, little choice.

Perhaps because I am not afraid of him, I find myself wishing Joshua would linger. I gather he is cripplingly shy or mute. Aside from the burns on his neck, he seems healthy and serves the officers with a smile. He is also the lamp trimmer, and he leaves greasy soot on everything he touches. If you have seen a cat inflate itself when cornered by a dog, you can imagine what this boy's hair looks like. Even so, he is the most calming presence on the ship.

On the rare occasion that these barbarians haul a bucket of seawater up to bathe, they use a paste that is more cinder than soap. As the ingredients are plentiful, there is no excuse for this, and I have undertaken, in these last days, the production of lye and proper soap. When I was an apprentice, my

Jesuit master smacked me with a ladle for daring to cook with unwashed hands, and now I cannot even think of cooking unless my hands are clean. I separated, as best I could, the white ash from Conrad's hearth and bundled it into several layers of burlap. Drop by drop I let water fall into this bundle until a few cups of cloudy lye accumulated in the pan below. This drip method can be done by hand only if one is a pirate captive and has plenty of time, though the rolling of the ship made handling the stuff an exercise in concentration. I came close to scalding myself badly as I mixed the lye with lard and added a bit of honey from the provision room for perfume. The soap is thin and must be kept in a bottle, but it is smooth and produces a healthy lather. I have taken to scrubbing myself raw in the privacy of my cell. I find it restores a bit of my sanity.

I have tried to lubricate the latch of my cell with the soap, but the gap between the door and the frame is too narrow for my thick fingers. For now I am obliged to wait for Mr. Apples, who lets me roam during the day and confines me at sunset.

Why, after so many years gone, is the spirit of my late wife so restless? There is no pit less worthy of Elizabeth than this ship, and yet, in the thump and hiss of the sea, I hear her call my name. Or, for a brief moment, amid the fetid and grunting odors, I think I smell her orange-blossom perfume.

Dearest Elizabeth, if you are looking over my shoulder now, I beg you: Go and rest. I will find my way to you at last, but I would not have you watch my bloody journey. Elizabeth, my blueberry, I kiss the page now — go.

Saturday, August 21
I have received a message from another prisoner! At least I suppose it is from a prisoner, though it may be from a mutineer or other like-minded soul. It reads simply:

YOU ARE NOT ALONE.

I found it slipped under the door when I returned to my chamber this evening.

Whence it comes and what may come of it, I do not know, yet I find myself reading it over and over like a note from a lover.

I have hidden it along with all of these entries in a growing manuscript of impromptu kitchen lists, recipes, prayers, and other scrawled jottings. This pretense will be enough, I hope, to fool a casual glance.

3

Use of a Spoon

IN WHICH I RECEIVE VALUABLE ADVICE
FROM A MYSTERIOUS FRIEND AND
WITNESS AN EXECUTION

Saturday, Later

This evening just before sunset I rose, still aching, to take inventory of the larder. On my way across the deck, I passed a dozen or so men taking their ease. They smoked, scratched scrimshaw, threw knives at rats, and one of them played a maniacal tune on a gourd instrument with keys made of hammered metal. Even as they lounged, they scanned the horizon for a corsair ship named *La Colette,* which, it seemed, had made a considerable impression upon them. It was clear they did not wish to encounter the ship again.

Mr. Apples was sitting on a stool among them. At first, I thought he might be rending meat, but on closer inspection, I saw the man was knitting, knitting ferociously; his enormous hands danced, yet his face was as still as marzipan. A skein tumbled out of his bulging pockets, his needles

41

clicked, and he hummed along to the music.

The wool was the same color as his hat and the same gauge as the cables of his scarf. Indeed, I noted that many of the crew wore some item that Mr. Apples must have knitted.

I made my way again down the companionway and abaft to the narrow pantry hold. With a lantern before me, I took stock of that chamber and felt desperate. Meager materials and these were they:

In Sacks:

heavy cornmeal, with scattered weevils
wheat flour, coarse
rice, polished
garlic, cured
raisins
dried figs
some type of white bean
walnuts
dried anchovies
coconuts
black pepper

In Barrels:

hardtack
molasses

lard

vinegar

limes

potatoes, buried in sand

rum

Madeira wine

panch

ale, bitter

honey, gritty with wax and what may be
wood chips

herrings, whole, pickled in vinegar and
garlic

In Boxes:

gunpowder-cured meat, which the men
call "Mary Sweet," tough as tarpaulin

onions, under hay

what must be cheese, waxed in balls

coarse grey salt

tea, pressed into cakes and smelling of the
earth

These are the desolate contents of the
hold; by far the most arresting are the rats,
so bold and so many. I understand now the
captain's predilection for tiger pelts, whose
lingering musk must offer some deterrent.

Certainly there are staples here to feed
the horde, but proper ingredients for cui-

sine? Butter, cream, mushrooms, fruit, ice, spices, fresh meats, eggs, preserves, crisp vegetables, sugar, bacon, sausage, sherry, etcetera — neither a scrap nor a drop of these. No herbs. Not even a carrot. Lord help me.

Concerning the cured meat, I've tasted it and I'm confident it is not pork. Though the tang of the gunpowder makes it hard to be certain, I think it is horse. I made the mistake of asking why the men call it Mary Sweet and was treated to several choruses of this song:

Mary Sweet was potting meat when she fell
    into the grinder.
She poured right in and filled the tin and
    that is where you'll find her.

Mary Sweet is given out once a day, and though the men complain about it, they look forward to it almost as much as to their wine rations.

Not far from the provisions, in a narrow hold, among unused torches and short lengths of rope awaiting splicing, Mr. Apples keeps a wicker basket full of scorpions. I had opened the basket and nearly stuck my head into it to discover the source of the faint odor of rotten oranges and dust when

44

Mr. Apples grabbed the back of my neck.

"Don't want to do that," he said.

"What is it?"

"Ain't food. Stick to the pantry."

I will obey. His rationale for such an unusual husbandry remains a mystery to me. There are, no doubt, many things twitching in the shadows of this ship that are best left alone.

Although I've wandered the ship considerably, I have not found my fellow prisoner. There are only half a dozen locked holds on the lower deck that might contain him, but I cannot go about knocking on doors and shouting without drawing undue attention. Despite my eagerness, I must pace myself. In my agitation, I've taken to running circles in my little cell. I wish I could say it calmed my nerves, but at least it distracts me for a few moments.

A few minutes ago, Joshua peered in, perhaps to see if I was recovered from my beating. I asked if he might bring me a crust of hardtack; having vomited my oats, my stomach was grumbling. He shook his head and tapped his ear. I assured him that no one would notice nor care if I had a bit of hardtack to dip in my panch. But Joshua shook his head again and cupped his hands over his ears.

With a sigh, I accepted that Joshua is deaf and mute. I mimed eating a small thing, and he disappeared and returned with a few dried figs. Bowing my head to thank him, I contented myself with them. It was just the sort of luck I was getting used to: here was the only person on the boat whom I thought I might trust not to slit my throat, and there was no easy way of communicating with him. I might as well engage my boot in conversation.

When he saw my pen and log, though, he showed great interest. After I had him wash the lampblack from his hands, we established that the boy can scrawl most of the alphabet, but few written words are known to him. He can read lips with some accuracy, but only granted ample light and patience. Two hours passed almost pleasantly as we ruined several pages of paper with jottings and sketches. During this time we arrived at a simple method of instruction: I write a word, he shakes his head if he does not know it, and then I proceed, by drawing and aping, to teach it to him.

If I am to be interned, I suppose it is good that someone should benefit — someone besides that hurricane they call captain.

Like all men of good breeding, Ramsey practiced verbal continence. When entertaining, he was a fine and theatrical orator. But during the mundane moments he spoke only when necessary, and, as his silences proved, little is truly necessary. Those who served him learned to take direction from the slope of his shoulders and the tone of his sighs.

Therefore, the rare moments when I saw Ramsey lose his composure stand out in my mind — as when he threw the doll into the fire.

I was haunted at the time by the vacancy in the house. Ramsey was a notorious bachelor, and, when we were not hosting, the silence itself marched the halls like a grim mistress. I was young, my Elizabeth and our unbaptized son were but a year in the grave, and my mind was wont to linger on morbid things. I concocted a story: I convinced myself that Ramsey had, himself, lost a child.

It's not uncommon for a young man to feel familial with an employer, and a charismatic man like Ramsey, a man of such poise, well, it's clear to me now that I came to think of him as an uncle of sorts. At least, I was trying to learn from him how to be a solitary man — to appreciate the nobility of a quiet room.

It was early fall when I found the doll in the woodshed. A nasty influenza had indisposed most of the servants, and Ramsey had sent them to their quarters rather than listen to their sniffling. This left me to fetch my own wood. I wasn't used to the chore and, while selecting logs, I stood too quickly and cracked my head on the sloping roof. Amid my raining curses there fell, from behind one of the beams, a toy soldier — a fine one with genuine silver buttons and a canvas uniform besmirched with mildew. The owner had fashioned a sword out of snipped tin and bound it tightly to the wooden hand. The doll seemed so out of place that I was afraid for a moment to touch it. If an actual child had plopped to the floor among the logs, I would not have been more stunned.

I immediately recalled a conversation I'd had with a woman at the market a few weeks earlier. She was a nursemaid, with a rheumy-eyed tyke on her hip. She spotted me picking through the parsnips and approached as if she knew me. "You're Ramsey's man, aren't cha?"

I said I was.

"Aren't you the lucky one? Fine house, isn't it? Oh, I know; I lived for five years there, tending to the boy."

Putting her finger to her nose, she winked at me with such import that I thought for a moment that I was talking to a prostitute. "But that's between us and the turnips, eh?" She laughed, then, and sauntered down the lane, the infant on her hip watching me unkindly over her shoulder as she went.

I had dismissed the incident, but as I stood staring at that doll, it came back to me, every word.

That night I placed the doll on a window-sill so I might consider it as I worked. It was my intention to return it to Ramsey in a manner that would express to him my deep empathy for his evident loss. I was puzzling over how exactly to do this even as Ramsey ate in the dining room.

I was preparing a caramel sauce for his pudding when Ramsey, as he sometimes did, came into the kitchen to compliment me on the goose-liver and leek pie. The soldier in the window caught his eye immediately.

"I found this curious object —" I began, but Ramsey snatched the doll and pushed past me, gnashing his teeth.

He burned his hand opening the oven and

pitched the toy into the coals. Flames licked it up at once. He looked not at me, nor spoke, as he stormed from the kitchen. I took my reprimand from this display and never mentioned it again to anyone.

That's not to say I forgot it. In fact I was deeply moved by the situation as I now understood it. Ramsey had had a son, by whom I couldn't begin to guess. It was clear to me only that the son had died. Before sleeping at night, I recalled the tiny silver buttons dripping so eagerly in the heat, the round head smoldering, the tin sword gripped tightly till the last.

It made me admire him all the more for his stoicism. In loss, Ramsey and I were family. Mabbot's merciless pistols have orphaned me again.

Mr. Apples, knowing that many things creep in the pantry, has given me a jar to hold any weevils or earwigs I sift out of foodstuffs. These the strange man will feed to his scorpions.

It strikes me with a shiver, as I write this now, that the pantry rats might be, themselves, a provision of a kind. I would not be surprised if these barbarians kept them as miniature livestock to satisfy the occasional craving for fresh meat. The thought dries my tongue and I begin to think, as I often do when faced with unpleasantness, of ways to gently and swiftly dispatch myself. But I am determined, if for no other reason than to spite the witch, to survive, indeed to stand victorious at the end of this ordeal.

How, though, to make a genuine meal from such a heap? Saint Paschal, attend to me and give me help.

Monday, August 23
Early this morning, I heard someone stumble right outside my locked door, then Mr. Apples yelling, "Damn your bones! You're as graceful as a potato."

To this a gentleman replied, "Give me a moment. It's the gout. Makes my legs stiff." This was no pirate. He had a proper accent, sounds that evoked the first curls of cream in strong tea, with the distinctly woolen-at-the-edges quality of a veteran pipe smoker.

Was this not my comrade? I rose and saw that the crafty fellow had secreted another message underneath my door. Gout indeed! The message proves that he is a valuable ally. It reads:

FLATTEN SPOON TO BEST LOCK.

I must try this at the first opportunity.

51

You've a friend, Wedgwood!

This afternoon, Mr. Apples was taking his gunners through their paces again, as he did every day, firing imaginary balls at invisible foes. The men went so far as to cover their ears, though the guns were dumb.

The bosun meanwhile had a crew caulking the seams of the deck near the forecastle. These men hammered wads of oakum and animal hair into the grooves, then poured boiling pitch over them. The smell would have driven me back below deck if a stark demonstration of Mr. Apples's power hadn't stopped me where I stood: One of the bosun's boys went to fetch a fresh bag of oakum and, no doubt in a hurry to be done, took a shortcut right behind the cannon crew in the midst of their fantasy battle. As he passed, Mr. Apples turned and drove his open hand under the man's chin with such force that the runner was lifted off the deck. His feet followed their momentum, and he twisted in the air to land facedown, sprawled like a scarecrow.

Pitching his voice so all hands could hear, Mr. Apples said, "That's just a kiss. If a gun kicks you, we'll scrape you into a snuff box to bury you."

With that he freed his crew to line up for

their grog. I was relieved to see the scarecrow pull himself up and weave his way back to his fellows, who seemed to forgive him for forgetting the oakum.

I found myself gazing at the cannon and considering the many shapes of violence. The hollowed sockets of those guns brought to mind the Cyclops staring blind with rage at the horizon after Odysseus had gone.

Mr. Apples broke my reverie. "You could cook meat with that scowl alone," he said, pulling yarn from his ditty bag. "What's the matter, Spoons? I didn't hit *you*."

"It seems to me," I said, "strength like that is a gift that could go to a better use."

"That swat'll save his life." He held up the gourds of his fists. "I was a pugilist. Is that the better use you're thinking of? I stood in a ring and crushed heads for the pleasure of a crowd. A bear can do that. That's what I was when Mabbot found me. These sailors could sign with any other crew, get monthly pay and chocolate to drink for the holidays, but here they eat mush and go months with no prizes. They hunt the Brass Fox, which is like trying to catch smoke in your hat. Why do they put up with it?"

"Why indeed?"

"Once you meet Mabbot, you can hardly go back to being a bear. You have two

53

choices: fight her or fight for her."

A full week aboard and I've made no progress toward the meal that will save my life. I have a better chance of building a cathedral out of vermicelli. In my despair, I can hardly lift myself from the sack of sawdust I sleep on and which I have grown alarmingly fond of. I try to imagine recipes, but my mind has the tinny echo of an empty flour bin.

I will spare myself the needles of remembrance. My survival depends on being present, focusing all of my energies on dodging the captain's threat. I must not linger on the sweet memories of my beloved Elizabeth, rest her, laughing with a jasmine candy in her cheek, nor of good men sharing a glass of port; nor will I linger on the softness of my down pillow back in London, nor on clean undergarments, nor on the view of the orchard from my kitchen window, nor on eggs — oh, eggs! Nor on the reassuring firmness and eager weight of my knife whistling so cleanly through a head of cabbage. I will not let myself catalogue the other friends I took for granted: my slim whisk, copper-bottomed pots, marble pastry table, and rows of yeast batters in various states of arousal. I shall not think once of my Rumford stove, my cast-iron castle, my coal-fed kingdom. For now I shall attempt to pretend that the things on hand here are the only tools that have ever existed. I must become like Adam, taking what is offered and inventing the rest.

The *Flying Rose* is modified, I've learned, in a few mischievous ways. For one, her stern is reinforced to support the two sleek black cannon, which the gunners have affectionately named the Twa Corbies. These long-range stern chasers are poised to destroy anyone in pursuit. Further, a good portion of the lower deck has been divided into small chambers, the better to hold stolen goods or prisoners like myself.

The vessel is always abustle. A seaman stands near the mizzenmast, ready to strike a large gong emblazoned with white enamel cranes. It is his job to generate the various rhythms by which the crew know their time and duty. While the sailors do indeed work hard and the ship is polished to a sheen, they also spend a stunning amount of time playing music, wrestling, whittling, or simply lolling about the deck, laughing and joking in a pidgin language that sounds like the bark of a sea lion. The ship's surgeon is a shameless drunk who refuses to rise from his hammock until he has had two liters of straight wine in his gut. God forbid I should ever need his attentions. Further, as far as I can see, Mabbot does not use compass or astrolabe but relies instead on Pete, a shriveled old savage of mysterious origin, calloused as bark, who sits upon a specially rigged chair out over the bowsprit and stares at the sea sunrise to sunset. While it is clear to me that poor toothless Pete has entered his second infancy, Mabbot says he is "counting the waves" and trusts his direction as God's word.

Mabbot takes a twice-daily walk, touring the ship as she goes, sometimes giving a two-word order. I have seen, as she passes, something moving in the deep pockets of her long coat. It is unsettling. The men in the berths whisper absurdities: that she keeps the plague in her pocket like a pet, that she has a wolf's maw where her generative organs should be. Such is the grip she has on their minds.

Her rounds bring her always to Pete, the little man at the forepeak. They speak, he points, sometimes they consult a map, then she returns to her cabin. It is a wonder the ship is not rotting in the deepest crevice of the seafloor, and yet she has made herself a menace to the Pendleton Trading Company for nearly fifteen years; indeed, her ambushes are the stuff of legend. The rumors of her resurrection after execution by firing squad and drowning are ridiculous, but I could be convinced that the woman has a pact with the devil. It would explain much.

Too, this ship is so full of Mohammedans I find myself wondering why God does not simply push it under with His finger as He did Gomorrah.

The men eat in the forecastle mostly, sitting on their lockers and holding their bowls on their laps. As a prank they invited me to sit at a small table, only to guffaw when my porridge slid across on a swell and dropped with a splat on the floor. In the future I must remember to think twice before accepting courtesy from a pirate and to keep one hand on the bowl at all times. Still, bit by bit, I allow myself to make simple conversation with the sailors here. Though I stammer sometimes at the sight of their pierced faces and lewd tattoos, I tell myself: *They're just men. Held together with wire and spit, but only men, after all.*

With one exception, I have not regretted these conversations. I have been obliged to linger in the galley, assessing my tools and resources, scant and rusty as they are. This has meant tolerating Conrad's long tongue.

A word on Conrad: I cannot call him a cook. Nor, having eaten so much of his fare, am I comfortable calling him a Christian, though he claims to be. He is a man, I grant. Many of the foulest things of the earth come from men.

His sores are in need of calendula. Happily we need not look at him while eating, for he wisely avoids the men at mealtimes. But having heard his wet cough, having smelled in the narrow passages the cheesy ropes of his braids, having witnessed, even once, his hobby of staring out at the horizon while his hand scuttles about his neck like a crab looking for some promising lesion to pick, one finds it hard to locate one's appetite.

How does this man, who would lose his post to a donkey on land, achieve such a position at sea? "Ship's cook," it turns out, is not properly a position but a punishment. Not only does he spend his days cramped in a steam-filled chamber, churning with a shovel enough food for an army, but worse, Conrad must bear the derision of the crew who look to a meal as one of the sole respites in a long hard day. Finding sand between their teeth and even the hardtack sour, they turn their frustrations upon poor Conrad. What pleasure they can't get by appeasing their tremendous appetites, they find instead in taunting the man who takes their hoots and howls with stoicism.

I have already learned that being at sea breeds romance and fantasy. Whether it is the monotony of the horizon, the confined perambulation, or the intoxicating ethers that boil from the deep I cannot say, but here men's imaginations bloom. Their women back home are, all of them, Helens, breasts like sleeping doves, petal cheeks, voices like glass bells; their inns serve not beer but nectar; their gardens grow peas the size of fists. These fantasies are ferociously strong, and, compared to them, Conrad's grey porridge is an insult. The man no doubt would have been cast overboard long ago save one of the captain's commandments: He that molests the cook becomes the cook. Stronger even than their anger at Conrad is their fear of becoming Conrad. Thus he is left in peace to make his bubbling abominations.

When not eating his "burgoo," the sailors tolerate him well enough. There are worse things in a pirate's life than a man who cannot cook and who talks too much.

As I am compelled to linger in the galley, Conrad takes the opportunity to fill my ears with his prattling. He considers me a compatriot, and I haven't the heart to correct him.

A central theme of his monologues is his admiration for the captain, which, from his tone, is not without a touch of the prurient. This afternoon, for example, he said, "Well we're on our way, aren't we? She don't lose a minute, the cap'm. Making up for time lost killing Ramsey. A mere holiday for her! But we're on track again. The grand pursuit!" He chortled above his cauldron of porridge. "Oh, but she's dogged as she is fair. She'll find him soon enough. She'll figure it out. Smart the cap'm, she took Ramsey by surprise, didn't she?"

"If it's all the same to you, we will not talk about Lord Ramsey," I said.

"The man was a dog."

"I'm quite serious, sir —"

"Strike me, then — do! Won't hit back." He lifted his chin, and I was surprised by the strength of my urge to wallop him. Instead I said, "You call her wise, but she put you here in this steam box."

"But I put myself here, didn't I? Punched the other cook in the eye, which fairly blinded him one side. Well, it was lashes for me, and now I'm the cook. How can I complain? If God were this fair, the world wouldn't be such a shit pile!"

"We will not speak of God nor of Lord Ramsey."

"Well, you've got your druthers, hain't you?" He made a rude farting sound with his mouth. "What'll we talk about, then?"

"Have you ladles? Tongs? A rolling pin? Where are the pie tins kept?"

He laughed again, which led to coughing. "I don't have your 'fisticated wit. Pots and spoons, that's what we got. Pots and spoons."

I took note of what I could find myself. There are some iron skillets, wholly unused by Conrad, rusted and in need of curing. Pots — we are flush with cheap pots. One fine rasp and several knotty and oversized wooden spoons . . .

Conrad went on: "It's the same pots we've had for the five years I been cook. Near round the world twice hunting the Brass Fox," he said. "The hunt is always in her mind. She won't speak it, but she thinks of naught else."

"What kind of weapon is the Brass Fox?" I asked.

"Weapon? Ha! The Fox is a thief — the King of Thieves."

"What does she need a thief for?"

At this he laughed hard enough to reveal several teeth made of cowry.

61

I wanted him to stop before he began coughing again, so I asked, "Is it treasure?"

"Sure it's treasure. But what type? Seen her, myself, chunk diamonds into the wake like sowing wheat. So it is hard to say, ain't it? Mr. Apples prawly knows, but he's tight as a barrel with no bung. Feng and Bai, well, they may know, 'pending on if they grasp the English tongue. But they're about as talky as my elbows. So that leaves those of us who don't know to speak on it. Grim has it that Cap'm is in hunt of the largest heap of gold ever heaped, left there by Ben Gaunt and his pirate 'federacy. Jawbone thinks she's looking for the wood of the true cross, but Jawbone was kicked in the head by a horse when he was short." Here Conrad tasted his gruel with a grey tongue — it was a sight I wish I had been spared. "Shash'll tell you she's looking for the secret city of immortals where everyone lives forever and grows tulips in their navels. Half the men have it she's looking for the egg of the roc, which is a fine theory, because I've seen one of them with my own eyes carry an elephant into the sky.

"Half the men believe she's looking for the antidote to the curse a widow put on her that won't let her sleep, which she don't, or don't much. Or could be a witched amulet to make her safe to musket fire, which, if there is such a thing, would be mighty handy and with many useful 'vantages, and worthy of a long search. Been shot once myself. Feel on this rib, you can make out the ball under the skin. Well, it still hurts. Man wasn't meant to carry shot around in his ribs — I'd rather not get another. Gimbal will tell you she's looking for a cure for the opium pipe, with that she could become empress of China and raise their army to break the comp'ny spine."

"The Pendleton Trading Company."

"What else? In my personal experience, though a person look complicated, deep down he is simple and likes gold. It's almost sure gold, ain't it? A mountain of it. Enough to make dukes of us all. Enough for her to buy the whole comp'ny a hundred times over. Whatever you do, don't ask her about it. She broke Gimbal's finger for his curiosity. Just reached out and took it gentle like she wanted to kiss him, then snapped it easy as a twig and held on to it until he thanked her for it."

"Thanked her?"

"Wouldn't let go until he did."

"Well, she's a fiend," I said.

Conrad looked at me so queerly then, it sent shivers down my spine. I must try to remember where I am and keep my opinions to myself.

Unable to really explore the galley with him in the way, I returned to my quarters, planning to try again later.

The man has me thinking about our destination. The sound of the wind boiling in the sails — I can hear it even now. We are, as he says, "on our way." But to where? I have been so preoccupied with my situation that I haven't given thought to our ultimate target. I am aware that pirates will sell a man into the slave mines for a penny. Yet more incentive to make Mabbot's repast memorable, indeed.

An odd bell brought me out of my brooding and onto the glistening deck. When my eyes had adjusted, I saw Mabbot pushing her way through the crowd gathered around a prone seaman.

Without preamble she knelt by the man and tugged his lower lip open. His teeth were dark with an oily residue. He was delirious, laughing and staring hazily at the faces around him.

Bai handed Mabbot a small wad of paper. She opened it. Inside were several shriveled flower petals enclosing half a ball of opium.

The crowd murmured.

Mabbot asked the sailor, "Did you eat this? You ate too much — you'll be ill."

"I'll not," the man said. " 'Pologies, Cap'm. Just a lark." He grinned and slowly got to his feet.

Mabbot handed the opium back to Bai, who chucked it overboard.

"Theater paint," Mabbot said wearily.

The crowd hushed as the bosun set quickly to work tying the man's hands behind him.

I realized that I had just witnessed a trial and sentencing. Before I could guess what punishment might be named after an actor's rouge, the bosun, with swift strokes of a knife, flayed the opium-eater's cheeks in arcs until the meat hung wet at his neck and his teeth grinned ghastly from the holes. The opium was doing its job, for the man looked surprised but showed no signs of suffering.

Ramsey had kept a small vial of laudanum, which he enjoyed frequently after an evening meal, but I had never seen a true opium swoon. Above all, the poor seaman looked sleepy; his indifference was frightening. Even as they bound his feet and lifted him toward the head of the ship, he looked merely annoyed, as if this were a prank they were playing on a friend who had drunk too much cider. He was trussed like a roasting pig to the bowsprit and left there.

Before long, the petrels that follow us converged upon him and began to make tentative jabs at his face. By evening the opium had worn off. He was entirely occluded by a frenzy of feathers, and I had to wad paper into my ears to block out his screams.

I moved as far as I could from the horror and encountered Mabbot at the stern bulwark overlooking a sea the color of jade.

"So gruesome," I moaned.

"I should have him write his lessons on a slate? Bend him over my knee for a paddling? He knows the law. He made a choice. Not all of us get to choose our death."

"A death sentence! For such a petty crime?"

"Petty?" Mabbot's own cheeks flushed. "For this pettiness ten *million* Bengalis starved in their own fields because the Pendleton Company forced them to grow opium instead of food. China herself is capsized! She can trust none of her officials to keep the tide of smugglers out. She has sprung a leak the size of the Pearl River and has lost all of her wealth to England's avarice. In a few years she will be a derelict. Look around you; not a few of these men have lost their homes and families to this pettiness. It won't happen to my ship."

"But surely he has learned his lesson by now."

"The lesson is not for him."

A month would not be enough time to prepare a kitchen here, and yet, with days left, I find myself loafing in despair, unable to begin the Herculean task.

Joshua showed up for reading practice again as if he were a paying pupil. Our lesson was slow and rudimentary, but it was a relief to forget my misadventure as we focused on a simpler world. *Go to market:* this one sentence required our entire attention for half an hour, and simply imagining life on land — the shady path I took past the church on my way to buy kale and a silverside of beef — was a welcome break indeed.

Joshua is quick to smile and has the devil's humor. He switched my panch with brine just to watch me pucker and sputter, then laughed like a crow in the corn. Here is a laugh to wake the dead; I suppose it is precisely because he cannot hear it himself that the bray is so utterly unfettered, loud, and raw.

The door to my cell is secured by a simple bolt. A monkey could manipulate it from the outside, but as long as I was on the inside, it was beyond my power. Until tonight, that is.

Due to my peculiar status as Mabbot's chef, and as only a madman would leap overboard, I am free to roam the ship except at night or when Mr. Apples considers it necessary to confine me. Nevertheless, if I am to have any chance of escaping, I must have my own key.

To that end I have stolen a cheap tin spoon from the berths, which I was able, after an effort, to flatten under my boot. This fits, as my comrade promised, between the cell door and the frame. By working it to and fro in agonizing increments, I can, with patience, free the bolt — or almost free it. I have chosen not to open the door completely for fear of revealing myself — once the door swings, I would have no way to lock myself in again, and my trick would be exposed. I must save this for a crucial moment.

4

Fiat Leaven

IN WHICH I MAKE CONTACT
WITH A FELLOW PRISONER

Tuesday, August 24

I have made myself a rudimentary calendar, little more than a series of grids on paper, and it is a frightening thing to mark every morning another day's distance from home and happiness.

After relieving myself over the bowsprit in the barbaric manner common here, I caught a glimpse of my fellow abductee shackled to the mast. He is a round man (though, judging by the hang of his clothes, he has lost weight) with an ample face and muttonchop whiskers. His naval officer's uniform is soiled and torn, but his jacket, despite the heat, is properly buttoned to the top.

When he spotted me and recognized, by my lack of response to the watch gong, that I was a prisoner too, this gentleman saluted. I was so moved by the gesture that I immediately returned the salute, only to realize that I had done so with the wrong hand.

When Bai saw this exchange, he wagged his finger at me. I was not looking for another beating, so I contented myself to sit and watch the prisoner from a distance. He returned my kind gaze. We shouted not, nor waved, yet the space between us was filled with volumes of sentiment. I don't know his name, and yet I feel more akin to him than to any other soul on earth. I would have sat there feeling the sweet relief of friendship for days if Bai had not come to shackle me, too, on another part of the deck.

The cause of this unwelcome treatment, I came to see, was the proximity of land: first the unmistakable musk of humus, then the irreplaceable verdant sway of trees, the amnesty of solid earth passing me by.

We anchored at Porto Santo. Mabbot and some others went ashore for a few hours while I could do nothing but sit and watch the palms swaying near the distant pier where little men cast nets into the water.

They released me hours later, when we were again at open sea. Near her cabin, I saw Mabbot arguing with the imperturbable Mr. Apples. They consulted a map, and, though they were too far away to hear, Mabbot's rage was visible.

■ ■ ■ ■

Today I undertook to establish that most basic of culinary foundations — a simple yeast sponge batter — not because I know yet how I will make bread in the ruins Conrad calls an oven but because I feel out of sorts without one. One may accuse me of superstition, but I feel a kitchen is not a kitchen, indeed a cook is not a cook, without a nice leaven batter rising gently beneath a clean tea towel. Even if I never find a way to bake, I will feel more secure knowing it is there. With a mound of dough warm and waiting on the counter, one becomes a mogul in the kingdom of bread, entitled to its myriad pleasures: the comforting weight of a rosewater manchet swaddled for the night, the coy tenacity of milk rolls, not to mention the smell of baking bread, which can turn the most refined dignitary into a boy begging for a nibble.

Such were my thoughts when I embarked on the task that, in a civilized kitchen, would have taken me two minutes. Instead, it took all morning and may not have worked in any case.

A basic bread sponge is easy enough to make: fine flour, a spoonful of the last sponge, clean water, and warmth. The sponge is stirred every day and fed more flour and within a week will bubble to show its contentedness. Any wife, brewer, or baker can do this while asleep. As an apprentice in Sanghen, France, sheltered in the Jesuit sanctuary from the feral convulsions and purges that had so rent our world, I learned simple civilities, such as how to make a sponge without the benefit of a starter. For this, one need only find a suitably sugary piece of dried fruit and use it in place of the dollop from the previous batch. Whereas a baker may use an ancient line of leavening dough, each batch carrying an enlivening pinch of its parent, the resourceful cook may sire his own line from the hearty particles of yeast that cling as a white rime to a raisin — and raisins I had in plenty. I was feeling capable if not optimistic when I encountered my first obstacle: lack of clean water.

Sponges aren't demanding, yet without clean water they will never rise. The water we drink here on the ship is cut with spirits for preservation, and the water we ride upon is salty as tears. This struck me as a defeating blow and sent me to my cell muttering in my frustration.

After an hour on my sack, though, I had

devised, in my head, a simple distillery, which might, with heaven's help, clean the water of salt. Seriously doubting that I would find the glass retorts or copper tubes needed to build such a contraption, I headed to the galley but stopped one last time in the pantry to peer around, and thank Mary I did, for there I rediscovered the sack of coconuts. Happy day! The water in a coconut is clean enough to wash a wound, and its sweetness will only make the sponge happier.

I had mixed the ingredients together, ignoring as best I could the coarse and musty quality of the flour, when I realized the second obstacle: lack of warmth. We are headed far south, I am told, following the captain's mysterious agenda, to round the gruff chin of Africa. But for the time being we haven't yet passed the Canary Islands, and while the days can be hot, the nights are cold enough to rattle my teeth.

My childhood guardian, Father Sonora, had a saying: "If it's too cold for you, it's too cold for the dough." Normally a bread sponge is left in the kitchen, near the embers of the fire, but I could not leave such a delicate thing in Conrad's reach, for I was sure he would step in it, spit in it, or eat it as soon as I turned my back. To overcome this impasse, I have decided to nurture my sponge as a wet nurse.

I have borrowed, from a heap of supplies, a kidney-shaped tin box, with a long leather strap. From the scraps inside, I surmised it had been used to carry tobacco, hardtack, and, it appeared, something furry. I cleaned it as well as possible with boiled seawater, dried it with the least-filthy corner of my shirt, placed my sponge within it, closed the lid, and hung it around my neck. It rests against my belly, where my body temperature will keep it in good health. In this way I will be able to monitor its progress and feed, mix, and moisten it as needed. Not since Abel ground the first flour between two river stones has a sponge been so arduously crafted. I will not know if I have succeeded for some days.

I was heartened, this afternoon, to hear the bosun call for "A Bible in every hand!" I should have guessed that, upon this ship, "Bibles" refer to the large white stones they use to scrub the decks. These little disappointments wear at me more than they should.

As the men chased my boots about the deck with their scrubbing, I overheard them talking again, with fear in their voices, about the corsair ship *La Colette.*

"She's fast enough to creep up and burn us to the waterline at dawn."

It was then that it struck me. "Who is the captain of *La Colette*?" I asked.

"The devil Laroche," was the answer.

Could it be the same Laroche whose accent made me nostalgic for my younger days in France? It had to be.

"Hah! I know the man!" I blurted, but even as the words left my mouth I knew I should not have uttered them aloud. It was an oafish mistake, but when Mr. Apples came to lock my cell tonight, there was no sign that my slip had raised any alarms.

Years ago I had been excited to have the legendary Laroche in the house, though I suspected that he was the fictional product of unscrupulous writers looking to sell more papers. The moment I saw his overcast eyes, however, and the restless intelligence therein, I thought, *It may all be true.*

I had pieced the scandalous story together from various places; parts of it I had read in the papers, parts of it were whispered by maids and footmen. Alexandre Laroche had had some terrible luck. The locket about his neck, they said, carried the cameo of an heiress, his fiancée for a time — could her name have been Colette? This detail I believed, and it endeared me to the man, for I had my own heart's grief hidden in a locket. But other bits seemed rather incredible: He graduated from the Sorbonne at the age of fourteen and, during his apprenticeship with Lavoisier, had facilitated many of the great scientist's breakthroughs before becoming one of the youngest officers of Napoleon's navy. For a time, Laroche was the hope of France. A mint was spent on his plans for a ship that would move under the waves like a fish. When I first heard about it I laughed outright, but he'd built a working prototype, or so the story went; the thing could rise, fire a broadside, then disappear again beneath the surface. With the ports of Europe blockaded, Napoleon needed a marvel, and Laroche was going to give it to him.

These kinds of tales, always delivered in a frightened half whisper, and describing how terrifically close England came to invasion or defeat, are as common as the boasts of the fearless heroics that saved us — inseparable as the soldier and his shadow. In this particular tale, our salvation came in an unlikely form. Laroche was demonstrating his disappearing ship to some officials, an admiral, and a cousin of Napoleon, I believe, when they were attacked by none other than the pirate Mabbot, becoming another casualty of her roving bloodlust. The air bladders, or whatever kept the thing afloat, were ruptured and everyone drowned except Laroche. Some will tell you that this was the decisive battle of the war, and indeed I shudder to think what would have become of us if such a ship had made it to Trafalgar. The loss of the ship ruined Laroche's career, and he was court-martialed to account for the lives of the officers aboard. His assets were seized and he was imprisoned. Only when Napoleon was exiled did Laroche walk from the jailhouse, his head bursting with new ideas. Colette, needless to say, had not waited for him; she had married a duke.

Despite his genius, Laroche slept under worktables in grimy warehouses, spending outrageous sums on new inventions and signing away his patents to settle his debts. He had fled France and lectured at universities on a variety of subjects but had never taken positions, preferring to spend all of his attention on new inventions. It was when he came to visit Ramsey, at the country manor in Somerset, that I met the man.

His arrival was quite the event. Naturally the staff had been whispering. Some had read transcripts of his lectures, and we had all heard his outlandish theories: that the weather could be controlled with magnets, providing they were large enough; that certain birds could be taught to speak and understand French but not English; that gold could be distilled from urine. I had seen an illustration of his proposal to send people across the channel in cannonball carriages. The carriage would be righted in the air with fins like a shuttlecock's. One rumor was confirmed shortly after his arrival: that he chewed every bite of his food exactly twenty-four times.

His composure was upright and solemn, like a candle flame in a still cell. I did not expect the celebrated scientist to dress like a funeral mourner, but black was his everyday color. Indeed he would have passed for a shadow in the hall save for the one piece of light he allowed himself: the faded cravat that needed starching and made him look as if his head had been served on a bed of wilted escarole. Even his suede gloves were jet and delicate as a woman's. He wore them, the waitstaff reported, throughout breakfast, and when Ramsey remarked upon it, the Frenchman's reply was this: "Some of my instruments require the utmost finesse. I cannot squander my sensitivity on the mundane abrasions of the world."

I had hoped to impress him that evening with my coq au vin (my secret was a sauce inspirited with ground andouille sausage), but, as it turned out, my time near Laroche would be less than pleasant for both of us.

The grounds to the east of the manor were little more than a green and gently sloping lawn, bounded by hedges. Its farthest edge was the boundary of Jessop's Wood, where the hounds were released in the spring. The hunting parties, sounding their bugles like the angels of the apocalypse, turned the green into a battlefield of ankle-twisting divots and slick mud, which the gardeners spent months trying to repair. In early fall, though, it was an almost meditative place, overlooking the ember hues of the forest.

As the manor was far from a good butcher shop, I had insisted on replacing the tough Tamworth hogs in the pens with spotted Saddleback shoats that I knew would provide tender ham and bacon positively tatted with fat. I wouldn't have bothered if I had known what was to become of them.

There was to be a demonstration of some kind that afternoon, and our distinguished guest had given me occasion to open some aged Gloucester cheese that had a wonderful caramel spirit lurking behind its peppery surface. My plan was to serve it at tea with currant jelly and manchets hot from the oven. But I never got the chance; the butler informed me that Ramsey wished me to help "provide our Laroche with an authentic target."

There is something about the power of an order. I was no soldier, and yet, though it seemed for a moment that my employer planned to shoot at me for fun, still I washed my hands and went out — such is the urge to be a sport, a good and willing man. When I presented myself, however, Ramsey sent me and another to wrangle the pigs from their pen out onto the green. We tugged and prodded them to the far end, just fifty yards from the edge of the forest. They were frightened, and we had to hammer a steel post deeply into the ground to keep them from yanking it free with their head-wagging. I had been feeding them apples and figs all week to sweeten their meat, and we struggled not to slip on their excrement.

Laroche, meanwhile, was overseeing the placement of a cannon upon a platform not far from the windows of the guest rooms.

Between the pigs and the cannon, most of the staff had muddied themselves in one way or another and stood in clusters near the house, whispering and giggling at the strange events of the day. After changing into clean pants, I stood with them, though I could not share their festive mood.

"Is it target enough," teased Ramsey, "or shall we put the geese out there as well?"

"It is sufficient," muttered Laroche, as he peered at his target through a glass and made adjustments to a sextant.

The learned Frenchman was indulging in what I thought was a theatrical display of fastidiousness. But I would come to learn that his precision was born of acute economy; he had but two of his peculiar cannonballs and could not afford to waste them on imprecise shots. As it turned out, one shot was sufficient.

The wait only heightened the staff's anticipation. The women clucked and covered their faces, while the men placed bets and offered their guesses at the nature of the missile. I took the opportunity to express my dismay to Ramsey. "I see we won't be having pork cassoulet next month," I said.

Ramsey was watching Laroche closely and muttered, "Rather we'll be having it tomorrow, I should say."

With that I was dismissed and considered retiring to my cheese but, like the rest of the crowd, I was too fascinated by the spectacle, especially when I considered this:

Ramsey never missed an opportunity to invite friends and investors to his manor for an afternoon of fun. Except for Laroche, though, no one of import was there. We were witnessing something of a secret.

Laroche proceeded to tamp and prime the cannon with swift, clean strokes. Then, with a magician's timing, he opened a box to reveal an iron sphere couched in coarse felt. The cannonball was riddled with boreholes, perhaps two dozen of them, set at regular intervals across its surface. He inserted a key into one of the holes, and the ball began to tick like a clock. He poured a glass of water over the sphere, then delivered it into the cannon as solemnly as a sleeping baby into a cradle.

A hush fell over us. Could we still hear the ominous ticking from inside the cannon, or were we only counting anxious breaths as we waited for the shot? Laroche looked to Ramsey, who nodded. Finally the moment was upon us. We all watched the gun, but Laroche had his eye on the distant, doomed animals.

Though we had been waiting for it all afternoon, the crack of the gun made us jump. Some even screamed, then laughed to cover their embarrassment.

There was a burst of grass as the ball

landed two yards short of the startled pigs and sat there in the soil like a dropped meringue.

There was just time enough for snickers from the men, when *WHAM!* the cannonball burst from within, sending shot from its holes. Behind a haze of smoke, the pigs could be seen on the ground — one lay motionless, while the other writhed and screamed like a lost child.

"Explosive shot," Laroche announced, "is not generally used because of the difficulty of fuses and temperament — it is as likely to destroy your own ship as the enemy's. But this weapon is different. There is no fuse to break off or fail in the mist. It works wet or dry, as you see. Simply set the spring for as many seconds as you need and fire. A single shot, even poorly aimed, is sufficient to undo fifteen men or punch through the enemy's magazine."

Ramsey began the applause and the staff joined him. Then he shouted, "Well — back to business!" But even as we turned toward our various tasks, I heard my name. "Wedgwood! You can do a field dressing, can't you? I trust you to sort what is fit for the table — the rest to the hounds."

Before I could object that the slaughtering was usually done by others, he sidled away with Laroche to get a closer look at the carnage. With a sigh, I recruited my sous-chef and a third man, and we set out with knives, saws, buckets, and tarpaulins.

I couldn't help but let disgust show on my face. It wasn't only that I had better things to do — the entire scene was offensive. A cleanly butchered pig suffers little, but even after the time we took gathering our implements, one of the pigs still groaned in its puddle of blood and piss. Ribs were shattered, and it was clear that the offal was pierced and leaking into the cavities, rendering much inedible.

Ramsey, though, took no notice of my chagrin, as he was positively fascinated with the effects of the demonstration. He and Laroche had taken up field chairs not ten feet away and were awaiting tea service. *Let them eat yesterday's biscuits,* I thought. Ramsey kept getting up to inspect the crater the missile had created and to peer at the pigs' bodies. At one point he even inserted a finger into one of the wounds, like Caravaggio's Thomas.

Returning to his chair, he placed his feet upon the still-smoldering cannonball and asked Laroche, "Is it safe?"

"As a cricket ball," answered the sober Frenchman. "Though a secondary charge is

84

possible, perhaps. The basic concept is da Vinci's — the clockwork, the *susciter,* is entirely mine."

Even with three of us working at it, the rude task took hours. At several points, as when my footing gave and I landed belly-down in a pile of viscera, I nearly gave up, but Ramsey had given us an order and it would not do to question him in front of the guest. Sense would have dictated that we wheel the carcasses to proper hooks and blocks, but, as I would come to see, Ramsey wanted something of a mess.

He smoked a pipe, and Laroche, who indulged in neither tobacco nor spirits, simply sat upright in his chair and looked toward the quince orchard where the bare trees turned the sky into a crackle glaze.

"After all this time," began Ramsey, "you must still think about the pirate who sank your ship?"

"She is a blight," said Laroche. "An *égoïste* — what is the word? — the worst kind of person — seducers, vandals, provo-cateurs — *égoïstes.* They ambush the pas-sages, terrify travelers and merchants. Like those colonists who threw your tea into the harbor, no? Or the crimson mob cheering the guillotine as it minced glorious France into suet. Mabbot is one of these. I am but a sweeper. My ultimate task is to rid the world of the *égoïstes*. They say the era of the Crown is behind us, but these revolutionaries, they all want to be kings. A million kings? No. Our future comfort lies in the corporation, in the unity of the shared goal."

Their tea delivered, and our hogs cleaned, finally, of offal, the gentlemen continued their interview as we began to saw off the heads.

Addressing Laroche in somber tones, Ramsey said, "It's a fine speech to deliver at parties. But if we are to work together, I would need an accounting of your personal motivations. Our arrangement will lack the safeguards of tradition. I must trust you as I trust myself, so I'll be perfectly blunt —"

"You wish to see my clockwork," Laroche said. "Are the springs and gears aligned? Are there hidden switches?"

"Just so."

"My casing is open; fasten your calipers to anything you like."

"A man of your talents should have his own fortune to rely on by now, I should say."

"I have not drunk or gambled my prospects away," said Laroche. "It is no secret that my future, my very name, has been sabotaged by Mabbot. It is no small thing to rescue a reputation, indeed to write oneself twice into history. It may sound like hubris, but would God have given me these gifts if He had intended me to fix clocks? No, tools are made for a particular purpose. It is an offense to heaven to misuse them. Since I left France I have spent all of my energies refining my designs, analyzing tactical methodologies — I am here at last because I am ready."

"It is this particular confidence that intrigues me so," said Ramsey. "How would you guarantee results?"

"The losses your company suffers yearly from piracy are a matter of public record. The cost of my expedition is but a fraction of that annual toll. If you had more promising options, you would take them."

"Don't mistake me," said Ramsey. "I've looked at the plans, and if they work as well as this toy here, your modifications will make for an impressive ship. But explain to me why should I spend on your one vessel what would buy me three warships?"

Laroche replied without a pause: "Pendleton gunships can blockade a harbor or shell a fortress, but one does not use a lathe to pound a nail. Mabbot defends neither port nor country — she takes her orders from the wind, spits on the rules of engagement.

Your navy cannot hope to defeat what it cannot comprehend. If it could, you would not be considering my proposal. You see, I speak not from pride but from the courtesy of clarity. I am no beggar, Lord Ramsey, I am simply the right tool for the task."

"I've learned, though," said Ramsey, "that matters of the heart are not particularly reliable investments."

"Heart doesn't enter into it. If a wolf eats your lambs, it is nonsense to hate the wolf. Only proceed out at once with a gun."

"But Mabbot robbed you of your reputation, your prospects," said Ramsey. "And am I mistaken, or did your fiancée leave you for a less disgraced man?"

Laroche sat stock-still, gazing out at the orchard where a flock of magpies suddenly lifted like a veil into the breeze and, with a distant clatter, settled again. He was so rapt in his meditation that for a moment it seemed he hadn't heard Ramsey's words.

Finally, he cleared his throat and said, "It is true, once Mabbot is dead, I will move into brighter days, but so will you — so will all civilized men. The wounds Mabbot inflicted are a gift to me. They are a daily spur to keep me from falling into sloth. You will back me not because I am the only man who hates her as much as you do, nor for my ingenuity, but because I am —"

"The right tool. Yes, you've said that."

They were quiet then, listening to the wet work of the butchering. We had been forced to make impromptu cuts to accommodate the shattered limbs and ribs. I had been taught that there is no knuckle too base for a stewpot, but in my ocher-slicked frustration, I sent pounds of good meat to the dogs that day.

Ramsey, knocking his pipe against his boot, said, "You paint the very picture of capability, Laroche. But how does a man poised over the precipice of total ruin sit so composed? Your name is hardly mentioned but a pack of creditors comes baying for your blood. I'll say it plainly: if I reject you, don't deny it, your next bed will be in a debtors' prison. You're so deeply in arrears that even the patent for this extraordinary weapon would buy you only, perhaps, a high window in your cell. I have seen men with better prospects on their knees, their cheeks shining with tears. You see, I know everything about you, except where your pride comes from."

Here, at last, I saw the Frenchman's composure flag — it was only in the tilt of his head and the pitch of his voice, ever so slightly strained. He stretched his neck as if it pained him. "What you call pride is but determination, and not fortune's caltrops, nor slander's whip, can slow me in my pursuit —"

"Dying of consumption in a crowded cell would slow you right down, I should say."

Almost too quietly to be heard, Laroche said, "Then you know my several motivations, my lord. I comprehend my position full well. You humiliate me in front of the servants, demand the details of my ignominy over the sound of the meat cleaver."

"Should I leave the pigs to rot? I did not acquire my holdings by letting things go to waste. I value a penny as a pound."

Finally Laroche looked at Ramsey, and in his slate eyes I saw a man whose suffering had become a kind of skeleton holding him upright. "I see the lesson, but it is wasted on me. I never hoped to dictate the terms of our arrangement." His gaze had returned to the horizon where the thorn of the moon was sinking. "If I am fit for the task, then for God's sake, use me."

After a moment, Ramsey stood and shook Laroche's gloved hand, and they went together to sign papers, or drink champagne or whatever one does to commemorate such an arrangement, leaving us to our disassembly.

■ ■ ■ ■

This account has, perhaps, painted an uncouth image of my late employer. A man of such responsibilities must occasionally negotiate the darker eddies of life's tide, and it would take a nimbler hand than mine to describe the ultimate righteousness of it. So I leave the details smeared on the page. He who writes our every story needs no annotation from me.

It is encouraging, nevertheless, to think that rescue may be on its way in the form of this eccentric and capable Laroche. In the light of the sun, I tell myself that my tribulations may soon be over. As the sun sets, though, I shudder.

I write here all I can, yet cannot express the fatigue I collapse under each night, worn to the bone with worry. I feel Hope and Fear beside me all the time, two woodsmen with a saw across my middle. They pull the saw in turns. It is everything I can do not to fall in two.

Wednesday, August 25
Conrad's verbosity is, at last, of some use. I asked him about the other prisoner and received this response: " 'At's Jeroboam.

Cap'm of the *Sinensis,* which is restin' happy on the bottom. Mabbot thought he had the Fox aboard; we broke her masts. 'At's why we went to England in the first place, only to find he'd left the Fox on the penal island they call the Fist. But Mabbot didn't waste the trip, did she? Got Ramsey, she did!"

"And the rest of Jeroboam's crew?"

"Playing cards with the squid."

"She's a monster. Why is he chained even at sea while I am free to roam?" I asked.

"You haven't fired guns at us. She keeps you without prejudice. But Jeroboam's earned her spite."

A captain! Here is an ally who knows battle. Here is a weathered crag on which to build hope. I have narrowed the possible chambers that might contain Captain Jeroboam to two. I shall investigate further.

Why it had not occurred to me before, I cannot say, but after seeing the men hoisting the longboats today on their return from Porto Santo, my head has split with an idea. The boats are always ready, and, if no one saw us, Jeroboam and I could away in one to try our luck for land. Two men upon the deck, by means of davits and muscle, can haul the boats up or down, and this while they are full of cargo. Jeroboam and I could manage this, I'm sure. Even if we were intercepted by strangers on open water, they could scarcely be more villainous than those who hold us now. The trick will be secrecy; the deck is never empty. Even in the dead of the night, I hear the graveyard watch clomping about and the stations calling "All's well!"

Thursday, August 26
I've located Captain Jeroboam. A rap on his door elicited a weary "What now?"

I slipped a note under his door. It read:

I am a simple cook but I have the resolve of a garrison. I am at your disposal, Captain, and ready to fly. Longboats in dead of night? Meanwhile keep you well. O. Z. Wedgwood.

It was tempting to write a longer missive, but I kept it brief so he might destroy it easily. I do not know what effect eating paper has on gout. I should not like to make things more difficult for the man.

It is a good omen that, today, my bread sponge batter has a faint but unmistakably intimate aroma of yeast. Like the smell of hard work that surrounds one who has just come in from picking apples. I must admit a certain motherly feeling toward this stowaway on my person. While I still don't know how I will use it, at least one of us is comfortable.

My labors have yielded a further spark of inspiration. In considering my scarce resources, I realized that I have privileged access to the provisions upon this ship, and this small advantage might be just enough to free me. A night watchman properly lubricated with food and drink is no watchman at all! This warrants consideration, but I must stay alive in the meanwhile, and that means cooking.

I have been forced to indebt myself to the carpenter, Kitzu, who is Japanese, thick, and bearded. He tends to speak in grunts. He is also a skilled fisherman. He drags nets and bait lines behind the boat, hanging like an ape from the railings. He adjusts and retrieves the nets with considerable strength and brings forth variegated treasures. Fish I have never seen, of all colors and shapes, beaked, spiked, soft, and armored. It is Kitzu's wont to choose a few to roast whole on sticks over a cresset, tossing the bones to the petrels who follow the ship. In this way, he and a few others break the unrelenting monotony of Conrad's cooking.

With Mabbot's dinner but a few days away, I stood by, watching him perform his feat, then begged to share a portion of his bounty. I had nothing to offer in exchange, save for my skills. So I am now beholden to this man; I have promised him something good to eat, and I cannot imagine what it will be. I implored him to keep our arrangement secret, for I do not know how jealous Mabbot is. Neither does Kitzu seem a man I would wish to disappoint.

But I must focus on my achievements: I have now, in a pail by my feet, a lovely spotted fish with an elegant stripe, which, I'm certain, is a type of cod. Further, in a bucket, a good handful of vigorous striped shrimp. By refreshing their water regularly, I hope to keep them alive until needed.

I am lost at sea. I have a single fish with which to preserve my life.

5
JEROBOAM'S PLAN
IN WHICH I VOW TO STOP MABBOT

Friday, August 27
This morning, to my surprise, Mr. Apples opened my door and dragged me to the deck. I cursed myself for not having shown more care in communicating with Jeroboam.

The deck was already alive with all hands, and I feared a flogging or execution was expected. I tried to gather my courage as I was shackled together with Captain Jeroboam. The man nodded at me with the grim composure born of gentility and hardship. Our wrists were connected by a short length of chain looped through the railing.

Up close, the poor man's body bore testimony to his ordeal. Despite the palm-leaf sun hat, his face was peeling and burned. His mutton-chop beard, majestic as it must once have been, now looked not unlike two frightened squirrels clinging to his head. Though it was scratched to opac-

96

ity, his monocle never fell from his eye.

"My good sir," Jeroboam intoned as soon as we were left alone. "A pleasure and a good thing, for now we have the strength of two!" We shook hands awkwardly, bending at the knees to accommodate the chains.

"If only we'd had more time to hatch a plan," I said.

"Oh, the plan is hatched, Quincy," he whispered. "This *is* the plan. But we must be patient, this is apt to take all day."

"Do they mean to torture us?"

"Jupiter, no. Not today. Today we're sacking the Fist, the island prison. You'll forgive the impertinence, but you wouldn't happen to have a spot of tobacco on you?"

"Sorry, no."

"No, of course not. Tighten up that chain, will you? After I tug, you give it a tug. Put your weight into it, Quincy! That's it. Ha ha. Slowly now."

By alternating our efforts, we began to use the chain to rasp at the railing.

"Don't look at it, Quincy, you'll give us away. We're just talking, you see. Gesturing, just passing the time, ha ha. Mabbot's shackled us here because she half suspects I've led her to an ambush."

"My name is Owen," I said. "Owen Wedgwood."

"Yes, I got your note. A pleasure. Now tug a little harder. That's the stuff, Quincy. You should know, fellow, that your capture was in no way a result of any disclosure I made to Mabbot. She came by Ramsey's whereabouts through another channel altogether. The devil himself whispers in her ear, I'd wager. Tell me, though — you were there — how did Ramsey fare? No, by your face I see the answer. Jupiter, what a pity! I've played cricket with the man and won't hesitate to swear that he was the very figure of good breeding! But you know that. And a lovely bowler. I've seen faster, but not a man bowls more elegantly . . . bowled, I should say. Take heart, chap, the tallest tree gets cut first."

The ship was abuzz, men ran to and fro carrying cannonballs and funnels of powder.

"No," Jeroboam continued, "I would have let her roast me alive before I so much as nodded in the direction of such a gentleman. I've given her a lesser prize. A rock, nothing more. You can see it now, there — see that guano-encrusted knob on the horizon? A prison. Mabbot is looking to crack it open and shake out the Brass Fox. I know he's there, as I delivered him myself, though I didn't know it was him at the time. Caught him with ten others near the Pearl

River, trying to pass as Chinamen. Not cowardice but prudence has compelled me to lead her to him now." He leaned in here, the curl of his whiskers nearly grazing my cheek — he must have been maintaining them with pitch and spittle. "Now give me your ear, Quincy. This prison was a French fort before we repurposed her to hold the scum of the seas. High walls and armed guards won't be taken easily, will they? Opportunity for Mabbot to catch a bullet in her heart, perhaps. But here's the meat: in the heat of battle, you and I will take the opportunity to make a quick move for one of the boats. Right? Right. Know any good riddles, Quincy?"

I did not.

The spit of rock on the horizon grew.

"We're getting closer. C'mon now, Quincy, give it a stiff yank, show some muscle! There you go. My ship was the Pendleton *Sinensis,* a third-rate ship of the line, armed like a man-o'-war! A proud beauty. Mabbot took us in a storm. Waves around us like the Carpathian Mountains. Shameful, reckless, there is not a cracker's worth of honor in her. She used her own ship to roll us, like pigs wrestling in the mud. It stained my dignity just to witness. Not proper. The codes of engagement mean nothing to her.

White horses breaking over both our decks and still she charged. Well, cheats lose in the cheating, as my father said. And my men knew it was no dishonor to lose that way."

"Who is the Brass Fox?" I asked.

"A worm and a freebooter — just like Mabbot. They're cut from the same cloth, those two. Anyone with eyes can see that. He's got some grand scheme, that one. He's not just picking pockets anymore — he's onto an altogether different game. He's kept mum about it, but they'll squeeze the truth out of him there on the Fist."

My wrist was already blistering where the shackles rubbed, and we had made but little progress through the hard wood.

"We're in the sauce, aren't we?" Jeroboam laughed. "But don't fret. Don't spend a second worrying, Quincy, Jeroboam has a plan. She tricked me, that's what she did. Didn't even get the opportunity to die with my crew, good men and clean-shaven every morning. That's how I ran my ship. Boot polish and tea at two. Other ships leave civility on the docks. The sea is a corrosive influence. Take a glance at this monkey crew and you'll see my meaning. Not on my deck! 'A clean face is an alert face.' That was our creed. 'If we die in the course of our duty, it shall be as gentlemen!' It's a distinction to sail with Captain Jeroboam. Where else does a sailor learn proper cricket while earning his stripes upon a forty-gun ship? Well, the proportions weren't quite right for cricket, but all of the basics, bowling, batting we practiced every day . . . Fielding we had to get creative with, of course. 'If you can catch a ball in twenty-foot waves, there's nothing that can upset you.' That was our motto."

Here he lapsed at last into a silence. We continued to grind our chain over the railing. My fingers began to go numb. It occurred to me that the man had perhaps not survived Mabbot's assault with his wits entirely intact. The stubborn perch of his ruined monocle unnerved me.

"I'm sure you did your best by them," I said.

At this he smiled sadly. "Only a few of them could really bat. I mean properly," he said.

"But what is Mabbot's purpose?"

"Who can tell? She wants to steal something. That's sure. The Brass Fox is the key she needs. The man could steal the royal commode with His Highness still upon it. But her ultimate goal? I don't know. Something ghastly, I assure you."

I could see a structure on the island now, a fortress of granite.

"When we see the opening, we must take it with all speed and courage," Jeroboam said. "A prison has plenty of nooks to hide in. We'll not get a chance like this again. Once we've escaped we'll bring back an armada to sink her. Have you a prayer? I've never had the tongue for it."

This finally was something I could do. "Deliver us, O Jesus, from all evil, from all sin" — even with our heads bowed, the man kept tugging on the chain — "from your wrath and from the snares of the devil."

"Amen. Just right," he said, looking relieved. "Are you married?"

"My wife is passed," I said.

"I'm sorry for you." He tried to pat me on the back, but the chain brought him up short. "Myself, I have the sweetest wife at home and yet I philander. You know the kind of smooth-cheeked women who carry baskets near the docks? Who are not afraid to look you in the eye? Of course, now, in the thick of it, I can think only of my wife."

"You'll see her soon enough," I said.

This, too, cheered him, and he smiled at me as if we were both already free.

The prison was perched upon low cliffs where it had a clean view of the sea. It had been built so close to the edge and with native stones that it looked like a brief extension of the sheer face itself. From a distance the squat structure looked disproportionate, like a child's sand castle. As we got closer, it was clear, by the action atop the walls, that they had spotted us long ago. Guards ran about making preparations. At the base of the cliff, sea lions lounged like drunkards after a bacchanal.

I flinched when the fortress guns fired. The water danced where their missiles went under, but none reached us. The sea lions barked out their own response, and then slipped enviably away.

"Unsporting!" Captain Jeroboam yelled. "They've only carronades. A prison is ready to guard itself from within, not from without."

Mabbot anchored the *Rose* fifty yards from where the crowns of foam marked the edge of the enemy's range. She shouted at Mr. Apples, "Aim well and take your time! Bit by bit!"

Mr. Apples went down the line of deck cannon, sighting over their maws and cranking them into position himself. Sometimes he would give a cannon a knock with his fist to make its angle perfect.

It was an eerie thing to watch him so at ease with the enemy's wrath landing so near. Occasionally I heard the whistle of rifle shot in the air above us, or the crack as a musket ball set itself in a mast. Bound as I was, I could do nothing but make myself as small as possible.

Mr. Apples was intimate with each of the guns and cajoled and patted them as if tending to a field of dairy cows. Their positions were locked, and the men marked their angles with pencils. Only after Mr. Apples had gone below deck to see to all the other guns did he give the order. "By the numbers and easy!" he shouted. "Fire!"

One by one, our guns, with a terrible rolling tempo, like the ticking of a monstrous clock, fired on the prison. The blasts were dreadful. I tried to cover my ears, but Jeroboam, still trying to saw through the wood, tugged the chain and I ended up slapping myself into the rail.

The first bombardment hit the base of the closest tower, making little mark save for a cloud of powdered granite. But what was just a scratch on the surface of the prison grew as each subsequent cannonball clawed at the wound. Mr. Apples's aim was unerring, and, slowly, a hole opened at the base of the tower. As a boy I had seen fellows stabbing at termite nests for fun. The result here was similar; the prison guards swarmed and scattered in great agitation, unable to prevent the slow erosion of their keep.

Mabbot, with a mug of hot tea, descended from the poop deck to confer briefly with Mr. Apples, then returned.

I yelled at Captain Jeroboam over the noise: "Isn't giving her the Brass Fox unwise?"

"I let her have this battle so we might take the war." Jeroboam put his finger to his nose. "We'll bring back an armada."

During the siege, one of the prison's cannonballs, by fluke of wind or powder, surpassed its range and punched a hole in the planks so near Mabbot that she had to dance to keep from falling in.

Mr. Apples rushed to her side. "Cap'm?"

"It's nothing. Keep at it, Mr. Apples," Mabbot said, irritated at the spilling of her tea. "Keep at it."

After an hour of this inchmeal injury, the tower, haloed in dust, leaned as if considering a more comfortable repose, then collapsed spectacularly, dropping in clusters off the cliff and into the tortured sea.

Silence and dust followed. Mr. Apples set himself to realigning the guns, then the terrible metronome started again, this time picking away at the adjoining walls. Only when a white flag unfurled from the top of the prison and hung like a parched tongue did Mr. Apples cease firing. Mabbot put aside her tea and checked the breach of her pistols.

"Trip the mudhook!" Mabbot shouted, and the anchor crew ran for the windlass while the rest readied themselves for battle. The *Flying Rose* jibed to position in the lee of the cliff, well beyond the arc of the remaining carronades. Longboats were lowered and, full of pirates, made for the beaches.

Mabbot shouted to the departing crew, "Not a prisoner harmed! Hear me! Don't touch the prisoners!" before disappearing into her cabin.

With all the boats gone to shore except Mabbot's pinnace, the deck was nearly deserted. Jeroboam, wheezing in anticipation, said, "Now's the moment, Quincy. *Now!*"

With a fierce yank, he broke through the weakened rail and nearly mangled my wrist in the doing. Off he went in a mad dash and I was compelled to shadow him, thinking, as I went, *This is the plan?* We ran flat-out toward the stern, heading for Mabbot's personal pinnace, which hung behind the ship, her little sails furled coyly. The elegant script on her stern read *Deimos.*

We scrambled from the quarterdeck to the

poop, and I was beginning to imagine what trouble sailing even that small boat would be for a pair so shackled when Jeroboam stopped in his tracks, stood straight at attention, and fell on his face. Though I tried, I could not hold him up, and, as he fell, he yanked me to my knees. His monocle broke with a pitiful sound. A short slender blade had pierced the back of his neck. Feng, who had thrown it, called for the captain, who emerged scowling.

She nudged Jeroboam with her boot, then turned a wry smile on me. "And you, Mr. Wedgwood, are you unhappy with our hospitality too?"

"No, ma'am," I quavered.

"Nothing you need?"

"Nothing, thank you, Captain."

She returned the blade to Feng, who cleaned it on the hem of his pants.

The weight of Jeroboam's arm pulled on me, and I was obliged to kneel near him. A breeze carried his palm-leaf hat over the rail. It danced for a moment in the air before dropping.

I was left alone. Occasionally a flurry of gunshots sounded from the prison above us, but they seemed distant and unrelated to me. The plan, whatever it had been, was horribly bungled. Things were far worse now, irredeemable. What folly to have put my hope in Jeroboam, whom I could no longer bring myself to look at. When I tried to stand and get some distance from the heap of him, his arm rose and tugged me back. He was my keeper now — even Feng left us unwatched.

I had had my fill of murder and corpses. A revulsion crept into me bit by bit, until it was everything I could do to stay where I was and not run screaming, dragging the bloody thing behind me.

Thus yoked with the dead, I witnessed the interrogation of the prison warden, who was brought at gunpoint to the deck. This man's keys had been ripped from him, belt and all, and he was forced to hold his pants up with both hands. Mabbot asked Mr. Apples a question with her eyes to which he merely shook his head.

A small heap of items, among them a tin cup, a prayer rug, and boots, were placed at Mabbot's feet. "These were in the jailer's chambers — he says they belonged to the Fox," Bai said.

Mabbot, her fury barely contained, demanded of the warden, "And where is the Brass Fox?"

The man pressed his forehead to the wood and raised his folded hands in supplication.

"Not here! He's not here."

"I'm beginning to grasp that. Where is he?"

"He escaped three weeks ago. We haven't had him for three weeks."

"Three weeks? Are you sure? Damn Jeroboam! Wish I could kill him again." She paced, fuming, then gripped the jailer by the hair. "Tell me why I shouldn't shoot you for incompetence. Did he just swim away?"

"He was delivered with a dozen other criminals." The officer moaned. "At first we didn't know who he was — he'd blacked his hair and given us a false name. When we discovered we had the Fox, we sent right off for instructions. Sometimes they want the notorious ones hanged in the public squares in London, it makes for a good show . . ." Here the man trailed off, remembering whom he was talking to.

"Give his head a thump, Mr. Apples," said Mabbot. "The contents are stuck."

The warden flinched and blurted the rest: "By the time we got instructions back, he'd flown." He held his hands up to show they were empty, as if he could be palming the Fox like a card.

"What were the instructions from London?"

"Immediate execution after interrogation."

"Without trial or even a last meal."

" 'Immediate' was the word. But we never got to do it. The Fox is not a natural man." The prison keeper wept. "Locks are nothing to him, he moves through the walls themselves. He took a hostage, one of the guards. There was a ship waiting for him. He had help."

"What ship?"

"A Dutch merchant, the *Diastema,* I think."

"Have you nothing for me?" Mabbot whispered.

"He left those things, a rug, a pipe, just things."

Feng returned on another longboat with a thin bearded man who covered his eyes against the sun. His overgrown nails and the grey stripes in his long beard gave him the appearance of a badger woken from its winter sleep. He was naked, filthy, and his ankles were swollen and suppurating where the shackles had been. By the angularity of his ribs, the man was starving.

"Who is this?" Mabbot demanded.

"That's Braga. He was in league with the Brass Fox," the jailer said eagerly. "Helped him escape."

"Bring him biscuits softened in a splash of wine, boys. Clothes for the man!"

The jailer stood in protest, but Mabbot kicked him down and placed her boot firmly on the buttons of his uniform. "By the looks of it, he's been kept in a hole for . . . how long?"

"Since the Fox escaped."

Mabbot pushed off from the jailer and made her way to crouch in front of Braga, who had ignored the clothes but was stuffing the hardtack into his mouth faster than he could choke it down.

"I know what loyalty the Fox demands," Mabbot said. "I won't ask what you think of him now."

Braga finally looked up from his food. He muttered, through wads of half-chewed dough, "Your hair —"

"We aren't talking about me, Mr. Braga. We are talking about the Fox. You would like to find him, I'll bet, to kiss his cheek or to throttle his neck for leaving you here in this pit. I don't care which. I am going to give you your freedom today, whether you help me or no."

"I don't know where he has gone."

"But you know where he has been, you know his secrets."

"Dug his tunnels around the Pearl River."

"Tunnels?" Mabbot stood, her brow shining in the sun. "So that's how he's out-smuggling the Pendleton curs. Mr. Apples, tunnels! Yes, Mr. Braga, you can help us. I'm offering you a position on my ship for as long as you like, and in exchange you'll tell me, and only me, Mr. Braga, all you know about the Fox. Is that an amicable arrangement?"

"Yes," the man said, "but . . ." And he looked at the jailer.

"But you have some unfinished business with your keeper," Mabbot said with a hint of disgust. "Make it quick. Bosun, loan our new shipmate a firearm. Trip anchor, Mr. Apples. Aloft and gather way. We didn't come here for tea and crumpets."

The crew moved up the shrouds like spiders to cast the gaskets from the sails while the jailer scampered across the deck begging, "Wait. Wait!"

Braga shot him twice in the head, dropped the gun as if it weighed too much, and began to bathe himself with a bucket and sponge.

Mabbot and Mr. Apples took the rug and other miscellany to disappear into her cabin, where I could hear their muffled argument.

The *Rose* was already wearing about, the sheets luffing anxiously as we crossed the wind and began to tack toward open sea, leaving the ruins behind us. A few other prisoners, wearing stupefied grins, had been brought aboard as recruits and, along with Braga, were given hardtack, panch, and a jovial tour. In my opinion, the disposition of the crew did not adequately reflect the horrors that the new recruits could look forward to. They explained the watch bells so blithely that I mumbled, "Oh, and they have 'theater paint' to look forward to, don't forget that!" As soon as I said it, I feared recrimination, but, happily, I was ignored.

A morbid petrel alighted and stared at Jeroboam's face, considering desecration. I shooed it away. I was being tested. Though I wanted nothing more than to be separated from Jeroboam's body, I could not bring myself to beg these pirates. To do so would give up the last shred of dignity I had. And so I stood there, until the sun set and the waning moon brought its cold scythe across the shimmering field.

Mercy appeared in the guise of Joshua, who, with Mabbot's keys jangling, unshackled me and led me toward my room. The moonlight was bright enough that I could see the child had no fewer than four cowlicks. It was then that a thought hit me like a pot dropped from the rafters: Joshua is the age my own son would have been, had he lived!

He is too quick to hide from; he saw my eyes watering and lifted his lantern to illuminate my face.

"Bring a book," I mouthed to him. "A book, next time. You can't write without reading."

In my room, I tied the dough tin again to my belly. I had hoped to leave the crude practice behind, but, it seems, I won't be escaping soon. I'll have to conjure a repast for the vixen after all.

As I pace in circles, my repugnance at the day's events has given way to a cold conviction: I cannot sit by as Mabbot callously murders every good man in the world.

Though I have no weapons, nor friends, nor money, nor hope of help, I swear that I will learn the scope of her mission. As an egg spoils from the tiniest crack, I will pierce the pellicle of her mystery and ruin her plans.

6
Dining with the Devil
IN WHICH I EARN A PILLOW

Saturday, August 28

I go, in my mind, to gentler times. Memory is a strange soup. My wife, when she was ready for me, wore a particular dress with a hem of lace poppies. It was her sign to me. She might say shyly, "A good day to go flower picking?" These days I can hardly recall her face and yet that hem is clear to me, its pattern burned into my fingertips.

Mr. Apples has either forgotten his duty or has been ordered to leave my cell open, for last night I was free to roam the boat deep into the night. Considering that it might be my last chance to see the stars, I moved along the bulwark, chilled to the bone as the graveyard watch went about their duties by lantern light. Cold as I was, it was good to stride freely under the filigree of the heavens. Still I am as far from freedom as I have ever been and daily getting farther; we push forever south with Africa

115

an occasional stitch of ocher on the port horizon. The ocean, whose essence is fluid and unresisting, is more prison than the staunchest bricks or iron bars.

I have examined the davits and blocks of the longboats again and am confident that they are not beyond my ken. If I take my time and lower myself very gradually, I believe I can manage the lines from within the boat itself. Further, I think it may be done quietly, as long as I move with deliberate pace. The moon is just a shaving shy of new. If I'm to have the advantage of darkness, I'll have to do it soon. In preparation I have waxed a small sack and filled it with dried figs, Mary Sweet, hardtack, and a flask of panch. I considered stealing the compass from the helm house but don't want to raise suspicion. After the captain has been fed and attention drifts from me, I shall make my move.

Monday, August 30
I am alive. The shrew is appeased, at least for the week. This is how I did it.

Yesterday morning I rose early, still unsure of my recipes but with a fire in my belly. I fasted, as is my wont when faced with an important job, taking only the smallest bite of hardtack dipped in weak tea. I have found that hunger improves my sense of smell and gives inspiration a clean passage. In any case my nerves would not allow me to eat.

Conrad had already committed his crimes for the morning, and so I banished him from the galley. I was alone and strangely energized by the task before me. I clapped my hands together to scare invisible demons from the room and began.

It is no great secret that cooking is, in essence, seduction. As with *amour,* pleasure does not bloom in the body so much as in the mind. One may be a "gymnast in the sheets," as the coarse say, but without passion and internal fire, without longing and anticipation, one may as well be doing calisthenics. So food. The most rarefied tastes on the unprepared tongue may be ignored or, worse, misunderstood. How then is the mind prepared for delicacy? As with Don Juan, reputation stirs desire. But even the best chef must entice interest, use aroma to flirt, caress and kiss with silken soups, reassure and coddle with a dulcet pudding.

Beginning at the end, I roasted walnuts and ground them to a fine crumb, then mixed them with half of my yeast starter, whose spongy surface, to my delight, was capped with a vigorous froth — evidence of its appreciation of the coconut water. To this batter I added flour, honey (warmed and strained through cloth to rid it of the grit), a pinch of salt, and a little lime juice and set it aside near the hearth. My heart leaped up when, an hour later, it had risen. I added a little more coconut water to thin the dough and spooned it onto a hot grill to make walnut crisp-cakes.

Let me sing the praises of wheat, for its powers seem bounded only by imagination. It can thicken, crisp, lend strength and flexibility, or emulsify. It is the bridegroom to yeast and is more sensitive to air, temperature, and moisture than any barometer. I should not be surprised to learn that God had, in fact, not made man from mud but from a sun-browned durum. I've had breads made with other grains, such as farro, millet, and potato — even at their best they are more deserving of mason's mortar than butter.

Then I set myself to the main meal. I mashed a cooked potato to a paste and dried it on the hot bricks of the hearth. Meanwhile I prepared the rice. Around my neck I wear a leather cord and a pewter locket filled with saffron, the favorite spice of my lost Elizabeth, rest her soul. It reminded her of sneaking tastes from the mulling pot as a child in her father's inn. At closing time, the dregs, raisins, cloves, cinnamon, and cider would have formed a thick paste in the bottom, and nothing approached that heavenly liquor, she told me, so much as the smell of saffron. After I lost her, cooking became my solitary devotion, and I have touched nothing more voluptuous than a butternut squash since. My unwavering focus in the kitchen, what others have called an obsessive attention to the viscosity of a sauce or angle of a cut cucumber, is, in fact, the only medicine I have for grief. That's not to say I have forgotten. When the tremors of life grow too jarring or when I fear I am losing touch with her memory, I open the locket, inhale, and hear the bell of her laughter and the soft graze of her arm by my side.

Of course I did not come to use the saffron easily. This was my reasoning: To leave the rice plain and be slain for it would be a class of suicide, frowned upon by heaven. Further, Elizabeth, should I meet her in that cloudy sphere, would not forgive me if, by reserving this memento, I met torture and death. And so I fed nostalgia to the grim jaws of practicality and tossed the scarlet threads into the rice as it boiled in seawater.

Such is the indomitable spirit of saffron

that even after years stale on my chest, it brought the rice to life with flavor and the color of a sunset. Or perhaps my wife leaned down and touched my efforts with a kettle-blessing to keep me safe. When the rice was still covered in water, I added raisins, which plumped pleasantly.

When the potato was dry, I powdered it further with my fist and used it to bread the filleted cod, adding black pepper and salt. I sautéed onions in lard, then fried the fish quickly, until the potato crumbs were golden, finally seasoning with a squeeze of lime juice.

The wine here is reportedly from Madeira (no doubt via some slain intermediary) and surprisingly good, if smoky. It hits the palate with a berry musk that sublimates to ephemeral lavender, all the while supported by a stalwart essence I can describe only as saddle leather. So it is true what they say about the enhancing effects of sea voyages on Madeira wine. Now that I know that the potation the men are rationed every day is this delightful, I might line up for it as the others do. The men call the gargantuan wine barrels "hogsheads," but to my eye they are properly firkins if not entire pipes. Each must carry at least one hundred and thirty gallons and several of these comprise the main ballast of the ship.

The sauce was a simple reduction of red wine, crushed garlic, peeled shrimp, dried figs, and salt — thickened with a simple roux. I say simple, but nothing on this rocking ship is simple. For decades I have enjoyed the meditative task of heating a handful of flour in butter to a perfectly roasted roux: the susurration of the wooden spoon in the pan and, as it darkens, the odor shifting from dry grass to wet terra-cotta and, ever so faintly, almonds. But here on the ship I must hold a pot with a rag in one hand and stir with my right, while at the same time dancing on the deck to the erratic music of the sea, hoping to avoid a bad scalding. Alas, for thickening a sauce, there is no replacement for roux.

For the occasion, Mabbot had provided miraculously intact china, with a blue glaze depicting horses running before a distant pagoda.

The cod parted in seams as if anticipating the red liquor I spooned over it, as I nudged the sauce-poached shrimp and figs around the edge of the porcelain. This was a moment that I struggle to put down in words. The arrangement of a meal on a plate is a sacred thing for me, representing the culminating moment not just of a day's work but indeed of my life's work, such as it is. It is an act that embodies untarnished hope for another's pleasure, a hope both ambitious and humble. Fretting falls away briefly and is replaced with an acceptance of the jumbled forms and flavors of the world, a feeling that things are as they should be. In short it is the one moment when my character is at its best. At least it should be. But how torn I had become, how lost, at the same time calmly wiping the rim of the plate clean while a voice in my ear whispered, *For a villain!*

I placed it, cakes and all, on a wooden plank and, lacking a proper silver lid, covered it with an inverted pot.

I kicked open the door of the galley, preparing to carry the meal out, and was met with a surprise. Unbeknownst to me — as focused as I was — my cooking had made a stir. The smell had enchanted the whispering men, who crowded near the door, sampling the air like so many alley cats, and had to be shoved aside by Mr. Apples so I could make my way to Mabbot with the tray.

Agonized in my knowledge that stumbling meant spilling not only the food but my life's blood, I navigated the slick wood, the pitch of the sea, and finally the dark companionway to Mabbot's cabin.

Rapping on her door with the toe of my boot, I was met by Feng. I flinched, remembering our last encounter at this threshold. This time, he stood aside to let me through the tiger-striped door. I stood, gaping.

Mabbot's chamber was unlike any I have ever seen: a strange hybrid of a sultan's pillow room, a duke's library, and a naturalist's laboratory. The entire back half of the cabin was windowed with thick glass set in heavy timber mullions. It being well night, the windows held nothing but our own reflections. During the day, though, they would provide a magnificent forty-five-degree view of the world behind. Upon the teak walls, fine oil landscapes and still lifes jostled for space. This bloodthirsty pirate had surrounded herself with scenes of tranquillity: a herd of distant cattle on a shady hill seemed curious about the pile of painted pomegranates just beyond the frame. The floor was thick with overlapping Turkish rugs. I smelled a cache of potpourri somewhere, heavy in cedar.

The cabin was of two levels, like the deck above: the bed, heaped with furs and hung with silk drapes, was on the upper; the saloon below contained a harpsichord and a small dining table. A stuffed pheasant perched atop a great mirror, its iridescent tail feathers unfurling all the way to the ground. Hanging on the mirror post was a grotesque and demonic mask with bugging eyes and scrolled tusks. Beside it a small door, ajar, led to an alcove. On a crowded bookshelf, a leaning stack of maps was braced by a human skull with a gaping hole in the brow, of the type made, I imagined, by a blunderbuss or perhaps a cudgel. This hole was filled by the languorous leaves of an orchid, its stalk reaching for heaven with a pristine burst of ivory flowers. Next to it, I spotted the brass bowl of potpourri that contained, my nose told me, the following precious items: cinnamon bark, bay leaves, rosemary, and cloves.

The captain was apparently a gardener. Rubbery vines crawled up the bedposts and framed the windows; potted ferns and plants with fanlike leaves squatted in the corners while, behind the bed, grew a citrus tree of some kind. With a deep envy, I saw, swelling upon it, the green buds of fruit. As if conjured by my covetousness, there appeared, almost hidden behind the tree, a small enamel bathtub.

Mabbot had been sitting on the plush chair near the bed, feet upon a carved stool, reading a book. When I entered, she removed her spectacles, sat up, and grinned.

"At last!" she said. In her lap rested a glistening ebon rabbit.

The table had been arranged with two settings of fine silver and china, candles alight. I set down the tray and turned to make my exit when Mabbot called in her jeering tone, "Forget something?"

"It's all there, madam."

"Sit, then!"

"I cannot," I said.

"Hemorrhoids?"

"I *will* not."

The rabbit leaped to the floor and darted under the bed when Mabbot rose. She approached until she was standing quite close. Lilac and sheepskin.

"Lively conversation and stimulating company can make a meal," she said. "Without it, the rarest delicacy has no savor. Don't you agree?"

"This is a depraved game," I said.

"I'm glad you see the fun in it."

Mabbot pulled out a chair and I sat, apprehensive and frankly exhausted.

She lifted the lid and gazed at the moon-pale fish on the bed of saffron rice, the figs and shrimp swathed in dark fragrant sauce. My blood beat in my ears.

Slowly, as if to tease, Mabbot took a crisp-cake, disregarding the proper order of things, and bit into it. I could not help but mark her face, which had grown quite placid as she chewed. The muscles of her jaw danced, lifting her ear under a curl of hair lightly, rhythmically.

Then she looked at me, her face lit with pleasure, and said, "Let's!"

She sat with the eagerness of a child and pulled a piece of the still-steaming cod onto her plate, then she apportioned some to me. She lifted her fork, waiting for me to do the same.

"It's for you," I objected.

"Why, have you poisoned it?"

With a sigh, I lifted my fork as well.

When Mabbot took the first bite to her lips, Feng coaxed, by memory and without mistakes, a Mozart minuet, haunting and delicate, from the harpsichord.

Suddenly, I was ravenous. Not having touched food to my tongue all day except to sample, I allowed myself to enjoy the first real meal since my capture. I had removed the fillet from the pan while it was still glassy in the middle and it had continued to cook by its own heat to a gentle flake. Between the opaque striations, wisps of fat clung to the crisp potato breading and resolved upon the tongue like the echo of a choir surrendering to silence. The saffron warmed all together as sunlight through stained glass blesses a congregation, while the shrimp sauce waved its harlot's kerchief from the periphery.

Mabbot, too, lingered on each bite, her face lovely with hunger. The captain knows how to eat, I grant her that.

"You're an alchemist, Wedgwood! What do you call this?"

"Call it? White fish with red sauce."

"Nonsense. That isn't a proper name."

"I'll call it . . . Hope of Rescue."

Mabbot laughed and was obliged to cover her mouth, which was still full.

"These plants — you must have fresh water," I said.

"Oh, just a little cask of rainwater, only enough to get them from port to port. I drink panch like everyone else. That and wine."

Feng finished the piece and left the room discreetly.

"By the way, everyone knows — you should too," Mabbot said, pausing here to regard me with such scrutiny that I shifted uncomfortably in my chair, "that Joshua, the cabin boy, is my personal responsibility. If I learn he has been mishandled in any way, I'll cut you into pieces so small even the fish won't find you."

"Mishandled? I'm teaching him letters! A thing that should have been done long ago!"

Her eyebrows rose at my outburst and she sat back and crossed her arms. "I see. Well, then, how does it go?"

"He has eyes. I don't see why he shouldn't read. It's slow going, but even a dog may learn many things if the teacher is patient."

"It's true," Mabbot said, appraising me with an unkind expression. "Even a dog." After several bites in silence, she said, "Tell me about yourself."

I took a moment to consider my situation. There was, at my core, a glow of gratitude for being alive while those near me had fallen. The murder of Jeroboam, which had so sickened and enraged me, also stoked this glow. This becoming woman sitting across from me was as grisly a villain as ever walked the earth, and yet I was more at home in the quiet of her parlor and the comfort of a good meal than I had been since my ordeal began. Taste and talk — these were the privileges of the living. I could refuse to make conversation and bring out the monster in her, or I could pacify and live long enough to escape. I obliged.

"My father was a cobbler," I said. "Or so they tell me. I was raised in the orphanage kitchen —"

"Where you learned that the cure for the dullest routine lay in a certain liberality of spices. *Saveur sans culotte!*"

"You may say that, yes. A duchess — she was a patron of the orphanage — came to view the grounds when I was twelve and already doing much of the cooking. She was a secret Jesuit, this kind woman, and a feast was prepared for her. She became a fan of my sauces and sent me to apprentice with a friend of hers at the Jesuit campus in Sanghen."

Joshua interrupted us with a bottle of wine and glasses. He couldn't help making fun of our scene; his lips were pursed in the dour pout of a sentry who had just eaten an entire lemon. He poured with the florid overarticulated gestures he imagined befitting a proper steward. Mabbot chuckled as he took a clownishly deep bow out the door. Another secret cache, this was an altogether different wine than had gone into the sauce. It came to my lips whispering a song of bees sipping on overripe fruit, of aging in an oak tub overhung with rosemary, of sleeping for a century in some sunken ship until the color of the waves themselves had soaked into the bottles.

"Sanghen?" Mabbot asked.

"Not far from Calais," I said. "Right

129

across the channel. Jesuits from all around Europe, all living on a valley farm. The land there was protected by our benefactors, and, as long as we stayed within the gates, we were safe from persecution."

"But that must have taken quite a lot of influence — one doesn't just wander between France and England in these days of strife, and as a Catholic, no less."

"I was fairly smuggled. But the monks have learned to look after one another; Jesuits fled the cities in droves to take refuge in our hidden monastery. We cooked for them all. My teacher had himself been chased from Bordeaux by a mob. As he said, 'Wars come and go, but people always eat.' When I was considering seminary, he said, 'Which do you like better, Pentecost Mass or the feast afterward? You'd make a terrible priest, but you make acceptable lamb galantine. God knows you love Him. Focus on the food.' This was a man who had made pies for the pope."

"You must make me a pie!"

"Cold butter and fresh flour is needed for crust. And real meat."

"We have lard . . . and Mary Sweet —"

"I'll try," I said.

"But go on. Orphans do tend to find their way aboard pirate ships."

"Captain . . . perhaps we can discuss less personal matters."

"Such as?"

"You don't speak like a pirate," I ventured.

"Do you know many?"

"I mean to say . . . you speak properly —"

"I am educated, properly, with great doses of impropriety. As an adolescent I was taken in by a wealthy man, a judge, who shared his knowledge and his fine things with me." Mabbot rolled a fork between her fingers languidly as she spoke. "It was there that I first acquired a taste for what he called 'the essentials': comestibles, wine, and conversation. They were subjects I excelled at. I was something of a project for him, a trained pet. He held parties at which I was the entertainment, the whore who could recite Ovid while hoisting her sails —"

I must have blushed, for she gave me a rather humane smile and said, "My, but you are a delicate flower, aren't you?" She patted my hand. I was so startled by this gentle touch that I yanked my hand away. Her smile didn't waver. "Don't fret, this judge didn't keep me long. When he tired of me, he sent me out. And I have been a wife of whim ever since."

"Ahem . . . Is the meal to your satisfaction?" I asked.

"Oh, delicious! Truly, you've earned next week's rent."

We finished our plates and Joshua reappeared to clear them. He brought more wine and poured; his little finger, hovering far from the rest of his hand, painted florets in the air. As a rule I never drink to inebriation, but now I allowed myself another glass. I was flooded with emotions, powerful and conflicting. The comfort of food and wine was a great relief, but it only highlighted the stark reality of my condition. "A week's rent," she had said. It will go on this way, week after week, unless my plan of escape proves good.

Mabbot's rabbit leaped onto her lap. Normally I am fond of pets but I couldn't bear its uncanny stare. I am beyond shame; whatever you may think of a grown man afraid of a bunny, you must take my word that this particular beast was misbegotten.

Mabbot seemed to be waiting for more conversation.

The rabbit peered at me as well. The thing . . . perhaps the stupefying swaying of the ship lent a certain unreasonableness to my perceptions. Nevertheless, I would prefer to be left alone in a room with a lion than with that lightless creature, who, I had convinced myself, could swallow my soul as one swallows a bean.

"This is Kerfuffle." Mabbot pulled on the beast's ears as if milking a goat, and the thing practically swooned with pleasure. "She's the softest," Mabbot said. "Give her a pet." I balked, but she pressed on. "Pet the rabbit, Wedgwood."

I had to lean to reach Mabbot's lap, and I could feel her breath on my cheek. The rabbit was indeed soft — the whole moment was much too soft, and I brought my hand back quickly, thinking: *This woman is a killer.*

Here we were interrupted by Feng, who rapped lightly on the anteroom door, then stuck his head in. Mabbot said to him, "The food is good, Feng, we'll keep him. Set it up." With that, Feng left again. "Tell me" — Mabbot leaned in — "if you were going to teach me to cook like this, what is the first lesson I would have to master?"

The wine in my veins mingled with the thrill of my life extended by seven days. "One mustn't confuse the nose with the mouth," I began.

"Certainly not."

"As with the harpsichord, to make a pleasing sound, one must hit several keys in harmony. Thus, flavor." I blushed here, feeling I had exposed my passion too much. But she didn't laugh. "The nose has infinite sensations, but the mouth has only six."

"This is fine." Mabbot beamed. "I miss refined conversation. Even in your sourness, you're a relief. My crew are good men, but they aren't dinner companions. Do go on."

"The flavors of the mouth have their analogues in life: Salt is the spirit of blood and tears, victory and defeat. Its color is red. Sour is a call to attention, a slap on the rump, the prick of a thorn admonishing you to attend. Its color is the yellow flash under a finch's wing."

"So you are a philosopher as well!"

We both drank. The rabbit was gone, then back again. It seemed to have the ability to dash in and out of darkness as one uses a door. "Go on, that's but two," she said.

"Sweet is the welcoming hand, the mother's milk, the kiss, the warm bed. Its color is the orange of dusk. Bitterness is the love behind a stern word, it is hard-earned fortitude. Its color is green. Astringency is a strong wind; it tightens and cleans, it invokes self-reliance. It is the blue of cold water."

These ideas had been brewing within me for years, but I had never spoken them aloud to anyone. The wine was stronger than I was used to.

She had closed her eyes and now leaned

back until her head rested on the chair.

"The Pearl Gate is the last flavor," I said. "Rarely spoken of. It lives in the dark slope of the soft palate. Only found in very particular broths, it is the taste that lingered after God breathed life into Adam. It is the flavor that animates the clay. It is violet."

When I suspected Mabbot had fallen asleep, I made to leave. At this, though, she protested. "Oh, a few minutes more! Poetry and passion, these are fine qualities. Just sit a bit longer."

"It is your turn, then, Captain. I've spoken."

"Fair enough. Ask me something."

"You said Ramsey had sent a corsair after you, that he fired red-hot cannonballs? He must be a considerable adversary."

"Relentless. He'd chase me to the moon to get his revenge." Mabbot was unhappy to be thinking of the man. "Laroche has a menagerie of infernal weapons. His gun rooms are lit, I'm told, with fireflies and fox fire, which give light but cannot ignite the powder. But I don't need to tell you, you have some familiarity with the man, don't you?"

So my slip of the tongue had reached her after all. "I saw him only at a distance," I said. "He spoke not a word to me."

She saw through my lie. A scowl from Mabbot is like the sleet-needled wind off of a frozen lake. It was the way one looks at an earwig that has just crept from the pages of a book the moment before pinching it in two with a thumbnail.

So I told her of the demonstration I had witnessed, about the pigs and the interview. The whole morbid scene improved her mood. I could have been describing an evening at the circus. "A rare spectacle to see a man sell his soul to Lucifer," she said.

It hadn't occurred to me before, but I realized suddenly that I could hardly count on a rescue by Laroche. "Now that Ramsey is . . . gone, Laroche won't be after you, will he?"

"We do not get the daily papers out here, Mr. Wedgwood. It will be some time before he learns about his financier's fate. But it'll only make him the more dangerous. Now those debts will be open to the Pendleton accountants, and they'll come after him to recover the expense. Once the company sees how much his strange ship costs, he'll be lucky to avoid a charge of treason. He'll have to bring my head smiling on a platter to keep his own, and soon! Poor Laroche!" The captain chuckled. "He's a victim of history, like the rest of us. He has the purity of a child — believes that what goes wrong can be made right. You have to admire his passion. He'd rather use his last penny on a bullet than on bread. I have nothing against him personally except that he's trying so hard to kill me. I suppose one does not get to choose one's nemesis."

"But you must have many."

She did not deny this. After a spell her gaze softened, and she resumed her habitual posture of threading her hands behind her head, leaning far back in her chair.

"The newspapers say you attack only Pendleton Trading Company vessels," I said.

"In my days as a privateer, I had no qualms and would sink any ship that dared to wet its hips. But now I dine exclusively on Pendleton meat." The captain rubbed her face. She was weary and, I saw now, older than I had first thought, with faint wrinkles at the corners of her eyes and a few grey hairs twined at her temples.

"But why?"

"We are surrounded by monsters," she said. "We can cower before them or we can pick one and sink our teeth in with the aim to give it hell. I have investments in the Pendleton Trading Company. I have invested all of my daggers into it. The unkind things in this world are countless. But my choice was made easier by certain personal offenses. In a way, Pendleton chose me."

"You speak as if the company is the villain. As if Ramsey was the rogue."

"I should," she said.

"But I watched you shoot him, helpless and unarmed on the ground." The memory inflamed me. "Is it a crime to be a gentleman — chairman of the most successful company in history? Shall a lord as lofty as this, who has dined with the king himself, be libeled? You murdered him without mercy, unprovoked, and unrepentant."

"You're right on all but 'unprovoked.' " She laughed. "Here sits a provoked woman — take it in. This is how a provoked woman turns her head, drinks her wine. Theirs is a noble piracy hallowed by the seals of gentry — while I take ships, they take entire continents and, oh, the plunder! Don't fret, Mr. Wedgwood. Pendleton has many heads. I have not killed the beast, I've only vexed it."

"Who is the Brass Fox? What is your aim with him?" I demanded.

"Now we are done."

Feng appeared and pulled me toward the door. I set my feet and tried to keep the anger from my voice. "Captain, when will I be allowed to return home?"

"But you've only just arrived." She looked genuinely hurt. "Give us a sporting chance."

"I am not in the habit of being mocked."

"Well, it comes to you naturally, then."

Shaking, I said, "I will not take insults."

"Take? Not take, that would make a pirate of you. No, they are given freely. In your company, I find I am positively wealthy with insults, and I don't mind lavishing them upon you."

"Home, Captain. When shall I be returned?"

"But where is home? Either you have none or it is here. By now Ramsey's estate is covered with dustcloths. Did the man have heirs? I ask you, did he?" Mabbot's eyes glimmered in the candlelight. "In that case there will be an auction. The great claw-footed tables, the Venetian lamps, the emerald-eyed lions, they will be dispersed, and then the manor itself sold. Another owner, another set of precious artifacts carted in. The other servants have already found jobs elsewhere, haven't they? What will you return to but strange faces, lack, and loss? Are you so eager to serve another master?"

"I prefer to choose my master."

"But here you lounge and loaf in the sun. I don't ask you to weigh anchor, brace a yard, or even mend rope. You cook but one day of the week. Is it not refreshing?"

"It's a wet hell."

"You won't make friends that way, Wedgwood. Where are your manners?"

Feng pushed me toward the door, but, in a fit of petulance, I snatched the bowl of potpourri on my way out. Feng looked to Mabbot, but she just smiled and shook her head. Thus I returned to my cell clutching the stale scraps, feeling I had somehow succeeded without victory.

Much to my surprise, I found that my cell had been altered while I was gone. My sawdust sack had been replaced with a hammock, a woolen blanket, and a horsehair pillow. There was now a small table with a pot and pitcher, a bottle of brandy, more paper, tapers, quills, and a bottle of ink to replace the lead ingot I'd been writing with. Under the hammock was a pewter chamber pot.

In my heart, gratitude curdled with resentment and fatigue. These meager comforts only made me long for home. I crawled into the hammock and fell instantly asleep.

7

FRAGILE VESSEL

IN WHICH I AM RESCUED BY AN UNLIKELY SHIP

Wednesday, September 1

I am finally well enough to make a record of my perilous escape from the *Flying Rose.* It is enough to say that I am happy to be alive — but I'm getting ahead of myself.

It began Monday night, as many terrible stories do, with a false smile.

I waited a few minutes after the gong brought the graveyard watch up: the men of the dogwatch wandered down to snore in the still-warm hammocks. This was the four-hour stretch when all of the berths in the ship were full, leaving only a dozen or so men on deck.

I used the flattened spoon to free myself, then wedged the door shut again with a scrap of canvas wadded into the hinge.

To forestall being spotted by navy patrols, the deck was kept fairly dark. The lanterns the men carried were blinded on the sides to pour light only on the tasks before them.

I made my way to the forecastle where they sat in a circle mending rope. The first part of my plan involved placing a large pot of soup in the middle of that circle.

Many of them had wads of Mary Sweet in their cheeks. A single scrap of Sweet could last a man as much as an hour. In this way it served like chewing tobacco, and tasted about as good. As soon as I lifted the lid of the pot, the men spat into their hands and chucked the meat into the darkness.

The soup was little more than a thickened court bouillon, but in the strange light reflected from the pot, I could feel the hunger of the men gathering like a squall. I had roasted the fish bones, head, and tail of my noble cod in a Dutch oven while at the same time caramelizing thinly sliced onions very slowly until they were almost syrup. To this I added anchovies and the milk of ten coconuts. I simmered this broth uncovered until it reduced by a fifth and added cubed potatoes last, being sure not to cook them to mush. With a splash of seawater for salt, a pinch of pepper, and a squeeze of lime, it was done: the commonest food I had thrown together in years and yet, I knew, the men would lick the pot.

"Moonlight stew," I said, forcing myself to speak confidently. "I don't know how you have survived Conrad's porridge. Mabbot told me the leftovers were mine to do with what I want. You'll have to share bowls, though."

The crew, holding the loose ends of the rope with their bare toes, leaned in with the tin bowls I had brought. A voice stopped them.

"Mabbot's orders?" It was Asher speaking, a handsome man with cleanly shaven cheeks, whom I'd seen shouting at the lesser seamen when the bosun was below deck. Around his neck was the whistle that conferred upon him the rights of sheriff and taskmaster.

"We could wake her," I said. "But I thought you were in charge of the graveyard. I was going to ask you if I could give some to the helmsman." I waited, with my head lowered in an almost imperceptible kowtow.

"I suppose it's all right," he said imperiously, then smiled like a schoolboy when the men gave him a cheer. I took this opportunity to pass a flagon of straight rum to the man immediately to my right, who, after a quick swig, passed it on. By the rules of the ship, these men generally drank nothing stronger than Madeira wine and now slurped at the flagon as greedily as I had hoped. The only thing more soporific than a hearty stew is a splash of strong spirits to boot.

Utswali, whose face bears the mesmerizing patterns of ritual scars, clapped me by the belt and pulled me down to share his soup with him. It was overcast — the darkness so thick that I nearly gave up my plan entirely for fear of venturing alone into such a void. A swig of rum helped steel my nerves.

"I'm off to sleep after I give a bite to the man at the wheel. Good night, gentlemen," I said.

The circle lifted their bowls to me in a heathen salute as I filled a tin cup and took it aft to the helmsman. He swallowed the contents in one gulp and burped "God bless ye."

It was time. With the men thus clustered about the soup pot at the head, I would have the stern of the ship to myself for a few minutes.

I made my way to where Mabbot's personal pinnace, *Deimos,* was swaying in the darkness. I trusted that the lookout had his eyes on the horizon, and besides, I could hardly see my own hands to work. I figured I had at least ten minutes of safety before the men started wandering the deck again.

I worked at loosening the knots of the davit lines, feeling my way around the stubborn knobs and bundles. What had seemed clear before was now a tangled mystery. I lost precious moments trying to be sure I was not, in fact, freeing one of the jigger-mast stays, which would have brought the sail monkeys running when they heard the unmistakable sound of the canvas luffing, like a calf coughing for its mother.

My heart drummed so in my ears that I was sure I heard the thumping of Mabbot's boots behind me, and I lost even more time turning to scan the shadows.

I climbed into the boat to feel my way around the davit blocks and stashed the waxed sack that contained my provisions and this journal securely under the foremost seat of the boat. By the insistence of the mist against my face, I guessed the *Rose* was moving at a fair clip.

The voice from the mast froze me with panic, until the actual words made their way into my ears: "All's well." An hour had passed already. The call would no doubt rouse the men back to work. Further, I was all too aware that the sun was racing the last length of its invisible track and that I had to be well and away before the morning crew stirred. I cursed the time I had lost sitting with them. It was probably near sunrise. I could not postpone this, for my ruse would not work again.

By the time I was confident of which lines were which, my arms shook with exertion. My mistake was to lean out over the water with one of the lines in my teeth to get a better grip on the block, for just then the *Rose* rolled and the pinnace dumped me out like a dumpling from a spoon. I was falling.

I saw, even as I dropped, the smug boat swaying but secure as an earring on the ship. Everything had the clarity usually reserved for nightmares. I had plenty of time to think as I plummeted: *My diversion was too good. Not one will see me fall.*

Then the water smacked the wind from my lungs and left me croaking like a frog. I saw then how quickly indeed the *Rose* was moving. By the time I had recovered my breath, the ship was already a dozen yards away. I tried to swim after it but my clothes bound my shoulders and knees. I kicked off my boots and struggled to remove my shirt, an effort that took considerable concentration, only to find the ship had doubled its distance.

I swam as if the devil were after me, putting my face full in the chilly water as I had been taught, for speed. But when I lifted my eyes, I was no closer.

"Haaalp!" I screamed. "Overboard!"

Could I hope she was awake and scanning the water from the cabin windows above her bed? What did I look like, a scrap of lint on black cloth?

"Haaalp!"

The ship disappeared into the endless pitch.

My prayers came forth as bubbles as I swam. I lost my direction but kept swimming. I swam until my arms were burning logs and my lungs a tangle of mucus. The waves came out of the darkness and I crawled up those low hills only to sled down the other side again and again. As I swam, I pleaded to the Trinity and to the Mother and to all of the saints starting with Augustine and not forgetting even Saint Gertrude, who eases fear of mice, or Medardus, patron of toothaches.

The east became a smear of pink.

With daylight upon the water, I saw the untouched waste of the second day of creation. The waves calmed and revealed a lathed horizon in every direction. Not a ship, nor land, nor smoke, nor evidence of man. The sea was clean of hope. I had become a crumb on the vast expanse.

When my arms went numb and stopped moving of their own accord, I heard myself pleading with the *Rose* herself, spurned madam. I would give anything to hug her dry planks, to be stashed safely in my gloomy chamber, close and damp as a lover's mouth. If allowed, I would make the *Rose* my permanent home. It was world enough for a humble life.

By the height of the sun in the sky, it was eight or eight-thirty. Mr. Apples might not see fit to open my chamber door to find me missing until ten or so. Even if they figured out what had happened and for mercy or vengeance decided to come about, they would be tacking against the wind, taking six times longer at least to retrace their course.

I was barely afloat then, using the last scraps of my energy to keep my lungs full and buoyant, kicking as little as needed to keep my face in the air.

The yawning void above me was matched by the depths below. Looking down, I felt vertigo, as if I were perched on the sharp lip of the moon. Indigo forms shifted in the fields beneath me like clouds herded by the wind. My eyes fixed on a pale dot no bigger to me than a beetle but unthinkably distant and therefore massive, directly below me. As I watched, it seemed to move and my eyes bugged with horror. If the thing came up, I would die of fright before it even touched me.

But was it moving or was it a trick of my brined brain? I resolved not to look down again and floated on my back. My ears filled with water, and this was strangely soothing.

A menu unfolded in my mind with the various modes of death and their relative degrees of agony listed beside. None of them cheap. Was dying of thirst less tortuous than dismemberment by shark?

As I paddled, something touched my outstretched hand, and I practically climbed out of the water shouting like a fool. But it was only a large mat of floating kelp. I pushed myself away before thinking better of it and returning to tear at the thick strands. I tied dozens of gas-filled bladders to my upper arms, around my torso, and stuffed more into my pants. Thus I was carried easily upon the surface and I no longer had to consciously control my breathing nor thrash with my feet. I hoped too that the dangling vegetation might fool passing sharks.

By now I was shivering almost constantly, though from fear, fatigue, or the cold I could not distinguish. My teeth chattered like tea service on a carriage. There were periodic pockets of warmer water, and though I tried to remain within them, they came and went without any regard to my efforts, and I only shivered harder at their passing.

The emptiness was vicious. Not a fish, not a bird. I had never seen such a lifeless expanse. I had heard of men who, stranded at sea, lost their minds long before their bodies gave out, and I hummed to myself in an attempt to fill the space around me. When I realized I had been humming the Mary Sweet song, I stopped and crossed myself twice.

I have never been particularly afraid of the dark, but as the sun dropped toward the horizon, my chest became a Pandora's box of panic and outrage. I finally saw sunset for the blood warning it had always been.

To my surprise, the temperature of the water did not change considerably when the sun abandoned me. Though it was clear that I would probably die of the cold, it appeared this would be a gradual death indeed.

The stars splattered themselves about me. I was grateful for the lack of moon. What tricks lunar light might play on me, I didn't care to find out.

With my belly to the sky, I crossed my arms over my chest, and still my shivering shook me like a marionette.

Thirst came on suddenly and with savage intensity. There was nothing to do but feel my throat curing like a strip of bacon.

A ship at sea is a cacophony of humming ropes, bells, swearing, hoarse hails, and wooden planks moaning against one another. Now the silence was deep and broken only by the occasional splash of water meeting water. I could even hear the crackle of the shooting stars as they struck the bowl of heaven.

Senseless emptiness.

I wanted to sleep, but thirst was drawing a woolen scarf down my throat inch by inch. My shivering stopped, and gradually I felt the tips of my fingers and toes going numb. Like some foolish prince in a children's tale, I felt myself transforming into a gnarled log of driftwood. Even with my seaweed buoys, I was obliged to kick and paddle occasionally, and increasingly my limbs refused to comply.

Sunrise pulled me from the underworld. It was unspeakably lovely, and all of my readiness to die vanished in that riot of light. It lasted forever. It seemed its own reward for the sweat and hand-wringing that fill our days.

Only a few hours later my joy had sunk again and I screamed my curses at the sun, that naked Satan. My chest was red as a boiled lobster and my lips split with every howl.

I must have slept, because I woke with the sense that someone was watching me. My wife, Elizabeth, paddled at the bow of a long black boat that stretched out to the horizon. Her hair shone with a brightness I could not look at.

"Take me into your boat," I begged.

Her dark wings sighed like the bellows of a great furnace. "Do you have the fare, Blueberry?"

"What is the fare?"

"Satiety," she said as she paddled off. Water from her paddle washed over my face and I opened my eyes. Her wings became the fin of a leviathan, the longboat the body itself. The whale sighed again, watching me. Then sank and was gone.

My thoughts turned philosophic. If I was not serene, I was, at least, surrendered. As a soldier broken on the field lies waiting, I waited. I was bitter and offended at the thought of my death, but there is a kind of freedom in having choice ripped away. Nothing more could be expected of me than to have the Lord's Prayer on my lips. How burdensome breathing was!

I took my place in a parade of flotsam:

driftwood, glass floats, corncobs tossed by some lucky revelers. The red ribbon around the neck of a corked jug caught my eye and I clambered toward it; the seaweed jewelry I had bedecked myself with made actual swimming a ridiculous effort.

The cork had been hammered into the jug and sealed with pitch. It took me minutes to pry it out with my teeth. Beer, wine, or poison, I would drink it. Tipping the jug back, though, I felt something dry meet my lips. Inside was a scrap of leather, hammered thin, bearing a message scratched with a charred stick:

MAROONED
SEND HELP
28S 98W

My giggles grew and soon I was laughing like a madman, my sore body wracked with spasms. Complaining about land beneath his feet — the entitled son of a bitch didn't know how lucky he was. I returned the message to its bottle and thumped the cork in place with my fist before flinging the thing over my shoulder.

The noon sun watched me try to drink my own urine by aiming the arc. A botched farce. The tears too were wasted in the brine.

The sharks, small but persistent, finally found me. I tried to lie still and closed my eyes. One of them tugged at my seaweed robes like a playful dog. Another sank its teeth into my shoulder, which was numb as wax. I would have prayed, but my tongue had withered in my mouth. A merciful cloud shaded my face, then slammed into me. The sharks scattered momentarily.

Either a ship was above me or my mind had finally snapped.

I heard gunfire, and one of the sharks wrapped itself in a gown of crimson. Quickly the others were upon it and turned the water into a roiling cauldron of cannibalism.

A net covered me, and I felt myself pulled from the water, my body suddenly taking on a terrible weight. Everything hurt. I could feel each knot of the net gouging into my tender flesh.

The planks of the ship, though, were radiantly warm, and I pooled there like soft cheese.

8
THE DREAMER

Half a dozen lascars were above me, wearing thin cotton shirts embroidered at the bottom and the cuff with a scrolling stitch. They offered a canteen, the contents of which unfurled like tender shoots down my throat. When my stomach gripped the panch with an angry fist and threw it up, the smiling men gave me more.

Between swallows, I coughed my thanks.

"Where do you come from?" someone asked.

"Escaped from the *Flying Rose.*"

At this I was lifted to my feet and dragged to an aft cabin, where figures sat before a table full of maps and charts. The forward wall was made of tarpaulin and had been lifted and tied to make a wide awning. My sunburned eyes seemed unable to adjust to the dim light beneath, but I knelt before the figures and offered my thanks. "Infinite gratitude," I said, "a thousand blessings for rescuing —"

As I began to make them out, my joy broke like a yolk forked. These were no fishermen. There were three of them, and each was more upsetting than the last.

The first was a figure so horribly burned that it took courage to look at him. This man's head was a tangled knob of scars. His ears, lips, and nose were gone, leaving him with a perpetual graveyard grin. He held a small brass bell and was seated on a crate watching over two figures seated back-to-back in quiet meditation. This ghoul put one finger over his bared teeth and hissed.

On the left was a woman whose obsidian hair cascaded over her silk wrappings into her lap. Her bare arms were festooned with bangles, and about her neck was slung a dagger in a filigreed scabbard. Her hands were the cleanest things I'd seen in weeks. Her spectacles sat primly on the end of her nose, and she did not even twitch at the bustle around her.

Her companion, though, was most upsetting. A handsome young man wearing a calfskin vest and a thick belt crowded with compartments, no doubt powder and shot for the pistol he scratched his knee with as we approached. He opened one eye to peer at us, and I recognized that stare.

"Captain," said the lascar holding me. "We have a guest."

"I heard the calls. We're meditating," grumbled the captain, and closed his eyes again. His oiled hair was thick and copper hued; when he spoke, it shifted with its own weight like wheat ready for harvest.

"But he says he's from the *Flying Rose*."

The captain leaped to his feet, clearly relieved to be able to arch his back, and peered at me with glee. The ghoul rang the bell and the woman rose with a scowl. "That was hardly an hour," she said, "and you fidgeted the whole time."

"Don't nag, Kittur," said the captain. "We have company! So that was the *Rose* we spied. That is too close for comfort." He lifted his voice to his crew: "Give a wide passage! She'll come about if she sees us."

I gawked, sure my sea-pickled brain was playing tricks. He had her gracious lips, her cheekbones, her hair. "Welcome to the other side," he said, and by his voice, by the freckles splashed across his nose, this was Mabbot's kin.

"What is this?" I begged, for I feared my troubles were far from over.

"Just leaped overboard, did you?" He laughed. "I understand, believe me, but at least I waited until we were ashore before I gave her the slip." His entourage chuckled. "Do you have a raga for the man, Kittur? Poor walrus looks half-dead."

At this the woman produced a stringed instrument, vaguely resembling a guitar, and the music that arose from it only increased my dizziness. I was not altogether sure I was awake.

The woman's henna-embroidered feet, the ghoul's angry welts, the mesmerizing sounds, these were spectacle enough, but it was the color of the young man's hair that made me stare.

"You're the Brass Fox," I blurted.

"But who are you, friend?"

"Owen Wedgwood. Ramsey's cook. Mabbot captured me when she killed him."

The dream music stopped and the ship went quiet. The other two watched the Fox, holding their breath, as he bent over me with a scowl.

"Did you say killed? She *killed* him?"

As I rushed to explain the events that had culminated in my capture, the Fox aimed the pistol at my eye. When I stopped in terror, he cracked the barrel against my forehead and shouted, "Speak!"

I blurted everything I could recall of the scene, even the fishes that attended the boat that carried me to the *Flying Rose.* Here the Fox interrupted me again.

"Too soon!" he yelled, and, with the slightest declination of his pistol, fired past my head and struck an albatross from the lines of the jib sails. As I covered my ringing ear, the bird fell and flopped about on the deck.

The ghoul spoke with a lipless sibilance. "Saves us the trouble, though."

"But too soon," the Fox growled. "The vultures will be circling. Shut up and let me think."

"Got to make it happen now. No time to go to the Congo."

"Gristle, shut your hole!" roared the Fox.

Kittur, setting her instrument aside, stepped past me and wrapped her arms around the Fox from behind. After a moment he softened against her.

"Gristle is right," she whispered. "We will enlist Africa when the time comes . . . if we have to. For now we head back to Macau and ready ourselves. It's time to send Mabbot a message."

"We rescue Braga first."

"Braga must wait," Kittur said.

"Mabbot has Braga," I blurted, hoping that if I showed no allegiance to her, they would think twice about killing me. I told them about the prison break and the strange bearded man Mabbot took aboard there. "He mentioned something about tunnels in China."

The Fox kneaded his forehead with his fists. "Damn all. What exactly did he say?"

"Only that they're near the Pearl River," I said.

"Nothing more? Nothing about what is in them?"

"Braga is loyal," said Kittur.

"Braga *was* loyal before I left him on the penal island. Things tend to go moldy in damp cells."

"All the more reason to move quickly," whispered Kittur. She pushed the Fox back to a stool, and he sat dejectedly.

"Shall we bring her about?" asked Gristle.

"Aye," grumbled the Fox. "But well to the west, and two men atop with an eye for the *Rose*. She'll spot us if we aren't careful."

As Gristle shouted orders and the schooner banked, I felt the Fox's eyes coming to rest on me again.

"A pet of Mother's — perhaps you'll carry the message for us?"

"You must deliver me straightaway to the nearest civilized port," I demanded.

"But you've only just joined us. Give us a sporting chance."

"God help me, I've heard that before."

It was then that I made out a figure lashed to the fore rails. My sunburned eyes had mistaken him for a bundle of oilcloth, but he was wearing the uniform of the guards from the penal island. His face was blistered from the sun, and his mouth was gagged with rope. I would have thought him dead except that his eyes were burning into me, begging for help.

Kittur and the Fox conferred in whispers. I took this time to assess my straits. I was out of the water but by no means saved. In my exhausted state, I'm ashamed to admit, I could not even imagine coming to the prisoner's aid. I was only steps from his fate, and my chief concern, it seemed to me, was to keep from being lashed to the bowsprit myself. But how to be of value to these brigands?

The Fox turned his attention to me, and, like a simpleton, I croaked, "I'm valuable!"

"Are you?"

"I can cook."

"And I can whistle 'Farewell Winsome Maiden' with my arse, can't I, Kittur?" asked the Fox.

To her credit, the woman ignored him and handed me a flask containing water, simple water cut only with lime juice — sweet nectar!

"Did you actually see Ramsey die?" the Fox was asking.

Wiping my mouth, I responded, "With my own eyes, I saw her do it."

The blood returned to his cheeks. Even in temper he was Mabbot's child. "To have seen that — I'm envious, I am. Who are you to have witnessed . . . but too soon!"

His eyes darted around the deck; perhaps he was shifting schemes of great weight in his head, or maybe he was only looking for another bird to shoot. I had a moment to take in the charts that festooned the walls of the cabin behind him.

The table was littered with logs and maps weighted in place with knives and a tackle block. Behind it were crates stuffed with books and scrolled parchment, their edges tattered and stained. If Mabbot's library had been stowed in a hurry, then nested in by a family of large rodents, it might have looked like this. It was the office of a madman, a shabby Napoleon bent on taking the world by alley and basement door. Our new course brought the wind into the space, and Kittur began to roll and stow logs. She was putting books in their place so swiftly that it was clear that this hasty library was hers as much as the Fox's.

"We have this in common." The Fox knelt

before me, examining my face. The man was wearing a cologne of crushed sage and turpentine oil. "Both kidnapped from my father's house."

"Ramsey, your father?" I choked on my disbelief. "It's known he had no heirs, and besides, you're the spitting image of Mabbot."

"No heirs but one." Here the Fox gripped my cheeks with both hands and wrung them as if to get whey. "He has plastered over my rightful place with lies." When I yelped, he let go and straightened his vest. "But we are prepared to correct that." He sighed. "The time has finally come! A flock of barristers won't stand against the argument I'll give them. In the end they'll see my way is easiest."

The man's features danced like shadows — now enraged, now bemused. This was a turbulent heart, and the welts on my cheeks told me that he had left a good portion of his sanity on some barnacled pier long ago.

"Is he really dead?" He tugged at his hair in wonderment. Kittur, obviously concerned by his pacing, took his arm gently and led him to sit again.

"The doll," I gasped. "The soldier with the tin sword. It was yours. I found it hidden in the woodshed."

"Did you?" The Fox draped his arm over Kittur, who watched him with concern. "I loved that toy more than a child should. Isn't it strange that you may be the only person in the world who remembers it, and I fished you out of the drink a thousand miles from England. What are the chances, pet?" He bowed his head until their brows touched.

She said, "There are no coincidences, *premi*. He is you. You are he."

"Was Ramsey still alone in that rambling palace?" he asked. "So crammed with furniture and yet so empty!"

Kittur stroked the instrument with her slender fingers and sang to her mate: "Here sits the son of warring titans."

Looking at me with unsettling interest, the Fox said, "You may be right, kitten, we're the same, this cook and I. What a strange thing to have in common with a man! Both snatched by Mother from Father's house. In my case, Mother's men threw me into a sack and carried me away screaming. Of course, you were too big for the sack, Owen? Ah, good, I pissed all over that sack."

"But you don't mourn Lord Ramsey's death?" I asked.

"Father would have drowned me in the

lake for looking like her if I wasn't such a valuable hostage. Mother at least took an interest in me. Taught me to slit a throat. Each parent told me that the other was a monster. And they both told the truth. And here I am, child of monsters."

"Child of truths," purred Kittur. The Fox smiled so sweetly then that I felt this whole thing might be one long practical joke — the drunken sound of the strings and this man's rude intimacy.

"Be careful, Owen," said the Fox, "if you listen to Kittur, she'll convince you that the entire world is being dreamed by a sleeping god: you, me, Mother, Gristle, even poor dead Father, all just motes in a single mind. What she won't tell me, though, is which of us are the figments, and which one the dreamer."

Kittur clucked disapprovingly.

"I have a hunch who it is," said the Fox with a wink.

"What is to become of me?" I asked.

"You mean when I wake up?"

"I mean, sir, which port will you be taking me to? How shall I get home?"

"Home? Kittur, the man wants to go home! Haven't you been listening? Once Mother *liberates* us, we never go home again — never sleep under that embroidered

165

canopy, never hear the clattering silver platters of almond biscuits with quince jelly coming down the hall, never hide again between the legs of the topiary elephants. But, then" — he leaned close and, with a firm knuckle, lifted my chin toward the glare — "what a canopy is this sky! After this, how could we go back to those suffocating halls? So we are torn, you and I! The mind is its own place, Owen. Make a heaven of hell, that is the trick. One doesn't do battle with gods until one is a god himself. Napoleon's mistake was to crown himself emperor. He should have crowned himself chief shareholder. We would all be working for him now."

"I have nothing to do with your feud. Please be honorable and set me to port somewhere —"

"Oh, I'm afraid not. You'll get a message to Mother for me. I need her help."

"I am not some pawn to be passed back and forth!"

"We have that in common too. Don't worry, it builds character. Speaking of Mother," he said, "what exactly is her course?"

"After you. That's all I know. To China, it seems."

"Not quite so far as that, no."

166

I found myself longing for the carmine balustrades and gilt trim of the *Rose.* True, Mabbot's ship was a prison to me, and fraught with its own dangers, but the son's ranting frightened me more than the mother's acid bon mots.

"We've had our differences, but I cannot manage this next part without her. You will tell her that. Remember my face. She must believe it was really me you've met today. You will tell her everything, won't you?"

I found myself nodding.

The Fox then whispered something to Kittur, kissed her, and went to the fore to peer east with a spyglass. She tossed me a small apple, which I ate in two bites. It was gone before I knew it and tasted better than anything I had ever put in my mouth. I was suddenly very tired. The instrument was again in her hands, and she began to play a song that sounded like the bombinating of a thousand bees.

Her voice was so lush that she seemed to be singing. "He's a great man. Did you see it in the eyes of the ship hands? They adore him." Her spectacles glinted in the sun.

"Madam, I assure you, I care not. I wish only to be returned to my life."

"Men who long for the past are already dead. Look to the future, Owen."

It was then that the lookouts called, "Sail ho!"

Leaning from the shade of the canvas awning I saw, in the rain-smudged north-east, the seed of a ship growing. The men on the masts called, "*Rose!*"

"Fly! Fly west!" the Fox shouted.

"The wind is with her," said the helms-man.

"That will change when she is abreast. We have twice her speed running. Stay the course."

The *Rose* advanced at an alarming rate as we beat windward with sickening lurches.

"How did she find us?" I asked Kittur.

"Her crow's nests are three times higher than ours. She probably spotted us as soon as we changed course."

I was so weak from my trial at sea that I feared a battle would be the end of me. No matter where I stood on the tiny deck, I was nearly trampled by the lascars lunging with lines or moving in a tight choreography to tack now starboard, now port. The schooner heeled at a frightening angle as we pushed into the wind. I found myself gripping the belay pins to keep my footing.

Soon the *Rose* was directly east of us, perhaps a mile distant, and changing her course to beat, as we were, against the weather. Almost immediately she began to fall behind as the schooner outpaced her.

I was making my way down the companionway to relative safety below deck when I heard the Fox yell, "Jettison the cook!"

The very men who had kindly pulled me from the sea now grabbed my arms and dragged me to the aft railing. There the Fox said, "Give the man a barrel!" and shook my hand as if we had just shared a pint as friends. "Here is the message: Tell her that it's time we worked together. I have a few things I need to set in order first, but she must meet me in Macau, on Coloane Island, northeast of the ruined temple. Follow the riverbed past the rocky hills to San Lazaro. There is a tavern there called the Serpent's Tail. Repeat it."

"Coloane Island, northeast of the temple —"

The Fox nodded to his men.

"No, wait!" I found myself in the water again, this time hugging an empty apple barrel.

To my horror, both ships were moving steadily away from me as the *Rose* followed the *Diastema* northwest. For ten desperate minutes I thrashed, pushing the barrel before me and hollering like a sea lion. Then, glory, the prow of the great ship

169

slowly turned as if noticing me. I realized that the *Rose* was, of course, tacking; what I had seen as moving away had, in fact, been the backswing of a wide serpentine course that came to sweep me up on its next pass. If the *Rose* had been running a narrow course, I would have been left, a grain in the field, and so I thanked God for tacking.

Rope ladders were unfurled against the hull for me to cling to as the *Rose* loomed. I had not made it halfway up the ladder with quivering arms when Mabbot screamed down at me, "Was that the Fox?"

"Aye," I croaked.

"Louder, man, and tell me — was it?"

As it was taking all of my withered strength not to fall from the ladder, I looked up at her and nodded. At her calls for redoubled speed, the bells rang out, and I could hear above me the crew tumbling about the deck trying to wring every drop from the adverse winds.

As I threw myself over the bulwarks to collapse upon the planks, the Fox's schooner was already shrinking toward the horizon. The climb left me completely flaccid, and once upon the deck, I curled up, unable even to shiver.

"We'll not catch her, Captain," Mr. Apples shouted.

"Here's an ugly fish," I heard Mabbot say above me. "Let's hope he tastes better than he looks." She nudged me with her boot and said, "Did you think I'd go without Sunday's feast?" When I didn't respond, she kicked me in the ribs. "Wedge, you had better have some information for us."

Even as I groaned, the twins dragged me to Mabbot's cabin, where, fighting to keep the apple from coming back up, I told her the entire tale. Mabbot paced in a tight circle as I related what the Fox had said. "If not for my bungled escape," I added, "we would have missed the man entirely."

"Work together?" Mr. Apples laughed. "Did the Fox say that? Captain, that smells strongly of horseshit. I can fairly taste it."

"But there *is* a plan here. Something ambitious — I can almost see it — tunnels in Canton, a patchwork army of angry men." Mabbot was kneading her temples with her knuckles. "He's captured with a gang of smugglers by Captain Jeroboam — which shows he's overreaching, getting reckless. After escaping the penal island, he flies east to regroup with his colleagues, deny rumors of his capture, set his things in order . . . then heads for the South Atlantic again to recruit slaves from the Congo. Who is he fighting if he needs men in every sea?

171

But now he's changed course again —"

"It was Ramsey dead," I said. "That sealed it. He said plans had to be accelerated now."

"But what is he up to? Fetch Braga — he's been more reticent than I'd like."

Braga was brought to the cabin and stood with his hands folded behind his back like a soldier at ease. The man had been pilfering garlic from the galley; even from where I sat in my puddle of seawater, I could smell that his grey-streaked beard was rank with it.

"You haven't told us everything you know about these tunnels," said Mabbot.

Braga was quiet for a moment, and I felt sympathy for his position. Only minutes before, I had been obliged to spew everything I knew to stay alive. Braga, though, managed to keep his dignity as he spoke with quiet calm.

"The tunnels we dug are not just for smuggling. The Fox is filling the chambers with a massive cache of black powder." He paused. "Directly under the Barbarian House."

This meant something to Mabbot, for her jaw dropped.

"Sounds like something you'd try, Cap'm," said Mr. Apples.

"He calls it his *insurance,*" said Braga. "Beyond that, I know what you know —

that he has spent his gold building a guerrilla army."

"But where is this army?"

"In the washing rooms of barons, in the cotton fields, in the holds of junks. On every continent, his fighters are waiting for the call to bring the opium empire crashing down. Pendleton has raised the army for him — slaves, lascars, starving farmers, opium addicts, smugglers risking torture and death for pennies. All waiting to feast on the corpse of Pendleton."

"But Pendleton has never been in better health."

"The weight of the entire Oriental trade rests on one rotten peg: the smugglers who bring the opium into Canton. Without them, Pendleton would have to go back to paying precious British silver for their tea. The empire would crumble. How many of the smugglers now follow the Fox? And he knows the price of every corrupt official who has dipped his toe in the Pearl River — he can give that rotten peg a push. And then, of course, he has his insurance."

"But even if he could break Pendleton's back, how would he stand to profit? He has never been much for selfless acts," said Mabbot. "And now this invitation to join him in Macau."

Braga shrugged.

"Your life depends on your honesty, Mr. Braga," said Mabbot. "If you have anything else to tell us, this is your last chance."

He only shook his head. Mabbot opened the door for him herself, and he left.

"With every answer, we get a sack of questions," said Mr. Apples.

"But we know the Fox is about to stage something dramatic," said Mabbot. "We know I am featured in it. What do you think my role is, water nymph? Mrs. Macbeth? He's got something grand in his skull."

"It's a show I'd rather miss."

"Heavens, no — orchestra seats, Mr. Apples. Anyway, we have our headings now, don't we?" said Mabbot. "And damn his fast ship, we can take our ease getting there. The men are itchy for a plunder anyway. First to Cochin China, then straight on to Macau."

"But it's a poison pie he's offering, for sure, Captain. A poisoned horseshit pie."

"I've noted your concern. Have you noted the heading?"

"Aye."

"Then to it."

When Mr. Apples left, Mabbot turned a sad gaze on me and asked, "Tell me, did you see my boy smile?"

I am now of a small cadre in the know: Mabbot, Mr. Apples, the twins, and myself. Of course Mabbot assured me it would mean my death if I spoke of her son to another soul, and given how she has kept her crew in the dark about it for so long, I take her at her word.

9

THE *PATIENCE*

IN WHICH MANY ARE PUNISHED

When I was feeling strong enough to walk again, I found the pinnace lashed as securely as ever with my sack of provisions still stowed discreetly under the seat, this journal undiscovered. After fishing a new pair of boots from a barrel of discarded and mouldering clothes, I went to make my peace with my saviors.

I owe my rescue ultimately to two men. The first is old Pete, the weathered ancient who watches the waves. After Mr. Apples found my cell empty in the morning, it was this old Pete's inscrutable reckoning that led the *Rose* back to find me. Mabbot had circled for a few hours in the waters where I should have been, and it was there that they spotted the *Diastema* on the horizon, recognizing it from the description the prison guards gave.

I offered the old man figs, but he eats only salted sardines with rice and that in the tiniest amounts. I sat with him but could not tell if he valued my company. His simple smile does not leave his face in any circumstance, even as he took in my scarlet nose and sun-blistered lips. He is as benign as a teapot. The events of the last few days have been brutally humbling, and sitting near this man in his wicker chair as he stares at the water does nothing but humble me further. I upbraid myself for not having recognized, at first sight, a saint in the flesh.

The other man is a more complicated story. Mabbot told me that Asher, the graveyard watch chief, had been ordered to "make right" my escape. The poor man hadn't slept, and it was he who finally spotted the *Diastema* from the nest. I made him a few savory griddle cakes of pounded cornmeal with onions, topped with slices of pickled herring. I found him moping silently in his hammock. He would not look at me, and when I handed him the plate, he threw it against the wall.

Joshua showed up for his reading lesson as if there had been no intermission, and I was glad for it. He showed me the mother-of-pearl inlaid box of ink and quills Mabbot had given him, but when I opened it, I screamed and dropped it; he had stashed a dead rat inside.

At first, Joshua's laugh frankly unsettled me, but when I hear it now, I cannot help but join in, even after juvenile pranks like this. In a world that feels, day by day, more soiled and fraught, Joshua's laugh can wash a room clean.

He brought too a tattered leather-bound Bible. It was a dramatically simplified missionary translation, with no sentence longer than ten words, but I held it to my forehead for a long moment before we sat.

Our reading lesson began, as any should, with Genesis. Translating these primal stories by gesture and drawing was arduous work. Joshua made it no easier. While his reading is confoundingly slow, his wit has the devil's speed. No sooner had a sentence been laid out than he had some objection to it. He knows many of these stories already, but he resists them with heathen vigor. The stick figure I made to represent Abel's wife he practically obliterated with question marks. In addition, he wanted to know who made God, and didn't He have a stick to kill the serpent with?

I set him to the task of copying sentences. For our next lesson I'll put together a less inflammatory curriculum. I think I'll ask the boy to write about his own family.

As I watched Joshua making the tentative loops and spears of the alphabet, I fought a strong urge to wrap my arms around him and pull him to my chest. I was worried for him; he was so thin and this sea life so treacherous. A reverie sprang up in my mind: I saw my late beloved Elizabeth at the door with her apron full of greens, I saw over her shoulder the apricot tree in bloom, I saw even the squirrel she fed despite the havoc it brought to the garden, and there at the kitchen table was Joshua, hunched over his letters, playing the part of our own son.

For a moment it was frighteningly real. A seaborne mirage. But the longing it set alight was so penetrating, and the remorse so ferocious, that, had Lucifer arrived with a contract and smoldering quill, I would gladly have signed my soul away for a single day in that dream.

I know I'm clinging to Joshua, carving him in the shape of my own grief. Of course, his shoulders are much too narrow to carry the weight of it, and besides, he is here willingly — the boy is a pirate, after all, there is no denying it.

These hysterical flights of fancy are yet more reason to find some way home, wherever that may be, before these weakening pieces of me finally break and madness rushes in.

This morning at sunrise, Asher was whipped for letting me escape. He walked, of his own accord, to the mast, where Mr. Apples tied his hands. It would have happened earlier, but Mabbot had wanted me present. All of us gathered, and she announced from the upper deck: "Punishment for dereliction of duty!"

The first lash brought a mournful cry from the young man. I went to Mabbot and said, "Please, let me stand in his place. This is my mischief."

"It *is* your mischief," she said. "But look at you. Your skin is still hanging from your fingers in folds. The sea has made you soft as a babe. That whip would cut you in two."

"Mabbot, please don't joke. This is not justice."

She looked me steadily in the eyes and said, "If I let you take the whip, what will you learn? What will he?"

The whip cracked and the poor man sank to his knees. When I averted my eyes, Mabbot said loudly, for all to hear, "Can you not even give him the dignity of witnessing his punishment?" And so I watched, sweating with shame, as the last strokes broke his skin open.

Afterward I went to him where he lay on his side under the hammock and tried to clean his wounds, but he would not tolerate me.

Thus I am caught in ratlines of reliance, and the more I struggle to free myself, the more entangled I become. I have never gambled, nor borrowed. When necessary, as a poor journeyman, I ate moldy bread rather than ask for flour on credit of my honor. Now, though, it seems I am daily indebted to a new scoundrel, men whom I would not have nodded to in the city streets.

Even so, yesterday I was heartened to have found fellowship of sorts. Eating supper with the men on deck, a bowl of gelatinous porridge before me, grateful to be still among the living, I stood and gave grace. I then announced my intention to observe evening prayers and invited any to join me. Expecting ridicule, I got instead half a dozen volunteers who followed me in prayer before bed, a sweaty bunch of fellows happy to bow their heads and whisper "amen."

I had been quite weak since my ordeal, my sea legs wobbly and my stomach eager to turn, but after this hodgepodge mass, I felt my strength returning. It satisfied something deep in me, and I slept better than I have in a long while.

Therefore, it was a shock when, today, I caught five of those same men prostrating and praying with the Mohammedans. Unable to contain myself, I scolded them for their sacrilege and got this response: "Gold ye may gamble. But sumtin' precious as a 'ternal soul, one is best taking no chances. Cover yer bets, man, for ye only look to break even."

This nonsense was delivered to me with motherly concern. From their expressions one might have mistaken them for missionaries guiding a lost savage. A better Christian would have stayed to show them the error of their logic, but with holy prayer compared to a game of dice, I was struck dumb and merely wandered away muttering to myself.

I may not be skilled at eloquent oratory, but for muttering angrily under one's breath, I have never met a more capable man.

When Joshua came for his lesson, I had already prepared a stick drawing of a family. I wrote *MOTHER* and *FATHER* beside the appropriate figures and *JOSHUA* beside a smaller one. Pointing to the patriarch, I asked, "What's his name?" with my face to the light so Joshua could read my lips.

Joshua put his fist on his heart, then tapped the thumb of his right hand against his forehead with the fingers splayed like antlers.

"No, write it here." I put the pencil in his hand, but he dropped it and made the gesture again. "The man must have a proper name," I said and moved his hand toward the paper, but he pushed it away and continued with his inscrutable gesticulations. I seized the wild bird of his right hand and put the pencil firmly in his palm, saying, "Whatever you wish to tell me, you can write. God made hands to hold tools, not to mince the air. You've only to learn to write, and you can express anything at all!"

But the impudent child broke the pencil in two and crossed his arms. Gathering all of my composure, I sharpened the pencil, taking the time to make a fine point, and placed it again in his hand. When he threw it down and began to gesture wildly, I pinched his ear, for effect, and said, "That is not the way to do it! Learn to write!"

The boy slapped me hard in the face. It took me so by surprise that he had turned and slammed the door on his way out before I could summon a response. I spent a good amount of time grumbling to myself. Perhaps I should not have laid my hands on him, but if he really wishes to learn the rudiments of language, he must apply himself. I cannot do all the work for him.

I wish Joshua's slap was the only insult today, but I must make a note to avoid Feng whenever possible. For no reason at all, while we passed in the twilight of the lower deck, the little man scowled and elbowed me, causing me to lose my wind completely. My ribs ache now with each breath. While a few here may be justified in their resentment, this man's cruelty seems quite gratuitous.

Friday, September 3
On this gruesome day I was the unwilling witness to the sacking of the Pendleton Trading Company ship the *Patience.* Although I've no desire to relive it, I shall note my impressions to be read, let us pray, at the eventual trial of Mabbot for piracy and murder.

During the night previous, we weathered a squall. It was a small one, the men said, though I could not tell if this was one of their jokes. I had tried to sleep and failed. It felt like I had been placed in a barrel and was rolling down a particularly steep and uneven hill. There were moments when I could not distinguish between the thunder and the clopping of boots on the deck as men ran about reefing sails or securing cannon. My hammock beat against the wall and tenderized me thoroughly. In my half sleep I wondered if Mabbot had foreseen this storm on the horizon and exchanged my sack for this hammock just in time for me to be flung about in it like a piglet brought to market. At one point, hoping to stave off nausea, I made the mistake of going above deck to see what the men were up to. As soon as I emerged, a great wave smacked me down, and only by scrambling upon the wood and catching hold of an errant line was I saved from being washed over the bulwark into the frothing void. Those seconds, illumed by the ghostly lanterns and the great shudders of lightning, were like another world, neither above water nor below it, a world of howling fear, and a darkness whose appetite was insatiable. Returning to my cell, soaked to the bone and shuddering, I resolved to tell the first priest I met that all the fire in hell had been long since dowsed.

Only in the mean dregs of morning did the storm pass and the ship calm itself enough for me to close my eyes. This is my excuse for sleeping well into the day. But that too was a mistake, for I had the misfortune to wake to cannon fire. God keep you from this fate. It is completely upending: the heart leaps up and tries to escape the prison of the ribs before the eyes are open. One may find oneself running, as I did, in an arbitrary direction, hands instinctively covering one's crotch, and slamming face-first into the doorframe.

But to the point.

I discovered, above deck, that our cannon fire had been a warning shot and that we were quickly approaching the *Patience,* which had been damaged in the storm and was making no effort to flee. The garish two-headed lion of the Pendleton Trading Company flag was impossible to mistake. Except for the broken mizzen yards of the Pendleton ship, the only sign of the storm was the mackerel-striped clouds above. Our crew was in a state of great excitement, and I had to push through a crowd of men at the bulwark to see the ship. Some of the men blew upon enormous tin trumpets, each easily twenty feet long. This colossal flatus that echoed off the sails of the *Patience* was meant, no doubt, to instill fear in our victims.

I have learned that although the oceans are vast, the shipping lanes themselves are rather narrow. Between the currents, winds, and storms, any ship hoping to make it to China and back dares not venture too far from the courses laid out in the almanacs. Though hundred-foot waves and mast-crushing winds sound terrible enough to me, nothing chills a sailor's mood quite as much as talk of the "doldrums." In these swaths of the ocean, nothing at all happens. Any ship slipping into such a zone becomes a windless island, and its crew castaways forced to eat rope and, eventually, one another. To hear them tell it, Mabbot's crew would rather row a live shark into a hurricane than find themselves in the doldrums. Mabbot's mischief, then, is made easier, for she needs only follow these safe routes and eventually she will spot a company ship on the horizon, like the *Patience,* homeward bound off the western coast of Africa, on the last leg of her long journey, with a belly full of cargo and hope.

The captain's upholstered chair had been brought from her cabin to the gun deck, and she sat there enthroned. When she saw me she beckoned and said, "Well, good morning, slumberbug. Bring a stool and join me. It will be educational."

"Mabbot," I demanded, "I forbid you to harm these innocents —"

"Ah, the barrister-at-sea with his customary objection." Mabbot sighed. "But hush now, darling, we're doing business."

The crew nearby had gasped at my tone, but when Mabbot dismissed me, they sneered and went back to work.

Because the view from the poop deck was better than from the quarter, I lingered near Mabbot. It was from there that I spotted, distant to the *Patience,* a cluster of boats. I held my breath with hope, thinking that it might be a fleet come to apprehend us, but those hopes were dashed when Mabbot said, "Good, then. You see? They've done the sensible thing and given us space. If they stay out there in their longboats, I'll let them live. It is better to have survivors to spread the word that the best option is surrender."

Thus we lay aboard the *Patience* without trouble or bloodshed. The men threw planks and ropes and stormed the ship, guns and swords drawn. But resistance there was none, and in only a few minutes the men began to emerge from below deck carrying their booty like a swarm of ants.

They brought pitch-sealed lockers first, carried by two men apiece, and set them upon the deck. The horns were blown again and all eyes were on Mr. Apples, who stood beside the chests and announced in a ceremonious voice, "Men, put down your worries and grab your cocks. It's bathing day at the sheikh's harem."

This was met with hoots and a general stomping on the deck, which subsided only when Mabbot raised her hand.

Then the chests were opened to reveal rows of clay pots whose narrow mouths had been plugged with resin.

Mr. Apples inspected them and shouted up to Mabbot, "Opium, Captain! Perfume on it like a lily stuffed up Satan's arse."

"I should say you know where to put that," Mabbot shouted down.

Mr. Apples nodded to the men, and they carted the locker to the port bulwark and dropped the whole thing into the sea. Fifty cases were thus disposed of. I could not say the exact amount but knew it was the sinking of a dozen fortunes.

"Mabbot, what is your purpose if not to resell your stolen goods?" I asked.

For the first time, Mabbot dropped her singsong tone and growled at me. "Stop your tongue."

But as the men brought more cargo for her inspection, her mood improved quickly. It was a parade of goods, a veritable market. At each item, Mr. Apples would call out the thing, for example: "Fifty bolts of green silk!" or "Saltpeter for an army!" or "Fifteen hogsheads of loose black tea!"

To which Mabbot would reply, "Ours." This meant that the item belonged to the ship in general. Once sold, its value would be divided among the men according to their rank. A tremendous amount of silk was thus deposited into the holds, also great casks of tea, loose and in cakes.

Regarding some items, such as a suede hat with a peacock feather, Mabbot would declare "yours!" and thus bestow it upon the man who had found it.

When Mr. Apples called out, "Small silver teapot! Cute as a monkey's shoe!" Mabbot declared, "Mine!" and the item was taken by Feng to a special hold. (I've learned to tell the twins apart, for Feng carries always a little leather-bound book, no doubt a heathen tract, tucked into his belt, dipping into it at moments of leisure.) Mabbot also claimed a rotund bottle of brandy, which was delivered directly to her cabin. Only a few items were thus owned by her, and if the men were upset by it, they showed no sign.

Though it seemed efficient at first, the event took all day. There was a ritual to it; they were reveling in their reward. It was this orgy of larceny, I realized, that made their hard days on the sea bearable, and they were not going to rush it. The air was festive, not unlike that of an Easter feast. A small group played a Gypsy polka on a flute, a drum, and an instrument like a harp but with fewer strings. Seamen danced with each other while they waited their turn to cross the planks from ship to ship. Mabbot was grinning — she drank a mug of tea and tapped her foot to the tune.

It was not at all the savage bloodbath I had imagined a pirate raid to be. The captain and crew of the *Patience* waited half a league distant, too far to make out individuals by sight, crowded as they were into twenty-foot longboats. No doubt the mood there was not so joyous, but from where I stood, I could see no signs of outrage. They could have been a flock of seabirds bobbing on the water.

The vast majority of the haul consisted of silk — a rainbow ton of it — satin, and muslin too, indigo dye, and, of course, tea. There were also several chests of silver ingots that Mabbot declared "ours."

After the larger barrels and chests had been lowered through the hatches by can hook and stowed, the personal items of the *Patience*'s crew and captain began to appear. With very few exceptions Mabbot declared these items "yours," and the men laughed and wrestled in their joy. They acquired boots, coats, hammered copper boxes, tobacco, hats, musical instruments, guns, swords, books, and trinkets of jade, ruby, and silver. Mabbot looked closely at every book before granting them to their finders.

The ship's manifest was brought for her inspection, and she gave it only a cursory glance before dropping it with disgust to the deck, where I picked it up. It was a ruled log — a great list of dates and places and goods. It was authenticated by Lord Ramsey's seal, and it hit me that these merchants had no idea that Ramsey was dead.

If I was reading it correctly, the manifest indicated that the ship was on its way back to England, with one more stop in Cameroon to pick up twoscore "long birds."

"What is a long bird?" I asked Mabbot.

"What indeed? Do you suppose they provide long eggs?"

Mabbot knew the answer, I was sure, but I didn't want to give her the opportunity to mock me, so I gave the manifest to Bai and forgot about it.

Then, to my surprise, the men hauled up a diminutive but lovely custom-built iron stove with a flat top for cooking and an ingenious box at the back for baking. Under her breath, Mabbot asked, "Can you use this?"

"Yes."

She told them to place it in the larder for storage. Mabbot also allocated for my use cabbages, which had kept relatively well in hay in the cool lower holds, and a sack of whole dried corn.

Then one of the men brought Mabbot a piece of paper that bore her likeness.

"A warrant! Five hundred guineas for my head. 'For crimes against commerce, nature, and the king.' A kind of poetry to it. Still, I'm a little insulted."

"Captain," Mr. Apples said, "five hundred ain't hardly crumbs."

"No, but this is my life's work, after all. One hopes for . . . Well, it continues: 'Her captor shall be thanked by His Majesty and granted a title within the Valley Suffolk.' Mr. Apples, is Suffolk a fine place?"

"Never been, Captain."

"Then it must be very fine indeed."

A box of correspondence emerged, full of London-bound letters from various officials and captains. Mabbot picked through these letters as the men stowed their goods. Most she ordered tossed into the sea, but one was addressed to Ramsey from Laroche. She and Mr. Apples read it together, chuckling.

"Good Lord," Mabbot said. "He's petitioning for more ships!"

"I told you, the man has ambitions," said Mr. Apples.

"If he had five of those damned things, he'd rival any navy on the seas."

"Thanks to God we've cut his patron down."

"Thanks to me," Mabbot huffed. She handed the letter to me, saying, "You might as well take a look, Wedge, it's a dead letter. Hard to believe a blowhard like that is so dangerous."

In a tight indigo script, the letter read:

Dear Lord Ramsey,

I trust this letter finds you, as always, in the excellent health that is your due. I thank you for the additional provisions — though I beg you again for a certain amount of free credit as the *épée solaire* requires unconventional maintenance and supplies, among them spermaceti for the gears, lenses, and leather. The balloon too requires spermaceti; no other oil burns pure enough and I've been forced to trade with whalers at open sea, which slows me. This is but an example of the frustration that simple specie would alleviate.

By your agents in China you must already know that the Brass Fox is gaining influence with the smugglers on the Pearl River. I fear that we are watching the blades of shears converge, but once Mabbot has been apprehended I will happily turn my attentions to that crisis. Let not the pettiness of villainy dampen your spirits.

When the path is made clear, progress and posterity flow of their own accord. We have learned this at great cost — the blood of revolutions, the might of crowns, all are swept aside by innovation and improvement. It matters not what language a man speaks; he holds a pen, he holds a plow, he holds a gun in exactly the same manner. We are all children of our tools.

As for our agreement that my reward for Mabbot's head shall be a complement of five ships under my command, I must reiterate that these ships, delivered in advance, would speed me to my target and sweep your path clear that much faster. I understand that your associates have expressed concerns about a privateer, particularly one of my extraction, commanding a fleet, but I know you to be a man of great influence and a harbinger of new methods.

I am every day closer. *La Colette* continues to honor her namesake; sophisticated but quiet, she does not dawdle, slender and lovely, and but a glance from her burns.

The balloon works exceedingly well (when I have oil enough) and will suit to supply an entire armada with instant communication far beyond the range of flags as well as providing a perspective once reserved only for God Himself.

I have not encountered Captain Mabbot since my last correspondence, which detailed my near victory, but be warned, by her reported headings, which are erratic as ever, it would seem she intends to make for the Canaries at least, and perhaps as far as to England itself. I cannot imagine she would be brash enough to advance upon London, but show some care and keep you far from the coasts until the shark is gone.

Included is another letter for my acquaintances in Paris. I would be grateful if you would send it along to the usual address.

Your Servant,
Alexandre Laroche

The letter burned my fingers — had it reached us in time, it would have saved both Ramsey and myself; we could have made a cozy retreat to one of his lordship's houses deep inland, far from the clawing of the surf, safe and sated on Yorkshire pudding and mutton with mushroom gravy.

How many hands had this warning passed through? How long had it languished in ports while the holds were filled with dumb tons of tea? "Keep you far from the coasts"! Lifesaving advice woefully delayed by the whims of weather and men.

When Mabbot saw me sitting on the deck staring disconsolately at the paper, she said, "Chin up, Wedge! I assure you, it's better to read his letters than to meet the man at sea. I know he charmed you on the field, but he's a moray on the water."

Finally, after all other goods had been apportioned, the men brought forth one final object. It seemed to be a statue of a savage on a wooden pedestal. Mr. Apples walked around it and peered at it from several angles before declaring, "Ahem . . . a trophy. From the captain's quarters."

Mabbot gestured and they brought it up for her to examine. It was no statue but a masterpiece of taxidermy. Though its features were that of a man, it was the size of a child, its skin very black. Its lips were pulled back in a perpetual snarl, its brow furled. It looked eager to heave its spear. It was naked save for the beads around its waist and the bolt through its nose. I could see no sutures, and its yellow glass eyes looked wet and ready to blink. It stood on a block of polished hardwood where a bronze plaque was secured. It read: SAVAGE HOTTENTOT OF SOUTHERN AFRICA.

I felt my humors sour and had to sit again. I had not, in the cruelest corners of my mind, ever imagined that men did this to men.

All eyes watched the captain; even the waves seemed to calm. She was, herself, still as a statue; the two stared at each other and neither blinked. I saw, on her temple, a blood vessel pulsing. Her lip trembled and she whispered something no one could hear.

Mr. Apples appeared beside her and sheepishly asked, "Captain, say again —"

"TO THE BOTTOM!" Mabbot roared as she rose. "Send the dogs to the bottom holdin' their rank hearts!" Her refined accent had quite disappeared and was replaced by a brined cockney.

The crew burst into action, running to man the guns and tugging at ropes to ease our sheets. "Now! Now!" Mabbot bellowed, her mouth wide as a well. "Place it 'pon the ship! 'Twill be his bier." Thus the Hottentot was hauled back and secured to the mast of the company ship. A barrel of bitumen was poured upon the deck and set alight. The fire moved quickly and within minutes had leaped to the sails.

Mabbot, blazing with rage, had drawn her jade-handled pistols on the distant longboats where the crew of the *Patience* awaited their fate. "*THIS* is yer precious comp'ny!" she hissed before firing both guns. On cue, our cannon battery fired. Of the half-dozen longboats I could see, two burst immediately into splinters. The others were rocked by the plumes of water the balls created. It was pitiful to see them scatter, rowing in all directions as our guns were reloaded.

Meanwhile, the conflagration on the *Patience* had grown, and I could feel its heat. I recovered from my shock enough to say, "Mabbot! You cannot simply murder those men."

At this, Mabbot did a most unwomanly

thing. She grabbed me by the throat with such force that something clicked and my wind was gone. Tugging me close, she whispered, "D'ye wish to join those noble men, those heroes in their boats? Then hide yer face from me!"

When she let go, I went to my knees, gasping. There was nothing I could do. The cannon burst out at the men sitting helpless on the waves. I made for my berth as much to hide from the horror as from Mabbot. On my way down, I passed Mr. Apples, who was carrying a bundle of smoldering slow matches. He slapped me on the back and laughed. "Captain sure fancies you, Spoons! Any other sailor would have been keelhauled for talking to her the way you do."

Though I did not watch, I am sure none of the Pendleton crew survived those awful minutes. So this is the terror that sells newspapers back home. Like a bad storm, she sows havoc as she goes. And what calamity will befall us when she finally catches up with her prodigal child?

When I next emerged, we were moving apace and the *Patience* was a smudge of smoke on the horizon. Below the setting sun, I could see the olive stippling of the Cape Verde Islands. Nearing the equator meant warmer nights, which was about the only good news I'd had in weeks. We were tacking against the southeast trade winds, which sent a ceaseless mist up over the bow. By chance, I spotted Mabbot flinging the door of her cabin open, carrying the stuffed pheasant that had stood upon her mirror. This she flung over the rail into the water, its plumage fluttering behind it.

Hope of escape is with me waking and dreaming, and has become its own cruel despot, whipping my imagination in sweaty circles. Too often I think it were better had Mabbot killed me. For if I managed to escape and survived the unknown perils of a journey home, I would arrive, as she so cruelly pointed out, at the wasteland of my former life.

I confess that there is a part of me, loathsome and cowardly, that wishes to be done with hope and call this ship home. It would be strangely relieving to give up and let myself become just another of Mabbot's men, loafing with never a decision to be made. This is the siren's call.

And so I find I must nurse my courage as tenderly as I nurse my yeast sponge, for it too would quickly dry up and perish here.

10

Sauerkraut and Theater

IN WHICH CABBAGES AND HISTORY ARE
MISTREATED AS WE CROSS THE EQUATOR

Saturday, September 4

While eating this morning, the men were whispering about the Brass Fox, and before I knew it they'd gathered around me. "Tell us what you know!" Conrad shouted. For he was usually the one who instigated these gossip parties. Simply whispering "Fox" was usually enough to bring the unctuous cook running.

"What can I know?" I have never been a great liar. "I hardly saw the man. I was half-drowned."

"I've told ye the truth," one man said. "Mabbot an' the Fox were lovers, sleeping on a heap of hoarded gold. But the Fox had an eye for the dairymaids, and on the day of their wedding, he left Mabbot holding her flowers. Since then she's been after him. Her plan is to marry him at noon an' kill him at one."

"That could be —" I said.

"Pig shit!" spat Conrad. "Lovers? They were no such thing. The Fox is the deposed duke of Portugal, this I heard from Short Jim. The Fox was betrayed by his own cousin, who sold the royal jewels to finance a rebel army. Now the Fox travels the world stealing the jewels back and slitting sleeping throats. Didn't he have that air about him?"

"The air of a deposed duke?" I muttered. "I couldn't say for cert—"

"Naw!" barked another. "The Brass Fox is a true fox whose skin was stolen. Everyone knows a fox is charmed and has riches aplenty stowed under the mountains. He's looking for his skin so he can return to his fox fambly."

This was followed by such bickering as made my exit rather easy. It is a position of strange privilege to be keeping secrets with Mabbot. No doubt, unholy grief would befall me if I told these men the truth I know. She has judged that her pirates would hardly be motivated enough by the return of the spoiled child to keep up the interminable chase, and so lets them conjure their own fantastic stories. Whatever Mabbot intends to do with the brat, I hope it involves a goodly reward for her crew.

Saturday already, and tomorrow I must feed

her again. Having heard the stories from a young age, we may take for granted the water to wine and multiplication of fishes, but making sustenance ex nihilo is no easy miracle, to say nothing of victuals that actually please the palate.

I have separated my stolen potpourri into discrete piles. These are the usable contents: five broken bay leaves; two sticks of cinnamon; a few fragile sprigs of rosemary; several cloves; what I believe to be anise seed (very stale); and a handful of small dried rosebuds. All of these have succumbed to the odor of cedar, that brute. Still, with a little heat, I might be able to coax their whispering voices to sing.

Here in the privacy of my scribbles, I admit that I feel a childish spark in me. Prior to this, all of my study and sweat, no matter the party or circumstance, had concerned no greater stake than the glazing of wealthy tongues. Now the game has changed. Despite the indignity, the debasement, despite my molten outrage, a piece of me is eager to meet this challenge.

I've added the cedar to my castile soap, and the result is quite refreshing. My cell affords me privacy, a rare commodity here on the ship, and I've taken advantage of it several times to crouch naked over a bucket to wash my clothes. Of course the seawater leaves a white rime no matter how many times I rinse.

It occurs to me that the sailors upon this boat, though slavish to their beloved captain, are not without wiles of their own. Did they not save the horrid Hottentot for last because they knew it would be the end of the party?

My botched attempt and subsequent pickling has me reconsidering my plans for escape. If it is to happen, it must be within clear sight of land, or at least of a rescuing ship, for I cannot risk being lost upon open waters again. My opportunity will, no doubt, appear suddenly, and I must be ready for brave action.

Eager to use the new cabbages before they wilted, I made sauerkraut, that loyal friend. The cabbages were of a Chinese variety unfamiliar to me, their leaves long and their taste mild, striking me as rather a hybrid of cabbage and lettuce. But the hearts were crisp, and I found myself stuffing my mouth like an old goat, so welcome was the crunch of a real vegetable.

I kneaded the shredded cabbage with salt

until it sweated brine, then packed it with a few cloves of garlic in a small wooden keg and set a rock upon it to keep the devil out. Sauerkraut will make my internment a little more bearable. It is one of the staples of civilized life that I had taken for granted and now feels to me like a blessed luxury. It has a hundred uses: it cures scurvy as well as limes while aiding digestion, strengthens the heart, sharpens the mind, and makes one's deposits as regular and well formed as those of an ox. Its juice can be drunk as a tonic and serves as a flavorful replacement for vinegar, while the kraut itself can garnish anything but sweet-cake. I assume that manna was something akin.

As it ferments, kraut whispers alchemical secrets. In two days, it will smell as agreeable as an old pillow still warm from night's use. In five days it will smell like a horse run to foam. The odor will then lessen as the vegetable begins its tart transformation. It will be good to eat in two weeks, but at five weeks it will reach the zenith of its power, its taste a violin bow drawn across the tongue. After six weeks it will err slowly toward slime. Like hams and men, it gets better with age only to a point.

Mabbot is correct in this: I do have more

idle time than I have ever had. Last week I spent it pacing and fretting. Now, after my misadventure in the sea, I take moments to appreciate the air and sun — my left ear, having been thoroughly irrigated, aches when I get too cold — and to watch Bai practice his slow martial dances while Feng angles for opponents over a specially made chessboard whose every square is bordered by half-inch runners that keep the pieces from toppling as the ship rolls.

The Chinaman has ruined chess for most of the crew. While he and his brother are usually as stony as gargoyles, the game brings out a surprisingly uncouth side of Feng. If he had invented the game, he couldn't take more pride in it. He will play anyone and takes as much pleasure in five-move victories as in the rare hour-long contest. He seems almost addicted to it, and few can face him on the board for long before he snatches their king with a cackle.

As hardly any wish to play him, he is not above bullying passing sailors into a game, saying, just loudly enough for them to hear, "Don't worry, I won't tell anyone you are a coward" or "You walk like a woman."

When he wins, as he inevitably does, he lets loose an almost girlish laugh and places his small hand on the loser's chest to say with mock concern, "Oh, don't cry!"

When I sat to play him, though, he swept the board into a sack with one quick motion and left me sitting alone. The man's hatred for me feels personal, though I cannot put my finger on the exact reason for it.

Chinkle, buntline, sheepshank, monkey fist — these sailors have as many names for knots as I have for cheese, and they make about as much sense. They've made a game of asking me to identify a given knot, then snickering when I answer incorrectly. They're happy for their loot, and today I've lingered at the periphery of the gangs taking their leisure, listening to their music and jokes, learning from them the complicated craft of keeping the *Rose* on her tack, which sails are royal and which topgallant, how to secure a line to a belay pin, and how to scale the shrouds. The men even gave me a hempen bracelet for having successfully climbed to the top of the mainmast and kissed the brass cap there.

I can attest that pirates do indeed sing, unceasingly and in ravens' voices, but not always unpleasantly, as they have plenty of practice and they harass those who break rhythm. Their themes are redundant and, more often than not, pornographic. But I suppose, if one wants hymns, one does not seek out pirates.

They are forever telling stories as well. On any given day, one can hear a variety of outrageous yarns about underwater kingdoms, scandalous assignations, or ghost ships. I admit I was interested to hear one sagacious sailor explain to several of us how Feng and Bai came to work with Mabbot. It was a wet oration delivered around a wad of tobacco in the man's cheek, and we all had to wait patiently while he spat over the railing every few sentences.

Feng and Bai, I learned, were the youngest of five brothers of the wealthy Tsang family, owners of a great silk-making house. "Their worms," the sailor said, "produced fabric so light an' airy that an entire bolt weighed no more than a sparrow. When their father refused to take a warlord's opium as payment, he was skewered 'pon a pike and the entire house was burned to cinders. The five brothers gave themselves to a Buddhist mystic to learn boxing. Then, years later, they cut their revenge from the warlord, his opium factory, his family, and his workers. But this bloodletting brought back neither their home nor their father, no, not even a single silkworm. Their grief was not slaked. They set themselves against the officials who had cooperated with the warlord. Scores died on their swords before they were eventually ambushed, tried, and sentenced to hang. It was in the Canton cell awaiting their death that they met Mabbot. She'd been captured by the navy and was awaiting transport to England, where the Pendleton Company planned to parade her in the streets before hanging her near the ports as a warning against piracy. Those of us left, myself, Apples, and a few more, used the hanging of the Tsang brothers as a distraction to break her out. Mabbot, though, refused to flee before she'd cut the brothers from the gallows with her own knife, while we fought off the guards."

"And what became of the other three brothers?" I asked.

"Mabbot could only cut so fast," he replied, and spat into the wind such that I was obliged to duck a brown string of saliva.

At sunset, I was ambushed in the galley by no fewer than a dozen men who, despite my screams, stuffed my head into a sack and carried me to the mizzen, where I was trussed to a plank like a stuffed goose. My feet left the deck as I was hoisted into the air to dangle helplessly from a spar. The sack was tugged from my head, and in the glare of sunset I saw nearly the entire crew assembled. Their grins made it clear that my pending execution gave them no end of pleasure. Even Joshua was there laughing with the rest of them, and that betrayal stung deeply.

To my surprise, only crusty old Conrad came to my defense. He croaked, "Aw, how'd he earn this already? He's only been aboard a few weeks! Cut 'im down!"

He was, of course, completely ignored. Mr. Apples stood imperiously on the poop deck so he would be eye level with me and asked, "Well, Spoons, what do you say for yourself?"

I had no heart to beg. "Is this a court?" I yelled. "Judge yourselves!" As I spoke, the impotent rage that has so darkened my breast burst forth. "Whatever offense you accuse me of, I redouble a hundredfold against you. I accuse and condemn you all, animals, brutes! Let my last words bring a blight upon your wicked hearts." I spat on the deck (an act I knew Mr. Apples in particular did not appreciate), and yet the men only laughed harder.

The deck rang with jeers as I was swung out over the water and dropped suddenly into the sea. I took a desperate gasp, and, though in the churning I could call no

211

prayers to my mind, I cleaved to the memory of a small wooden Saint Ignatius that stood above Father Sonora's oven. It had been darkened by soot and its face polished to a shine by Sonora's custom of touching it as he passed.

Swimming was impossible, and I rolled into the increasingly chilly murk. When my chest began to heave of its own accord and my nostrils filled with the fiery brine, my ropes went tight and I was hoisted up into the light and dropped back upon the deck, where the laughter of the men continued.

I was untied and someone shouted, "He has spunk, I give him that!"

"That he does." Mr. Apples chuckled before announcing: "Owen Zachariah Wedgwood, having crossed the equator on the *Flying Rose,* you are hereby initiated into our distinguished ranks as captain's cook, idler, and general jackass." He placed a wreath of seaweed upon my head and whispered, "Do not spit 'pon my deck."

"Piss!" I shouted.

"Spoken like a gentleman. Now, boys, the fun's over, back to your posts."

I have approached Kitzu for fish again, but as I have not paid him for his last contribution, he scowled at me and made as if to give me nothing until, finally, he tossed at my feet a speckled and frenzied eel, as one might throw crusts to a dog. The rest of the catch he gave to the crew — as I moaned. Among the knots of seaweed in which my eel churned, I found a small but lovely herring and took that too, and placed them both in a fresh bucket of seawater in my chamber.

After our tiff, Joshua continues to avoid me. I am already missing the lessons with him. I had come to rely on them as a precious, if temporary, diversion from the enervating madhouse of this ship. Now there is no break from my anxious pacing, my worries about how to make comestibles from sawdust. Nevertheless, if the boy wants to learn, he must come to me and make amends.

It doesn't help that, instead of learning to read, Joshua is being taught to fire cannon. I tell myself I shouldn't worry — that the boy got along well enough before my arrival — but I cannot keep myself from loitering nearby while they walk him through the tamping of the barrel and the pricking of the charge. I lurk despite knowing that the crew bristle to be watched by an "idler."

Today, Mr. Apples laughed at me. "What's the matter, mother hen? Your boy growing up too fast?"

To this, I answered, "Would that he grows well and tall and with all of his fingers intact! He is clever — much too clever to be manning brute weapons!" This last remark earned me such scowls from the gunmen that I rushed straight to my chamber.

Saturday, Later

This evening the men erected a small stage upon the deck, complete with a curtain, lanterns, and a motley orchestra, to put on a bit of theater that they had been preparing. On the whole, it was a rude and rudimentary farce, little more than a medium for artificial blasts of flatulence and an excuse to flounce about, smacking one another's arses with oars. But those watching lapped it up. Indeed, they barked themselves hoarse with laughter. Mabbot sat at the front in her upholstered chair, smoking an ivory pipe carved from the tusk of a walrus. Having a view of only the back of her head where her red braids parted, I could not tell if she was still upset about the *Patience* incident.

The "salt opera," as the men called it, was preceded by a few individual offerings. First Asher plucked a haunting tune from a bean-shaped guitar. This was followed by stoic

Feng himself taking the stage and commanding rapt attention with his perfect posture. He took from his belt the mysterious little book, and I readied myself for a pagan sermon. Instead, Feng spoke, quietly and mostly from memory, a Shakespearian sonnet:

As an unperfect actor on the stage,
Who with his fear is put beside his part,
. . . O! let my looks be then the eloquence.

If I hadn't been so well acquainted with his merciless fists, I would have thought, from this quiet delivery, that he was a tenderhearted schoolboy, trying to woo a maid.

O! learn to read what silent love hath writ:
To hear with eyes belongs to love's fine wit.

After the stomping and simian hooting that serves as applause here, the stage was ceded to the evening's main entertainment. The show, taking its inspiration from legends of Mabbot's exploits, was the sort of infantile horseplay that I would have walked away from if I had not been arrested by the costume of one character. By his blue coat and the outlandish mustache made of twisted coconut fiber, it was clear that the man was impersonating my late employer, Lord Ramsey. When he strode across the stage, he was met with boos and hisses. With horror, I perceived the actor wore not just any blue coat; it was, in fact, his lordship's actual coat with the grisly stain upon the lapel. Honor and duty obliged me to march up and rip the thing from the desecrator's frame, but I was easily shoved to the deck by those watching before I could touch the man. Fantasies of bloody vengeance rose in me, but I was painfully aware that I was in the wolves' den, and that there was nothing to do but witness and pray for rescue.

Between the rude crotch-thrusting, which evoked levity every time, and the toots of an old tin horn that stood in for broken wind, a rough plot emerged. The protagonist, ersatz Mabbot (played by Mr. Apples in a horsehair wig, his bosom stuffed with pillows), pranced about the stage with a small papier-mâché ship ingeniously girdling his tremendous waist. Shortly "she" was seized by navy ships and, despite delivering frightful blows upon their heads with her scabbard, was imprisoned in a cell made from a dangling net. Here, she croaked out a falsetto tune:

Life is a drop of water on a stove,

A mouse on a miller's stone,
Without hope of rescue,
I shall die here all alone . . .

Mr. Apples's talents are admittedly impressive. He can negotiate the arc of a cannonball as well as the waltz of knitting needles. He cannot, however, sing. Alas, the audience disagreed with me, clapping as if it were Handel.

The genuine Mabbot, in full view of this farce, didn't stir. The evening's entertainment was apparently an attempt to improve her mood. I couldn't imagine seeing herself played so artlessly would please her, though.

If the drama thus far had been based upon fact, it now swung shamelessly into falsehood as a strange thing happened upon the stage. Ramsey arrived to free Mabbot from her confines and made this apocryphal speech: "Hannah Mabbot, Tiger of the Seas, harken! I offer freedom for your skills! Use them for England! Spain nibbles at our bread! France sends our merchants to dine with Davy Jones. The foreign devils trade in slaves and opium. Protect us, Privateer Mabbot, sail forth and protect us!"

To this, ersatz Mabbot agreed, and immediately there appeared upon the stage men waving French, Spanish, and Portuguese flags, sailing along in their own paper boats. Forthwith and with balletic flourishes, the stage-Mabbot engaged in swashbuckling, dispatching them one by one. Down they went, thrashing and moaning. Here was used, to clever effect, a red kerchief. Whenever a character expired, this rag was fluttered about the wound to indicate spurts of blood. It was then seized and reused by the next victim. This single cloth embellished and stitched these murders into a grim yet somehow lovely choreography.

But while Mabbot was busy perforating foreigners, Ramsey wrung his hands devilishly and tweaked his mustache. Making a show of his secrecy, he produced a box marked opium and delivered it to a man in a coolie hat, much to the outrage of our audience. Further, he brought forth a man in chains and sold him for a fistful of coins. This treachery elicited hoots and screams of derision from the crowd, who implored Mabbot to turn and see what they saw, but she was busy clearing the seas for the trading company. When her work was done, she sat, mopped her brow, and smoked a pipe. Here Mr. Apples mirrored exactly the real Mabbot watching, much to the delight of the crowd, going so far as to whip a braid over his shoulder just as Mabbot did.

At this point Ramsey and, by his tricolor cockade, a Frenchman came forward to conspire in stage whispers. This Frenchman wore black from his spats to his bicorne hat. To him Ramsey gave a few of the coins and sang:

Laroche, with your ingenuity,
You are the man for me,
Pendleton grows stronger.
Hannah Mabbot, full of wrath,
Of competition hath cleared our path.
We need her no longer!

They shook hands and Laroche, his paper hat askew, drew his sword and sprang upon Mabbot. They fought.

Eventually, Laroche shot Mabbot who clutched her breast and fell into a sea of blue cloth waved by stagehands. As Laroche stepped forward to sing his victory song, though, Mabbot emerged behind him with a demonic twinkle in her eye. As the audience murmured, she plucked the bullet from her chest and tossed it over her shoulder. This time Laroche was sent yelping and covering his arse to protect it from the flailing Mabbot was giving him.

Mabbot, searching for Ramsey, ran to every corner of the stage, while he, still fingering his mustache, lurked just behind her at every turn until she gave up. Then, when Ramsey sat down to a celebratory meal, Mabbot appeared and shouted, "Tell the devil I'll be late for tea!" and shot him. When the red kerchief fluttered, Mabbot danced a jig over his body.

These, then, are the stories the wicked tell themselves that they may sleep.

The ending prompted a clamor of cheers and applause, which lasted only until the real Mabbot yelled from her chair, "Lies! Defamation!" The ship went silent. The actors, clutching their wigs to their chests, stood pale and attentive. Mabbot rose and turned her terrible visage upon the crowd. She drew her pistol and said, "That is not how I dance. I dance like this!" Shooting her pistols at the sky, Captain Mabbot performed a jig of her own, her light hops punctuated by the clopping of her boots. Mr. Apples joined her, his false bosom bouncing. The crew erupted in cheers, and music played, and the bacchanal continued well into the night. From my chamber, even now, I can hear hedonism galloping to and fro above me.

Could it be true that Mabbot had worked for Ramsey — was he, even as he ate my sauces, waging hidden wars against foreign competitors? It would mean Mabbot and I had been paid from the same purse. Even I, whom Ramsey called "an Englishman with a French tongue," cannot believe the world is that muddied. I never considered my French apprenticeship to be unpatriotic. What skills I learned I used to the benefit of England. And besides, though despots may whip the world to war, a brioche did not sail against Trafalgar. Cathedrals were never shelled with chèvre. The one exception to this rule is the boiled cabbage I encountered in the monasteries, which is a weapon in a bowl. The proper way to treat a cabbage leaf, of course, is to blanch it ever so briefly, wrap it around a piece of thinly sliced ham, and dip it in hollandaise.

Sunday, September 5

If I had needed further confirmation of the folly of sailing, I found it today.

Nothing written, nor painted, nor sung by a poet, could have prepared me for the violence of the southern African seas. The sailors call the wind there the "Roaring Forties," and use it to fling their ships around the cape and into the Indian Ocean. If ever a man was stricken with hubris, those waters hold the cure. With no cloud in the sky, the waves, which the men call "greybeards," rose to the height of the topmasts and played with our ship like it was a child's toy. The shock of seeing walls of water circling the *Rose* would have sent me cowering below, if my vomiting hadn't prevented it. I hung from the railing like a sausage as the deck dropped out from under me. Again and again we crested those mountains to rush headlong into the indigo valleys. Only by Mr. Apples's hails to the men on the yards and the swift hands of the helmsman did we survive.

So we are cutting foam now toward Cochin China, for Mabbot has an ally there she wishes to recruit before reaching our ultimate destination: Macau. There we will meet, at last, the Fox — we are closer than ever to the goal that has preoccupied her for years. What exactly the redheaded fiends want from each other, whether or not we will make it that far, and what may happen when we finally arrive, God only knows.

The papers would have us believe that Mabbot is, like some mythic squid, a peril that rises from the deep at random to pull ships down, a singular and senseless hazard. In fact she is but one character in a convoluted tragedy whose entire cast seems to be comprised of villains. Even as we hunt the Fox, we are hunted by the navy and

Laroche, who are in turn also after the Fox for undermining trade in the ports of China. The *Flying Rose* is a link in a chain of enmity that manacles the entire globe.

Monday, September 6
Yesterday, when the *Rose* finally emerged from those godforsaken seas, having rounded the cape, I rose, still queasy, to pray for myself and all lost souls. We were jibing with the wind now, the southeast trades carrying us swiftly north. The men were slung like cats on the yardarms, exhausted.

I embarked on bread from my yeast batter, which, through daily feedings of flour, had fully matured into a tumescent mound, sighing contentedly when poked. Bread necessitated shoring up the primitive oven of brick and iron grates. Despite the great promise of the little iron stove hauled from the Pendleton ship, I still cannot use it. I have told Mabbot that I need someplace to set it up, there is no room in Conrad's galley, and, further, I will need a chimney to vent the smoke. Mabbot was in a sour mood when I approached her about the matter — she said, "You expect me to make you a second galley?"

"If you want proper nourishment, a proper

kitchen is needed," I said.

She huffed and our conversation was over. So I've been forced to become a bricklayer as well.

Conrad talked at the back of my head as I worked, his syphilitic breath moistening my neck.

"Don't know hunger till ya been adrift a fortnight on a ten-foot longboat with eight other men. Don't know hunger till you've stewed yer own belt in brine an' ate it an' liked it. That is hunger . . ."

Ignoring his rants did not deter him in the slightest, but at least he didn't seem to take offense. Not even when I drowned out his prattle by cracking walnuts with my boot heels.

The weevil-tainted dough didn't rise as much in baking as I had hoped, but the bread was hearty enough, enlivened by the anise seeds and walnuts, and would serve my purposes.

"Rare honor to enjoy the cabin the way you have," Conrad prattled on. "Well, you must've charmed her, I guess. But soon enough we'll all be living the life of steak and cherries once we get our share of the Fox's treasure . . ."

On my way to and from the larder, I passed the men repairing sails after the depredations of the Roaring Forties, and heard this gossip regarding our notorious Brass Fox: "He's no simple man. You heard the prison guards. Fox went right through the prison walls. Which of you seen a man what can do that? Clear as my face that the Fox is Satan's own bastard. Sired on a corpse and raised by witches. He's searching out the pieces of the true cross with which to unlock the gates of hell and bring it 'pon the earth."

It's evident that a pirate has no more truth in him than a goose has milk. Mabbot might actually spread these wild rumors herself, for it keeps the crew from the notion that has begun to push into my mind like a stubborn weed: that what fuels her fanatical hunt is neither treasure, nor revenge, nor great schemes of conquest, but something far more menacing, the single-minded urgency of a mother lion searching for her lost cub.

I saw Joshua trading gestures with the man on the crow's nest and had to admit that in certain circumstances it is an elegant improvement over hollering oneself hoarse. There are others on this ship, their hearing blasted by cannon retort, who use Joshua's signs to communicate. In fact everyone here knows at least some of the boy's hand language and can express the basic elements of this life — ship, rope, rock, gun, wind, wine, and land — in this silent method. The boy came to me to learn reading and writing but, after all, what are his signs if not a writing on the air? — and more eloquent for the dramatic facility of the face, which can deliver meaning better than any punctuation. I have, until now, considered his method of communication primitive. I should have known better. The boy is surrounded by brutes and yet surpasses them in all respects. I have been too stern a schoolmaster. It seems I have more amends to make.

Encouraged by my meager success with the oven, I moved to the deck to build, from pots and grills, a smoker.

The eel I handled thus: After cleaning it, I rubbed salt and a little honey into the body cavity and coiled it on the grill of the improvised smoker above a small pile of red-hot embers. These coals I covered with a handful of steeped tea leaves. The lid I left slightly ajar and returned every ten minutes to add more coals or tea until, with the daylight waning, the eel was finally done. The honey had caramelized into the meat, which came easily from the bones. As for the smoke: when one has been on the road, tired and rained on, and catches, long before seeing any sign of a house, the faint but unmistakable odor of a chimney and with it the promise of drying off next to a fire — that is the feeling that the tea smoke imparts, not the actual arrival but the comforting nearness of home.

I took the smoked eel to the galley and was interrupted there by Mabbot, who arrived to watch me cook. She said not a word but leaned in the doorway, simply observing me.

In general protest, I greeted her not, nor made conversation of any sort, pretending I hadn't seen her. But she was not deterred and stared with great interest at my every movement.

Never had an employer interfered so. Even Ramsey, who fancied himself an amateur cook, had never examined my every move thus. She seemed to be noting the exact angle of my wrist as I chopped, the strength of my grip as I kneaded.

Ignoring her as best I could, I boned the herring, then boiled and mashed it together with garlic, rosemary, salted anchovies, and a handful of white beans.

I knew then what a mouse must feel with

a cat nearby. Indeed I felt the long whiskers of her gaze against the nape of my neck. It seemed the heat from Conrad's hearth was increasing, and I began to sweat profusely.

At last, when I could no longer stand her silent scrutiny, I turned and barked, "What is it, then?"

Mabbot chuckled and, after an infuriating silence, said casually, "I saw Ladislav Dussek perform when he was in London. I had good seats. Very close. I could see even the velvet nap of his cravat. Every one of the improvements he had made on his piano are now de rigueur for any serious piano maker. The man was an innovator, a genius. He bent the very wood to the will of the music."

"But what is your point?"

"All his imagination, his technical facility, his vision, what would it be if he could not stand to be watched?"

With this she walked away. I muttered, "Did the man play sonatas on a barrel of moldy flour?" As I heard her boots moving away on the deck, I let my voice rise till I was yelling at the sky: "Was he performing on cheap tin pots?" I slammed the pots together. "They can't take heat! I might as well be boiling beans in wicker!"

It felt good to vent my frustration thus.

But even an hour later I could still feel the tickle of her gaze upon my back.

Though I would have preferred to have an egg for the noodle dough, I made do with the right ratio of water and lard, kneading it long enough to keep it together but not so long as to toughen it.

On a ship it is hard to distinguish desperation from genius, but I must congratulate myself for today's resourcefulness. While I was searching vainly for a rolling pin, it occurred to me to try a cannonball. I have to admit it works well enough for pirate pasta.

I bravely investigated the mysterious cheese in the pantry. The crust of each fist-sized ball was hard, grey, and bland, but toward the center the cheese had aged to a fine white crumble with threading dark veins. The smell was sharp and bodily, somewhere between Stilton and Dorset Vinny. My best guess was that it was sheep's milk, and it would serve my purposes quite well. I decided to call it Pilfered Blue.

Well after sunset on Sunday night, my tray laden, I approached Mabbot's cabin and stopped, hearing voices inside: Mr. Apples and the captain in a heated conversation. Though I didn't follow it entirely, they seemed to be discussing preparations for Macau.

"I want to try this diviner," Mabbot said.

"Thought you despised witches," Mr. Apples grunted.

"I despise charlatans. But this woman doesn't err. I've used her before. Does it not feel like a fool's errand that he has simply invited us to Macau? I want to be sure we're not wasting our time. Braga knows the smuggling tunnels around the Pearl River, but he doesn't know what to expect in San Lazaro."

"But Laroche is about, almost certain, Cap'm. He is somewhere in these seas guarding the tea routes. They'll miss the *Patience* soon. For all we know, they've found the Fox themselves. Bait for a hook."

"I've no choice but to bite," Mabbot said.

"Could wait until the season is over, hide out for a patch, give the men a spell — they love beach revels. They're shit-brained for mangoes. Then, when Laroche is tired, we'll head in swift and find the Fox."

"We cannot slow now — we've come so close. By minutes and hairs we've missed him. Time to redouble our efforts."

"I'm only saying, Cap'm, that the men are tired, and now they've got silver burning their pockets, itchin' to spend a little."

"They'll have plenty of time to buy whores and chocolate once I've found my Fox."

11
One Woman's War

IN WHICH MABBOT REVEALS HERSELF

Where was a heavy silence, and worried that they might sense my presence, I knocked. The door was opened by Mabbot herself. Mr. Apples replaced the maps in the chart cupboard, locked it, and then disappeared. I set the platter upon the table and stood silent while Joshua brought the china and candelabra. I helped him set the table for two, smiling at him all the while, but he ignored me entirely, leaving as soon as the places were set.

It was then that serendipity and my own oafishness brought us closer to understanding the Fox's plans. While setting the table, I spotted a new pattern on the bed: clusters of pink and tan that, upon closer inspection, revealed themselves to be poppies woven into a Turkish rug. Mabbot saw my eyes linger. "Do you fancy it?" she asked. "It's one of the trifles recovered at the prison. A variation of prayer carpet, perhaps.

Quite fine, but I have more underfoot than I know what to do with."

"It would make my cell warmer, that's sure," I said, stepping closer. "It seems nice and thick. I thought for a moment it was a map. It's so dim in here."

At this Mabbot looked at me as one looks at a friend long missed. "A map?"

"I thought this blue strip was a sea, and these green humps, hills. The blossoms could be . . . of course, I see now that it's only flowers."

"How silly of you." A moment passed as she stared dreamily at the rug. Then she screamed, "Apples!"

A moment later her faithful second-in-command burst into the room with a knife drawn for blood. Mabbot, disregarding the alarm she had invoked, pulled him by the arm to the bed and patted the rug. "Cork-brained Wedge thought this elegant carpet was, can you imagine, a *map*."

Mr. Apples chuckled. "And a Bible is salad to a goat."

Mabbot traced her finger along the patterns of the rug and said, "Right. But then, if we pretended this was, *in fact,* a map, what might it tell us?" He studied the flowers, then blinked at Mabbot in surprise. The two pirates looked at each other with growing

pleasure. "These vines and these blossoms
—"

"Tunnels and chambers! That clever bastard."

"It's his warren under the Pendleton
warehouses. But I'm hungry," said Mabbot.
"Wedge has been working all day on whatever succulence he has hidden here. Draft a
copy of the rug and show it to old Pete, and
to Braga. No one else sees it."

"Yes, Cap'm." And with that Mr. Apples
rolled the rug up and whisked it out the
door. Mabbot slapped me on the back and
said, "I knew you'd prove useful, Wedge. I
just didn't know how very."

"I guess I'll not be getting that rug to
warm my floor."

"Remember all those times I didn't kill
you? And coming about to pull you from
the water after your little swim?"

"Fair enough."

"Oh, don't pout. I'll get you a damned
rug." She glanced about and laid her hand
upon a dog-eared book. "And here, it's a
prison Bible, handwritten. Warden said it
belonged to the Fox, but my boy is hardly
God-fearing. I know you like that sort of
thing."

She handed me the leather-bound book,
which, with a quick perusal, I could see was

only a fragment of the New Testament, Mark or Luke perhaps. I was touched by the humble manufacture; I could imagine a prisoner coming to terms with his wickedness by writing the word of God out, letter by letter, in some damp cell. There are many roads to salvation.

Mabbot and I, in our strange ritual, sat quietly before touching the victuals. She was still brooding. I took the moment to say grace, softly, aloud. She glared at me with storm-water eyes. Her hair was still in braids, and her brow and neck were exposed, browned from the sun and densely freckled. Those freckles were hypnotic in the candlelight, trembling where her pulse danced, cinnamon shaken into a bowl of milk.

I must have become transfixed because Mabbot cleared her throat and said, "Are we still praying?"

I removed the pot I used for a lid to reveal the meal.

"Three courses," I announced. "Herring pâté with rosemary on walnut bread. Tea-smoked eel ravioli seared with caramelized garlic and bay leaf. And as *touche finale,* rum-poached figs stuffed with Pilfered Blue cheese and drizzled with honey."

Slowly, begrudgingly, a smile softened her

features. She passed her nose over each, inhaling deeply, before spooning the glistening ravioli onto her plate. We ate without speaking. It was gratifying to do away with courses and take each taste as it called to me, every so often sipping wine to clean my tongue.

Blotting her lips with a silk damask napkin, she said, "My dear, you've proven yourself again. What do you think about while you chop and knead? Help me forget this ship for a minute."

The ravioli slid voluptuously about the plate, attended by the firefly aromas of bay leaf and garlic. Their skins were tender between the teeth, yielding at the last moment to an eddy of smoked eel. I chewed for a moment before answering.

"I have begun to think of the mouth as a temple, of the kind that Adam and Eve might have made in a cave. The temple is open on both ends. On one side is the known world, lit by the sun and in the order nature and man have designed. On the other end is darkness and transformation. Between these poles of birth and death, serenity and insanity, lies taste.

"It is our greatest grace, a gift reserved for men alone. A dog sups on gutter filth, and a horse eats grass; they have tongues yet do not taste. Taste is the sense that was most defiled by the transgression of the forbidden fruit; it was this betrayal of the most intimate of the senses that so angered the Lord and sent us wandering out here."

Then, thinking I might have won a certain degree of influence, I suggested: "Both of our lives would be made considerably better with but a sprinkling of shaved black truffles."

"I'll have my boys find some next we land."

"I doubt your men could. Truffles are a cook's treasure, buried in rare and secret places. And the wrong mushroom, Captain, would make our last meal."

Mabbot considered this as she chewed. Finally she said, "You're a strange man, Wedgwood." She served herself a second helping of the pâté. "Where does this strange man come from? Do we know each other well enough yet for you to tell me?"

"Perhaps not, Captain."

"Is that how you play? She must show hers first? Very well, I'm happy enough to talk about myself, I so rarely get to. But it must be a fair exchange.

"Someone birthed me, that much I'm confident of — the rest is hearsay and heresy. I too am an orphan. Mine was a city home. I spent my first years in a many-roomed house where the mold made fantastic patterns on the walls, where the rain came and went freely through holes in the roof, where mice enjoyed great privilege and opportunity, where nothing was expected of us save obedience. We didn't complain of being rented out to sweep chimneys or glean orchards or sort coal. At the proud age of ten years, some of us little damsels — I say 'little' only because we were terribly thin — were brought to another house altogether where the beds were soft and well used and we were given company, sometimes a dozen times a day. Tell me, Wedge, do you know what a merkin is?"

"I can't say I do . . ." I stammered.

"Well, that's a credit to your character, probably. They're itchy, leave it at that."

Mabbot was sniffing the food again, enjoying its aroma with a vitality I had never witnessed in Ramsey, but the grim tale she told kept me sober.

"Who does not love a lovely child?" she said, with a half smile. "Who can resist having a little fun? The world came to me; I had neither to move nor speak and great men came to play: barristers, lords, men of industry, indeed even royalty. Oh, the fun they had! Fun enough for a lifetime, I

238

should say. One gentleman brought his daughter's nightclothes for me to wear. Believe it. God dug no deeper pit than a man's skull."

I could only blink at her. Each word out of her mouth was worse than the last. I felt suddenly naked and pulled my jacket tightly around me. Did no one protect her? I saw her as a child on a filthy mattress and could not hide the horror on my face.

She said, "You little daisy, Wedge, you blanch so easily. I'll move along. Feeling quite undeserving of the gifts we were receiving, my friend Evangeline and I stole out one night and slept in alleys and upon the rooftops of London, during which time she acquired a stubborn cough. I left her blue and wheezing upon a doctor's doorstep.

"The street is where I studied the fine art of availing myself of people's latent generosity," she continued. "I never took more than my share, nor from those who couldn't afford to replace it. Nevertheless, men with clubs didn't appreciate my lifestyle — but the fun we had in those jailhouses! You may think wardens and officers a dull bunch, but they like to play with a child as much as anyone. From there to the orphanage, from which I flew again like a spit seed. I was housed for a time by the judge I told you about, then on to other cities to escape my reputation. I shaved my head to hide myself; this hair can be seen, I'm told, from quite a distance. Well, it was seen by a privateer you may have heard of: Sean Corey, the Rake of the Great Horn. I liked this one. Oh, I did. I kept him warm in those frozen waters for six years before we were ambushed. He was captured and leaped dancing from a gallows in Newfoundland. You can imagine my disappointment. I led the ragged survivors to reclaim our ship from the admiral who had seized us, and deposed him myself."

"Deposed?"

"Deposed his neck, mostly. With a salad fork. It earned me the respect of our crew, and they elected me captain, and that was the beginning of my career, I suppose. I was still dressing as a man back then. But look at me, going off like a teakettle. Your turn now, Wedge. Fair's fair."

Mabbot took the last two ravioli from the tray. Here, at last, was a true appetite, who had seen the caverns of death and yet clung hard to life, who chose daily where to be in the world. I had thought myself content to cook for lords and ladies whose natures were passive, to whom things were brought. Cooking for Mabbot was altogether different. She had nothing but what she took. For her, my cuisine was well earned and relished with a vigor that made my palms sweat.

Of course, she was a tyrant and a criminal, but when she ate, I saw in her a radiant life, a deep hunger, and an almost pious reflection on each moment. When she swallowed, her nostrils flared like those of a running horse, yet her hunger was sophisticated. The ladies I had served in the past knew how to hold salad forks and discuss the latest fashions, yet their palates were blind. Mabbot claimed each dish as Moses's men claimed the land of milk and honey.

I took myself a fig, considering what to tell her. It had cooled in the sweet amber glaze. Inside, though, the cheese was still warm, and the liquor of the stewed fruit and salty tang of the aged cheese made me speechless for a moment.

"That good, is it?" Mabbot said, reaching for one herself.

Surrendering to the seduction of the food made me pliable. Why hold anything back? What would silence win me?

"I was left on the back stoop of the monastery in a crate of freshly dug potatoes, one muddy lump among many," I told her. "So I assume my mother was a farmer. The potatoes must have been her way of offering payment to the monks for my care."

"How do you know it was your mother?" Mabbot asked, taking the fig in small bites and letting it dissolve in her mouth.

"At times, I imagine I can remember her voice," I said. "Who knows? There I was, gnawing with my one tooth the slick nub of a potato. Father Sonora found me on his way out to gather mushrooms. He did not pick me up right away but left me on the stoop in the cold until he came back, his apron pregnant with morels. Only when he saw that I was still there, not crawled away, nor retrieved by a regretful mother, nor devoured by a hungry dog, did he kick the crate inside, accepting me as another of God's burdens. He must have felt some guilt about this later, as he confessed it to me more than once. As a boy I was sensitive to the cold. I still can't bear it, and he blamed my time on the winter stoop for my infirmity.

"Because of my frailty, I couldn't room with the other boys who slept in the dormitory with their breath making clouds above their faces. I thrived only in the steam bath of his kitchen. When moved into colder chambers, I wheezed so frighteningly that I was allowed to sleep on a cot near the curative heat of his stove all the time. I was nursed on warm goat yogurt and spoonfuls of Father Sonora's *cocido,* a dish too sublime to be called bean stew."

"A Spaniard?"

"He'd been sent by Rome to help reestablish a Jesuit diocese and had ended up in the kitchen of the orphanage. He said, 'Apparently the Lord would have me serve Him by serving you breakfast.' It was a stroke of luck for me; I grew up eating roast lamb skewered between mint leaves, empanadas stuffed with ground beef and olives, and each summer when our garden finally gave up a few tomatoes and cucumbers, we celebrated with gazpacho."

It was surprisingly comforting to say his name. It reminded me that I had another life before this one. Just the thought of Father Sonora made me weepy, and I forced myself to keep talking.

"His soup was nourishing, but it was his bread that stays with me. Sonora was a master baker, and though I know exactly how he made his loaves, to this day I cannot re-create their crusts, crisp as sycamore bark."

"I thought you said your father was a cobbler."

"This was what the monks told me. Probably a kindness to spare me from feeling a bastard. I was Sonora's ward, and he, grumpy old man, was my earth and sky. Eventually I was forced to sleep in the dorm with the other orphans, but when we were given free time twice a day, once after matins and once again before vespers, whereas the other boys played, I went back to the kitchen to sit near the hearth and watch him work."

"You didn't like their games? Let me guess, tried to protect the cat that they tied spoons to? A valiant knight even then, weren't you, Wedge?"

"A knight can fight. As you well know, I fight about as well as a pillow."

"That's an insult to pillows. At least they can take a beating."

"Sonora was cantankerous and had a heavy hanging lip with a hairy mole. He pretended to be frustrated, but he never hit me the way the other monks did; he was gentle. I loved him fiercely. He was overly fond of vinegar, though."

Mabbot's eyes were closed again, but she had not fallen asleep. "And?" she demanded.

"And what?"

"Go on. Did you ever avenge a lover with a fork?"

"Perhaps another night, Captain."

"Well enough."

I felt, with a shudder, the rabbit brush past my feet. After a moment, I asked, "You know the sailors Theodore and Finn?"

"I know my men."

"Then you have seen them holding hands?" I asked delicately. "Going everywhere arm in arm?"

"What of it?" Mabbot asked.

"You tolerate it? I'm not naïve; I know what happens aboard a ship, but those two . . . they've sewn their hammocks together. It goes beyond brief physical comforts."

"Indeed it has progressed unforgivably to sweetness and, sin of sins, right on to love." Mabbot laughed.

"Call it what you may, in God's eyes it is a crime."

"I have seen crime." Mabbot leaned close and her glare was back. "I have been trod under it. I have, in my haste and fury, committed crimes, a few, and I'm paying for them even now. If, looking down, God ignores the screaming and steaming gore and chooses to be offended by those two doves, He is an ass or an idiot. I do not abide either."

Hearing heaven thus insulted would, just

weeks ago, have spurred me to violence, but now I merely shifted in my seat. I ventured another subject, one which had been bothering me since the "salt opera."

"So it's true you worked for Ramsey as a privateer against the French *guerre de course*?"

"It was a different crew I had then," Mabbot said. "Almost twenty years ago. I didn't know then what a devil Ramsey was. But eventually I learned how the tea-opium-slave wheel turned, how *he* turned it. It's not hard to be ignorant on land — you go to your market and you buy your tea and that's that. But I had seen too much to pretend I hadn't. Ramsey had directed me to the Bay of Bengal, where the French were harassing Pendleton ships. I didn't have to sink but a few of them to realize they weren't French but Bengalis with French guns, trying to defend their coast. A small revolt that I had crushed almost single-handedly. I went ashore, I saw the opium farms, I saw the starvation. Wedge, you only cooked for the man, but, you see, I had killed for him, protected his routes, I helped it all happen. I couldn't sit by."

"And you were with child?"

"I didn't know it. I had torches and a good portion of my crew — we were on our way to burn Ramsey out of his house when we were ambushed, I barely escaped. He had smelled my shift in loyalties and was ready for us with a garrison of musketeers. With a stroke of his pen, I went from legitimate privateer to hunted pirate."

"Your men have fabulous stories about the Fox," I said. "Just today, I heard this: You and the Fox, working together, long ago, put your hands on a map to Eden, the actual garden, and stole the fruit of life, dodging the while swipes of the flaming sword. At the last moment, though, the Brass Fox abandoned you while he sneaked away. You, cornered by furious angels, pleaded and swore to bring him back for divine justice."

"That's good." Mabbot laughed while picking her teeth with a blade. "I hadn't heard that one."

"The Fox said that you taught him to kill. He said he sailed with you — that you took him from Ramsey's house in the middle of the night."

"You're such a stubborn weed, Wedge. I'll tell you only if you swear to keep it to yourself."

"I'll not whisper it even in my sleep."

She leaned in to say, "The Brass Fox is Cain himself. He cannot be apprehended because he is protected by the mark God gave him. He comes and goes as he pleases."

"Mabbot, you're as bad as your men."

"I should hope I'm considerably worse."

"I'm asking, Captain," I said. "Help me understand. You would have me eat with you as if I were not a prisoner swept up in the course of your adventures. So here I am, my life suspended for the sake of this hunt. I'm not appeased by fairy stories. I met the man, I saw his features — he even speaks like you. He claims Ramsey as his father. Is it true or no?"

She sighed and considered me for a long time before speaking. "It is. Ramsey stole him from the nuns where I had left him, just a tyke. I took him back as soon as he was old enough to sail. It was a mistake, perhaps, to bring him aboard so young — no, youth has nothing to do with it. Some are too soft for the sea at any age. But what choice did I have? I couldn't leave him with Ramsey — the loneliness of that rambling house with the servants whispering in the shadows like ghosts. Can you believe Ramsey never spoke to the child? The boy looking like me didn't make it any easier for him. It is not good to have the gaze of a man like Ramsey on you at an impressionable age. A man of influence, a man whose flatulence is attended to by a thousand shareholders, and to see in that gaze nothing but disgust. A glance like that is a sharp awl, and my Fox was soft wood. By the time I got him, he was desperate for attention, but if I merely tousled his hair he would fly into a rage. I couldn't touch my own child; he was like a feral dog that way, but praise, oh, he was a puppy for that. Tell him he was clever, and his grin would nearly cleave his head in two." Mabbot's own smile lit the room for a moment, then quickly disappeared.

"My boy saw a thing . . . a murder in the barracks. There had been a feud earlier in the night; one seaman felt another had cheated him at cards. This seaman waited until the cheater was asleep, then held his head and poured molten lead into his ear. This, by the way, is why gambling is forbidden on my ship. My son saw it all from his own hammock. He didn't speak for a week after that. We've all seen worse, but, as I said, Leighton . . . the Fox, he was sensitive. It's not a pretty thing to witness, a man killed that way, but, from the way he shivered, you'd have thought it happened to him. It may as well have, he was so changed after.

" 'Soft children become hard men.' Who

said that, Wedge? Or is it 'Sweet children become sour men'? Some have survived lead in the ear for a time. The metal cuts right through the fatty parts and cools deep inside, like a lump of ore, sometimes in the skull, sometimes in the neck, there for good. Once you see a thing, once you know a thing, it's in you forever. Maybe it's one solid fist, or maybe it's got jagged petals. So the flesh becomes a purse for the blade. They go mad from the pain, or the lead poisons them slowly. Luckier to die right away.

"I had high hopes for my boy; I held nothing back. I could teach him how, but I couldn't teach him why. His anger had no target, he would aim at anything. He sank a tunny boat with her crew aboard — for fun, like shooting a cow. I couldn't have a loose cannon like that on my ship, but I couldn't leave him to be shot by marines. It was in Calcutta that he just disappeared. He's been chewing through the guts of the world ever since. I tracked him through opium dens, carnivals, caves, forests, deserts. He makes enemies everywhere he goes, sets bigger and bigger fires . . ." She trailed off.

"And you've been chasing after him, putting out his fires?"

"In a manner of speaking." Mabbot

sighed. "Tell me, Wedge, what do you really know about the company — about their trade?"

"China is a nation of martinets, that much anyone knows, who insist that we move all the tea in the world through the little porthole of Canton alone — their stubborn intractability in taxes and free trade are an impediment to progress."

"And opium?" she asked.

"To be perfectly blunt, if the Chinaman has difficulty with moderation, why should English commerce suffer?"

"You are the scholar, aren't you?"

"I have never claimed to be a diplomat nor a historian. I am interested in China as the source of tea and spices. My world is the kitchen. My skirmishes are fought in the skillet," I said.

"How poetic. A feather in the cap of ignorance. This war surrounds you. If you have hidden in a kitchen and kept your hands clean, it is because you have been allowed to."

"I'm no innocent, Captain. It's not play to be raised a despised Catholic in England and yet be loyal to her. Our orphanage survived only by the mercy of a protective benefactor. And then to have been secreted in a barrel across fortified borders to clean duck with my French chef while our nations were busy gutting each other for the plums of the New World and the pits of the Old. I'm no schoolboy. I have walked the edge of treason and have not crossed it."

"It may be why I like you, Wedge. You've been rolled in the surf to a luster. But here's a little bedtime story: The Pendleton Trading Company, of which your beloved former employer controlled the lion's share, was established to bring you your precious spices and, of course, tea. How we love our tea. But what could England offer in exchange? The Chinese aren't fond of jellied eel, nor of fog. No, we paid silver, and before long China had all of it. It couldn't continue. Happily, England found the solution in Bengal, India. There grows a lovely flower —"

"I know what opium is."

"Then you know it cannot be grown in England. Crucial it was for the Crown to own Bengal. A bloody coup but worth it, for, at long last, the Pendleton Company had something China wanted. And how the tide has turned. They've gotten all of their silver back and all of the Chinese silver as well. It's a propitious arrangement: Their country on its knees, selling anything they can put their hands on for a pinch of smoke.

Pendleton forces Bengali farmers to grow the opium, sells it to the Chinese for mountains of coins and tea, and comes home fat as a cat in the bacon barrel. Cannon, coolies, opium — the staples of transatlantic commerce. Long live the king." After a silence she said, "I am not as fond of bloodshed as you may think."

"You make your way on a sea of it," I objected. "Not a stranger approaches but you fill him with shot."

"We are at war. Your ignorance doesn't —"

"Yes, yes, the opium."

"The opium, the slaves, these are but ripples on the surface. Our struggle is deeper and older. We battle princes of power, kings of industry, popes, the rich who gnaw at the bones of the poor."

"And on your side?" I asked. "What armies do you have?"

"Only the few of us who are awake. We fight each in our own fashion. I've had the bad luck to be awake from a very young age."

"How do you hope to win?"

"Naturally there can be no hope of winning," she said. "That's what makes me so dangerous."

"And your son. Which side of this war is he on?"

I had pushed too far. Her mood properly curdled, Mabbot showed me the door.

12
THE *DIASTEMA*
IN WHICH WE ARE BITTEN BY THE FOX

Tuesday, September 7

The call from the foremast of "Ship ho!" brought all to the deck to see a schooner adrift a mile from our bowsprit. It was the *Diastema,* the very ship I had met the Fox on, only now lacking any sign of sails, rigging, or crew. The massive profiterole clouds stacked in the sky made her look the more pitiable. A lone yellow flag punctuated her mainmast, and our crew took it to mean there was illness aboard. We assumed the weather gauge so as not to be downwind from a plague craft.

"She's adrift," Mr. Apples announced, "and stripped of apparel and cordage — cleaner than a nun's backside. Mayhaps mutiny?"

"Anyone care to bet he's still in there?" Mabbot scowled. "Well, Mr. Apples, at least say hello."

Mr. Apples fired a shot that took the flag

right off the mast. The only answer was a graveyard stillness.

"We're not far from the Sunda Strait," said Mr. Apples. "I don't trust a prune on a plate like this, Captain."

"Longboats!" Mabbot ordered. "Twins, five others, keen for ambush. Muskets. Get the surgeon's camphor for our kerchiefs."

Mabbot called to me, "Well, Wedge? Aren't you curious? There may be a larder for you to pillage." As I climbed into the longboat, she chuckled. "See? You're a pirate through and through."

Mr. Apples halted the men readying the davit tackle for our descent and whispered urgently to Mabbot, "Captain, this has my tapeworms dancing."

"If it is an ambush, Mr. Apples, I'll need you here with the advantage. Eyes on the horizon, and if so much as a gull shows its feathers, fire a shot to inform me."

We were already being lowered to the waves when I saw with chagrin that Asher, the poor young man who had received a lashing for my escape, was in the boat with me, giving me a scowl so searing that I suddenly didn't care what was in that larder.

As we neared the *Diastema,* her stillness worried me. The ship seemed to be holding her breath. When we pulled alongside, Asher threw a line, shinnied up, then secured a jack ladder for us to climb.

The other men tied their kerchiefs about their faces. Mabbot, seeing I had none, sighed and pulled a silk square from between her breasts, doused it with camphor, and threw it at me. "Can't have you giving me yellow fever, can I?"

The cabin, which had been glutted with charts and logs, was now cavernous and bare. The deck was bereft of lanterns, blocks, and lines — some pinchfist couldn't stand to leave anything of use, it seemed — and therefore offered an unobstructed view of the endless horizon. The effect was both exhilarating and discomfiting. The schooner was rolling on the surf, and I tried to find the exact center of the deck where the motion was slightest. No sooner had I done that than Mabbot said, "Asher, you are Wedge's chaperone."

"Yes, Captain!" Asher said, as he took my elbow with an eagle's grip. It was his opportunity to redeem himself, and my arm would bear the bruises of his determination.

"Tightly below, gents, and eyes open," Mabbot said.

Feng opened the companionway door, and immediately we smelled it. The men paused, but Mabbot urged them on: "Below, boys!"

Once inside, the men lit candles, then clustered about Mabbot, their muskets and sabers making an urchin's shell. The forecastle was empty. We made our way to the aft holds, the smell of rot and shit getting stronger with every step. The camphor hardly helped.

Just beyond the aft mast, the bulkheads had been walled to form a chamber where the odor was becoming aggressive. One of the men tugged his kerchief down to retch. Mabbot sniffed. "Well, we might have a plague after all. Don't touch a thing. Wedge, no provisioning here." Food was the last thing on my mind anyway. Asher didn't relax his grip.

Just inside the doorway we heard the unmistakable buzz of blowflies. I resorted to breathing through my mouth with the captain's kerchief clapped over it.

The corpse sat with his back against a chest, as if guarding it. Disturbed by our approach, a cloud of flies rose from the body and into the air. The face of the dead prison guard was animated with maggots, now laughing, now crying. His stomach had given way, and he sat in a skirt of his own offal.

I panicked. I had slipped somehow on the

slick walls of the world and fallen into hell, where the flies wove their black shroud about me.

One man was even worse off than I, for he dropped his sword and bolted into the darkness only to knock blindly into the corners of the chamber, swallowing flies with each gasp. He was a young carpenter's mate with a tattoo of a bluebird on his neck. The darkness, or the smell, or the sound of the maggots doing their wet work on the corpse — something had unmoored him.

Mabbot hissed, "Quiet!"

When the seaman's orbit came close to me, my own terror gave way to action. I seized his head in my hands and drew it to my chest, whispering, "Stay still." Asher helped me hold the man, and while he whimpered, he had at least stopped struggling.

"Thank you, Wedge," Mabbot said. "Well, let's see what kind of treasure this poor soul couldn't walk away from, shall we? Wedge, do you smell that?"

"How could I not?"

"Not that — something under it."

Bai lifted the lid of the chest, which was empty and seemed much deeper than it should be. He inserted his candle to illuminate the bottom.

It came all at once, the shouts, the push for the door, all of us running full-out because of what we had seen: Bai's flame had sparked a web of fuses whose courses spread down into the hole beneath the chest. Before I even understood what I had seen, Mabbot screamed, "Run, fools!"

Tapers were dropped as we emerged from the chamber and scrambled in a herd toward the companionway. Mabbot had been pushed toward the light of the stairs by the twins. This lower deck was shallower than that on the *Rose,* and Asher, who tried to stay close to me even in this blind rush, cracked his head on a beam and fell. As I bent to lift him, I was knocked over by those behind me and trampled. Asher and I were untangling ourselves when the first explosion threw us forward. My cheek was split against a timber. Smoke and water coiled around me as I made it finally into the light, only to find the deck beneath me had risen in a splintering wall. I would have been crushed if a spar hadn't come swinging to pitch me in an arc over the water.

The schooner had become a grenade, and chunks of burning wood hit my back even as I flew. Several bursts on top of one another lifted a crest of water. I dove beneath the waves to avoid being mangled, but another explosion flattened me as I swam. It felt as if all of my air had been forced out through my ears. At last I found the surface where the *Diastema* was nothing more now but the stern, turning in the water like the arse end of a diving duck.

But what had I seen? A body rolling past me as I came up. Though the air burned like brandy, I filled my lungs and dove again, groping through the sooty currents. I caught a foot and tugged toward the surface. The body seemed eager to find the floor of the sea, but I pulled with all my might. Near the surface, even as the need for breath lit my lungs with phosphorus, it occurred to me that I might be towing the rotting corpse. I bawled like a newborn when I finally had air again, sucking at the sky, and saw that the man I had pulled from the deep was Asher, lips and eyelids blue. Pulling him over a still-smoking spar, I beat on him until he gasped and puked.

The next thing I remember, I was being wrapped in a blanket on the deck of the *Flying Rose* with Asher beside me, breathing but weak.

Whosoever finds this record, I warn you, avoid the sea. Calamity hides in every wave, and the floor of the deep is paved with bodies. If you must eat fish, catch them from a creek.

My ears rang and my eyes throbbed. I felt as if I had shoved my head into a hornet's nest. Mabbot and the twins had made it into the longboat and, though shaken up, were considerably drier than I was. The three others were burst, burned, or drowned.

Panch was brought for us, and someone presented Mabbot with a strip of salt-cured ham, more evidence of the hoarded treasures the crew kept in their lockers. When it became clear that Mabbot was not retreating to her cabin, a chair was brought for her, and she sat there with a blanket across her shoulders like a mantle, staring out at where the stern of the *Diastema* was now sinking out of sight. Her panch was replaced with hot tea.

The crew stood in dumb clumps until Mabbot said, calm as could be, "Mr. Apples, do the men have nothing to do?" They jumped to their duties even before he began to roar orders.

"You see, Wedge, what I'm up against?" Mabbot said. "I should have anticipated it; the Fox wouldn't leave a toy like that for the navy to pick up. And he does love his hellburners."

Mr. Apples was upset. "Madness to waste even a small ship —"

"The Brass Fox isn't mad," Mabbot chided. "He is ruthless. It isn't a waste if it confuses the hounds. If we catch him at sea, negotiations will be on my terms. He's buying time to get to his den."

"You call that buying time?"

"If he wanted me dead, he would have made those fuses much shorter."

I was dismayed to hear admiration in Mabbot's voice. These, then, are the games that Mabbot and the Fox play. It was a wonder they hadn't set the entire globe aflame.

Asher was shuddering on the deck beside me, still alarmingly pale. I tried in vain to get him to drink some panch until Feng shoved me aside and helped him to his hammock in the forecastle.

After drying my hands and face and with humility heavy as a veal calf on my shoulders, I went in search of Joshua. With the exception of my meals with Mabbot, my lessons with Joshua had been the only moments when I did not feel death's very teeth upon my neck. Our time together tethered me to a gentler life, and while he has shown that he does not need me, it is clear that I need him. The singed hair on the back of my neck testifies that life is short and my stubbornness serves nothing.

I found him on the forecastle deck mending his hammock. "I'm sorry," I said — and said it again to be sure he understood. He ignored me for a moment, then pointed out for me the distant strip of Madagascar, thin as a vanilla pod on the water, and sniffed the air. Was it an aromatic mirage or did the wind actually carry the perfume of that sumptuous spice drying on racks in the afternoon sun all the way out to our musty ship? But the smell disappeared just as quickly, and the land shimmered and slipped behind the rim of the horizon.

Sitting beside him, I made the gesture I had seen the day we quarreled: the thumb on the forehead, fingers splayed. Joshua used his finger to trace the word on the deck: *father.* Apparently it was a word he already knew how to spell. We took turns tracing more words — *mother, brother, boat, money,* and *storm* — onto the planks and I learned the proper hand signs for each. I went to get paper, and we spent the remaining light trading words this way. I learned dozens more, among them: *poor,* the fingers touching on a patched elbow; *grief,* the hands dropping down the body; and *death,* like closing the back cover of a book. If I was to learn about his family, it would be in his words, not mine.

By sunset, the horizon's opalescent glow had filled my heart. It seems I have my pupil again, and have become one myself.

Thursday, September 9
Last week, to repay Kitzu for the fish he gives me, I prepared a simple candy that he may use to rid his mouth of the taste of Conrad's insults. I simmered diced coconut meat in a mixture of molasses, honey, and rum until thick, then kneaded and twisted dollops into knobs to cool. If I'd had butter, they wouldn't have been dense and black as asphalt, but Kitzu loves them and is happy to chew on them like a dog with a rawhide. When he passes me on the decks, he slaps me on the back and shows me his darkened teeth.

Seeing some sailors snacking upon strands of kelp they had dried on the bulwarks gave me another idea, and I set about puttering in the galley to calm my nerves. Boiling the *Patience*'s dried corn in ashwater, I made hominy, which, after it had cooled, I drained and placed in a jar with seaweed, garlic, a pinch of the precious rosemary, enough brine to cover it all, and a splash of sauerkraut juice. I'll have pickled hominy in a week or two, and with any luck I'll have

265

something to serve it with.

The sea here in the middle of the Indian Ocean is the color of pewter, but at intervals great patches of jade and turquoise embellish the surface. To me they are lovely, but the older seamen scowl at the blooms and mutter about typhoons. Before we reach Cochin China, we must first pass through the narrow passage between Sumatra and Java. There, I am told, we can look forward to heavy naval patrols, and perhaps Laroche himself waiting to pounce.

After our misadventure together, I could not help but try my apologies to Asher again. I made lace-edged golden crêpes on a tin inverted over a boiling pot. For having been made without eggs, they were surprisingly good.

As a young man in the monastery, I suffered a passionate crêpe-mania. I argued with my chef that a well-made crêpe was the pinnacle of civilized achievement — its simple elegance masking the rigors of mastery, like a ballerina's pirouette — and that it was a universal medium for any ingredient. Smoked smelt, lemon curd, horseradish — there was nothing I wouldn't smear on a crêpe. My teacher indulged me because, he said, he had been an ignoramus once too. Like many youthful convictions, mine was as short-lived as it was fervent. I stopped eating crêpes for every meal, but not before I perfected the pouring of the batter, the motherly flip and fold.

The best crêpes, I know now, are simple. For Asher I made a sauce of raisins stewed in rum and drizzled it over the rolled crêpes. I found him on the forecastle deck. He was surrounded by comrades huddled near, listening to him tell the story of the fireship *Diastema*. I knew I had chosen the wrong moment, but they had all seen me, so I had no choice but to walk right up to the man.

"Asher —" I had intended some eloquent explanation of my motives and circumstances, but the words did not come. "I'm sorry," I said, and held out the wooden trencher.

It was a long quiet moment, and when I was nearly ready to hurl the crêpes over the rail myself, Asher took one from the tray and had a bite before passing it to the man next to him. The tray made its way around the deck, as if I had apologized to them all, and I was finally able to take a long deep breath.

I had made to leave when Asher called after me: "Wedge!"

I turned to face him.

"How did the ship burn?" he asked.

"Like hell itself," I said.

"And the corpse?"

"Froze my blood."

Asher made room for me to sit beside him and continued his story to the delight of the others, who occasionally looked to me for confirmation. When he had finished, they insisted that he tell it again as the sun set.

I found myself lying on the deck, talking to a clean-shaven Italian they call Chicken. He'd been brought aboard years ago to tend to the hens and small Oriental pigs that once inhabited crates on the deck. "After the men slipped on manure during a chase," the man opined, "Mabbot ordered a great feast, and I've been scrubbing decks with the rest ever since."

There is a game the men play here. On clear nights the stars are close enough to tickle one's nose, and the men take entertainment lying on their backs making light bets on the number and direction of falling stars. Gambling is forbidden by their contracts, so the men bet not money but only trivial things, calling them gifts. In this way trinkets circulate among them: etchings of brothel girls, withered nubs of sausage, perfumes, mostly tobacco. I have found that I have a knack for the game, though I have nothing to bet and so cannot technically win. Still, men, in their goodwill, have rewarded me for my luck, and in this way I have acquired a jar of salted olives and, to my delight, half a small bottle of olive oil that Chicken drinks as a tonic.

It is not a bad thing to be among men looking at the stars and laughing. Without faces, or scars, or clothes, a voice fits right in, finding its course across the sky with the others.

13

La Colette

<u>IN WHICH JUSTICE CATCHES UP WITH US</u>

Friday, or perhaps Saturday, early October
I am lucky, they keep telling me, to be alive.
Much has happened and none of it kind. I
am not the man I was. My mind is still beset
by fog and wind, but I can recall the events
of September 10 clearly enough.

It began with a balloon.

We had passed through the Sunda Strait
between Java and Sumatra just a day prior,
and I thought I felt those island gates closing behind us.

A sharp wind had scraped the sky free of
clouds and brought a quiet that I had
learned to associate with coming thunder.
Mabbot and Mr. Apples stood on the quarterdeck peering at the sky with what he
called a "big an' close" but the civilized
world calls a telescope. To my eye the thing
in the sky was just a speck, but through the
lens, which they eventually granted me, I
saw what looked like an Oriental paper

lantern hung on the vault of heaven.

"Laroche's smoke balloon," Mabbot said.

"I've seen them only in illustrations," I said. "It looks so small."

"They can see the whole world from up there," she said. "They can spot the lump in your pants. You'll see a flicker, a twinkle . . . See there? The man in the balloon uses a mirror to communicate with Laroche. Giving our location and direction. Well, Mr. Apples, you were right again, *La Colette* is here. Now, where can we hide?"

"His corvette is near twice our speed and her guns have better range —"

"I know that," growled Mabbot. "I asked where you think we should *go*. Bangka?"

"Never make it."

"What about the black corals of Nasik?"

"Yesterday that might've give us the edge," he said. "I doubt Laroche's maps have them clear as we do. But 'twould mean going full about. If Laroche is astern, he'll run us down —"

"There is nothing else near. He'll catch us at open sea otherwise. At least the weather gauge will be ours."

"The sun will be his, and besides, a Frenchman knows how to fight from the lee."

They stood in silence. The wind tossed

271

Mabbot's hair, and chill bumps rose on her arms. She said, "We have little choice."

Mabbot returned to her cabin while Mr. Apples hailed the helm. The deck banked sharply, and then pitched as we came about. The crew scampered to trim the yards, sheet to royal, and the masts groaned like timber in a bonfire. The watch below, feeling our change of course, began to gather upon the deck. Word of the balloon had spread. A few of the men had their own telescopes, and these were passed around. There was a jarring acceleration as the *Rose* began to gallop, and I felt I could feel her appetite, her oak and canvas curves turning the air itself into speed.

Suddenly there was nowhere I could stand without being buffeted by the furious preparations for battle. Noise and calamity, which only afterward did I begin to comprehend. Laroche's ship, *La Colette,* had been spotted, directly between us and the shelter of the reefs. Bells rang out. Every man was running. One sailor stood with a speaking trumpet to his mouth, shouting, "Laroche's ship! Do not gaze at the ship! Do not look!"

A clangor of gongs and hails and always the refrain "Do not look!" When I peered to catch a glimpse of the distant ship, Mr. Apples clapped me so hard on the neck that my knees buckled.

"Don't. If you value your sight," he said. He was wearing the smoked-glass goggles, which I had thought merely a souvenir. I shuddered to think what kind of trauma could cause such reverence in these fearless men. It was apparent that they had suffered considerably the last time they encountered Laroche.

Mabbot had reappeared, this time in her green coat and red boots. She wore suede gloves, and her wrists were hidden by frills of lace. Judging by her dress, she confused battle for a ball. She was shouting, "Bring us alongside! Chains on the yards! Douse the sheets with alum!"

One powder monkey running past me with his precious cask moaned, " 'Tis hardly noon and no clouds. He'll sink us sure this time."

Another sailor took up the trumpet and shouted, "*La Colette*! Buckets at the ready!"

It was all I could do not to be trampled by the river of men brandishing muskets and locking the free cannon in place.

Then a thing happened that I would not believe had I not witnessed it myself. When *La Colette* was only half a mile away, I saw, with a corner of my vision, a light bloom from the ship like a second sun rising in the southwest. Resisting the urge to examine this wonder, I averted my gaze only to feel a sudden blistering heat upon my neck and back, as if someone had thrown boiling water upon me. Utilizing my native cowardice, I dropped in an instant to the deck and scrambled behind a rope barrel. From there I saw, with fright, a spot of light so bright I was sure an angel of the Lord was traveling about the deck of our ship. This lozenge of white heat, perhaps a foot in diameter, moved from the bow to the quarterdeck in the blink of an eye, darkening the wood where it went. When it hit men, they cried out and dropped, but some of them, trapped as they were in the shrouds or high upon the forecastle with no shelter, could not evade it, and I watched as their clothes smoked and their hair burst into flames. They were illuminated as with the glow of divine grace, yet they screamed in their agony and were horribly burned.

This thing I have witnessed with my own eyes. A terrible weapon.

The light flew about the ship with abandon, maiming as it went, before fixing upon the base of the mizzenmast. In a few seconds, the wood there was aflame. Men appeared with buckets to douse it, and, at great expense to themselves, wrapped the mast with layers of wet felt blankets that smoked and steamed and smelled of hell but didn't burn. These men kept the mast wet and continued to douse other fires with their buckets. The odor of burned skin, alum, and cooking wool made me want to retch.

My back stung, but I felt I had escaped a very bad burn. Only at that odd moment did the happy thought rise in me that I was near rescue. I hunkered in my hiding spot behind the barrel and prayed with all of my being.

Mr. Apples had positioned himself near the cannon on the main deck and looked toward our attackers, serving as eyes for those loading the barrels. In addition to his protective smoked-glass goggles, Mr. Apples wore long leather blacksmith sleeves. Those manning the cannon crouched and scrambled like crabs, eyes shut tight. They took their aim from his shouting, but waited until we were in range to fire. Joshua was there with them, his back turned to danger, his smoldering match ready.

Then I saw, in great detail, as if time had slowed, the planks of the starboard main deck leap up like leaves in a wind and scatter as a cannonball blew through and erased half of a longboat on its way to the sea. My prayers were on my lips. Another ball missed us by feet and lifted the water in a white bloom that drenched me where I squatted. Only then did I hear the distant retorts.

Our sailors ran in circles, doubling lines and packing guns. Another iron comet tore through the forecastle like the finger of God.

Young Finn ran before me, one of the unnatural couple whom Mabbot called "doves." As I watched, he made the mistake of letting himself look toward *La Colette.* It was the briefest slip, spurred, no doubt by the irresistible need to gauge the nearness of danger, but, like Lot's wife, he got no reprieve. The light passed over his face just briefly. A frightful calm stilled his features for a vanishing moment just before he fell to his knees clutching his ruined eyes. I could not hear him screaming over the deafening noise of the hull groaning as Mabbot pushed her ship at top speed toward our attackers.

The bark of Laroche's guns grew louder by the heartbeat.

Here, all of my life's ambitions had been reduced to one very short-term goal: survive the attack long enough to be rescued. But, as the searing light moved to the mizzen, I reasoned that rescue would be impossible if our ship sank first.

When the mainmast began to smoke and flame licked the canvas, I found myself picking up a bucket that had been dropped by a man in agony. I joined the train of sailors rushing to quench the fires that leaped up about us.

Mabbot stood upon the quarterdeck, wearing her own smoked-glass goggles and looking out toward our attackers. Feng and Bai stood with her, their backs to the light. Mabbot's voice carried even over the percussions of hell: "Speed! Speed sou'west! Prepare guns! Prepare our gifts!"

I cannot say how much time elapsed as I ran to and fro with my bucket. Long enough to see many more burned. Long enough to feel the air about me sucked away by a cannonball and to witness a man broken in half like rotten tinder. I admit that my legs quivered and I was moved to abandon my efforts and hide, but the air was so charged with shot, smoke, and that swift light that I felt it safer to keep moving.

Mr. Apples's battery had begun to fire, and each retort shook the planks beneath my feet. I could no longer distinguish between the enemy's guns and our own.

The light had grown larger and, it seemed, weaker, no longer eliciting screams as it struck men. Indeed it passed over me again, and I dropped but was not burned. It was losing its power as we closed the distance. Our captain had a plan.

"South! South! Toward the channels."

Then we were upon Laroche's long-waisted ship. There it was, not thirty yards away, a salamander insignia upon her flag. The corvette was menacing with canted masts, two gun decks, and brass fittings so highly polished that they cast a rose glow on the rigging and sails. To call the ship experimental would be generous — it had been built to Laroche's own maniacal specifications. The entire hull was copper green, and the head was armored with iron plating to protect against the Twa Corbies; the rivets there made the ship itself look like a weapon.

Their deck was the same hurricane of shouting and frenzy as ours. Men on each ship took cover and exchanged rifle shots. I crouched behind my barrel again, using my water bucket as a helmet, and peeked out now and then to see how close we had come. Only when it was near enough would I take my leap to freedom.

Making our reckless flight to the south, we were wrong to the sea, and the waves lifted the starboard side of our ship such

278

that, at intervals, even the ocean completely disappeared from view, replaced by an endless sky, then the same rail would dip almost to touch the water, and men hiding behind barrels and cannon were exposed to shot from above.

Mr. Apples, his ox-yoke shoulders swinging wide, hurled a basket onto the deck of Laroche's ship, where it broke open; dark clumps scattered like quicksilver. I saw that the contents were alive, and I recognized then the scuttle of his pet scorpions. At the time I thought it a ridiculous attack, but as I write this, I understand that it was not a weapon of battle as much as of vengeance and the sowing of fright. The creatures sped for the cover of shadow and small places; *La Colette* would be haunted for weeks by venomous beasts hiding in the murky nooks and crevices that ships are comprised of. They would never be accounted for entirely — and periodically a sailor, pulling on his boots or reaching for a coil of rope, would be stung. Men would feel the caress of scampering legs in their sleep. Captain Laroche might well have to find a whole new crew due to the superstitious nature of sailors, who would no doubt call the ship cursed.

But these thoughts were not in my head

at the time. I had become a simple animal, pinned where I was with fear. Meanwhile our ship continued to be ripped apart, now less by cannon than by rifle shot. I didn't know a ship could be so thoroughly ventilated and yet float.

14
ETIQUETTE FOR CLOSE COMBAT
IN WHICH I LOSE MUCH

When our vessels were five yards close and the waves rocked *La Colette* such that her deck was made plain to me, I saw, with clarity, the marvelous contraption that had so burned the *Flying Rose.* A dozen large mirrors were positioned at distances upon the deck, and some on rigs were suspended out over the water. These swung upon swivels to reflect sunlight to the center, where a great moon of silver sat, concave and polished to a high sheen. This collecting dish was positioned behind several large lenses that, in turn, rolled upon tracks and could be adjusted to focus the terrible beam.

This is how men spend their days on earth.

I was considering my leap to freedom, reassuring myself that, despite this furious attack, Laroche was Ramsey's man, like me, when my thoughts were stopped by the sight of Feng swinging from a severed stay line across the divide and landing in the shrouds of Laroche's ship. From there he dropped to the deck and, evading Laroche's crew (who had not yet truly appreciated his presence among them), made straight for the solar weapon. Producing a cooper's hammer from his belt, he shattered, with lithe and efficient strokes, the glass lenses one by one and moved on to the central dish itself, where he put two great divots into the silver before he was beset by Laroche's marines. They surrounded him and he used his hammer as a weapon, making short swift arcs that landed with staggering speed on one sailor after another, now breaking a knee, now caving a temple. This crowd moved about the deck, for Feng would not let them corner him, and they left behind them a trail of broken men, some impaled on their own swords. He ducked and leaped like a flame, dodging the falling bodies, all the while writing invisible ideograms in the air with the hammer, each punctuated by apostrophes of blood.

My vision obscured by smoke and the rolling of the deck, I was able to witness only brief moments of this melee, but it was time enough to see Feng cut down a dozen men. They would have had more luck catching the wind; he had a manner of slinking askance, slipping behind them even as they lunged. The sailors seemed confused to find their wrists broken and their jaws unhinged by that appalling hammer. One, taking desperate action, dropped his sword and lifted his blunderbuss, but Feng did not flee nor flinch. Rather, in a wink, as the gun was aimed, Feng went to the soldier as easily as one hugs a friend. The gun fired safely under Feng's arm, and three soldiers behind him dropped, gripping their red bellies, felled by their comrade's shot.

All the while, rifles and cannon continued to mutilate the air, scattering wood and bone like confetti. As more men moved to intercept Feng, our gunners gained advantage and many of Laroche's men found themselves riddled with crossfire.

Only when a net was thrown over Feng did his choreography slow. I heard Bai's steady voice addressing Mabbot behind me: "Captain, with your permission?" Mabbot must have nodded, for Bai flew to *La Colette* in the same manner and began to disperse soldiers, severing Feng's net with his tasseled sword. The brothers, unstoppable and moving as one, cut the tether on the spanker boom and swung it out over the gap. This they used as a bridge, dancing across the narrow spar to the cheers of our crew and returning to Mabbot's side. I saw that Feng had suffered blows and lacerations. Still, the glow upon the twins' faces showed their satisfaction with the foray.

During these events, I became aware of the figure of Laroche himself, a long shadow on the foredeck, using his sword to punctuate his orders. The brass buttons, running in parallel rows down his coat, glinted in the sun as he orchestrated the vicious assault.

Our ships were even closer now, the rails half a dozen feet apart, but I saw with horror that we were passing Laroche's ship quickly. We would get no closer. This was my only chance. I set my timid heart aside and focused on the receding glimmer of my promise to myself. To return! Nothing else mattered.

I rose in panic, my prayers to individual saints abandoned for one single, childish refrain — "Heaven help, heaven help . . ." — and I ran, though the waves were against us and the deck rocked beneath me. I ran as straight as I could toward *La Colette* with no other plan than to leap, grasping at the beams and ropes of the liberated yardarm that swung drunkenly near our rail, or to fall into the water and swim if need be.

As I reached the rail, the waves brought

our vessels level and there, standing opposite me upon the French deck, was a young naval officer, with the salamander upon his breast and the pink of battle upon his round face. My savior. I stood full at the railing, arms raised in excitement and shouting my own name: "Owen Wedgwood! Owen Wedgwood!" But I saw no kindness in his face. A breath before he raised his rifle, I imagined how I must look to him: hair matted, beard untrimmed, eyes wild with desperation. Was I not the picture of a bloodthirsty pirate? I dove to the deck just as he shot, and rolled, hugging the shadows of the quarterdeck.

Only when I tried to scurry to more promising shelter did I ascertain that the ball had passed through my lower leg; there was a sickening grinding when I put weight on it. I slid in a slick of blood, fairly pinned to my position by rifle fire. For minutes I was racked by an infantile melancholy; if the pope himself had shot me, I could not have been more disappointed.

Then pain broke into me, the cacophony of war again filled my ears, and I was reanimated by the desire to live. With pandemonium severing the stays of creation around me, I crawled to the galley, where, in agony, I squirmed into Conrad's enormous cauldron for shelter, pulling my useless leg behind me and praying for a smashing victory by the attackers, but not so smashing that it resulted in my death. My last thought before darkness took me was that Mabbot's warrant had said nothing of taking her alive.

I woke to a chorus of moaning of which I was the baritone. I was chilled to the bone, though my neck and fingers felt as if they were on fire. Someone had been pouring rum into me; my beard reeked of it. The moaning of the others, burned or shot around me, came and went with the light.

Days passed as fevered minutes. I had, at one moment, clarity enough to know that I had been rescued when I felt on my skin the blessing of sunlight and beneath me a bed of down. Real down! Further, I was no longer among the dying but alone. I daresay I smiled despite the pain, which had grown to consume my entire right side. Fever rattled the shutters of my mind.

Then my dreams of rescue scattered like bats when one of the twins, those agents of suffering, hovered above me, pulled back my eyelids, and clucked, "He is dying."

Mabbot responded, "Do not stop your ministrations." Her voice was soothing and calmed me, and I found myself wanting her near, which only confirmed the severity of my delirium.

Yea, do not stop your ministrations, my heart pleaded. Whatever occult arts you possess, whatever bitter herbs and incantations, spend them on this body. I no longer cared where the body lay, in an English bed, upon a pirate ship, on a desert island, or floating upon an iceberg — only that I should not die.

This was Saint Anthony's agony. Various demons presented themselves to me. Chief among them was the ship's surgeon. I would have preferred a gargoyle perched above my face. I could not tell who stank more; we were, both of us, positively soaked in spirits. I realized, with a clarity available only to the fevered, that the good doctor was, in fact, Death himself, passing as a member of the crew this whole time, patiently waiting to gather us up. I spent myself cursing and trying to beat him away. These spells were periodically interrupted by slaps or cold water splashed upon me.

I learned later that we had barely survived Laroche's assault by reaching the black coral channels, as Mabbot had hoped. These channels can be navigated only by toothless Pete, the cryptic ancient who sits at the bow.

La Colette's hull was compromised by the shallows, and we limped to this island river, deep in the convoluted bays of Selat Nasik, where we've hidden to make repairs.

In my fever, I was also visited by gentler phantoms: A plump hare ran through a dark forest pursued by something malignant. I ran to protect it, or at times became it, feeling the evil at my heels. I quite exhausted myself trying to keep up as it ducked behind giant trees and turned down narrow paths. And when I spotted its white tail disappearing into the muzzle of a cannon, I lunged in after it, shouting. The cannon was much longer on the inside, and I crawled for some considerable time before emerging out of an oven, unscathed, in the small kitchen of my journeyman days. My beloved Elizabeth was there, alive and young and real in every detail, from the loose sweep of her hair to the lavender hue of her apron. I wept to see her and kept at it until she offered me some of the soup she had been preparing and soothed my back with her soft hand. She was encouraging me to swallow the thick dumplings floating in the soup, saying, "If you don't chew them, you'll choke."

This was my old life, before pirates, before even Ramsey. My first position was working at the inn for the widow Hamilton, who always had something to say about my "French airs" but who paid me well. This was the season, perhaps even the very day Elizabeth finally conceived, that downhill slope that would take them both from me. But here she was, well and vibrant. In my anxiety that fall would come and snatch her away, I looked up from my soup and saw, through a window, the hare caught in the jaws of a large reptile. I watched as it was swallowed, passed as a grotesque lump through the serpent, and emerged on the other side slick and black as bitumen.

At this I woke.

I heard the surgeon say, "It must be done."

Mabbot replied, "Then, steady and clean, do it."

My leg, when I was conscious to it, was swollen and lay heavy as a slaughtered pig upon the wooden cot, for now I was no longer on the down bed and must have dreamed that too. The pain was ungodly, and I was grateful when they filled me again with rum until darkness asserted itself.

When I next woke, the surgeon was gone and one of the twins was spooning a foul ocher tonic into my mouth. There was, beside me, a crate of Spanish moss or cobwebs or the like, and this they were applying to my wounds. The sharp pain had been replaced by a crushing weight, as if my foot had been clamped within a carpenter's vise.

I heard one of the twins say, "No more rum. He must feel this to heal."

The pain worsened and I wept. I cried out and groaned until I slept, for I was sorely exhausted. Without the rum's kind parasol, I was exposed to a torrent of pain. The twins forced gruel and their foul potions between my clenched teeth. I begged them to release my foot from the vise.

Then it was morning, which morning I could not say, and I was truly awake for the first time since the attack. I was again on down; in fact, I was in Mabbot's cabin, in her bed, with nothing but a sheet wrapped around my loins. The twins were nearby. Mabbot was reading in her chair next to the bed and, I realized, holding my hand gently. When I snatched my hand away, she looked up from her book and smiled.

"You certainly curse like a pirate," she said.

"Lie still," Bai said. "The needles."

I looked upon my body and with mounting anxiety saw that my belly, knees, and forearms had been perforated with needles like the map of a conqueror. On my chest sat small mounds of smoldering incense.

"What witchcraft — ?" I coughed.

"This witchcraft," said Mabbot, "bore you through a fine fever; your foot was full green before the surgeon did his part."

My foot was hidden somehow, sunk into the down mattress. I lifted it and saw that there was nothing there but a stump, bound thickly. Just below the knee my foot and calf were gone.

"What have you done to me?" I cried.

"You didn't want that old thing," Mabbot said. "It smelled so bad even the sharks won't eat it. What a bother. Your escape attempts aren't so good for your health; let's skip them altogether from now on."

"Fiends! Devils!" I tried to rise, but Feng placed his palm on my forehead and pinned me where I was. I swept my hand across my body to remove the needles and incense.

"These good men have performed a miracle," said Mabbot.

"Took my foot!"

"The surgeon took your foot and promised me you'd be dead in a day. You are not dead. You owe that to the twins and their medicine."

"Return my foot!"

"Well," Mabbot said. "Our guest is unsatisfied with our hospitality. Get him out of here."

After plucking their machinations from my skin, the twins lifted me toward the door.

"Wedge," Mabbot called, stopping us. "Don't imagine that you're excused from your contract. Now more than ever we must stick to our tasks. I'll give you a week to collect yourself; the following Sunday I shall dine as usual." I saw then that her cheeks were blistered and her arm was bandaged from the battle.

"I'll pitch myself into the sea before feeding you again!" I spat.

"Of course, that is your choice. Oh, and the men will gossip about your time here. If you encourage any untoward rumors, I'll rip your equipment off to verify your story."

Leaning upon Joshua once again, I saw, on my way from Mabbot's cabin, that we were anchored in a river surrounded by lush jungle. The ship was in pieces, the bowsprit cut entirely away, its lines loose in the wind, and a great log on the main deck was being lathed to replace her. Men sat in circles repairing the sails, which were beginning to look like a child's first quilt.

I was locked in my cell, dim and cramped after Mabbot's luxurious cabin. Over the course of the next few days, I mostly slept. My fever returned in fits. Joshua appeared to wet my forehead with rags, to empty my chamber pot, and to feed me gruel and more of the bitter sauce that the twins concocted.

I confess here, as I have no proper confessor, that in my delirium I demanded that God restore my body whole. My petition, if not ignored, was at least denied.

When the twins appeared to check my progress two days later, I grabbed Feng by the wrist and howled, "If it is no longer there, why does my foot ache so?"

"Do you want the medicine? You act like a child."

"Can't you make it stop hurting? I still feel the foot."

"It will take time."

15

DEAD MAN'S STOVE

IN WHICH WE LICK OUR WOUNDS AND JOSHUA TELLS HIS STORY

I can tell you that the soul of man is neither a vapor nor a prick of light but a body of limbs in the image of our maker. I know this because, though my foot is washed up on some beach without me, yet the spirit of my foot remains, attached and itching. This is why the Lord has ordained that we shall rise whole upon our judgment, for to be separated from one's own flesh with no way to scratch an itch is hell.

The twins, then, are not only Mabbot's bodyguards but her personal physicians as well. I can't blame her for preferring their arcane methods over the surgeon's. They massaged the stump, which I tolerated only by biting upon a belt. They also massaged my knee and thigh and hip, which proved quite welcome. The smoking herb — mugwort, they told me — was pinched from a small teak box and rolled between their fingers into cones. These they lit with great diligence upon my chest and thighs. They managed to remove these piles of ash just before the fire reached my skin. They also let blood from my back and shoulders with cups.

It was clear they were attending to me only through a direct order from Mabbot. In my mind I renamed them "Stoic" and "Silent." As my strength slowly returned, though, so did my curiosity.

"Is it true that Mabbot cut you from the gallows with her own knife?"

Feng left rather than engage me in conversation, but Bai said, "She saved us as she saved you."

"She did not save me," I said. "She kidnapped me."

"The rope was around my neck. Yours is around your mind. Just hope she can cut fast enough."

In this way I was, day by day, mended, though not in the way I wanted. Rather than being relieved, I felt my spirit moving with each session into and through the pain until I wore it thinly, as a mantle. My foot I could still feel, especially in the mornings, but its crushing ache had softened to a throbbing.

I found myself growing an entirely new body. I've thinned and resorted to tying my pants with a cord of rope, as the others do.

What is left of me hobbles around on the crutches that the surgeon gave me.

Thursday, October 7
This week has passed so quickly, though I have done nothing but sleep and eat. I manage to snore even through the noise of Kitzu and his crew of hammermen pounding day and night to restore the planks and bulwarks.

Today, with effort, I made my way above deck to find the ship greatly improved. The mosaic of fresh planks was being sealed with pitch boiled from the trees. Moreover, sailors came back from the deep jungle bearing baskets laden with fruit — bananas and pineapple — and two frighteningly long-tusked animals, dead and swaying from poles. They looked like demonic pigs to me, but the men called them "babirusa" and claim they do taste like boar.

When she passed on her rounds, I waylaid Mabbot and asked to be excused from my duties.

"I should think not," she huffed.

"I cannot stand without these crutches," I said.

"A heron stands on one leg."

"A heron does not cook!" I shouted.

She considered for a moment, then said,

"Joshua will be your hands. Even a dog may learn." Mabbot laughed and went upon her way, leaving me waving a crutch impotently in the air.

From the mirror in the berths stares a gaunt, bearded stranger. Like the story of the man who fell asleep in the fairy ring, I've woken to find the world I know in ruins. I still ache for freedom, but Mabbot's curse has come true; I can no longer imagine what I'd be escaping to.

My yeast batter had suffered from my neglect: under a dried crust, mottled with mold, the dough was now very sour. I salvaged it by cutting out the core and mixing it with fresh water and flour. What a thing can endure and live through astounds me.

Reading in my hammock, I saw the adulterations almost immediately. The Bible Mabbot had given me was written in a small expert hand with Jesus's words in crimson ink. Thinking that the Sermon on the Mount might soothe my nerves, I had gotten to the end of Matthew's account when this passage stopped me:

And Jesus followed the dry bed north until he came to the burned mill and turned directly east and walked to the third cache marked by the cairn. He saw there fifteen carronades and twoscore French carbines. These are owed to Xiao Wei who promises one-sixteenth-ton black powder delivered to the tunnels . . .

My confusion was quickly replaced by outrage. I had opened a Bible for God's word, but what I slammed closed was a thieves' catalogue. Similar blasphemies punctuated the entire book, describing hoards of ammunition and silver, and exactly how to find them. In the passage that should have related Jesus curing the blind, it said:

As he went along, he saw a man blind from birth. His disciples asked him, "Rabbi, if this man could, what would he see in the Southern Cache?" Said Jesus, "Thirty hogsheads of black powder, thirteen hogsheads of saltpeter, and a dozen carronade sans ammunition."

I clutched the book to my chest and considered my situation. Then I went through it with a pencil; it was easy enough to spot the false passages. I rose and crutched my way to Mabbot's cabin. When the captain herself opened the door, I thrust the book into her hands, saying, "I've come to accept that I have little hope of returning home until you've finished your business with the Brass Fox. I'm giving you this in the hopes that it will speed us along. I expect it will." I tapped the book in her hand. "Lists, directions, names," I said. "Your son —"

"Lower your voice!" Mabbot hissed.

The Fox," I continued, "evidently coerced a scribe to disguise his logs. The parts that will interest you tend to lie near the end of each chapter. I've marked them. The parable of the vineyard is little more than a list of officials and the amounts they've been bribed."

"Mr. Wedgwood, you're a genius; I'm not paying you enough."

"You are not paying me at all. Let me make it clear that if I thought that this information would put an innocent in danger, or that it would keep you from justice for even a moment, I would have kept this to myself. But if a petty vendetta with another rogue is all that keeps us out here, then make your pact, or whatever it is you intend to do. The Brass Fox is just another name I wish I had never heard.

When you are done, I should very much like to be taken home."

By the curious glint in her eye, this was the first time she had even considered freeing me. "When I get my Fox," she said slowly, "we can renegotiate your employment."

It was something. For all of her villainy, Mabbot's word is not inconsequential. Every day we get closer to Macau, to the tavern called the Serpent's Tail, where, I am sure, only calamity and mischief waits, and yet, for once, I am eager to get there. If I am to return to a familiar light, it seems I must first plumb the darkest tents of this carnival world.

Now that I am moving about, Joshua has come by for his lesson. I have remembered, for the most part, the signs he taught me, and he has conveyed in his own language how he came to sail upon the *Flying Rose*. It was a halting story, for I had to stop him every few seconds to help me with a particular sign, but through his patience, the following emerged.

He was born into a family of which not a one could hear, if I understand correctly, on an island near Cape Cod in the former colonies. The island is populated by the deaf, a heritable trait, one assumes, or perhaps a result of bad waters. Joshua learned his hand language there, and, he assured me, upon the island even those blessed with hearing use the signs rather than the tongue.

Joshua's father worked his hands to burls by hauling nets for other men. His mother washed clothes for half the town and, Joshua swears, never slept but labored to save each penny. Though she baked pies every Sunday, Joshua never tasted a single one, for they were all sold and the money stashed in clay jugs. Finally the day came when his father could buy his own boat.

"We had the boat for only half a season," Joshua explained. "My father and brother went out every day while my mother and I sold the fish at the market. I hated gutting and scaling all day. Then my father invited me to come out on the boat, but my mother said I was too young, that I would be bad luck. So the next morning I snuck out of the house and hid under the nets. My father knew I was there, but he didn't say anything." As his hands shaped the story for me, tears welled in the boy's eyes at the recollection. His fingers now churned a vicious storm before my face. His cupped hands, signifying the boat, rolled and shuddered under the force of the gale. "Father told me to hold the brace line, but I couldn't. I lost it, and the boom knocked them into the water. The sea took them because I was weak."

This, at least, was the basic story, though my pen can't paint the scene as cruelly as his hands and features did. The hurricane pushed his broken boat deep into the Gulf Stream, and strong westerlies took him the rest of the way to the edge of Mabbot's hunting grounds, where she found him half-dead on the deck. He has been with Mabbot for three years since. He has sworn not to return home until he can buy his mother a proper house to replace the drafty shack he grew up in.

"I didn't know anything," the boy said. "When I'm old enough to captain my own ship, when I'm rich, I'll go back." After a solemn moment, Joshua seemed to be ready to continue with our writing lesson, but I was too horrified by the thought of his mother, widowed and alone, thinking the boy was dead.

"When my wife died," I tried to tell him by means of drawings and rudimentary signs, "I thought it was my fault, for not keeping the windows sealed against the cold, for not having money enough for a better doctor. There is no end to that kind of" — I struggled to find the right sign — "heart-wringing. If your mother is still alive, she cares not about ropes or storms. Go home. She will weep with happiness. She will thank God. At least let us try to send her a letter."

"What do you mean?"

"Mr. Apples could not have held that rope. You were just a child —"

"No, what do you mean, 'if she's still alive'?"

Here my patchwork communication failed me. "I meant nothing. Only that people die on land as well. The grief of losing everyone at once, that can make a mother ill."

Despite trying to fight them back, the tears spilled down his cheeks as his hands shredded the air with their speed, far surpassing my comprehension. When I begged him to slow down, he laid this out for me: "It's my fault. Everything is gone. I have nothing to give her. Better she thinks I'm dead. If I can bring something good back for her, I will. If not, I will stay dead."

It is hard to know how much the boy understood of my fumbling. When he left, he was deeply agitated. I would like to blame the gestures, but it was a sobering conversation in any language. I suppose that, in his grief, he had never considered that he might lose her too. She was a fixture, as constant as the lighthouse on the sandy bluff he had drawn for me. Like countless young men before him, he is on a journey to find the cures for the toil and poverty he'd left behind. The *Rose* was the place to prove himself strong and brave, and, with the wraiths dispelled, he would arrive home with stories to tell, as the son in a fairy tale comes home with a golden duck. Clumsy as I may have been, I hope I've cured him of such notions. The good things of the world are around the hearth. We'd all be better off at home.

I can imagine, though, that Joshua simply may not want to return to that world hollowed by grief; better Mabbot's swagger and the silver luster of adventure. What can I say to that?

We creep about in the filigree inlets of Nasik Island, whose southern coast is surrounded by smaller islands and their coves, like a toppled nesting doll. When we gather way, we go slowly, owing as much to the shifting tides as to our wounded ship, and the men have been exploring the turquoise rivers with longboats. It is a humid world of sudden rains and shimmering mirages — a "malaria paradise," as the men call it. Jutting crags festooned with cormorant nests loom suddenly into sight, then disappear just as quickly behind lush canopies and low clouds. The calls of monkeys and mournful birds are caught by the sails and cascade onto the deck. Where the sun touches it, the sea is a tranquilizing blue that shifts to slate again when the light goes. We are oft surrounded by granite cliffs and walls of verdant foliage, whose susurrations are cousin to the whispers of the sea. After so long on the waves, it is a strange thing not to be able to see the sky without looking up.

Such is my luck. Here I am near land with plenty of opportunity to duck and away. But when I look to the looming jungle, brash with the calls of animals, I feel the weakness of my one leg and the vapors that come when I am too long upright. Moreover, the forest is thick and tangled, and I can imagine myself wholly consumed, if not by tigers then by the vines themselves. There are no signs of civilization. Until I fully recover from my injuries, I am better off on the ship than lost in that swallowing green.

Friday, October 8
There are others aboard who are worse off

than I, those who have been horribly disfigured or mutilated. In all, twelve were killed in the battle or died shortly after. Of the entire threescore crew, fully half of us are significantly wounded, and not a man aboard does not bear at least some mark from the attack.

I have exchanged pleasantries with Finn and Theodore, Mabbot's "doves." Finn's eyes are blasted and wrapped in thick cloth. He will never see again. Theodore leads him about tenderly, reads to him, and fetches panch. At an earlier time I would say this was divine punishment for sodomy, but I witnessed the battle myself; Finn was blinded by man, not God, and though I know no sparrow falls but by His will, I must also consider my own injury. If Finn sacrificed his vision for unnatural acts, what have I traded my leg for, I who have been chaste since my wife's death and attended mass weekly until my kidnapping? And one must also wonder where poor Finn would be now without his companion, who loves him no less despite his infirmity.

When the gong brought the groggy new watch up the companionway like so many wooden figures from a cuckoo clock, the retiring shift wasted no time lighting their pipes or tumbling below to fill the still-warm hammocks. Mr. Apples took his breaks with the rest of them, and I found him sitting at the base of the mainmast with his needles and yarn. He chewed as he knit, the sinews of Mary Sweet grinding between his teeth.

"Has Laroche no other duties than to hunt us?" I asked, hoping for a reassuring word. I'd come to the wrong place.

"Not a one," he answered. "If the man sleeps, he dreams of Mabbot's steaming heart. He's got none to report to 'cept Ramsey, no particular lanes to protect, and his ship is greased with company gold. At least it was. 'Twill be interesting to see what happens when his provisions go and he learns his master is dead. It'll add to his determination, but it will gall his crew. They're used to getting paid, and who knows how he'll handle them. For now, though, we chase the Fox, Laroche chases us, and around the world we go!"

"But if Mabbot was working for Ramsey when she sank Laroche's prototype, doesn't Laroche have reason to hate them both?"

"Ramsey's got a knack for setting his dogs at each other's throats. He paid Mabbot under the table; no one knows she was his privateer. The stories of Mad Mabbot the Demon Pirate cover Ramsey's tracks. But suppose Laroche is smart enough to see through that? Matters not one bean. Ramsey was the only one who would underwrite his vessel, and now Laroche has this last chance to prove himself. We may be the only ones who know his damn machines work. If he brings Mabbot in, he'll be a hero in any nation — he could take a mink-seated sinecure, or become an admiral, or sell the plans for his ship and retire on the profits. But if he fails, well, what is he but the cracked charlatan who floated balloons over the water? If you had only the two choices, gilded fame or nameless death in a debtors' prison, wouldn't you fight hard for the first?" He paused here to pick a piece of grey meat from between his teeth with his needle.

"Strange thing is, Mabbot likes Laroche. She says, 'By the discipline of his crew, and his own grit, Laroche should be pinned to the ground with medals. Children sing songs about captains who aren't worthy to wash his decks.' " Mr. Apples chuckled, somehow amused by this glut of bad news. "But history will not know him; his glory is writ on the waves with a knucklebone."

As if to confirm my decision not to venture out, some Malay-speaking natives emerged from the forest today bearing scowls and ancient Portuguese blunderbusses. With crew members doing their best to translate, they expressed their unhappiness with our use of their teak trees. Mabbot herself negotiated with them, giving them silk and tea, no doubt saving us from considerable unpleasantness.

The repairs that can be done only near land are given priority as all are concerned that Laroche will discover us. Has *La Collette* been repaired? Is the balloon aloft and searching? These are the fears that animate the watches. Mr. Apples drives the men hard and has even threatened to use me. Every day, though, the sailors are granted an hour or two before sunset to relax and play their Gypsy songs. Mr. Apples seems to prefer not to walk the land but smokes his pipe and knits while looking out at the men frolicking at the edge of the forest.

I have had my first taste of fresh water since my capture. A clean spring was found deep in the forest, and ten men had the task of refilling our stores by carting empty barrels out in wheelbarrows and bringing them back full. If not for my foot, I would have volunteered for the chore, only to get a chance to wash my hands and face in that spring. I contented myself instead with the casks they set on the deck. Soon they will adulterate it with their spirits to keep it from spoiling in the moldy lower holds; in the meantime I'm glutting myself with it. It's strangely freeing to note that fresh, clean water is better than anything I have ever fumbled together over heat.

The men were preparing one of the babirusas by lining the body cavity with banana leaves and stuffing it with embers. They planned to roast the entire catch in a pit, but I convinced them to salt and smoke a good portion, assuring them that a little ham would do wonders for everyone.

I also struck a deal with a few of the men: if they would share with me their gathered victuals, I would give them a portion of whatsoever delicacies I made. Dozens of men fairly surrounded me with their offers, but, leery of indebting myself to a hoard of pirates, I chose my prizes carefully.

In this way I came to own shares of two spangled pheasants piping in wooden crates, six baskets of mangoes, uncountable unripe bananas, two bags of pineapples, three pails of yams, coconuts, one green papaya, dandelion greens, cilantro, mint, basil, a single ginger root, and an intriguing herb the men call lemongrass, whose odor is true to its name while erring ever so faintly toward pine. Most exciting of all: seven quail eggs.

More than anything else, more than Laroche's furious attack, more than the ridiculous salt opera, more than the painted vistas that unrolled before the *Rose,* it was these new ingredients in the hold that impressed upon me how far I was from home. Cooking with these would make me a citizen of the world, a vagabond. Still the nearly visible scent of these herbs, the shameless heaps of mangoes, the ocher stripes of the bananas that seemed to be ripening as I watched, all whispered to me of undiscovered pleasures.

The men also filled a barrel with bitter citrus to replace our limes. After tasting one, Mabbot winced and said, "Tastes like turpentine, but it will stave off scurvy."

"Pure superstition, Captain," I responded. "Everyone knows scurvy is caused by onanism."

Mabbot gawked. "A joke? Has Wedgwood made a joke?" She shouted down to the riverbank where the men were making charcoal, "Chaps! Twice the wine for every man, for dry old Wedge has found his sense of humor!"

■ ■ ■

Saturday, October 9

Joshua appears to help me putter in the galley. Near the hearth, as I am still weak, I collapse upon a stool and direct him with a crutch.

It is an agreeable arrangement, as we both have eyes and hands, and while he kens my yelling only half the time, he understands a gesture fully and immediately. His signs are efficient and poignant, and preserve the quiet I prefer for my work. Little by little, I am coming to fluency.

To me, the tiny galley is a gauntlet of shifting coals and sloshing pots, but Joshua waltzes with the room and never stumbles. His nose is far better than mine was at his age. He can detect the lightest traces of an aromatic. Further, the boy can handle a knife with great dexterity even as the cutting boards slide this way and that.

It seems he can learn anything I can teach and faster than I would have expected from any pupil. The boy is a prodigy, and I wish I could send him to an academy.

The men are already eating the bananas, green though they are, and the mangoes are disappearing at an alarming rate. I must talk to Mr. Apples about enforcing rationing. In the meantime I have started my exploration of this new world with a peculiar recipe indeed: pineapple-banana cider. I spent half an hour poking about the hold with a lantern to find the ripest fruit. The bananas are squat, almost rust-colored now, and very fragrant. With Joshua's assistance, I mashed and boiled them into a thick paste. When it cooled, we added pineapple juice and covered it to let it ripen. In a few days I will strain the contents and add coconut water. If necessary, I can add small pills of the yeast dough to quicken the liquor. In this heat, the cider will be ready in a few weeks.

When I feel the phantom foot cinched within the invisible vise, I am forced to beg for help from the twins. Their needles, their massage, their smoldering mugwort, and their bleeding cups are the only things that keep the soreness at bay. The effect of their care is instantly soothing, and I feel my spirit appeased. The surgeon had demonstrated his one use in sawing off my leg. Unlike that foul and drunken butcher, these doctors treat the body whole — humors and spirit as well.

I have too much time to ponder my fragility and the care those ebon-haired twins have shown. My thoughts inevitably become confused: Could it really be black magic if it soothed so completely? Had God given their land this saving knowledge but not the means for eternal salvation? Such questions make my nights long indeed.

Sunday, October 10
This morning Joshua, grinning like a split melon, woke me and, though I had not yet had tea and was not in the mood for games, led me out of my chamber, across the deck, and down the starboard companionway to a hold that used to contain great coils of rope. The place was transformed. The hull now framed a port window of wooden slats. The air was sweet with pitch and sawdust. The hooks that used to hold mattocks, spikes, and other tools were now hung with pots and spoons. The little iron stove had been set up against the back wall and secured to the floor with bolts, its chimney poking through a hole still ragged from the cooper's saw. Behind the stove, the wood had been shielded with a sheet of hammered tin that reflected morning light from the window. It was a small kitchen, even smaller than Conrad's galley, but it had a proper stove, a basin stand, and a block for chopping.

As I marveled, Mabbot appeared in the doorway behind me and asked, "Will it suit?" She was hiding something behind her back.

"Much better, Captain," I answered. "It will be cramped with Joshua and me — I'll need a stool. But I'm glad for it."

"Thank Kitzu," Mabbot said. "With all the repairs, the man hasn't slept since we anchored. Something else" — she held out a copper box that I had seen pillaged from the *Patience*. Inside, the box was divided into tiered chambers, each with a lacquered lid, and these held a selection of ground and whole spices: sage, turmeric, cumin, ginger, mustard, cinnamon, asafetida, mace, cayenne, and cloves. I felt like an emperor receiving the treasures of a new country. The odor rising from the box was like a clambering vine wrapping itself thickly around my head, musky with the deep minerals of the earth and dusting my shoulders with a rainbow of pollen.

"I could have used these in weeks past."

"Last month I was in no mood to make gifts."

It was a ransom of spices, a small fortune, and yet out here, with no buyers, they were worthless as ash to all but myself. Only my presence imbued them with value.

Despite my decision not to brave those jungles, today I spent several hours upon the riverbank, bathing and enjoying the blessed constancy of soil with the other men. I forget for long moments that I am a prisoner, and then I am so frightened at having forgotten that my heart races and sweat beads on my brow. Though Mr. Apples keeps his eye on me, I must not slacken in my search for freedom. I am still thin, though, and after only an hour upon unfamiliar terrain, my shoulders ache and tremble from the crutches.

Monday, October 11
Today the *Rose* was ready for open seas, but Mabbot insisted that we stay and gave the men a full day's rest. As a result, and though it was only midday, the men not on watch were quite drunk when a ship was spotted approaching the mouth of the river, causing a panic.

Happily, the vessel was merely a Japanese whaling ship, and emissaries from both were sent to meet in longboats to trade tobacco, spices, liquor, and spermaceti for Mabbot's lamps. I went along.

It was a strange impromptu marketplace we made, four small boats rocking in the tide, tethered to one another by thrown ropes and goodwill. Kitzu translated, though we had to wait long spells as he gathered news of his homeland from the whalers. The others spent tremendous amounts of silver wheedling knives from the Japanese and suggested I do the same. Instead, I convinced two of the whalers to row back and bring me samples of every foodstuff in their galley.

Paying with silver pieces Mabbot gave me for the purpose, I thus obtained a pot of fermented paste Kitzu called "miso."

I cannot say for certain what it is made of. Kitzu tells me miso is comprised of "winter rice and beans." Neither rice nor beans ever looked, smelled, or tasted like this, and so I know Kitzu is having fun at my expense. The paste has a rich, meaty smell, and I've been assured by the whalers it will keep for a month at least. Kitzu told me it would last ten years, proving that the man is either lying or confused. Still, it is wonderful stuff — would that I could have bought an entire barrel, for, first thing upon regaining the *Rose,* I boiled a bit of water, and the miso made an excellent broth that will serve well as a replacement for beef bouillon. Further, I bought a pot of savory black soy liquor — salty but, though I cannot yet imagine what to do with it, no doubt valuable.

Macau is deep in the South China Sea, and Mabbot has plotted a course past Cochin China. When the evening tide allowed, we finally left our river retreat and headed again for the vast dark expanse, hoping to put at least a full night between us and Laroche, wherever he may be lurking. The crew is wary, as am I, but there is nothing I can do except focus on my own tasks.

In anticipation of Sunday's meal, I have taught Joshua the quick and kind way to wring the neck of one of the pheasants kept in wicker cages. We cleaned and plucked it, then hung it in a lidded cauldron in the cool lower holds to age along with a small pot of the salted gizzards, heart, and liver. Such provisions make me feel almost wealthy.

16
Teaching a Dog
IN WHICH MABBOT SURPRISES ME AND I RECEIVE A GIFT

Friday, October 15

We are again surrounded by sea, and though I loathed to see that fertile and giving land disappear, I knew that it was nothing but a mermaid's song. My only way home is to press further into the wilderness.

I am beginning to learn how to watch the sky for weather. The lavender furls on the northern horizon are as lovely as they are ominous; I'm told they are distant monsoons and that our course will bring us to meet them. Just as haunting are the boat-sized manta rays that fly in languid flocks under our hull.

While I was explaining to Joshua how to make mirepoix to anchor a sauce — a purely fanciful exercise, as we have no carrots or celery — I was interrupted by Mabbot, who threw a bundle of clothes at me and demanded that, prior to our next meal, I shave. The clothes were finely sewn and included linen pants and a silk under-shirt. An entirely different class of garment from the stiff and salt-crusted canvas clothes I'd been wearing for weeks. I guessed they had come from the captain of the *Patience.*

"I cannot wear the clothes of a murdered man," I said.

"Then wear them and live," she replied, and left. But her threats no longer have the sting they used to. I do not doubt that Mabbot, in a fit of rage, could have me flung overboard, but, though I do not wish to die, I no longer tremble at the threat. I now have some intimacy with death, and like the hops in a beer, it has both embittered and forti-fied me.

Mabbot is nothing so much as a spoiled child playing with dolls. She props me in a seat to make tea-talk, and I find myself charmed. When bored, she throws tantrums and lashes out. My task is merely to survive intact and to remember that I must not come to like too much the dark beauty of distant storm clouds or the dreamlike flavors of island fruits — to remember that, though it seems a pale shadow now, my real life awaits me somewhere beyond this roll-ing deck.

I have made an audit of the foodstuffs

loaned me, the portions I owe and to whom. These men know to come to my chamber on Monday morning for their leftovers. My contract with certain members of the crew has borne a curious phenomenon. Men have begun, a few times a day, to knock at my door offering trinkets such as mother-of-pearl boxes or mummified monkey's hands. One offered to wash my clothes, which I would have agreed to if I had another set to change into in the meantime. (Better to do it myself than wait naked while a pirate disappears with my clothes.) They all want me to cook for them, and I am forced to turn most of them away. One man, though, offered a small bag of dried tomatoes (of an uncertain age but still piquant) that he had been rationing.

This man I kissed on both cheeks, though I am not known for displays of affection. I have been unable to put down this bag of tomatoes for fear it might disappear, and instead keep it in my pocket. I still wear my tin of yeast dough upon my person as well, feeding it when necessary and taking a comfort from its familial smell.

The surgeon, it seems, does have one other skill. When he's not passed out or lopping limbs, the man whittles naked women from

Kitzu's scrap wood. He churns out various poses at an alarming rate and trades them for rations. These shameless fetishes, which the men call "Pine Pennys," proliferate until one cannot take three steps without his gaze falling between the spread legs of a doll stashed in the crook of a bulkhead or tucked into a seaman's belt up to the bulging mammaries. This is the surgeon's chief occupation.

Some of the men rub them for luck. A nervous energy is growing day by day. We're closing in on Cochin China, and while some are excited to be closer to apprehending the Fox, others worry aloud about the naval patrols that guard the tea routes here. While the occasional sight of a distant shore is a poultice for my heart, those around me feel that we'll soon be fenced in by Borneo and Malaysia. "Too easy to trap us there. We'd have to have wings to find open water," they say. Mabbot, though, is undeterred, driving us at top speeds into the heart of Pendleton territory.

My returning health has renewed my dreams of escape, though they are now infused with a draft of hard-won cynicism. As often as not, these fantasies end with me eaten by a leopard or pressed into service in an emerald mine. I know next to nothing of the lands we visit. The explorers and merchants who have conquered these jungles have all been valiant and well funded, escorted by guides and pack animals. How would I fare with my sack of figs and my flattened spoon? Further, those explorers were imbued with God-given courage and an insatiable lust for adventure, whereas I have been known to pay too much for beef at the Smithfield market for fear of harsh words.

And worse, my mind moves beyond the uncertainty of escape to the uncertainty of home. Perhaps I'll find myself again on the stoop of a monastery, that family that has never turned its back on me.

Deeper and deeper into the barbarous regions we go, and every step away from the light of civilization brings us closer to Macau and the den of the Brass Fox. I tremble to witness the end of this bloody story. He has been nothing but trouble for me, and any man who could so enslave Mabbot's mind must be a monster, indeed. I cannot help but breathe the heathen vapors here and find myself racked with an unholy anxiety — a premonition — that we shall indeed find the Fox waiting for us, just where he promised, and somehow, at that moment, I shall be lost for good. His words haunt me: "We never go home again."

Sunday, October 17

I have worked, at last, with the raw materials of my craft. I am enjoying it while I can, for I know it won't continue; soon enough I will be again the blacksmith without a hammer. Today, though, we made a proper feast.

Before sunrise, Joshua and I set the neck, bones, and feet of the aged pheasant to simmer with onions into stock, later adding a little of that mysteriously seductive miso.

Pie crust has never been so hard-won. The winds are hot and dry, and even on the lower deck, one feels the sun warming the planks overhead. To properly chill the water and lard, we corked them in clay amphorae and sealed them tightly with wax. With a little help from Kitzu, we fastened the jars to long fishing lines with lead weights and tossed them into the sea behind the boat to spend the day in the frigid depths.

The sun-dried tomatoes we soaked in a little hot water to ready them for a puree. The yams turned out to be inedible by way of density. If I were a cabinetmaker, I might have the tools for converting them into something useful. Perhaps this is one ingredient better suited for Conrad's galley than mine.

There is a particular terra-cotta pot that Conrad tended to use as a midden for dirty spoons, onion skins, etcetera. This we washed thoroughly before letting it soak in clean water.

We quartered the pheasant, then floured and browned it in a skillet. In a little lard I sweated garlic cloves, lemongrass, onions, and the minced gizzards, heart, and liver of the fowl. Lemongrass is too fibrous to leave in the gravy, but its aroma is a welcome addition to my world; it has the energy of lemon zest but with a broader range that reminds me of a Riesling wine.

Though I had gained some facility clopping about the open deck with my crutches, here in the galley things were more difficult, what with the close walls, the slick floor, the knives, and the spitting oil; my right hand was usually occupied by the mundane task of keeping me from toppling into a boiling kettle. Therefore it was dependable Joshua who chopped, fried, and rolled. Having to manage most of these tasks by proxy was confounding, both because I missed having my hands in the mix but further because I was forced to articulate, in a language not my own, methods that, though they came as simply to me as paddling to a duck, were nevertheless quite nuanced.

The pie dough was the most difficult, for a crisp and flaky crust is dependent on perfect ratios, temperatures, and texture, normally gauged by experienced hands. I was so frustrated by my incapacity, I found myself yelling at Joshua, who was much chagrined and undeserving of my outburst. Though he could not hear my pitch, my demeanor and visage struck him like a blow, and he turned his back on me for a moment to shut me out.

When the tomatoes had softened, we pulverized them in a coconut-shell mortar with a single anchovy, a splash of Madeira wine, olive oil, and a pinch of cinnamon. This sauce was ladled into dishes to be cooked with the eggs and, at the last minute, basil, whose tiny purple leaves whispered of anise.

The terra-cotta pot was now twice as heavy, having absorbed much water. Into this we put the lemongrass gravy, the browned pheasant, some crumbled sage, mustard, a dash of ginger, and a cup of pheasant stock. I covered the pot with its lid and placed it into the hot oven to braise. This wet-clay method, invaluable for dry or gamy meats, was taught to me by a fellow apprentice in France. He was a comrade for only a few months before being excused for an overly enthusiastic crème flambé that managed to incinerate half the table.

Joshua deftly peeled and arranged sliced mango upon the tart crust. We then glazed it with a brandy-and-honey reduction before baking.

By way of apology for my outburst, I reserved some of the dough and made a smaller tart for the boy alone, adjuring him to enjoy it in the privacy of the new galley, lest some pirate snatch it from him.

Fortuitously, the few remaining unripe bananas are starchy and amenable to savory treatment. Just as the slices were browning at the edges, I tossed in a pinch of sage. Once fried, they would make a wonderful bed to anchor the piquant gravy.

As the pheasant braised to a glistening brindle, I found myself shaving and pulling on the lavish *Patience* clothes, pinning one pant leg up to keep it from dragging. How can I explain, except to say that I too need a moment's respite from this salt-chafed existence? After such a base tumble through the gutters of the world, I'll take any excuse for civility, even if it is pure theater.

When I showed up at Mabbot's cabin, with

Joshua carrying the tray behind me, I found the dining room lit with a multitude of candles. Mabbot wore a low-backed gown of sage green and a blue-diamond pendant festooned with pearls. Her hair had been pulled up and away from her neck, secured with a jade comb. Her face, enhanced by rouge and dusted with powder, could have been carved from cream marble by Michelangelo himself. She seemed a wholly different person, not only in appearance but in behavior as well, for the raiment clearly embarrassed her, and she fidgeted at the hem of her gown. Rather than meet my eyes, she pretended to be engaged in arranging the candles.

Joshua stared so candidly that I had to physically shove him from the chamber. I was suddenly nervous to be standing close to a woman of such admirable proportions. Further, I found myself worried for her name: that she should not be alone with a man sans escort. This old reflex struck me as so absurd that I couldn't help but laugh.

Mabbot misinterpreted me. "Am I so amusing? You think this is burlesque?"

"Oh, no, you look a princess."

Mabbot squared her shoulders and roared, "I'll not be mocked at my own table!"

I took her hand and, tugging at it to entice

her to sit again, said, "Hannah Mabbot, I've not a pinch of insincerity in my blood when I say that you look radiant. Let's have our little soiree. See? I've put on the laced shirt; my beard is gone."

She sat and said quietly, "It's just that even I need a moment of elegance now and then. Maybe it is a little ridiculous."

"Ridiculous or no, we take our pleasures where we can, and the repast tonight, I must say, is deserving . . . You're radiant," I repeated.

"You won't think so when this damn corset pinches me in two. You clean up decently yourself . . . Joshua is glad for your lessons, you should know. I haven't had the time to give him the attention he deserves. I thank you for it. You've got decency, Wedge. What delicacies have you wrought?"

"Quail eggs and basil shirred in ramekins with sun-dried tomato puttanesca, braised pheasant with dandelion greens and *jus de l'île* over pan-fried banana, and a confetti of pickled hominy *à la mer.*"

Mabbot put her chin in her hands and gazed at the victuals for a moment before saying, "Aren't you clever."

"A bishop from Rome showed me how to make the puttanesca, though he called it simply *'dal mare,'* and suggested I confess it as a venial sin every time I made it, just to be safe. A stove is a wonderful invention," I said.

"I have to agree. What a banquet!"

"And, of course, I had proper, if exotic, ingredients — couldn't we go more often to land?"

"If only I could arrange it every day, Wedge. Alas, I have more pressing matters and much water to cross."

"What exactly has the Fox done to set the world against him?" I asked.

"He has stolen women from sheikhs and fish from penguins," Mabbot said. "But it's the opium that really matters. He's taken entire warehouses of the stuff. Worse, he's wooed smugglers from Pendleton, and they are the linchpin of the empire."

"But that's your game, isn't it? I'd think you'd want to give the man a medal. Or is it hubris? You want to be the only thorn in the lion's paw?"

Mabbot took a moment to carve herself a leg of pheasant, and I was worried I had offended her, but after wiping gravy from the rim of her plate with a napkin, she continued.

"If that were all, I'd leave him be, but he's slipped into the well. He doesn't destroy the stuff. He smuggles it into China himself.

The Pendleton Company wants my head for tangling their routes, but he redoubles their grief, taking their profit while undermining their market. He's dancing a jig between the lion and the dragon."

"Why not let him?"

"I'm not content to have one devil swapped with another. And now he has some scheme to outdo Pendleton? No, I'll not let him become another opium baron."

"And when you catch him?" I asked.

"A civil conversation. He's clever enough to recognize reason. And besides, he said he was ready to work together, didn't he?"

"What if he lied?"

Her face clouded over so quickly that I sat back, feeling the need to take cover. But beneath the icy glare, I saw a weariness that far surpassed my own. There was indeed a heart beating furiously in those depths.

She sighed. "It's almost certainly a lie, or worse. But this may be my last chance to . . ."

"Stop him?"

"To set him straight. I've not been this close to him for years. How can I not try to put it right? But let's not ruin our appetites with this — your work deserves better."

Without another word, we began to eat. I was hungry, but no appetite would excuse the way we set upon those dishes. We shoveled food into our mouths in a manner ill befitting our fine attire. Bears would have blushed to see us bent over our plates. The pheasant, still steaming from the oven, its dark flesh redolent with the mushroom musk of the forest floor, was gnawed quickly to the bone. It was a touch gamy — no milk-fed goose, this — but it was tender, and the piquant hominy balanced that wild taste as I had hoped it would. The eggs, laced pink at the edges and floating delicately in a carnal sauce, were gulped down in two bites. The yolks were cooked to that rare liminal degree, no longer liquid but not yet solid, like the formative moment of a sun-colored gem.

Whether cast by the menu itself or by another unseen force, the spell was upon us, and we ate until our bellies bulged and we had to sit back in our chairs groaning. And all the while my mind wrestled with what I had seen in her eyes. One does not choose madness. Was Mabbot not a prisoner too?

After only a few minutes of intoxicated burps and happy rocking, Mabbot eyed the brandied mango tart as a pugilist eyes a rival. She carved herself a slice and, with the very same knife, which she wiped quickly upon a towel, reached between her shoulder blades and cut the uppermost tethers of her corset to make more room.

After dessert we sipped on strong cups of tea, one of the luxuries we can afford to take for granted here in the trade routes.

"Delightful," she said. "If only for a little cream."

"Don't speak to me of cream, Captain. I dream about milk at least twice a week. I run naked with milk running in rivulets from the corners of my mouth. I even miss humble parsley — zounds, how I've taken that weed for granted! And butter, I'll not describe my butter dreams, they're too depraved."

Mabbot chuckled. "We must leave something for dreams."

"Anyway," I said, "I credit Joshua with much of this meal."

"So your apprentice is working out?"

"Very amenable, an amazing young man."

"So even a dog can be taught, after a fashion?"

"But Joshua is not a dog!" I nearly shouted. In my ardor I spilled my tea. "He learns more quickly than any assistant I've ever had. If I'd had him on land, in a proper kitchen —"

"Oh, shut up, Wedge, I wasn't talking

about Joshua. I was talking about you. You're the dog." Mabbot was laughing out loud now. "You stubborn cur. But you learn. And this *food,* Wedge. Kidnapping you was the best decision I've made in years." She beamed.

I folded my arms and took to looking at the floor.

"Let us take a little stroll and watch the moon."

"I don't stroll as well as I used to," I said.

"We don't have far to go."

Mabbot waited patiently as I navigated the ladder to the poop deck by placing my crutches up first, and then supporting myself with an iron grip on the top rung.

We stood between the Twa Corbies, watching the moon in silence for a long time, each of us lost in our own thoughts. The strangeness of my new life impressed itself upon me, this intimacy with notorious criminals, this chaotic tour of the globe. And this woman, for she was, despite her savagery and unnatural predilections, an undeniably lovely woman, a more fascinating character than I had ever known. Her arm, when the ship rolled, occasionally brushed against mine, and though I am sure she noticed it too, she made no effort to distance herself. When a crutch fell, she picked it up for me.

"I want to understand, Hannah," I said softly. "Please don't get upset . . . the opium — of all the injustices in the world —" I found myself stumbling over my own tongue, not wanting to ruin the rare moment of peace between us. "That is, as you have pointed out, the world ignores the opium trade, but for some reason you cannot."

"Your papist ears are itching for a confession?" Mabbot chewed her thumbnail while she considered my face. "Do you recall my young days as a bed warmer? I had a friend in that brothel. She was older than I was, but she lacked a certain . . . numbness that the rest of us had, a knack for leaving the body while the men batted it around. She felt every grunt and hairy grip. I watched her face wasting away, every day more gaunt, and her red-rimmed eyes . . . So I stole a tin of opium from a coat pocket, easy enough while the gentleman snored, and told her to eat a little before. And it worked. It helped greatly."

Moonlight fell on her brow, on her nose and lips.

I whispered, "Where is the confession?"

"That's it. I made it easy for her, for *them*. I might as well have chained her to that bed. She didn't cry anymore; she disappeared completely. When I ran away with Evangeline, this one stayed for the opium pipe."

"A childhood mistake turns you into a pirate?"

"Do you really think, after all that you've seen, Wedge, that I'm out here atoning for my crimes? When I learned how Ramsey had used me, when I learned how the Pendleton Company really made their money, that girl rose up in me; she reaches for the sword with my hand."

"It's true, then, that Ramsey's ghost sits at the heart of the story, having pitted you each against the other?"

"In his scheming to own the globe, he sowed the sea with privateers and assassins, leveraged the Royal Navy to his will, and even forced the Crown to allow him to raise private armies in Africa and India. The devil himself could not keep so many pawns in place."

"And to think I made biscuits for the man."

She shivered. "Let's get back inside before the crew starts asking questions about this dress."

Hopping in the undignified manner my new proportions demanded, I escorted her to her door, then made to leave, but she beckoned me back inside. I leaned upon my

336

crutches while she dug in the chest at her bedside and produced a bizarre item, much like a wooden chalice, with a stem of polished teak and a rounded base. Its cup was full of moleskin and a knitted wool pad; the whole was adorned with a heavy leather strap and buckle.

"It was a collaborative effort," Mabbot said. "We'll have to fit it to match your stride."

I could see their hands in it: Mr. Apples's yarn thick and soft, the wood oiled to a handsome sheen by Kitzu, the leather worked to velvet suppleness. It was a gift of considerable forethought, even beauty, but how could I feel grateful? The thing revolted me. The seductive complacency I had felt just moments before dissipated in an instant. I felt that if I accepted this thing and wore it, then they would, piece by piece, take all of me and leave me a leather-and-wooden puppet. I feared, frankly, for my soul.

I said, "I wouldn't need such an abomination if not for you!"

Without another word, I took my crutches and hobbled out, leaving her holding the artificial leg.

■ ■ ■

Tuesday, October 19

Today the surgeon and Kitzu came to fit my peg to my body, and though the process filled me with a number of unpleasant emotions, I cooperated. Mabbot has it in her head that I should wear it, and after all, it would be nice to walk rather than hop. After the measurements, Kitzu took it away, then brought it back a quarter inch shorter and left me with it.

Deeper and deeper through the South China Sea we go. Every day I feel some grim terminus approach. By her tenacity, one would guess the captain intends to drive us to the tattered edge of the map. She is her own planet moving on a stubborn mission against the sweep of order.

17
Sabotage
IN WHICH WE VISIT A WITCH

Wednesday, October 20

I spend much of my time learning Joshua's hand language, though there seems to be no end of it. It's our arrangement: he learns to read, I learn to sign. If I am falling behind, it is only because he learns so quickly. He corrects me now without hesitation, jumping upon the slightest mistake and mocking my errors. He is frustrated with the way I move my face, particularly my eyebrows, and goes so far as to push at my features as if to mold them by hand.

Wednesday, Later

It is late, but I write by candlelight because I am too anxious to sleep. I saw Mr. Apples and Mabbot discussing anchoring tomorrow in the Phan Thiet port of Cochin China. This may be my last opportunity to escape, and I must take it. Again, I have packed myself some meager foods for a journey. When the party leaves tomorrow, I will wait for them to get some distance, free myself from my cell if need be, then make to the dock.

I stride with my strange new appendage the three steps to my hammock and back and forth like a caged tiger, until a spot has worn in the wood where my peg lands. The strap has to be very tight to keep it from slipping, but each day I can wear it for longer stretches.

Thursday, October 21

I was upended early this morning when Mr. Apples threw my door open and announced, "The cap'm wants you should join us."

I could not tell him I had other plans, and so, soon enough, we were moving swiftly in a longboat toward a pier. There were six of us: Mr. Apples, the twins, a Cochin seaman, the captain, and myself. In the harbor were half a dozen fishing boats, little larger than canoes, occupied by figures in wide straw hats. I watched as one hauled a net full of shimmering fish out of the water. The green-furred hills bunched toward the mouth of a wide river. Close to the inlet were several ships with roofs instead of masts. They looked like illustrations of Noah's ark.

"Hulks," Mr. Apples told me. "Floatin' warehouses. When a ship's been patched too many times and is too weary for open sea, she gets pastured."

"If the Fox is headed to Macau," I asked Mabbot, "why stop here?"

"There is a man, an old friend of mine — well connected, a first-rate smuggler before the malaria slowed him. He's the only person I trust to take me into Macau. He knows the countryside there. And with any luck his grandmother is still alive too."

"His grandmother?"

"She knows things."

As we walked down the dock, ruby-eyed herons judged us from their perches on the gouty trees above. Bai carried one of the pheasants we had captured on the island, still squawking in its sack.

A pair of unshaven French soldiers sat smoking in wicker chairs at the foot of the dock, their uniforms sagging open in the heat. As we neared, they stood and aimed their muskets halfheartedly. Mabbot's stride didn't slow until she was only a few feet from the taller soldier, who was obliged to take a step back to keep his gun trained on her.

"I'm Captain Hannah Mabbot. That's my *Flying Rose*. Do you know me?"

No doubt the soldier had seen the scarlet flag of the *Rose* even as she anchored. Now he was taking in Mr. Apples's barrel chest and the swords on the hips of the twins. A prod from his subordinate steeled his resolve, though, and he rattled his blunderbuss and growled, *"Je ne parle pas anglais."*

Mabbot pulled a ditty bag from her belt and emptied it into her palm. She offered the half-dozen silver crowns to the man. "Do you know me now?"

He took the money with relief and returned to his post, where the other soldier bickered with him for his share of the toll.

Walking upon solid ground took some getting used to, as the path came up and met my peg in a jarring manner. The air was alive with the odor of ox dung and the paternal musk of the earth itself.

"Did you just end decades of enmity with thirty bob?" I asked. "France is poorer than I thought."

"Mercenaries," Mabbot spat. "Those men aren't French any more than I'm English. If we don't get near their hulks, they won't give a fig about us. Besides, France knows my work. They should be paying me."

The forested hills were riotous with birdcalls. I had been eager to get to land, but the jungle was uncomfortably close, and the stories I had read about cannibals and man-eating tigers seemed suddenly quite vivid. The insects alone were enough to make one pause: the flies converged on us as we left the shore, and every few paces a new beetle or spider crawled across our path, each more grotesque than the last.

At a bend in the river, we came to a derelict village consisting of dozens of stilt houses arranged in a rough circle around a boggy meadow. Most were abandoned; others looked to have been razed by bandits and bad weather. The slopes of the nearby hills were scored with fields, but there was no movement there. Weeds had choked the ditches, and feral dogs ran in the wastes. At the peak of the hill sat a church, quiet and dark, its cross jutting into the sky like the hand of a distant swimmer. Several huts had long since burned, their bamboo skeletons grim in the yellow light. Moreover, the Cochins here seemed to be ill. They lay at the doors of their huts looking gaunt and exhausted. A handful of children, their bellies swollen unnaturally, clustered about us begging. Mabbot tossed them sacks of hardtack and pickled herring — our lunch — and when they had bolted these and still were not appeased, Mabbot was obliged to smack at them with a reed to clear our way.

Why the captain wanted me on this day trip, I couldn't fathom. She seems to anticipate my attempts to escape, though I hide this log very well in a sack of stale tea. I have even gone so far as to leave a decoy set of innocent musings out for a snooper to discover, yet I have never found evidence of the pages disturbed.

Two older boys ran up bearing a rusty musket and a sharpened stick. Just as Bai leaped to intercept them, they fell to their knees and held the weapons over their heads.

The Cochin seaman interpreted: "They think you are the Brass Fox; they are ready to join your army."

For once Mabbot had no witty reply. Her face curdled, and she left the boys kneeling in the dirt.

Mabbot started her search with the closest stilt house, bowing deeply as she poked her head in and inquired after a man named Huynh.

It seemed that each villager she spoke to wanted something for the information. Since we had already given away our food, it was slow going. Enormous flies kept biting the back of my neck.

As we walked past the huts, a woman sitting in a doorway, her body emaciated and covered with pox scars, clicked her tongue at me. She caught my eye and pulled her robe open to reveal a thin breast, offering herself.

I averted my eyes and hurried to catch up with the others.

"What happened here?" I asked Mabbot.

"Opium happened! Oh, missionaries and French militias did their part. But mostly this is a poppy blight. It works so well in India, why not grow it here? This is what I wanted you to see. This was a thriving market. I used to rely on this place. But now . . ." Mabbot spread her arms and twirled as she sang out in a gilded voice, "Opium *Yāpiàn!*"

"Opium is not a magic spell," I said. "Opium per se cannot do this. Sloth and greed, the weakness of men, do this."

"Wind and your opinions," she said. "Opium turns hardworking men into lizards. Isn't that magic? Many here are addicted now, but it didn't start that way. These hills used to be green. Rice paddies, melons, oxen, ducks. Then the warlords forced these families to grow opium exclusively and took all the profit for themselves. As a result, the farmers starved. Those who resisted were massacred. They smoke now to dull the hunger."

Just as she entered another hut, I asked Mabbot if I could visit the church. She nodded at Feng, and he followed me up the dusty hill.

It was a mud-and-wattle construction with an arched door and flaking grey paint. Feng stayed outside with his eye on the stilt house while I went in. Even before I adjusted to the darkness, I could sense that the place was empty save for the flies. I dipped my fingers into the urn of dingy water and crossed myself. The nave was littered with kneeling benches. The confessional was little more than an upright casket with a turmeric-colored curtain. Flies circled before the crucifix, which was rough-hewn and gory. I knelt on one of the benches with some difficulty.

"I am sorry for having offended Thee," I whispered. "I detest my sins, and I dread the loss of heaven . . ." I trailed off. The chapel of our orphanage was a simple place; even so, my heart was inevitably soothed the minute I entered it. Now I felt nothing but a growing sense of unease. Never had I seen a church as desolate as this. But wasn't this fitting for me now, rank as I was, forgetting my wife during moonlit strolls with a brigand?

I rose, clumped toward the apse, and

chuckled at what I saw there: a potbellied pig and a mangy pye-dog sleeping together on the floor of the altar. I lay down next to them on the cool bricks, and they made room for me. I felt the muscles of my neck relax. It was very quiet, blessedly so, and I closed my eyes. Then Feng hollered, "Wedgwood!" It seemed Mabbot had finally found her man.

By the dour faces on the family crowded into the hut, it was clear that Mabbot's smuggler was on his deathbed. Most of them left to make room for us, but one young woman sat at his feet, gripping his swollen ankles, as if defying us to take him from her.

His sunken cheeks were pallid, and I could smell the rot on his breath even from where I stood near the door, an almost sweet stench, like the paste found at the bottom of an apple barrel.

"Mabbot," he whispered as she knelt by the cot. "I'm no good."

"I can see that, Huynh. I guess you won't be taking us into Macau."

"Be careful, the Brass Fox has people everywhere now."

"Tell me."

"He steals opium from Pendleton warehouses, he has smugglers, tunnels, and he trains even fishermen to fight. He has an Indian woman with him — she was part of the Bengali uprising. She has thousands of farmers ready to fight with her. People call him 'hero,' they say he's going to free them from Pendleton. I have cousins sworn to him. They say the day is coming."

We all waited while the man recovered his breath. When Mabbot put her hand on his brow, the young woman at his feet stood, scowling.

Huynh said something in Cochin, and she sat again. "He wants to stop the Pearl River trade," said Huynh, "the tea, the spice, the silk, the opium — everything."

"Impossible."

"If enough smugglers and farmers stop work, the warehouses will stand empty. They have the harbors . . ." We waited while he coughed. "They are close enough to slit the right throats. It would take months for Pendleton to bribe new harbormasters. If he controls the river, he can strangle the trade, at least long enough to make a real panic in the investors. You know all of Europe would jump at a chance to squeeze into England's territory."

"But why?"

"They say to free the people." The man chuckled, a dry papery sound. "Sounds like something you'd do."

"But it doesn't sound like the Fox."

"Maybe he'll surprise you." The laughter became coughing, and suddenly the man was exhausted. "Either way, he's going to make a mess of things. Why not let him?"

"You know I can't do that, Huynh." Mabbot placed a hand on his shoulder. "What do you need?"

"If Grandmother can't cure me . . ."

"She'll outlive us all," said Mabbot.

"Maybe something for my family."

Mabbot withdrew a small sack of coins from her coat and, without hesitation, handed it to the young woman, who received it with a stunned expression, then quickly bowed.

Mabbot touched his shoulder again and said, "Goodbye, Huynh, we'll play cards together in the next world."

"And I'll let you beat me like I always did — you're a terrible loser," said the dying man as we ducked into the light.

We made our way beyond the meadow to Huynh's grandmother's: a tiny hut overhung by moss-choked boughs. The toothless crone waved us in. Mr. Apples, too big for the door, stood guard outside.

Mabbot offered a live pheasant in the sack, which I realized was the very one I had been planning to stuff for Sunday's dinner. I was about to object when Mabbot, via the translator, addressed the old woman: "Thank you for seeing me again. I'm sorry, but we have no chicken. Will this do?"

The crone reached into the sack and removed the pitiful bird, which had molted in its agitation.

Mabbot laid a large map of the South China Sea upon the dirt floor of the hut and weighed its corners with stones. She also gave the old woman a gold coin.

Mabbot pointed to the Macanese island of Coloane. "Is the man I'm looking for there?"

The crone shooed us until we had pressed ourselves against the walls of the hut, then she sat before the map. Holding the pheasant upside down, she rocked with her eyes closed, muttering to herself. The pheasant became quiet and closed its eyes as well.

Then she twisted the head of the bird cleanly off and let it run in blind circles, leaving a wet calligraphy upon the map. It hit the wall of the hut between my legs, where it loosed its bowels and finally collapsed.

What had I expected, on an outing with pirates, than to witness a satanic ritual?

The old woman threw slivers of etched

bone across the map, and then she and Mabbot consulted it.

The witch placed a curled nail on the island that was now bracketed between a bone and an arc of blood.

"Is he telling the truth?" asked Mabbot. "Is he there now?"

"He is waiting for you. He is there, but not telling the truth."

"The man doesn't wait. Where will he go next?"

"He will wait. But it is *rất nguy hiểm*. . . very dangerous." The witch picked up a bone and tapped the markings on it. "This is bad."

Friday, October 22

Last night my slumber was traded wholesale for a series of upsetting events.

With the witch's bloody warnings tainting our course, the *Rose* is finally en route to the rendezvous with the Fox, moving relentlessly through the pitch toward Macau. As if Laroche and the naval patrols were not enough to make me long for English shores, our own crew, it seems, is now more dangerous than ever.

In the deep of the night I was getting the only sleep I would get, worn out from the walk to the witch's hut, when I became aware of a figure in my cell. At first I thought it a dream, but after a period I was convinced that a person was indeed standing near the door watching me as I slept. When I reached for a candle, Mabbot said, "Good, then, you're awake. I'm not the only one who can't sleep on a night like this."

I had no idea what kind of night she meant; in my cell, nights were much the same. I was groping for a match to light the candle when Mabbot, without hesitation, sat upon me in my hammock, forcing me to make room for her. Wine from the bottle she was wielding sloshed upon my face. She said nothing, just sat there with her back to me and her legs dangling over the edge, leaving me in a most awkward position. After a time I heard that she was weeping quietly.

"My boy," she whispered, "my Leighton!"

Completely unnerved by this scenario, I resorted to a tactic most common in prey animals: I froze and hoped to be forgotten. Eventually, though, Mabbot lay down in the hammock with me and passed out completely.

Her snoring filled the darkness and I squirmed to extract myself without waking her, no small feat, as she had left little room between me and the wall. When I had finally untangled myself and confirmed that she was still asleep, I strapped on my peg and left the chamber in nothing but the stained canvas sack I used as a nightshirt, quite unsure of my plans.

One may accuse me of protesting too much, and no doubt, under different circumstances, I may have taken time to be tempted by base motives with a woman thus undone in my bed. I was all too aware, though, that Mabbot is no milkmaid. Those who trifle with her tend to meet dramatic ends.

Unable to think of any other option, I made my way across the chilly moonlit deck to the officers' berth, a narrow chamber on the starboard side of Mabbot's cabin where the twins and Mr. Apples slept. I rapped upon the door.

I stood at some distance from the berth with my hands up, trying to appear as unthreatening as possible. When Feng answered, I said, "The captain is . . . indisposed . . . in my cell. Please help me."

Very soon we had made it back to my room, where the twins tsked and muttered while lifting the captain from my hammock.

This confusing development would have been enough to keep me sleepless for the rest of the evening, but, as it turned out, we weren't the only ones awake. As the twins carried Mabbot through the purgatory lamplight of the lower deck, an explosion shook the air. The clamor woke even Mabbot, who blinked in horror at what we saw as we emerged above deck: the steerage blooming with flame.

As every hand crowded the decks in confusion and Mr. Apples called for buckets to quench the flames, it became clear that we were not under attack; the moon was bright and the only thing upon the water with us was the dark line of the Cochin China coast. It could mean but one thing: a saboteur was among us.

Someone had pilfered a cask of black powder and set it off just below the wheel. By luck the helmsman was resting in his cot and relatively unharmed, but the wheel itself had fallen through the deck and was in shambles. Only by a swift bucket line was the conflagration smothered.

When one has been a long time upon the sea, one would rather see blood hemorrhaging from one's own navel than to see a hole in the deck. Men worked in shifts to jury the rudder, holding their breath as best they could through the smoke.

Mabbot refused to go to her cabin and, somewhat sobered, brought her great stuffed chair to the deck and said, "If aught has a fight to pick with me, best they do it here in public, like men."

Trying to stay out of the way of the sailors rushing fore and aft, I crouched behind Mabbot's chair. In a brief respite between shouting orders, Mr. Apples and Mabbot conferred in hoarse whispers.

"We're close enough for someone to row back to shore," said Mr. Apples, "but all boats are accounted for, Captain."

"If the powder room itself had gone up, we would have sunk in minutes. No, this saboteur wants only to cripple us. Give Laroche time to find us. Someone wants to switch sides. How is it, Mr. Apples, that one of my own men is vying for the bounty on my head?"

"I can't see it, Captain. If anything, they love you too much."

"Then why is there a hole in my bloody deck?"

"Maybe this one." Mr. Apples jerked his thumb at me, without so much as a wink. He was never one for subtlety.

"Wedge didn't do this tonight," Mabbot said. "I know that much."

Mr. Apples went back to herding the crew. Happily, the rudder had survived intact, and while a new wheel was being built, the helmsman could shout his orders to those who steered below by leaning into the tiller like half a dozen mill mules.

The hole in the deck might have proved calamitous if not for the skillful and swift repair by Kitzu and his gang, who patched it with boards and rags soaked in pitch. Soon I was drafted to help lathe planks for a proper repair.

It was a glorious sunrise — strata of silver and pink, like an abalone shell held over the earth — and we worked right through it. As a result, my back is seized and my hands are stiff as antlers. Some portion of the booty looted from the *Patience* has reportedly been destroyed by the blast and water damage, though I haven't had time to assess this for myself. I assume the tea and tobacco is most vulnerable, followed by the silk.

So there is a traitor aboard. Naturally gossip pollinated every ear as we worked, and the theories were varied and convoluted. Some suggested that the saboteur was a spy for Laroche, which might explain how *La Colette* has tracked Mabbot so efficiently. Opponents of this view argued that such a spy would have to leave communiqués at port, which would require Laroche to know our course in advance, or to have messengers ready at every harbor in the hemisphere. Many assume that Pendleton, once they learned of Ramsey's murder, will have doubled or tripled the bounty on Mabbot's head, and no one has come closer to claiming it than Laroche. Some argued that the saboteur was trying to capitalize on the prize before Laroche could. This plan would require delivery of the *Rose* to the Royal Navy, which would mean that naval ships were near. The simplest and most logical theory was the one Mabbot had already hinted at: the saboteur hoped to slow us long enough to defect to Laroche's crew, changing the bet in the middle of the game.

Mr. Apples, who had been bellowing orders with the demeanor of a bee-stung bull, finally ended the gossip with a threat. "So much whispering! The one thing we know about saboteurs," he said, "is that they love to whisper."

18
LOST TREASURES
IN WHICH I AM MISUNDERSTOOD

Friday, Later

After a late and tense breakfast, Mabbot spoke from the quarterdeck to all hands.

"What a calamity, a blow struck from behind! But what the powder has done to the hull, we must not allow done to our spirit. Speculate you may, whisper you will, but you shall not accuse a fellow without reason and proof. We are a fine crew, the finest upon the sea, and we are so because we are a family. Well, that, and because we are so very good-looking!" This goaded a begrudging chuckle from the crew. "We will not allow a worm to defile our trust! Be vigilant for the saboteur, but more, be vigilant against idle gossip. Only as a family do we survive. Bind yourselves together. Do not be alone. The rotten kernel will float to the top!"

She paused a breath before issuing the law: "Who gossips maliciously receives ten lashes! Who accuses without proof loses an ear! Those who do not have ears left to lose shall lose a toe, Charlie." There was more laughter at this as all looked at Charlie, who had already lost both his ears in melees. "But if you bring me true proof to identify the traitor, you will win this purse." She hoisted a leather sack and let it dangle in the air. "Ten gold!"

This she tied to a spike hammered to the mizzenmast.

Someone is no longer Mabbot's loyal soldier, no doubt spent by this endless and costly pursuit of a shadow. Isn't Mabbot herself showing signs of weariness, for what was that episode in my chamber? So much grief is tangled in the Fox's tail.

It is hard to articulate how profoundly my emotions are crossed by these recent events. To have a villain among us who would see us drown or blown to bits is discouraging, to put it mildly. On the other hand, this same shadowy figure may be my best ally, for through him I might find a path to rescue. But how to align myself with such skullduggery without getting myself killed? It is all very confusing.

I have spent hours imagining the mind of the saboteur and have concluded that he must have plans of escape. If there is indeed a way to take one of the longboats, perhaps in the dark of the night, and meet up with agents of the Crown, or even France, I should very much like to be on that boat with him. But if the plan is as poorly worked out as Jeroboam's, well, such a situation has no appeal, for it is my chief desire to place my good foot upon solid earth as a free man once again, not to burn and drown as a result of some disgruntled sailor's sudden suicidal machinations. If only I could find a way to know his intentions. But here I must tread very lightly indeed.

Saturday, October 23
We have, each of us, lost much.

The sabotage of the steerage had us stalled for half a day before we were on our way again at three-quarter speed, Mabbot assuring us we would put to land and make repairs as soon we reached the Paracel Islands, which lay just days ahead on our course toward Macau.

We had not been sailing an hour, though, when the bells rang out and all hands went to the deck.

Laroche's balloon was again above us.

Conrad passed me on the deck. "Smoke from the fire brought him to us, and nowhere to run," he groaned.

"Aye," Mr. Apples said. "From that balloon he'll have seen us right off. We stick out like a cock in the cloister."

Mabbot conferred with Mr. Apples, and soon the orders went out through the booming horns: *"Jettison all cargo! Everything but provisions!"*

When this order was met with some hemming and hawing from the men, Mabbot disappeared into her cabin and emerged with a heavy chest. Behind her the twins brought stacks of her books and cases of fine wines.

As all took heed, Mabbot kicked the chest at her feet.

"Today we must buy our wind. These are my personal jewels!" she shouted, opening the gilt-inlaid case to show them. "Pearls, lapis lazuli, gold. And these, my books, which you know are the jewels of my heart. And this, my wine, which is too good for you scoundrels!" This brought nervous chuckles. Mabbot, with no further ceremony, threw the case of jewels overboard as the men watched; the box tumbled in the air and sent the treasure in a sunlit arc before disappearing into the pea-soup sea. The twins pitched out her books and wine. She said, "There will be a time to meet Laroche in battle, but for now we put our hope in speed. The greedy wolf gets shot. We must be swift. We love our silver but consider this: What would you pay for your life?"

Her sacrifice had motivated them. "A penny for life!" Mabbot shouted, and they responded as one, "A penny!"

Then the men drew from the various holds their hard-won hauls. Tons of silver and silk were thrown over the rails. Strong and brave men wept as the eager waves devoured it all without a trace.

"We will have it again!" Mabbot shouted. "We will earn it back and more!"

Thus the entire plunder of the *Patience* went to the bottom.

The men even tore the stove from my galley and pitched it into the foam. My heart ached considerably then, for the stove had great use here upon the sea, while silver had none.

A young sailor was caught pocketing a brick of silver, and I hid in my room as he was bound to the mainmast, stripped naked, and flogged thrice for every ounce of metal. Even as I write this, I can hear him cry out. At least it isn't theater paint.

Of the magnificent treasure this ship carried yesterday, only the little purse of ten gold pieces tacked to the mizzen remains.

Thus purged, the *Flying Rose* lived up to her name and cut through the water with, as Mr. Apples put it, "foam between her teeth," leaving behind that ominous balloon, which leered at us like a swollen eye until cloud and distance finally erased it from the face of heaven.

To calm my thoughts, I racked the frothy pineapple-banana cider today as best I could and bottled it, securing the corks with cord and wax. A quick taste told me it would not be aged enough by Sunday.

As Mabbot has sacrificed her personal cache of wine, I have undertaken to give our next meal as much support as possible in the form of a simple but refreshing beverage. I boiled the fresh ginger along with lime juice and what little zest I could scrape from the ossified lime skins. To this I added honey and the few precious anise seeds, then took it off the heat and strained it. While it was still warm, I added small pills of yeast batter and covered it to let it come alive.

To throw my lot in with an unknown saboteur or to retain an allegiance of apathy with my own captors? This is the puzzle that has kept me awake all night. It is a wonder that the planks of my cell have withstood my clip-clop pacing; any softer stuff would have worn through as I tread hither and yon over the arguments. How strange to admit that I feel safer siding with Mabbot than with someone who may very well be an agent of the Crown. Safety, though, is for lapdogs. Yet such a saboteur could just as well be working only for himself, or for a cabal of outlaws depraved enough to make Mabbot look like Mary. These are the racquets that have been batting my shuttlecock mind about.

I am writing here to cement my decision: let this be a contract with myself — to action! If I am to die, I would rather it be in pursuit of freedom than in a coward's sloth. I will try to make myself known to the saboteur. To do this risks exposure, and, ironically, I rely on Mabbot's word for my safety, for while I may make myself suspicious, I trust her crew not to accuse me without sufficient proof.

Saturday, Later
Tonight in the berths, for the purposes described above, I stood, as I sometimes do, to offer grace and instead made this encrypted speech: "Lord bless this food and bless us together and each alone, for together with You is a joy while to be alone is

a terrible thing, indeed. Not alone should a man wrestle with the order of things but in league with friends; one may take great comfort though he be surrounded by unkindness. Whoso is alone among us, let him find friends."

It was obscure, to be sure, but it is a dangerous game I am playing, and my safety lies in prudence. My goal was to communicate to one by dissembling to all. Immediately upon sitting, though, I was beset by doubt. I could just have easily broadcast my traitorous tendency to all while missing the one. My mind became a stewpot of worry. Fears rolled, steaming, to the surface only to drop back under before I could fork them.

I was prepared, in case the hidden saboteur did not catch my meaning right away, to find some other means of making my intentions known. I was surprised when, immediately after the meal, I was approached by a thin seaman named Gimbal. Gimbal looked at me with portents and put his finger upon his nose and indicated that I should follow him into the companionway, where he whispered that I was to meet him two days hence, at the foremast, at midnight.

■ ■ ■

Monday, October 25

I am full of bats and starlings about meeting with Gimbal tonight.

To pass the time I set myself, these last days, to the task of Mabbot's weekly feast, which, without the proper stove, was an exercise in prestidigitation.

It may be that Mabbot's cold threat has ebbed. If I failed in my duties, would my life really be forfeit? Yet I find myself continuing the pursuit of flavor for the sake of my own sanity. It calms my soul. If I lost this vocation, I might die by my own hand. Therefore I continue to re-create the progress of culinary history with wads of dough as a boy re-creates epic battles using only twigs and stones.

To compound the loss of the stove, Kitzu's catch yesterday was meager. The man can be forgiven, for if this ship floats it is thanks to his ceaseless hammering; the steerage is nearly fixed, though the wheel has yet to be lashed to the rudder. Kitzu reserved for himself a handful of small silver fish and left for me the roe, two squid the length of my forearm, and nothing else.

Joshua cleaned and grilled the squid while

I started on the white-bean and onion soup, a comfort made possible by the last of the basil and the surprisingly tender salted pork provided by the babirusa.

Meanwhile, we simmered crushed pineapple to a near jelly. Finally, Joshua sliced a mango as thinly as the knife would allow, while I improvised a cornmeal-and-flour biscuit dough and rolled it out.

I dressed again for my weekly date with Mad Hannah Mabbot, the Shark of the Indian Ocean, wishing I had more than one pair of this dead man's trousers.

Mabbot too had a limited selection, for when I arrived, she wore the same gown. Her pearl necklace had been lost to the sea.

We sat in silence for a moment before I complained, "I was on my hands and knees for two hours today, trying to coax the heaps of coals into a manageable pile without burning the ship to the waterline."

"You've made a worthy sacrifice," she said. "We all have. The men will be bitter for having lost their silver, though it saved their lives. It is a complicated thing. With money in their pockets, they become lazy and contrary. Heavy and slow, as does the *Rose* herself." Under her breath, she continued: "A small part of me is glad to be rid of it. When my men are hungry, with death upon their heels, they work hard and never complain and enjoy their own company. They sing every night."

"But did the stove really need to go? How much difference —"

"The stove was destined for the bottom, Wedge. We merely contrived not to have the ship go with it."

"You'll taste the difference."

"I have come to trust your genius. Show me."

"Grilled squid and green-mango salad with cilantro, mint, and a pinch of cayenne," I announced, lifting the cover to reveal the meal. "White bean soup à la babirusa, garnished with pilchard roe, and, to finish, pineapple cobbler."

"You see?" Mabbot said, kissing my forehead. "You're unstoppable."

The early evening was spent in a very pleasant fashion with heavy attention to the feast. When we could not eat another bite, I popped open a bottle of ginger beer, which made quite a mess, gushing as it did. There is little alcohol in it, but its effervescence finished the evening perfectly. I'm emboldened by the success of my ad hoc yeast, and it has given me hope for the banana cider. I was so content with things that I felt brave enough to pose a question: "If the Pendleton Company is busy flooding China with opium, who is delivering afternoon tea to the civilized world?"

"It's a fancy piece of finance," Mabbot answered. "The ships arrive empty; not a single shilling comes from English coffers. The Pendleton Company buys tea on credit, sells slave-grown opium to eliminate that credit with a substantial profit in addition, then heads home with ships full of tea, silk, and silver."

"I thought China allowed trade only through Canton."

Mabbot laid out a map of the South China shore and pointed to an imperial-looking structure. "For the sake of the tea trade, China allows Pendleton to occupy this little patch of land at the mouth of the Pearl River. Every cup of tea you have ever had was a once a leaf under that roof. The Chinese call it the Barbarian House. It's a warehouse, a fortress, an embassy, an outpost, and a front for the biggest criminal operation in history. It is the reason England is rich while the rest of Europe is planting in salted fields. You know, Wedge, you're positively handsome when you're not being a boor!"

I saw her point. Or rather, I believed her. I had heard of the opium trade, but I had no idea it was the foundation of the Oriental shipping industry, let alone the reason for the English presence in India. Our little interview was proceeding with an uncommon courtesy. I have to admit that there is a certain thrill in seeing the world through Mabbot's unflinching eyes. I had not known secrets this large could be kept.

I pushed on. "But if China knows the Pendleton Company is smuggling opium, why do they tolerate it?"

"England's navy could strangle them in a matter of weeks. It's all China can do to keep them restricted to the Barbarian House. All of the Pendleton officials this side of the world live there in lavish quarters above the warehouses, fat and happy. After five years a young officer can return to England wealthy enough to buy a duchy. But I'm sure Ramsey told you that."

I ignored the barb. "I'd thought you'd have attacked the Barbarian House by now."

"It is a heavily guarded harbor. I could never get close enough."

"Yet the Fox manages."

"Braga tells us he dug an elaborate system of tunnels at the mouth of the Pearl River. Braga helped design them but says they braid together with natural caves, a labyrinth of pits and slick slopes. He says the rug map is the key to navigating them."

"Can't Braga be your guide in Macau?"

"The tunnels are for smuggling into Canton. The Fox's lair in Macau is far enough from Canton to hide but close enough to sneak back in when he needs to. Braga claims to know nothing of it."

"Are we really going all the way to Portuguese China?"

"Pish, Macau is right around the corner, a few hundred nautical miles."

Here I reached for an itch only to find myself scratching the peg. "The frustrations of a phantasmal foot," I said.

It may be rare, but Mabbot laughs like spring itself. She's shown great tact about my peg. Moreover, much to my relief, she has not yet mentioned having visited my chamber three nights ago. If not for the twins' witnessing it, I might believe I had dreamed the encounter. For all I know, Mabbot does not recall it. I certainly do. The event has played out regularly, in various permutations, in my fancies since.

Tuesday, October 26, Early Morning
Judging the passage of time as best I could by the moonlight sweeping across the narrow porthole, I made to exit my chamber at midnight.

371

Thus, agitated and mistrusting, I met Gimbal at the fore and followed him, without a word, down the starboard stairs into the bowels of the ship. On the way he said, "You're late. Anyway, hurry on, we'll be glad for a new face."

"We? There are more?"

"Oh, yes. Half the boat, one time or another, has come to our meetings."

Before I had time to weigh the wisdom of joining a full-blown mutiny, we arrived at the door of a damp hold used to store empty barrels and crates. When the door was opened and my eyes adjusted to the dim light of the lanterns, I saw a most salacious scene, one that might have leaped from Bosch's canvas. Ten men or more lolled upon heaps of burlap in a concupiscent tangle. I saw then why so many of the crew winked obscenely when certain rope knots were mentioned: Wasn't I seeing here the monkey fist, the slippery Spaniard, and the ten-fingered glove? Such a heap of blasphemy it was that I could scarce tell whose limbs were whose; rather, they seemed to be one beast, reeking of the body's own sea-foam.

Someone shouted, "Need a seat, Spoons? There's room on my lap!"

There is, no doubt, a proper and Christian response to such an offer, but I was so shocked that my only thought was to excuse myself as quickly as possible. "Ah yes, right! Do go on without me. I have a sudden case of the shits." With that I turned and fled to my chamber and spent the rest of the evening watching the door.

If the sight of those actions aroused in me certain unwanted pressures, it is only because I have long been sequestered in this unholy environment with no friends but these. The kerchief is not lifted clean from the gutter.

Wednesday, October 27

Despite the watch and the unease that saturates this ship, the saboteur managed to strike again last night. This time the fire, fed by oil, considerably compromised the port holds of the lower deck, not far from my own chamber. These holds, being recently emptied, held little of value, but Mr. Apples says the starboard hull is sprung not far above the waterline. We now have no choice but to find timber on the Paracel Islands, which the crew is loath to do for fear that Laroche may trap us in the harbors there.

At noon, Mabbot tacked a piece of wood next to the purse already dangling from the mizzen. She read the inscription aloud:

"Two full shares of our next haul! And for the saboteur, theater paint!" At this, a roar went up.

The folly of early Tuesday morning has taught me that one must not trust in hidden messages for communication. If I have hope of finding the saboteur, it will be through vigilance and keen perception. In this I am no better suited than anyone else. All persons have become suspects. He will be difficult to find, for the entire ship is after him, and if he has even the brains of a crumpet, the man will not make the mistake of announcing himself.

Everything has become so confused. I despise this saboteur despite his being perhaps my only true ally. I find myself fantasizing of bringing him to Mabbot for punishment. I am on a steep slope indeed. If I escape, it will be to peril, and unwritten pages, but they will be, at least, my pages. Better to die in the attempt (I tell myself again and again) than to live a hundred years as a captive or, worse, a pirate. I will have my life back, bereft as it may be.

As for my oath to bring Mabbot to justice at any cost, well, those words were written long ago, it seems. Boiled long enough, even garlic loses its bite, and I have been so thoroughly boiled. These scribbles indict

not Mabbot so much as the entire filthy
world.

19

THE CULINARY USES OF A CANNONBALL

IN WHICH TRUST IS BETRAYED

Friday, October 29

Today we've set anchor off the shores of the western Paracel Islands, which are scattered crescents of sand and palms, like the crumbs left from God's earth-making. The men shuttled across the shallows in the longboats to cut timber for Kitzu's repairs. The atmosphere among the crew has grown quite sour, and twice Mr. Apples was obliged to stop quarrels himself, lest they spread into riots. The men pop and spit like fritters in oil.

To my benefit, they were all so distracted that they took no notice of me as I made my way around the ship making preparations for departure. It was clear I would have to swim, but that has always been a strength of mine, and, this time, the sea was warm and calm. Even with my attenuated figure, I was sure I could do it. I had spotted a series of fishing villages along the coast that, by my estimation, could be hiked or paddled to in half a day.

As this was unfamiliar land, full of natives and who knows what kind of savagery, I decided that, in addition to my usual bag of figs and water, I must bring with me a pistol, dry and with enough shot to defend myself or, if needs be, hunt small game in the eventuality that I am stranded longer than I'd like.

I had made my way to the gun room, where I knew a number of pistols to be in lockers. To be sure no one saw me, I ducked in quickly. After letting my eyes adjust to the dimness, I jumped with fright when I saw three figures, Feng, Bai, and Asher, huddled in a conspiratorial nature.

I had clearly walked into a secret meeting, and they were not pleased.

Bai leaped to his feet. "You were listening?"

"Listening? No. I heard nothing."

He tapped my chest with his finger and said, "You heard nothing." It was no longer a question.

I was then escorted back to my cell and locked in.

Friday, Later
An hour later I used my spoon key to free

myself and make my way to the deck again. To give Bai the impression that I had been freed legitimately, I lingered awhile near Mr. Apples who, along with the bosun, was orchestrating the stowing of freshly hewn planks. I was not able to regain my previous freedom of movement. Everywhere I went, Bai, or the captain, or Mr. Apples seemed to be near. Even if I could get clear enough of them and leap into the water without provisions to take my chances unarmed, then surely the boats that were forever going to and from the shore with lumber would see my splashing. A cowardly part of me smiled inwardly — I would have to remain safely aboard the *Rose*. I circled the deck, cursing myself.

But ho, what have I seen?

I have been so confounded by my craven relief at not having to swim to those dusky sands that, until I began this entry, I had not properly considered what I had witnessed in the weapon room. Was it not a clandestine meeting of saboteurs? No doubt the insidious twins have decided to sell Mabbot for the prize and take the *Rose* for themselves.

I must admit I am disappointed and frankly frightened, as I know I can never be in league with those two. Even Mr. Apples seems to like me more than they do. Further, if they succeed in any form of mutiny, I am sure I'll be cast into the sea or set adrift or simply executed on my knees. This is a rebellion I can neither join nor survive.

Saturday, October 30

Today Mabbot sentenced eight sailors for "gambling, untimely inebriation, and maligning one another's mothers." In punishment the men were attached by the hip to lines and hung over the rail to chip the hull clean with chisels. If I had understood the gravity of the punishment, I would not have complicated it by requesting that Mabbot include in her sentence that the men return with whatever mussels they should find. The rest of the crew agreed it was a fair and fitting punishment, as the men had been witnessed drinking well before their watch was over. It might have been dealt with swiftly by Mr. Apples if their play had not escalated into a brawl. This, Mabbot would have to make an example of. She stated, "We do not fight among ourselves."

The severity of the penalty was made clear to me only when the men were allowed, after several hours, to return to the deck, bleeding from hundreds of gashes. At first I thought they had attacked one another with their chisels, but their wounds, I came to understand, resulted from being buffeted against the razor-sharp barnacles of the hull. When one man fainted, Mabbot ordered the other seven to tend to him. He was revived only after much massage and attention. The eight sat wrapped in blankets and huddled together for warmth, while Mabbot addressed them: "We're friends now, aren't we?"

"Yes, Captain," they groaned as one.

"And all of us well-bred?"

"Yes, Captain."

"Good, then. Get back to work."

Such is the strange justice upon the ship. In any case, the sailors' suffering won me a bucket of mussels for tomorrow's meal.

Sunday, October 31

Curry intimidates me.

Ramsey had acquired the taste from his early trips to the tea plantations and tended to request it when his guests included young women; it is no secret that his lordship enjoyed a bachelor's privilege. At such meals, Ramsey was inordinately garrulous, and his story of hunting a tiger never failed to elicit gasps from his audience. It was no different from any hunter's tale; a man-eater had managed to circle around and leap upon our hero from behind. When the animal breathed its last, the guests would applaud and Ramsey would bow.

My own performance was never as satisfactory. The guests didn't know how curry should taste, and so I wasn't as concerned with their reaction as I was with Ramsey's, who would let me know the morning after that the curry was "not quite the thing, I'm afraid." Like the naturalists drawing fabulous creatures based on hearsay, I was trying to perfect a dish based on a tea merchant's romanticized travels. Cumin and turmeric, chili and ginger, any one of these in the wrong proportion can ruin a dish, and with all of them fighting it out, I was lucky to do as well as I did. Looking back now, I wonder if my attempts weren't corrupted by the boorish associations I had with the dish. It was rare to see the braggart and playboy side of Ramsey, but I particularly disliked it.

His tale never failed to end with the rather breathless description of the felled beast itself: "The pelt which had been dusted with a hundred Oriental spices in the fields, the tongue which had lapped at the bones of a hundred coolies, eyes which had seen ten thousand sunsets. At the last moment I hesitated, but the ghosts of his prey called to me, saying, 'Avenge us!' I took aim and fulfilled my duty."

It's no wonder I couldn't get it right; I hadn't really wanted to.

This morning I woke early to try again. There is no excuse not to; I never had spices half as fresh as those that Mabbot gave me, which sing even from their closed box.

A few of these were not ground, and I set to the task of rolling the cannonball over them. The missile serves for a pestle almost as well as it did for a rolling pin. If I ever work in a proper kitchen again, I may have to bring one along.

As if woken by the smell, Joshua arrived to help me, and soon we had freshly powdered cinnamon, mustard, and cloves to mix with the turmeric, cayenne, cumin, and ginger; curry is a multifarious potion.

As the cinnamon broke under the cannonball, it struck me that all I had to do was follow that one note, and it would show me where to go. We built it pinch by pinch and took turns sniffing at the pile, debating whether to sharpen it with a touch more mustard or anchor it with cumin. When we lost the cinnamon's hum, we knew we had gone too far and had to turn back. This was no dead tiger. We were creating, we decided, a fabulous tree, and when we were done, we could smell cumin's muddy roots, the callused bark of mustard, the pulsing sap of the turmeric, all the way up to the sunlit blossoms of cinnamon.

Such a rich dish demanded a bright counterpoint, and the papaya was just the thing. It was not quite ripe and so had the satisfactory crunch of a cucumber. The black seeds glistened like roe in its womb, and though Joshua didn't like the smell of it, he was willing nevertheless to julienne the fruit and toss it with lime and a touch of honey. As the babirusa had been curing for such a short time, the flesh was very supple, and the thinnest slices, almost translucently pink, were reminiscent of a mild prosciutto. These streamers we tossed until they entwined sensually with the marinated papaya.

I must say that I'm delighted with the simple elegance of rice steamed with lemongrass.

Wishing to preserve the tenderness of the mussels, we saved the curry until just before serving. The powdered spices were roasted dry for a few minutes to release their perfume, then combined with a little lard and shredded coconut meat. Anchovies and miso provided a savory foundation for the sauce. We simmered the mussels in ginger beer, and just as they opened and released their brine, we combined all into a steaming archipelago.

To my dismay, Bai was lingering in Mabbot's cabin when I arrived.

Unsettled, I presented the meal immediately: "Green papaya and babirusa salad, curried mussels over lemongrass rice, garnished with a bouquet of cilantro."

"Good, then!" Mabbot said. "Damn ceremony, let's eat."

When Bai left to fetch hay for the rabbit, I leaned in to whisper, "Captain, I'll say it straight: the twins are the saboteurs."

Mabbot turned grave. "This is serious," she said. "Do you have proof?"

"Indeed. I saw them with Asher having a secret meeting in the munitions room. Quite clandestine."

Mabbot took my hand and, checking to see that we were still alone, said with gravity, "My God, but how can it be?"

"I know it must come as a shock —"

"It is indeed a shock that you don't know what proof is." She cracked a smile. "Such a simple word. Even a child knows the definition of 'proof.' Didn't you hear my conditions? If you accuse without evidence, you lose an ear. I'll excuse it this time only because you already lost your hoof."

"But what proof would satisfy you? You ask too much!"

"I know that."

"Then why?" I demanded.

"Now the crew is watching, waiting. They will police one another, and that will make the saboteur's job difficult until I find out who it is. Meanwhile we won't execute an innocent only to have the saboteur emboldened."

"But I've just told you —"

Here I was interrupted by Bai, who came in with a bundle of dried alfalfa for the rabbit. He pretended not to hear, but I was sure he knew what I was up to. I will be lucky not to be slain in my sleep. When he strolled out again, Mabbot whispered, "How do you know *I* am not the saboteur?"

"What nonsense —"

"Is it? A saboteur brings them under my skirts. Not that they're prone to mutiny. These are good men who love me as they can. But this last year has been a hard one. I have spent much of our winnings on my hunt. Incidents like this tend to draw out the discontent as the leech draws out the bad blood. Now, though, with a devil aboard, the men are neither bored, nor listless, nor rich, nor fat, which upon a pirate ship are hardly benign traits. Left too long, those qualities can lead to discontent and indeed sabotage!" She laughed so hard the tea splashed from her cup and the rabbit came to lap at it.

"Your stubbornness will get us both killed," I hissed.

"I'm not only stubborn, Wedge," she said, "I am also captain of this ship and all that happens upon it."

A note: The pineapple-banana cider is good enough for a pirate ship. It would be excellent if I had a proper champagne yeast and not this tin of dough I carry around on me. Still, even though it is more sour than one would like, the fruit essence fills the nose and calls to mind the sun-dappled island beaches, which is enough to lighten the spirits.

Tuesday, November 2
We took another Pendleton ship today: Captain Wesley's East Indiaman the *Trinity,* freshly provisioned and not two weeks into her journey home.

This time the engagement was bloody from the first, as the venerable trading vessel had few guns of her own but was escorted by two smaller gunships, each quick to turn and bristling with cannon.

These hardly deterred Mabbot. She dove right in, seeming to relish the challenge. Our men cheered when she ordered the battle flag raised, a black field with a white hourglass, signaling to our enemies that their time had come.

Our opening shot landed near enough to wet the sails of the first warship. When it gave chase, we fled; Mabbot herself took the wheel. Our pursuer covered the distance alarmingly. We skated a mile east, but in minutes the ship had halved our lead. This was what Mabbot wanted.

She sang out, "Twa Corbies!" and the crew cheered. The gunship was maneuvering to seize our wind and bring its starboard guns in line for a broadside when our two stern cannon roared. The missiles knocked a hole in the gunship's breast large enough for men to spill from it like seeds. This, then, was the purpose of the *Rose*'s reinforced aft and the heavy long-range cannon mounted there: to send devastation into a pursuing ship. Our foe listed and her sails cupped the waves.

We made another pass at the stationary Pendleton ship, but the second escort would not leave the *Trinity*'s side. "Wear about and ramming speed!" Mabbot called, and soon we were racing with our bowsprit aimed to pierce the cow-belly of the *Trinity*. We traded shots with the second gunship as we approached, and our fore topgallant was splintered by a lucky ball. At the last minute we veered off course, missing the *Trinity* by meters and putting the fat ship between us and the gunship as an impromptu shield. At our closest, three of Mabbot's Sandwich Islanders dove into the sea between the ships, belts fastened with air bladders and waxed sacks of tools and petards.

During the ensuing calamity, we spotted the airy course of a homing pigeon, rising from the *Trinity* like hope made visible. It circled thrice, gaining its bearings, before setting off north. Mabbot screamed, "Apples! Apples! Apples!" I was watching the flight with tremendous envy when Mr. Apples's rifle sounded and the distant bird tumbled to the sea.

Sailors on the deck of the *Trinity* fired rifles and muskets while the escort moved to flank us. Our men returned fire only enough to cover for the others, who were throwing planks and lines to board the merchant ship. The swimmers, unnoticed by the enemy or too low for her guns, converged upon the gunship's prow as she approached. They clung to the hull with hooks and tacked their bombs below the waterline, bearing the onrushing sea like crabs bracing themselves in a heavy tide.

Meanwhile our crew had boarded the trading ship and, after a brief but valiant skirmish (Mr. Apples and the twins, working together, are a terrible force), captured the captain and two chief officers. These poor men were hung by their feet over the side of our ship, bellowing their outrage. The warship escort was therefore forced to fire very carefully indeed so as not to destroy the *Trinity* behind us nor the fragile bodies slung across our hull like jewelry upon a dowager.

The swimmers had made it back to the *Rose* and were climbing the jack ladders with war whoops when the petards they'd secured detonated — five muffled pops. The men on the deck of the warship went into a panic, climbing the masts as she capsized, then sank with terrifying speed.

This was the efficient malice of Mabbot's mind. From my hiding place behind the rope barrel, I saw firsthand the unnatural and cruel techniques that had allowed her to wreak havoc upon the routes for so long. While her enemies plotted approaches and speeds and angles of wind, Mabbot had already picked their pockets and poisoned their tea.

It is said that even the most powerful wrestlers may be brought to their knees by the strategic twisting of a single finger. Mabbot's enemies fell so quickly about her that they seemed eager to perish. If I hadn't seen the devious devices she employed, I would have believed, as so many do, that the woman was a demon.

It was clear to me then why Ramsey had been forced to hire the Frenchman, for only Laroche's mind matched hers for sinister twists. Knowing Mabbot's motives — even beginning to believe that they might be honorable in their way — did not make watching these skirmishes any easier.

When the shooting stopped, Mabbot, to my great relief, lowered the *Trinity*'s long-boats into the water, cut down our prisoners, and allowed the crew, officers included, to swarm into the craft. They were forced to watch from their crowded and rocking boats as we picked the *Trinity* clean.

This was a less festive event than the previous sacking, as Mabbot seemed eager to gather way. All loot was hurried through the hatches and into the holds to be inspected and sorted later.

In the bustle, the men brought to Mabbot the cage containing the remaining three

Pendleton homing pigeons. She considered them for a moment, then handed the cage to me with a twinkle in her eye, saying, "I'll know, won't I, if you misuse these?" Also recovered from the ousted captain's personal stash was a barrel of wine, a bag of almonds, an ingot of chocolate, and a pod of Brazilian vanilla beans. It seemed the man had good taste. To the sailor who had recovered these treasures, Mabbot gave half the chocolate. The wine she took for herself. The rest she gave to me.

As the crew worked, they debated what to do with the *Trinity* itself. The same discussion was being had in several places at once, and these were the several voices of the argument:

" 'Twould be a scandalous shame not to take command of such a prize, and a good chance to rid ourselves of the saboteur, for he'd likely be among them that go."

"But would ye like to sail with a skeleton crew of which the turncoat is such a large portion? And besides, such a fat wallowing ship ain't good for anything but carrying tea, and I dunno any who is ready to become a trading company."

"Could be sold at auction."

"But ye'd as like be hanged as paid for her."

By general consensus it seemed the massive ship would be scuttled once she had been picked clean.

Beset by curiosity, I made my way to the *Trinity* to look around. (Not trusting my peg, I crawled across the boarding plank, much to the delight of the rest of the crew.) I aimed to discover whether the huge vessel had a proper stove.

In fact, there was a well-provisioned galley directly adjacent to the captain's cabin containing an elegant Treadwell stove that was, alas, too hot to touch, let alone abscond with. I was looking at it dejectedly, noting that it was almost big enough to hide a man, when I was inspired to find my way to the *Trinity* crew in their longboats and throw my lot in with them. This flimsy notion was quickly rent by reality; we were in the middle of the South China Sea, and those poor souls had a grim chance of making it to any shore. Besides, I had read the accounts of desperate men resorting to cannibalism in open boats. Hard to believe I wouldn't be first choice. After all, the last time I tried to surrender myself, I lost a leg; I cherished my remaining limbs all the more for it.

The *Trinity* was an enormous vessel and the haul was commensurate. In addition to seemingly endless lockers of tea, bolts of silk, and barrels of pepper, the holds were packed to the ceiling with teak, cotton, and porcelain ware. I went to watch as the last of the booty was pulled into the light. I caught sight of the silver on the deck of the *Rose* before it was lowered into the hatches. The *Trinity* crew had melted it down into flat ingots for easy stacking, and what a stack it made; even from a distance it took my breath away. Several fortunes, naked and glinting in the sun. The soft skin of the ingots made me want to chew them between my teeth like a batch of caramel. How much opium had been sold for this shameless pile? What could it buy? A cathedral? An army?

This was Mabbot's promise to the men ratified, for they had indeed regained their sacrificed treasure and then some. The *Rose* was fat and heavy again, but Mabbot couldn't deny her crew their payment. The *Trinity* contained so much cargo, in fact, that much had to be left where it was.

There was, however, something that would not be left: our men brought from the lowest holds a parade of small dark heathens. These people, Philippine Islanders, were bound together in groups of ten, their necks clasped within long boards like communal stocks.

The heathens squinted in the light and were covered with their own filth. One woman could not reach her child, who was locked two spaces behind on the board, and yet stretched for her and moaned and wept. Even as they were led to our boat, she reached for her daughter, who was quite ill and was being fairly dragged along by the lurching of the others in a manner most unsettling.

I had seen figures from Siam and Kampu-chea washing the laundry and tending to the gardens of the gentry I had served. These were the lowest servants, to whom even the other maids rarely spoke. I swear I had not known that they were thus pro-cured, and in fact would not have believed it before today. But there was no denying it. These were the "long birds" ordered by the manifests. Whereas some were sent to dig diamonds and harvest cotton, these people were being abducted to London to carry night soil and morning water. There were close to forty of them, and a sailor called across that there were a dozen or more dead in the holds.

I had seen Lord Ramsey's signature on the manifests and could no longer pretend that he was clean of this. I felt the creaking structure of my past, riddled with holes, sink out of sight. I was again floating alone upon the empty sea without shelter or direction.

Our men led the coolies as gently as possible to our ship, with much confusion and cajoling. It was too much for me. I shinnied back to the *Flying Rose* and made for my berth, but Mabbot beckoned.

When I went to her, she merely stared at me. I tried to hold my tongue, but after a moment I blurted, "They may be better off in a Christian land. Who knows what dirt mounds these workers call home?"

"Workers." Mabbot was grim.

"Trading in slaves has been outlawed these twelve years."

"What does that say about your trading company?"

"By Christ, woman, I didn't found the Pendleton Company! I have no stock in it. Why do you hound me so?"

"I am fond of you, Wedge, can't you see that? I'm only taking you through your lessons."

"I am no schoolboy."

"Then be a man. You ask why I do what I do," Mabbot said. "But what will you do?"

I gave her my back and hurried to my chamber. Would she have me ride the seas waving a cutlass? Drink the blood of my enemies? As I paced, my wooden peg mark-

ing the passing seconds, I saw again and
again the woman reaching for her child, and
it brought me back up to the deck.

As Asher and Mr. Apples set about picking the locks of the stocks with an unsettling familiarity that pointed to much
experience, I knelt beside them and whispered, "What can I do?"

Mr. Apples didn't bother to look up from
his task. "Aren't you the cook?"

As I went to the galley, I saw that the *Trinity*
was indeed being set alight; it would be a
colossal bonfire, but I didn't pause to watch
it.

I had planned to make a simple potato
soup, but Kitzu too had been moved by the
coolies' emaciated frames and soon dropped
at my feet a writhing net of dangerous fish:
two conger eels, a banded dragonfish (whose
quills, he told me, carried a potent poison),
and a shuddering red octopus.

As I could not hope to know the captives'
tastes, I committed myself to one of the
most comforting foods I had ever known:
bouillabaisse.

When I arrived at the French monastery
where I would spend my apprenticeship, I
was weary, thin, and frankly terrified.
Without uttering a single word of greeting,
my teacher sat me down and served me

bouillabaisse. This stew is made from the most humble fishes, each added one at a time to a lusty herbed broth, thickened with potatoes, and finally topped with a spicy cream. I had become a foreigner in a hostile country, despised as an Englishman and a Jesuit, my entire life carried in a small rucksack, yet this soup filled my hollow belly and told me that I was safe.

Joshua and I filleted the dragonfish wearing the smithy's gloves to protect us from the quills. While I would have liked to have my saffron again, I found myself, for once, grateful for the ingredients on hand. Bouillabaisse is often accented with orange peel, but I realized that lemongrass made a much more substantial aroma and admirably carried the baser seasonings of dried smelt and bay leaf.

We were gathering speed again as I puttered, and I felt strangely blessed not to be on the longboats with those villains but here with these.

To make rouille is difficult enough in a proper kitchen, but without a real whisk or thickening egg yolks, I knew I had a serious challenge before me. With my steadfast cannonball mortar I powdered hardtack, adding just enough broth to produce a paste, then crushed in garlic and cayenne pepper.

With a whisk made of three forks lashed together, I whipped this paste while Joshua poured in the thinnest drizzle of olive oil until we had a hearty cream.

After the cubed potatoes had begun to soften in the broth, we added the fish, one at a time, letting the embers beneath the cauldron slowly die. To keep them from becoming too tough, the octopus tentacles, sliced into coins, went in just as the soup stopped simmering.

The rouille covered the surface with a rich sheen before spreading throughout like a fog at sunrise.

As we served the stew, I heard several of the crew complain that the coolies ate better than they did.

Two of our seamen spoke Tagalog, and they were kept busy explaining to the guests their change of fortune. While they ate, I asked Mr. Apples what would become of them.

"S'hard to say," he answered. "Villages probably burned by the Spanish, families massacred. They may take to shore the first place we anchor. Some may stay on. Some of our best men have come to us this way — Utswali, Kinsha, Blue — they were all found in chains."

I spent the rest of the day helping dress

their wounds and setting up canvas tents on the deck. It turned out that these drafty quarters were not for the slaves but for the crew. Mabbot has given the forecastle berths to the women and children for the time being and has made it known that we were going to change our course to deliver the islanders to their home. Conrad grumbled about this, about the scuttling of the *Trinity,* about how quickly we would run out of food with this many new mouths to feed — mostly I believe he was sour because he had heard the men praising my soup.

20
KILLING THE MESSENGER
IN WHICH I SEE MY ERROR

Wednesday, November 3

It has been demonstrated today that I am hopeless with knots. Even after several lessons, I am no closer to understanding their wicked convolutions. I've been trying to make myself more useful since our guests joined us, but, in a dramatic demonstration of my ineptitude, I managed to free all three stays (no easy feat) of a loose cannon as it was being transported. The cannon, weighing at least five hundred pounds, picked up speed and plowed through a barrel as easily as through fog, nearly crushing a man who saved himself only by climbing a mast like a monkey. The metal beast certainly would have killed someone if not for the swift and strong men who intercepted it with ropes and nets. I have been forbidden from touching a cannon again, and we're all more comfortable for it.

The Philippine Islanders, having been

pushed from their mountain homes by Spanish ranchers, were tricked into boarding the Pendleton ship by company men who offered to provide armaments and support to win their land back. They'd been kept in the hold for weeks as the ship waited for propitious winds. They're eager to return to the island to find their lost families. Despite their ghastly treatment, and having reason to distrust any crew, they are nevertheless some of the kindest people I have ever encountered. They break their circles to make room for me to sit and, having nothing else to offer, present their soup bowls for me to eat from. They embody the finest of Christian traits while despising the church. For the latter I blame the Spanish. I tried to remedy the situation; through a translator, I related the story of Jonah. After listening politely, they returned the favor with a story about a bird that kills by devouring a sleeper's shadow. I did my best not to be frustrated, but the rest of the afternoon was squandered on similar heathen fables.

Thursday, November 4
Bai and Feng have continued to convince me of their guilt, for I have seen them passing notes again with Asher.

With Macau so close, Mabbot is increasingly distracted and pensive. She pores over maps and takes private meetings with Braga and Mr. Apples daily, preparing for our rendezvous with the Fox. Despite many efforts, I have been unable to catch her alone. At Sunday's meal I will strive again to warn her of the twins' malevolence, for I have a sinking suspicion that it will be my last chance.

Friday, November 5

This morning, after Joshua cleaned and plucked the three pigeons, I hung them to age. I took the time to shell some walnuts and soaked the meats in ale.

Of course I considered setting one of the pigeons free with a plea for help bound to its claw, but Mabbot is smart enough to count three birds. God knows what would happen to me if she saw one in the sky rather than upon a plate. I am fully aware that to willfully kill a Pendleton pigeon is a treason against England. But the rationalizations that assert themselves are hard to gainsay:

1. The birds would have died anyway by Mabbot's command. Better they should come to some use.

2. I have had my moral fabric so tarred by

my long and complicated association with these pirates that I cannot hope to salvage myself by petty attention to the proper use of company correspondence animals.

3. My opinion of the Pendleton Company has, I have to admit, been not a little shaken, and my loyalty with it. While I do not hope to spend my life among pirates and thieves, I cannot, on the other hand, continue to give my allegiance to the trading company, nor to the Crown that funds it, for I have seen with my own eyes their atrocities.

The proper way is lost to me; my compass spins. I therefore give my entire attention to those works that seem to me incorruptible: the application of heat, the proportion of seasoning, the arrangement of a plate. When robbed of all pretensions and aspirations, with no proper home nor any knowledge of what discord tomorrow brings, I still may have a pocketful of dignity. The Roman pomp and raiment have fallen away, and I see at last the glory of washed feet and shared bread.

Saturday, November 6
In order not to draw attention to ourselves, we set anchor within sight of Palawan Island, where the wind sends the palms

swaying.

I'd seen little of the captain until we were close to the Philippines. Then she emerged to order that her personal pinnace, *Deimos,* carry the islanders to their destination. "Load it with as much food as it can carry, five pistols, shot, and gunpowder," she said.

"Shall I sail her, Captain?" Mr. Apples asked.

"They can sail, can't they?"

"But how shall we retrieve the pinnace?"

"Shan't," Mabbot said. "It's a gift."

"Captain —"

"You'll see to it, won't you, Mr. Apples?" With that she went back to her cabin and did not emerge until we were speeding again toward Macau.

The last I saw of our guests, they were reefing the sails of the pinnace, their faces stony as they gazed at the slow undulations of the palms. Between the Spanish soldiers and the predatory company, their fate is precarious, but they are determined to fight for their farms. As Mr. Apples predicted, a few male cousins have stayed on, preferring to throw their lot in with Mabbot.

Saturday, Later

I made the mistake of leaving my yeast starter in the galley while I helped Kitzu clean the crabs he had caught on a baited line during our brief anchor. I returned just in time to catch Conrad dumping the dough into a bucket of salty slop. I salvaged the poor thing by washing off the outer portions and fed it with fresh coconut water and flour. These barbarians are not to be trusted. Hereafter the yeast batter shall remain on my person no matter what.

Sunday, November 7

I woke early to grill onions and garlic for the *mole.* When I was a boy, a missionary returning from Mexico visited the orphanage and made the dark velvety sauce whose feral aroma so inflamed my young imagination that I convinced myself, somehow, that it had been made with panther's blood. When the fathers declared it too sensual for the boys, I worried I might never get to taste it and begged the missionary to share his secret with me. It was the first recipe I committed to memory, and, though it did not call for blood, it was for me a magic incantation, a litany of rare ingredients, whispered only in the deep of the night when all others were asleep. I promised myself that I would someday taste the forbidden *mole.* Unfortunately it would be years before I had the freedom to attempt it myself, and by then the recipe was barely a tattered recollection. I have tried to re-create that sauce many times since, and did not truly succeed until today.

The ever-useful cannonball crushed the chocolate and ale-soaked walnuts easily. Missing the miso, I made a quick stock from discarded crab and shrimp shells and black soy liquor. I minced grilled onions and garlic to a near paste, enjoying its caramelized breath. I would have liked a few whole chili peppers to roast but made do with powdered cayenne, black pepper, and a pinch of cinnamon. I wet two sea biscuits with just enough lard and stock to moisten them, and threw them into the pot to mingle with the other ingredients.

The pigeons I prepared by dredging them in flour and browning them in a skillet with lard and smoked babirusa ham. I then placed them in the terra-cotta pot and braised them in a little brandy before ladling in the voluptuous sauce and letting them simmer for fifteen minutes.

The wet terra-cotta mitigates burning, but braising in Conrad's hearth still requires banking red coals into a crescent and worrying over the position of the clay pot minute by minute.

The last of the potatoes went into the crab

croquettes. After grating and salting the tubers, I squeezed out as much water as I could and put the liquid aside to settle out. In half an hour the starch had precipitated. I poured off the water and stirred the starch back into the potatoes (such are the humble measures of an eggless world) along with the virginal crabmeat, black pepper, and dried cilantro and set them aside for frying.

Joshua, on his own recognizance, prepared a warm sauce to crown the croquettes. I offered suggestions for the ingredients — a shaving of Pilfered Blue, anchovies macerated in wine, etcetera — but his dark eyes sparkled when he understood that I would not be looking over his shoulder. "I'm trusting you," I told him. "Make it simple and balanced." It took an effort to keep from peering into his pot, but I remember well the first few times Father Sonora asked me to take on a soup or sauce myself. There is no replacement for the sense of accomplishment one feels at having made his own sauce; it lifts the chin.

The pleasure I took from preparing the dessert was libidinal. The vanilla and dried rosebud simmering in brandy sent waves of intoxicating aromas washing over me. When the spirits had nearly evaporated, I threw in the crushed almonds, dried coconut, and just enough honey to bind it all together.

I noticed, tonight, as I pulled her chair out for her to sit, that Mabbot is getting modestly plump. Her jaw is not as severe, and there are two lovely creases ringing her neck. It is a gentle improvement, and I cannot help but take a little credit.

She saw me looking and I hurried to my seat, embarrassed.

"Crab croquettes with *bagna cauda*," I announced. "Braised squab napped with chocolate *mole,* and, finally, vanilla-rose amaretti."

We set to it. The scents that had so inspired my cooking, just hours before, deferred temporarily to the textures of the meal. The croquettes tsked and whispered when bitten into; inside, the delicate fingers of crabmeat parted reluctantly, like lovers holding hands. The squabs were indecent in their steamy terrine. The *mole* slid off the meat and sent dark rivulets under the tongue.

After twenty minutes of nothing but pleasurable murmurings, I finally remembered the urgency of my secret. Putting my finger to my nose, I leaned close to Mabbot.

"Those twins, Captain. Something must be done."

Mabbot sighed and dropped her fork onto her plate.

I pressed on. "I saw them again, whispering very heatedly, with Asher. The three of them trying hard not to be heard. They speak Mandarin, so I cannot know what it is they were saying, but it was urgent and secret and terribly suspicious!"

Mabbot dabbed at her lips with her napkin. "This is distressing."

"I'm glad to hear you say so!"

"But, if a mutiny is afoot, why not join them, Wedge, and free yourself?"

"Bloodshed is not my way."

"More likely you figured, and rightly so, that those two would never have you in their club." She laughed, and I couldn't help but smile a little myself, so contagious was her mood.

"In all honesty, Captain, given the choice, I would far rather be your captive than theirs. But you of all people know what they are capable of. I urge you to act soon, now, this instant. Catch them by surprise. It is the only way."

"You will not let this be, will you?"

"But how can I?"

"Very well. This is not how I would have had it. Don't you know that nothing happens upon this ship but I hear it? I know their secret, Wedge, or rather, Feng's secret, for it belongs rightfully to the one and not the other. But a ship is a small world indeed, and even those two cannot have any real privacy." She took a sip of cider and sighed. "Feng is with child."

I was sure I had misheard.

"Your face!" she said. "Why so shocked? Though she moves like a fury, and though she goes as a man, nevertheless she has a heart like the rest of us. Asher is her lover, and, no doubt, they were discussing the inevitable dilemma we face when she begins to show, which will be any day now."

"But —"

"A woman, even escorted by her loyal brother, cannot go easily upon a ship of pirates. Mine is a special position and hard-earned. I was a man upon the seas for fifteen years before I showed my real face. Well, now you know. Of course, you are forbidden to tell another soul. Alas, I fear I shall be wanting new bodyguards in a few months. I don't suppose you will take up training as a pugilist?"

"But —"

"As protection, your width would make you an asset, though for that I could just as well stand behind a barrel." She laughed. "Have I hurt your feelings?"

"How can it be?"

"The Shaolin monks wouldn't teach boxing to a woman, but she had sworn revenge along with the rest of her brothers, so she became a man. I assure you, there are many of us passing in the halls of power. We are not all so content to spend our lives in the kitchen. In my early days, I shaved my head and wore breeches. There was no other way."

She must have seen me trying to remember which twin was which, for she said, "That's right, you were pummeled by a woman. Properly wrung out like Monday's laundry. But I'm sure she'll oblige if you want a rematch."

"What man strikes a woman?" I mumbled.

"Yes, of course. Present your chivalry. It is a sturdy shield."

It was finally clear to me why Feng had bullied and bruised me in the dark passages: it was in retribution for Asher's flogging! I had caused her guitar-playing lover to suffer, and she couldn't let me pass without knocking the wind out of me every time. My head in my hands, I felt laughter rise up, uncontrolled, reckless. "I surrender," I said. "You talk circles around me and I cannot hope to keep up. But then, you have the advantage, as I am bound by good manners."

She laughed too and we laughed together, and I felt something important slip from me. Once gone, I could not say exactly what it had been, only that I had been holding on to it ever since this horrible story began, as a man fallen from a cliff clings to a stalk of nettle; that bitter weed had kept me alive. Now that I had let go, I was falling and I would not be the same.

Perhaps I was feeling the effects of the cider, for I noted again Mabbot the paradoxical beauty, her bearing upright and yet relaxed, her eyes soft and sharp.

We had been looking at each other for some moments before I was properly aware of it. Suddenly anxious that she would see the admiration in my eyes, I mumbled, "Ah, I'll retire now, Captain," and felt the heat of her gaze again as I made my way to the door.

21
WOLVES AND SHEEP
IN WHICH I ATTEMPT A FINAL ESCAPE

Tuesday, November 9

We have reached, finally, Macau — a coast like shattered terra-cotta.

The ship is alive with anticipation. Word has spread that the Fox may finally be within reach, though what this means is, as always, contentious. Some say we will soon be tossing out our silk to make room for his gold, while others believe that the Fox's smuggler army will join the *Rose* to take on Laroche. The excitement is but a thin veneer over the anxiety of being in very dangerous waters; not fifty miles away is the Pearl River, where the Pendleton office sits and oversees the filling of ships with cinnamon, tea, and porcelain packed in straw. That means first-class warships roam these seas, ready to defend the heart of England's trade with China.

After sending a longboat crew to secure our landing, Mabbot set about provisioning another with maps, guns, and food for a full day's excursion. I begged to go along, citing a longing to get off the ship and feel the blessed soil beneath me. Truthfully, though, the recollection of my unfettered laughter in Mabbot's cabin and our locked eyes frightened me, and I felt I must find an opportunity to flee before I lost myself completely.

There were nearly two dozen of us: Mabbot, Mr. Apples, Mr. Braga, the twins, myself, Joshua, and a pack of Mabbot's best fighters, hungry for action. Macau was known to be a country of thieves and highwaymen; no matter who planted their flag there — Spain, China, or Portugal — the reputation for lawlessness only grew. As we rowed closer, the rust-colored hills baking in the sun and wreathed with smoky grey trees made me regret my decision to join the party. This was a landscape of caves and hidden valleys — precisely where bandits refined their craft. I asked, "Are the Portuguese sovereign here?"

"The Portuguese have no cavil with me," Mabbot said. "Neither the Dutch."

The waves fairly threw us upon a beach so rocky my peg could find no purchase. If not for Joshua's help, I would be stumbling there still. We stowed the boats under some low-hanging bushes bordering an inlet and followed the creek.

The sailors went before us, hacking through the brush with mattocks. To my relief we left the river stones behind and crested low, parched hills. Mabbot, consulting the chicken-blood map, took some time to get her bearings, and I did too. The landscape offered nothing more promising than dust devils and lurching black beetles.

"Doesn't Braga know the way?" I asked Mr. Apples.

"Braga only knows the tunnels at Pearl River. The Fox never took him here nor told him how to find it."

In the distance was a mountain with a peak shaped like a blade, and we made for it. I quickly fell behind with Joshua and Mr. Apples, who had been charged, apparently, with watching me.

Though the terrain was rough and dry, it felt good to be on land. Even the coarse weeds struggling in the cracks of the clay fostered a brotherly feeling in me. Bowing to a strange compulsion, I picked up a pebble and popped it into my mouth, sucking at it like candy. I could tell the captain felt the land-happiness too; her walk was jaunty. When she tossed her coat over her shoulder, I could not help but admire her waist tapering to flare at the hips. I tried to imagine a man to match her, a character absurd enough to marry Mad Mabbot. There could be no taming her, but at least one would not lack for humor or adventure. And too, she loved to eat.

We passed some abandoned barns whose walls had been used for bills. Glued over the rest was posted Mabbot's warrant, similar to the one we had seen on the Pendleton ships. There was a drawing of her, and, in three languages: "Cannibal Pirate Mabbot! 15 Ingot Gold Reward."

Mabbot frowned as she stared at it. "Are my eyes really so far apart?"

The poster was ripped up and we moved on.

The walk was long and I had plenty of time to chat with Mr. Apples. "I thought Portugal had no cavil with her," I said.

"That's a Pendleton poster." Mr. Apples laughed. "Lies grow wings. Truth grows bunions."

He was distracted, looking at the distant hills, no doubt worried about bounty hunters. I was glad to have him nearby.

I asked, casually, "So is this it? Will we finally find the Brass Fox?"

"Cain't say. He doesn't tend to linger, though Macau would be a sensible place to call home. Plenty of scoundrels to enlist, and the rare sheriff is easily paid off. In Macau you don't ask questions." Mr. Apples grunted, stopping for a moment to stare at some animal scat, then picked up his pace. "Even if he ain't here though, sooner or later we'll have him. He's running out of tricks and showing signs of sloppy. He's tired."

"I'll remind you that I met the man," I whispered. "I know Mabbot isn't after gold. What does she hope to accomplish?"

"Spoons, you're not half as clever as she says you are." He coughed and spat a thick wad of mucus upon the ground. "Think it through: Mabbot teaches him how to sail, how to shoot — more important, *who* to shoot. But turn around to find he's off and smuggling opium. He steals it from Pendleton and sells it to buy more smugglers and mercenaries, building his own little empire. He's become the very thing she hates, what she's given her life to fighting. If it were your child, could you just let it go? There's a hundred reasons for the captain to kill Ramsey, but what would make her risk her ship to walk in on your little feast like that?"

"She's trying to clean up the mess," I said, beginning to see it. "Undo all of her mistakes."

"But with every passing day, the Fox becomes more and more like his father. Captain thinks she can make him see it her way. Between you and me, it's too late for that. I've watched him kill fishermen and there was nothing in his eyes but fun. The man is a whetstone. Here's a better question: When it comes time, can Mabbot put an end to it?"

After making our way over a great valley of hard-packed sand, we took a break at noon under a gnarled and leaning soot tree to eat and catch our breath. There I removed my peg to massage my stump and let the pad air out. We had only started our repast of figs, dried fish, and hardtack when Mabbot set off again, kicking up dust, and we were obliged to pack up and follow.

Finally we crested a hill and entered a valley fed by a wide river. The trees here were thick and shady.

At first it looked like an avalanche site, but as we neared, the shape of the temple emerged from beneath the creeping vines and cascading boulders. The heads of the stone Buddhas had been knocked off by the vandals, who had, no doubt, dispatched the monks as well. The place was haunted by long-faced monkeys who rocked on their haunches and eyed us warily. Several of them squatted where the statue's heads had been.

Behind the temple was a low hill bestrewn with chips of brick and rotting wood, and beyond that lay a scab upon the earth — San Lazaro. Even from a distance I could tell that the town was a misbred place where we would not find any rudiment of civility. As we moved past the sun-blighted fields and ramshackle hovels of the outskirts, a pair of half-feral dogs circled our party and snarled at us, practically choking themselves on their outrage. I half hoped Mr. Apples would shoot them, but apparently Mabbot and her crew were used to such welcomes and they ignored the beasts.

San Lazaro was a model of Babel after the fall — a cacophony of cultures. The foundation of the town was crumbling cob and wattle, little more than holes of mud painted with grey lime, like something crabs might make on a riverbed. The warring empires had built over, around, and through the cob leaving a haphazard quilt of architecture and influence. Board-and-batten structures from bygone eras leaned conspiratorially against half-built Romanesque towers. A stockade, built in a hurry for a fight that ended decades ago, was occupied now by rats and muddy children who peered at us through the cracks. Several houses in a row were made of red brick, probably as officers' quarters, and now served as stables for squat spotted horses. The sour smoke of burning dung hung over the mottled rooftops. At one intersection there was a proper English house, complete with columns and shutters on the windows, but it looked as if the original owners were long gone — the entire building had been painted an oxblood brown and was bedecked with mirrors and ideograms dangling on strings from the moldings.

The people here were as varied as those on Mabbot's ship but — and I thought I'd never say this — less welcoming. Their races were impossibly muddled from generations of careless rutting.

Cackling men baked adobe bricks in the sun while, nearby, a bearded ancient offered songbirds and crickets in tiny wooden cages. A water buffalo ate lazily from a pile of filth in the middle of the street despite the whipping the boy on its back was giving it. A stooped Oriental sold skewers of blackened meat from a cart to passing ruffians.

I considered buying a basket of red melons from a street hawker when it struck me how easily one might get lost in such an environment. Here, among these thieves and rascals, was my opportunity, at last, to take my leave of Mabbot. I decided that I must approach the situation with the utmost care.

We watched an elephant, every bit as monstrous as they say, carrying a load of bricks, herded by a man with nothing but a bamboo switch. I marveled that such a powerful frame could be thus humbled. In a story, I would have leaped upon its back, and we would have bounded to our freedom together.

We passed a vacant lot where penned sheep were nosing in the dust for whiskers of dry grass. Seeing this, Mr. Apples gave a start and shouted, "Sheep! Cap'm, may I? Cap'm, with your permission?"

Mabbot sighed and said, "With speed, and mark our direction. We'll not wait." At this Mr. Apples set off looking for the shepherd.

Joshua saw my grimace and asked with his hands, "Where is Mr. Apples going?"

I tried to explain, with my limited signs, that a man, particularly a vulgar pirate, had appetites of the flesh and that, in the absence of a rightful marriage, those appetites could turn toward his fellow man or, worse, beasts. I then explained hell as best I could, though in all our lessons I hadn't learned the appropriate signs for such things. And so I made do with invented gestures and

421

the little vocabulary I had. I was at it for some time. For all of my effort, my morality lesson emerged thus: "All men body hunger bad. God becomes sad. Hot place bad, long time very hot . . ." and etcetera. Joshua gave me a look that told that he seriously doubted my sanity. Then he signed, "You need more practice."

I couldn't argue. In any case, the time to act had come. With Mabbot preoccupied and Mr. Apples having his fun, I had my first real opportunity for flight. Remembering my vow to free myself, I seized on the moment and asked Mabbot for a silver piece to buy melons. She didn't even look at me. "Take Joshua and be back with Mr. Apples or we'll leave you here." Obviously more concerned with finding the Fox than with any of my doings, she carelessly dropped three silver pieces into my palm. I pocketed them with a pounding heart. They would go a long way toward passage back to England on some merchant ship.

Feng gave me a suspicious look as I walked away but did not move to intercept me. I gave her my foulest moue and she just shook her head in disgust.

Only a minute later we had rounded a warehouse and were out of sight. My chest grew tight at the thought of liberation, and for a moment my fear was gone. I clapped Joshua over the shoulder and hurried down the alley. We found our way to the ruin of a burned cathedral. Ducking behind its only remaining wall, we finally slowed and Joshua asked, "Where are we going?"

Glorious freedom. I was shaking like an aspic and felt a rush of pleasure at being on my own for the first time in months.

"We'll just wait here for a moment," I signed.

I wandered a bit farther through a narrow passage of stone and saw what looked to be a civilized portion of San Lazaro. The sun shone on several brick houses and not a few fruit trees. In the distance a woman was hanging laundry from a line, and this simple vision of domesticity was enough to bring tears to my eyes. By the time Mabbot became suspicious, I would be hidden in a small but clean room, paying some family handsomely for my keep. Eventually the *Rose* would have to leave port, and then I would be free to find work on a civilian ship and begin my journey home.

This was it. My heart had already begun down the happy lane, but I turned to say goodbye first to Joshua. I gave him a manly slap on the back and issued a stern command: "Wait here for five minutes, then go join Mabbot." I didn't have time to explain, and I couldn't have the boy following me, so when he started to ask questions, I gave his shoulders a stiff squeeze and let him see the stern resolution in my eye. "Five minutes," I signed. "Then go find Mabbot."

My opinion of the auspicious street went sour almost as soon as I began to clump down it. The glares I got from the men on their stoops told me it would be folly to ask for shelter. The woman I had seen hanging clothes had ducked inside and slammed the door. Two thick-armed men had come out of their homes to follow me. As soon as I could, I turned back toward the main thoroughfare. I'd thought that any city would be preferable to life aboard a ship, but now I began to miss the company of our muscled crew. I went at a quick pace, looking for signs of an inn or boardinghouse where I might hide until the *Flying Rose* had left the harbor.

I found myself in a labyrinth of stinking alleys and cul-de-sacs, which forced me to move like a rat through filthy puddles and narrow overhangs. Wanting only to put distance between myself and Mabbot, I lost my orientation and rounded a corner to find I had made a circle and was looking down an alley I had already traversed. This time, though, a child in rags, even younger than Joshua, stood in the middle, as if to bar my way. In his right hand he held a bone — from the looks of it, a thighbone. He raised it to his face, sighted over the pocked gnarl at the end, and pretended to shoot me. I hurried on, coming close enough to confirm that the bone was probably human. Even as I passed him, he filled me with imaginary shot, pausing only to reload with invisible powder. The child did not smile or even seem to be enjoying the game.

That was when I heard Joshua wail. A most distinctive noise. The boy never used his voice except to laugh, and I knew at once that he must be very scared. The sound brought me full about and now, finally, the bone-bearing child smiled.

Joshua would, no doubt, find his way back to Mabbot; his mind was excellent and full of resource. I turned and resumed my winding hunt for shelter. My knee and hip were already burning with friction and fatigue from the uneven ground, but I ignored them, half galloping, my free arm swinging as a counterbalance to every stride.

Seconds later I heard Joshua again. This time it was a long howl. Maybe he was only looking for me, but he sounded truly scared or in pain. Poor Joshua needed me. Escape would have to wait. I reversed my course and began to run, if my clumping lope could be called a run, toward his voice.

Trying to plot the straightest course back to Joshua, I was obliged to cut through the alley with the odd child again. As I passed, the urchin caught my peg with the crook of the bone, and I went sprawling into a puddle bubbling with algae. I rose, snatched the bone from the child, and might have given him a good thrashing with it if I had not heard the wailing again. I kept the bone and made for Joshua.

Reaching the ruin, finally, I saw two men had cornered Joshua and were stripping him of his clothes, despite his struggling and screaming. His nose had been bloodied, but Joshua fought them with undiminished fury. They seemed to be enjoying the challenge of picking him slowly naked, taking their time and making sport of his terror. The brutes had not seen me, and I crept behind the largest one and raised the femur to take a crack at his head. Before I could swing, though, the odd child leaped onto my back and clawed my face. Blood and grime blinded my right eye as the ruffians turned on me. In the scuffle I managed to get my back to the wall and pull Joshua protectively under my arm. The men facing me had, each of them, been branded between the eyes. By the dimensions of the scars on their brows, I'd guess that the tool was a red-hot coin. What manner of fraternity meted out this kind of initiation, I did not care to know.

The scarred men, silent in their duty, began to wallop me, each in turn, about the face, belly, and groin.

Falling upon my back, I covered Joshua with my body and tried to kick the men with my peg, but I was quickly reduced to simply rolling away, as best I could, from the worst blows. The men said not a word, and with the clarity that comes of fearing for one's life, I saw when they laughed that their tongues had been cut out. These were escaped convicts.

A kick to my head clapped my teeth closed on my own tongue, and as blood filled my mouth, I fought to stay conscious.

Then the beating stopped, and, peering between my fingers, I saw Mr. Apples breaking the men apart with the thighbone. Not a word was spoken, and the sounds of that grim weapon powdering their jaws and necks was worse even than the pain of the beating. Joshua tried to kick me off but, wanting to spare him this sight, I kept his head beneath me until the men had fallen and Mr. Apples, hardly even sweating, reached down to pull us to our feet.

"Having a good time?" He coughed as he shook the gore from the bone. "Do ye want this for your stewpot?"

I spat a stream of blood and reassured myself that my tongue was still attached at the root. Joshua was weeping and I held his wet cheek with one hand and with the other signed, "Sorry, sorry!" The blood on my hand left a crimson circle on my chest.

Mr. Apples considered the bone for a moment, then handed it back to the odd child, who immediately aimed it at him.

"Captain will be waiting," Mr. Apples said.

He picked up his backpack, which was stuffed so taut with wool that it looked like a giant tick. This he slung over his shoulder and headed off whistling as if on a Sunday picnic. After helping Joshua with his shirt and sandals — to my great relief, the boy had no serious injuries — we made after Mr. Apples as quickly as we could. My body still tingled with the acrid liquor of fear, and I knew when that subsided, I would feel the bruises I had received. Worse, though, was the guilt. My stubborn thoughts of home had almost gotten Joshua killed.

In my gratitude for his intercession, I tried to make conversation with Mr. Apples.

"That is," I huffed, "some fine wool, Mr.

Apples . . . You'll do beautiful things with it."

"I'll have to wash and comb it first. Wish I could get my hands on some proper dye."

"I could give you some turmeric, perhaps. It makes a fine color, and a pinch goes a long way. Or we'll find you some lichen. The monks used to dye their robes a handsome ocher with nothing but boiled lichen and urine . . . I must ask you, why didn't you use your gun on those men? No complaints from me; I'm grateful just the same."

"I like to use broad strokes. A gun jams, a gun misses, and often as not, even if it hits, the thing will just keep coming. My hands don't jam nor miss —"

Joshua interrupted us to sign, "See? He only wanted wool. He didn't want to fuck sheep —"

"You're right!" I signed with my one free hand.

Joshua considered me for a moment before signing, "Your brain is cracked."

I couldn't argue.

We caught up with Mabbot at a great banyan tree whose trunk had been decorated in patches with hammered lead and crude figurines. When she saw Mr. Apples, she yelled, "Where have you been? I'll not be kept waiting on account of your fondness for — What in bloody heaven happened to them?"

"They were making friends," Mr. Apples said.

"Enough! The tavern is just there," said Mabbot, pointing to a brooding windowless building with a small red door. Above the door hung a flag that featured a writhing serpent eating its own tail.

Braga said, "If the Fox is here, it is because he wants to be found."

"And I want to find him," said Mabbot.

"I don't trust it."

"Then stay here with them." Mabbot chose ten men to stay with Braga. The rest of us followed her into the tavern.

22

THE BRASS FOX FOUND

IN WHICH MABBOT'S HUNT ENDS

The Serpent's Tail was long and narrow.
There were several thick oaken tables along
one side of the tavern — in craftsmanship
and dimension, they were little more than
stumps — and a tin-plated bar on the other.
Above the tables, a narrow set of stairs led
to a loft, which was hidden by heavy tapes-
tries. There were armed men, fifteen or
more, near the back wall, where a single
open door cast a dusty light upon the
sawdust floor. By their surly silence, I assumed they were the Fox's men, and that
they had been expecting us.

I was standing behind Feng, who was
shifting her weight on the floor with her
head cocked. Then, as if deciding that the
sawdust there was not good enough, she
guided Mabbot away from the bar toward
the tables. A sweep of my boot revealed
wooden planks beneath the sawdust; those
that were directly beneath me seemed to

shift independently of the others — I was standing on a trapdoor. This was one of those bars where one may take a single sip of beer and wake chained to a galley oar and bound for the gold mines. I followed Feng's example and moved closer to the others.

Like armies staging for a battle, our factions glowered at each other across a no-man's-land of empty tables and reeking piss buckets. Sheets of leather, emblazoned with tattoos of sinking ships and mermaids, hung like pennants from the rafters. The blows to my gut had left me decidedly nauseated and I gagged when I realized what the pennants were: the tattooed backs and bellies of dead men, preserved for posterity — a grisly museum of former patrons.

Mr. Apples announced, "Hannah Mabbot is here for the Brass Fox. Where will we find him?"

The men at the other end of the building neither answered nor moved. Mr. Apples took two steps toward them and roared, "Speak!"

The Fox finally parted the loft curtains and showed himself; his hair, oiled to a deep bronze, nearly brushed the top of his high starched collar and cravat. His polished boots clacked as he came down the stairs.

The horribly scarred Gristle carried his pistol and bandolier. "Do show a little patience, man! You've only just arrived," said the Fox, as he strolled to a table in the center of the room and sat down.

We all turned to Mabbot; she was frozen, her eyes locked on her child. For a moment, it seemed she would stare at him forever, then she regained her composure and joined him at the table. "But we have been waiting for much longer than that," said Mabbot, "to see you."

"Well, you see me now."

"I do," said Mabbot softly.

"Wine!" shouted the Fox. Gristle ran to fetch a pewter tankard and quickly poured two glasses. Mabbot waited for the Fox to drink first, then emptied hers in one gulp.

Mr. Apples pointed to a series of wooden kegs lashed to the rafters. "That's not wine."

"Those keep things from getting out of hand," said the Fox. "The barkeep puts enough powder and shot in them to ruin anyone's day. It encourages civility."

"They could be full of sand," muttered Mr. Apples.

"Care to take aim and find out?" the Fox taunted.

Mr. Apples rolled his shoulder and stared at the cask above him, clearly considering whether to try to jump and grab it, but Mabbot tsked. "We're not here to quarrel. Let's talk somewhere quiet."

"We'll talk here," said the Fox.

Mr. Apples huffed, the veins on his neck rising. "Captain, I don't like this —"

Mabbot shut him up with a glance. Like a chastened dog, Mr. Apples grumbled and retreated. "Give us some room," she said, and we all backed toward the front wall to give her the semblance of privacy at the table.

Gristle refilled their wine. Mabbot did not take her eyes off the Fox's face. "More and more the handsome man," she said.

"I credit the buttermilk baths you gave me every night before singing me to sleep!"

They laughed together, and it echoed off the rafters. The Fox's men shifted, looking as disconcerted as I felt. Of all the strange things I had seen thus far, the bared fangs and blue underbellies of the misbegotten globe, this was most unexpected. Surrounded by the bristling ruffians, in a city of cutthroats, in a world turned by the forks of avarice, here at the center they were laughing. It was all too brief, though, for now the Fox was draining his glass again, fortifying himself for what was to come.

It was then that Kittur padded slowly

down the staircase from the loft. Her eyes were bright behind the spectacles, and I saw fear there. For some reason this upset me more than the shoddy grenades dangling above us or the posturing brutes. She knew what was about to happen, and it was not good.

"And who is this? Won't you introduce me?" said Mabbot.

But the Fox only winked at Kittur, who pushed past the assembled gang and made her way out the back door. I decided then that we would be safer waiting outside with Braga and the others. My hand went to Joshua's shoulder to guide him toward the front, when two of the Fox's ursine men came in and stood barring our escape. One held a medieval iron club with a knobbed head; by the blackened lacquer in its grooves, it had not been cleaned since its last use.

An expectant hush fell upon the tavern. Only the soft scuffing of boots in sawdust and the clink of weapons against buckles could be heard as Mabbot and her strange son looked at each other.

"You know the next part, Mother Goose. You must have guessed." A lock of hair fell into his face, and Mabbot pushed it behind his ear. He let her.

"Tell me," said Mabbot.

"I do wish there was another way." The young man lifted his glass again but seemed to lose his thirst all of a sudden — staring into the wine as if seeing an insect there.

"How good can this plan be if you can't even speak it aloud?" Mabbot prodded.

"Are you so eager for the noose?" The glass came down hard and shattered in his hand. The explosion seemed to calm him. He pulled a shard from the meat of his thumb without so much as a grimace and watched the blood trickle. "Your sacrifice isn't unappreciated." He sighed as he stood. On cue, his men drew their sabers and guns.

"Are you still having nightmares?" Mabbot asked casually.

"Oh, they never stop, do they?" purred the Fox. "They only merge one into the other."

Mr. Apples and the twins had taken up fighting postures, ready to meet the mob as they came, but Mabbot remained stubbornly, insultingly seated. She said, "You have just this one moment to explain yourself before things get impolite."

"Impolite? Will courtesy bring the couriers to my door with my inheritance in a saddlebag? If I powder my hair, will Pendleton recognize me for Ramsey's heir? No. I must make my case in earnest, or they will not hear me."

The Fox's men were rocking on their heels, just waiting for the sign to rush against us.

Mr. Apples grunted. "It's like I said. Nothing here but ambush, Captain. It's time to be on our way."

Mabbot grabbed the back of his belt and yanked him behind her, like a trainer keeping a bear in check. "We've come all this way, Mr. Apples. I will have this out."

"And why, exactly, have you come all this way?" asked the Fox.

"To stop you — to *ask* you to stop smuggling opium," Mabbot said.

"Ah yes, the poor smoke-eaters still have your sympathies."

"They do, and besides, it is far too dangerous a game. Pendleton will —"

"But which is it? Is it wrong or is it dangerous?"

"Both!" Her voice broke, and, for the first time, I saw Mabbot frantic. "You must consider the forces you're playing with."

"Am I really listening to Mad Mabbot council me on prudence?" The Fox's men snickered.

"I can trust my crew," said Mabbot. "But you're betting on the winds. You cannot trust a bribed man."

"What, then, shall I be? A tailor, perhaps? Or a baker? Something safe and plain, is that what you were preparing me for when you taught me how to cut a man above the knee where the blood cannot be stanched? When you showed me how to break a neck with the butt of my pistol?"

"What do you want, Leighton?"

"What do you have?"

"Do you want an apology?" Mabbot's voice was barely audible now.

"*That* would be very interesting indeed."

"I'm sorry."

Here Mr. Apples clenched his fists so hard I thought I could hear the sinews straining deep in his forearms, but he kept his mouth shut.

The Fox, drinking this moment in, leaned forward and asked, "What *exactly* are you sorry for, Hannah?" The blood from his thumb pooled in his loose fist.

"I did not —" Her voice seemed to come from the bottom of a well. ". . . Whatever you needed, I didn't have it."

For a moment, it seemed the Fox was moved by her words. Then he shook the blood onto the table, where it made darker clouds in the spilled wine. "Enough," he said. "It's already decided."

Mabbot said, "Think it through. Pendleton would never give shares of the company to a known brigand, let alone Ramsey's shares. On the other hand, if you decide to act sensibly —"

"Is that what you call your petty skirmishes? Sensible? You waste your time with piecemeal scraps in lonely seas. They build them faster than you can sink them. Pointless. You never dared go for the heart. Forever foaming at the mouth about slaves and opium to convince yourself that you're something more than a bloody cutpurse. What exactly is my birthright? What scrap of this filthy clod can I call home? Have I no better fate than to be hunted down by privateers and bounty men? No, I'll take what is mine. I'll not be ignored. You mistake me, Mother. I didn't ask your permission, and I don't need your advice."

A wave of his hand brought Gristle and the others forward, their pistols and muskets fixed on Mabbot. Some held ropes and shackles.

"It would seem we're at an impasse." Mabbot sighed.

"Then you'll come without a fuss?"

A look of disgust twisted Mabbot's face. "Just where are we going?"

"Let's not make a scene, please. We're not

really at an impasse, are we? You're out-gunned. Though, believe me, I would much prefer to do this gently. Maybe you'll escape from the gallows. You've done that before. Regardless, I'm handing you over to Pendleton to demonstrate my sincerity as a company man." He turned away, and to his men, he shouted, "Take her whole — don't bruise the lady."

At this Mabbot finally stood. Her poise was broken. She swayed and had to brace herself on the table. "Whole for the gallows? Oh, Leighton." She moaned. "What have you become?"

"Become?" He turned, and, to our astonishment, the man was crying. "What a sweet thought: to become. But I was *made,* wasn't I? What could twist the sinews of my heart? Yes, Mother, I remember your lessons — every word. What hammer and what chain? In what furnace was my brain? Come, you remember it, don't you? Well, for good or ill, your work is done. Go easy, you've earned your rest." Tears made sooty streaks upon his face. The room was bristling with drawn weapons. Mabbot's crew had formed a tight nucleus around her, and their every gun was cocked and aimed at the Fox.

"You'll be my peace offering," he said softly. "That is the *sensible* thing. You see, I have thought it through — thought it through to the letter. The papers love nothing more than a captured pirate to parade down the streets, and they'll paint me a patriot. If they still refuse to negotiate, I'll sink my teeth in. I'll strangle the Pearl River to a trickle and let the tea barons starve for a few months. And if needs be, I'll drop their warehouses into hell. Nothing speaks quite so eloquently as a well-placed bomb." He was proud of his plan, and by the wet eagerness in his eyes he wanted her to be proud too — proud of her boy, even as he hanged her.

Mr. Apples could stand no more. With a single stride he crossed the distance to the Fox and lifted him like a sack of beets, one massive arm around his throat.

In a pinched falsetto, the Fox said, "She won't let them harm me. Take her!"

Then the fighting began. The blow to my head earlier must have been worse than I thought, for the tavern seemed to me a grisly dance hall, goaded into motion by the music of grunts and screams. Men cleaved to each other in urgent passion. To my relief, out of respect for the bombs hanging just above our heads, the guns were not fired, but swords and daggers glinted in the lantern light, and there was no escape from the sound of bodies colliding and the clotted mewls of men drowning in their own blood.

Looking for shelter, I crawled toward the bar. It was then that the trapdoor opened and more thugs emerged like spiders, grabbing at the feet of those above and dragging them below. I turned and scampered in the opposite direction. The twins had seized Mabbot under the arms and were carrying her, despite her struggling, toward the front. They had not made it ten feet before a wave of brigands forced them to stop and fight.

Mr. Apples, with a blade in one hand and a wooden stool in the other, was sweeping through the Fox's men like a reaper in the wheat. I was cowering with Joshua behind an overturned table, looking for a safe moment to dash out, when Braga and the reinforcements burst through the front door.

And the shooting started.

One of the powder kegs was immediately shattered, spraying sand over the writhing melee. There was the briefest pause as the fighters took in this information and reached for their guns. Every pistol in the world went off then — the keg might as well have been filled with powder and shot. The tables, the chairs, the whole building shuddered with the violence of the retorts. Gun smoke immediately filled the long room while brilliant seams of sunlight cut across the murk, as the bullets knocked holes into the walls and ceilings. The lanterns hopped and danced in a furious jig.

Thinking the trapdoor must lead to tunnels away from the pandemonium, I tugged Joshua a few feet toward it before our path was blocked by a dying man — I could not say for sure whom — who fell in a heap before me, trying weakly to pull a blade from his back while blood dribbled from his mouth.

Then I was hit.

I felt the bullet immediately and fell again behind the shelter of the table. Upon examination, though, I found that it was not my skin that had been pierced but the tin containing my yeast sponge batter. The ball had made its way into the tin case and lay lodged in the dough.

A lantern had shattered and spilled oil upon the rear wall, where the flame spread eagerly.

Feng and Bai were occupied warding off the attempts to seize Mabbot while she wove her way through the carnage toward the back, where the Fox stood guarded by a handful of his men. She had not drawn her pistols and she waved her hands in the air as she went, crying, "Hold! Hold!", but her voice was swallowed by the roar of the guns.

I watched as the brute with the wrought-iron club threw his meaty arm around Mabbot's waist and swung her to the ground like a sheep for shearing. With a knee on her neck, he began to tie her wrists with rope as Feng and Bai fought desperately to reach her.

The Fox came at a run from the other side of the hall, ducking Mr. Apples's windmill arm, and shouting, "With respect, didn't I say? You do not touch her but with respect!" He shoved his own man off of Mabbot and reached down to pull her to her feet. That briefest moment is frozen in my memory, the two of them holding hands in the eye of the storm with the battle converging upon them from every direction. Perhaps it is precisely because everything was, just a breath later, utterly torn, that this moment seemed to last much longer than it could have, lit with a trembling light.

Perhaps the Fox was about to say something — his mouth was open — but already some careening pistol ball had made its tunnel into his forehead. He looked up at the ceiling and fell backward. Mr. Apples and the twins scrambled to reach Mabbot as she dropped and pulled her child into her arms.

Through the thickening eddies of smoke, I saw Mabbot on her knees, her face gone pale, holding his leaking head to her chest. There she rocked, as if comforting a baby.

Feng made it to her side just as Gristle lifted his blunderbuss and fired. Mabbot and Feng fell in a heap.

Bai rushed to his sister while Mr. Apples seized Gristle's gun and swung hard. Even as the stock broke the head of a nearby ruffian like a melon, Mr. Apples reached out and crushed Gristle's throat in his enormous fist. The few remaining brigands had begun a hasty retreat through the trapdoor rather than face Mr. Apples without their leader.

Joshua and I clung to each other until the tavern became still. Peering from behind our table, I could see that nearly all of our crew lay among the dead or wounded. Only Bai, Braga, Mr. Apples, and two frazzled seamen still stood over their fallen fellows.

Then another shot rang out, pinning a boutonniere of blood to Mr. Apples's shoulder. The sniper in the loft reloaded behind the curtain as the others dragged Mabbot to the shelter of the bar. Mr. Apples made a move to charge the stairs but took another shot in the thigh and fell back. Behind the bar, Bai was worrying over Feng and Mabbot, who both lay motionless.

Except for the crackle of the rear wall burning, the tavern was quiet enough to hear the click of the sniper opening the chamber for another round. I saw then, as if in a dream, Joshua run a third of the way up the stairs. He pitched a lantern into the loft. There was a pop and sizzle as the sniper's powder box went off all at once; a moment later the shooter fell through the air, his head and hands blackened, to the sawdust floor and writhed there in the deepening murk.

The next several minutes are hard to recall. The fighting had stopped, but the smoke and flames forced us to flee the building; when Mr. Apples gave us the nod, we moved as a band through the front door, carrying three bodies and leaving the rest to burn. There was no sign of the Fox's surviving men, but a crowd of townspeople had gathered, and, when they saw us emerge, several of them braved the fire to see what could be salvaged from the building.

Mr. Apples moved quickly despite his wounds and gave Mabbot's entire bag of silver to a passing woodsman in exchange for a grizzled mule.

Mabbot was insensate but breathing, a wash of blood streaming from her temple down her neck and back. Feng was dead, her heart cloven by the force of the blunderbuss. Bai had slung his sister over his shoulder and would not put her on the mule but instead made his way quickly toward the coast on foot. We followed, ever on the lookout for another ambush.

The two remaining seamen carried the body of Leighton, the Brass Fox, slung between them, as Mr. Apples ordered. One sailor balked, "But it's hardly treasure."

Mr. Apples took the sailor by the hair and lifted him kicking into the air. "Having trouble hearing me, man?"

"No, sir!"

I gave Joshua a kiss on the head before Mr. Apples lifted him and carried him like a hero on his broad shoulders. Because of my slow gait, I was obliged to ride upon the mule behind the unconscious Mabbot, who left a trail of pattering blood. Mr. Apples called for Bai to let us put Feng upon the donkey, but Bai would not let go of his sister, nor slow down. He carried her as if she weighed no more than a bundle of flowers.

"Knew this Fox was trouble!" one of the seamen grumbled.

"It hardly matters now!" I barked, surprised by the desperation in my own voice.

Ignoring me, he said, "Cap'm shot, an' for what? A kiss from the boy? Is this corpse our hard-earned prize?"

The sailors received from Mr. Apples a glare so chilling that they shut their mouths and did not speak again.

By the time we made it back to the boats, Bai had laid Feng out and wrapped her face with his own shirt. The dragon tattoo made a dark storm on his back. Though his face showed signs of weeping, he was stony as we approached.

"How is the captain?" he asked.

"Breathing" was all I could say.

When we got back to the *Rose,* Mr. Apples carried Mabbot to her bed, and then left to shout orders at the crew. He was worried that Laroche was not far off, and we tripped anchor and set sail to hie south in a hurry.

Meanwhile, Mabbot, still bleeding from the head, wouldn't rouse. Neither would the good doctor, who lay pickled, as usual, in his hammock — it's the good doctor's prerogative apparently to requisition as much wine from the hold as he pleases, no doubt for the sake of keeping wounds clean. Bai, as still as an idol, sat next to Feng's corpse on the deck and stared out at the water. Asher keened and rolled his face upon Feng's bloody chest, his hand cupping the slight swell of her belly.

In her cabin, I arranged towels under Mabbot's head, then felt through her hair, gummy with drying clots, searching for the source of the flow, but could not ascertain the edges of the wound. Finally, distraught by the unceasing blood, I ran to fetch Mr. Apples's wool shears. I began to hack through her hair, thick as a bear's and sopping. Once I began there was no stopping, and soon enough I was surrounded by great tentacles of her legendary locks. Eventually I had clipped her to a rugged half inch. Although I could see grey hair sprinkled here and there in the scruff of her scalp, she seemed younger thus, almost girlish, thin and vulnerable.

I steeled myself to examine the extent of the damage. The wound was revealed: a gash from her eyebrow to the back of her skull, as straight as a saber's cut. In places the tissue was sliced clean through and the grim white of her skull showed like teeth between bloody lips. Upon the bone itself, the bullet had left a shallow groove in its course. But for this scrimshaw, her skull seemed as solid and stubborn as ever.

Still, it was a heavy injury, and I doubted she would wake. I heated a blade over a lantern until it glowed. I rinsed the wound in brandy and pinched it shut with one hand. With the other I crossed myself and rolled the blunt edge of the red-hot blade as deliberately as I could over the length of the laceration, searing it shut and filling the room with the smell of burned hair and grilled steak.

I blistered my finger in the process and was bringing it to my mouth when something nearly broke my nose. Mabbot had woken to punch me in the face. She sat up, her visage a terrible muddle of confusion and rage, rolled her eyes, and fell again senseless. She was very pale and, except for her shallow breathing, looked lifeless. At least the bleeding was done.

"You're welcome," I muttered, clutching my tender nose.

I went again to fetch the surgeon, and when he would not rise, I followed Mabbot's example and punched him square in the face. It did not wake him, and I turned to leave, then came back to punch him again; it felt so good the first time. I left him to his drunken oblivion and returned to Bai. Kneeling next to him, I begged, "I will watch over Feng, if you'll only go and see the captain."

He stood and went. When he returned, he

450

said, "I've put needles in her ear. Nothing more can be done until she wakes."

Every few hours an argument breaks out on deck about what will become of Mabbot, or whether Laroche is nearby. Mostly, though, the men argue about the Brass Fox, for his death has only stirred their fascination:

"That ain't the real Fox in the hold. The real Fox can't be killed."

"We should sell him to Pendleton for a bounty."

"Nah, we should find his hoarded gold! The man had a mountain of it!"

"Hush! His spirit will wreck us if you don't show respect."

"Drink piss, spirit! It's Mabbot you need to worry about. He's her blood. Bite your tongue or she'll flay us all when she wakes."

Mr. Apples is busy cracking heads together to keep the peace.

Thursday, November 11

My own injuries are nearly healed. Mabbot, though, has been asleep for two days. The wound upon her head no longer bleeds but has swollen around my hasty surgery. She sweats profusely in her sleep, and every hour I pull her upright and spoon coconut water and Bai's fever medicine into her parched

451

mouth. I've lived during this time in the stuffed chair beside her bed. I even tolerate the rabbit to nest in my lap.

Mr. Apples has announced that we are tacking back toward the Sunda Strait, much to the delight of the crew, who believe that this place is bad luck. He will not, however, give us any further indication of our destination.

Friday, November 12
I was asleep and drooling in the chair beside her bed when Mabbot's voice woke me.

"You must think I was most . . . reckless, in the tavern." She was sallow and stippled with sweat, but her eyes were keen.

"I'm in no position to judge," I said.

"None?"

After a silence, I admitted, "I too have been undone in my time. I lost my wife in childbirth. The child too."

"You loved her?"

"If not for godly counsel, I would have buried myself with them."

"Then you're familiar with the immodesty of grief." She spoke so slowly and softly that I was obliged to kneel at the side of the bed with my ear close to her mouth. "Tell me, Wedge, is Leighton . . . How was he left?"

"He is here, Mabbot. We've put his body

in a hogshead of Madeira to preserve it until you should wake. Mr. Apples has posted a guard."

She seemed relieved, and I thought she'd fallen asleep again, but she said, "I'll take him to America, find a cottage there, like the one in the Canaries where I nursed him. They're not hunting me in the Americas; they too hate the Pendleton Company . . . maybe I'll stay there. My sails are slack."

I let her rest and rushed to the galley to prepare some broth. To heal, one needs a soup of real marrow bones. I used what we had — salted babirusa and dried fish — and cursed as I cooked. I added molasses for her blood, wishing I had even the lamb knees Ramsey used to throw to his hounds.

When I returned to her cabin, though, Mabbot had lapsed into a coma and would not wake. I pushed the liquid into her mouth, mopped it where it dribbled out, and hoped some of it made its way to her belly.

Friday, Later
She has been in and out of consciousness, and to my rising alarm, the infection and fever have grown worse. The surgeon's visits are impotent and insulting. She has lost so much already, I will not let him bleed her,

and he mumbles that nothing more can be done. Today as he leaned his drunken frame over her, I couldn't hide my outrage.

"Have you considered amputating her head, good Doctor?"

"I can hear you, Wedge," Mabbot said softly.

"The fever must break," the doctor said. "There is nothing for it."

Bai prepares the bitter medicine and comes to assist with her toilets, but otherwise he sits upon the deck looking out at the horizon day and night.

"Lonely as moonlight on a spoon, that one," Mr. Apples remarked.

While I was busy nursing Mabbot, Bai had set Feng's body upon the sea in a bier of lashed planks and watched the spot on the horizon where it had disappeared as if he could still see it.

Tonight, as the sun set, I mounted the deck to offer my condolences to Bai, but the rigging stopped me. Even to my untrained eyes, it was clear that the ship was severely disordered. The yardarms were topped at opposite angles, and the topgallant sails were set on the mizzen while the sheets sagged loose and lazy; a ship in this state could have caught the winds only in a strange dream. It looked as if a great hand had reached down and tousled the ship. I asked Mr. Apples, "Is this the discipline you keep? Captain Mabbot indisposed for a few days and we've come to this?"

"We've scandalized the ship out of respect for Feng," Mr. Apples said. "Don't fret, in an few hours we'll clean her back up. I never took you for a bosun."

I found Bai at his vigil and sat beside him. I had misunderstood and maligned him. There was no denying it — the man had spared no effort in saving my life. I made an attempt to reach him in his grief. I said, "I've had this pain. To tell you it will go away would be a lie. It will never go away. But, if you live long enough, it will cease to torture and will instead flavor you. As we rely on the bitterness of strong tea to wake us, this too will become something you can use."

For his stoniness he may not have heard me at all.

Saturday, November 13

Mabbot's wound has suppurated. I watched, worried, as the surgeon lanced it, and, when he left, I dressed it with the grey tree moss the twins had used on my injuries.

Later in the afternoon Mr. Apples came to Mabbot's cabin and stood looking worried over her for many minutes, so I said, "Tell them that she is healing."

He nodded gratefully.

"Tell them that I am cooking for her, that in a few days she will be her terrible self again."

23
BROKEN BREAD
IN WHICH A SACRIFICE IS ACCEPTED

Monday, November 15
I feed the rabbit oats and dried alfalfa. I feed Mabbot broth and, when she can chew, rice gruel and crushed garlic to fight the infection. I have pleaded with Mr. Apples to let us go to land to get some fresh meat, but we have set out for safer regions and are days from any port.

These are the details of my hands and eyes. I haven't yet tried to write of the strange doings of my heart, for I am shocked by them and perplexed. Mabbot's infirmity has filled me with horror. I long to see her fortified, lifted, and healed until she can mock me with that ferocious tongue — until she can rage into the wind. I putter about her, washing sheets, wetting her brow, petting her head when she is restless, and humming the tune Father Sonora sang while he worked, the only comforting song I know. But for hours at a time there is nothing to be done, and so I allow myself to look, just to look at her as I have never looked at another human being — her cheekbones and full lips, cracked now by thirst, the eyebrows that were thunder's cousins now loose and elegant arches. The hand I hold, with its calluses and muscles and freckles, is unlike any other.

I long for her vigor to return, and yet I cherish these moments of quiet with her. Even Kerfuffle gnawing at my peg is tolerable.

In short, I am disastrously in love.

Tuesday, November 16

Some men have set up an altar and burn sandalwood outside her door. There are always a few lingering there, waiting for news. I try to give them encouraging words.

Of course, I worry what heaven and my lost Elizabeth see when they look down, but I have given up trying to accommodate them. I feel quite unable to make good with the celestial host when there is such imperative in front of me. God, in His infinite knowledge, has given me precious little and has allowed much calamity.

As for Elizabeth, if she knows anything, she knows that she lives in the purest parts of my heart. But she must also see that I am no longer the man she wed, that I have lived lifetimes since then, and that, if I am not yet to be called into the clouds, I must contend with the stains of this world, the blood and the sweat and the love.

Mabbot, for her part, seems grateful to find me near when she wakes, and once, fatigued by the effort of eating as I propped her up, she dropped her head upon my shoulder and rested her hot brow against my neck. We sat there pressed against each other for some time.

I do not know if, in her delirium, Mabbot has understood about Feng's loss, but she has not asked for her, and so I must assume she has.

I've taken to reading to her, and though she sleeps through most of it, it calms both of us.

Wednesday, November 17

In her sleep she calls out to Leighton. Today, from her pillow, she told me of his birth. Though I tried to convince her to conserve her energy, I also hoped that speaking the story might serve as a purgative, for it has become clear to me that her fever is fueled as much by grief as by infection.

"I needed a safe place," she said. "I was

young and getting so heavy. The crew had disbanded, Ramsey hanged so many of them. I took my silver and bought a small house in the Canaries. Chickens in the backyard, a creek that ran straight to the sea. I had Leighton there, by myself. One minute I was screaming alone, and the next moment there were two of us — he filled the world. A woman came to clean and cook a few times a week, but I didn't let her touch him. Such a bright light in his eyes, from the very first."

Here I forced her to eat some rice gruel with salted pork and sauerkraut, coarse fare but the most nutritious thing I could give her. It hurt her to chew and so I mashed it well.

"This woman heard about the price on my head in some tavern, and she turned me in. She was remorseful enough to warn me before the men arrived. Well, you may imagine, one cannot run with an infant. I left him with the nuns in Ireland. Don't hate me, Wedge, I had no choice. If they caught us, we would have rotted, both of us, in a cell. I didn't know Ramsey would find him. I came for him as soon as he was old enough to sail, my ten-year-old prince."

"I know, Hannah," I said, trying to calm her. "You worked so hard to keep him from becoming like Ramsey. I understand why you had to find him again."

She said nothing, and for a moment I thought she'd fallen asleep. Then she said, "Let him be as cruel as his father, I don't care, only let him live! I hunted him because I feared he was going to get himself killed. I may be a terrible mother, but I am a mother yet. I bungled it all. My Leighton! Whose shot killed him, Wedge? Did you see?"

I hadn't. Mabbot's tears were as fierce as her anger, each sob like a dagger in the gut. It was too much for me to bear and I pressed my hand to her cheek. "He drank from my body," she said, and finally slept. I went to fetch Bai for more medicine. The bottle of tincture is nearly empty.

Thursday, November 18

Mabbot's fever has worsened. I wrap her in blankets and still she shakes and cries out for warmth. She has been delirious all night. It will not relent and she twists, fighting phantom battles, clawing at her own skin until I am forced to hold her wrists.

The swelling about her scar has abated, but the fever is deep within her, and though I spooned the last of the medicine into her, I doubt she will survive. This cannot go on.

To make things worse, there is a storm

bearing down upon us and no hope of outrunning it.

Friday, November 19
The ship rolled and lurched as if swung on a pendulum. Mabbot's bed is nailed to the floor, and I had taken a prayerful position clutching one of its posts as the stuffed chair and the dining table slipped from their notches and became lambs hopping about the cabin. I reached to keep Mabbot from slipping out of the bed and felt, with alarm, that her breathing was very light.

I had no idea what to do. I shook her, but she did not rouse.

"Mabbot," I said, and again louder, "Mabbot!" But she was limp as a rag.

I put my lips to her ear and shouted, "Hannah!"

"Mmm?"

"Where are you off to? You mustn't leave us without a captain. Can you hear me? Hannah, I would not have you die."

"Wedge," she groaned, "you daisy."

"Only hold on. Who will give Pendleton hell?"

"I've cheated death a dozen times. Now he is come with an army."

"Pendleton will be victorious, vindicated —"

"You're trying to inflame me. Let me sleep, Wedge, I'm so cold."

Her teeth clattered like horses' hooves. I used rugs and ripped the tiger pelts from the door to lay over her, yet she shook as if buried in snow.

Then I got into the bed with her.

I took off my shirt to offer my warm skin and held her there trembling against my chest as our vessel spun in the darkness.

I must have slept too, for when the waves had calmed, she woke me with a soft laugh. Her hair was wet around her ears, but her face was clean and open. She was through the fever.

"Hello, Mr. Wedgwood." She laughed again, her arm encircling my waist.

"Forgive the presumption," I mumbled. "It was to keep you warm."

"Oh yes, my chills," she mocked me.

I rushed to rise from the bed, but she held my arm and said, "But I'm still a little cold."

"I didn't think you'd make it. Apparently, bullets can't kill you," I said.

"God favors the beautiful," she answered, and then slept.

Mabbot's jibes filled me with hope. She needed only this little help, this one spoonful of soup at a time. I stayed and held her, the soft tufts of her shorn hair against my

463

chin. She slept and I lay awake, in wonder and, for the first time in years, happy. I was deep in unknown waters, but I was home. Mabbot had fought her way into me, and she was stronger than I. Now that she was in, there was nothing for me to do but love her.

When she woke again, I went to fetch water. She drank an entire carafe. When I went to fetch more, I found a full pitcher waiting just outside the door — Mr. Apples had seen us together.

Saturday, November 20

I spent the night holding her while she slept.

In the morning Mabbot noticed Kerfuffle first. As she said, nothing on the ship is hidden from her, for she seemed to sense the rabbit was gone. The heavy chair lay on its side against the bookshelf, and by the angle of the rabbit's leg underneath, it was clear the animal had been crushed.

Mabbot groaned. "Is she not breathing?"

I righted the chair and replaced the heavy logs that had fallen during the storm. The beast was still, already stiffening as I lifted it.

"A windfall for your pot," Mabbot said, turning her back to me as she pulled the covers tightly around her.

"You're joking."

"Do you imagine that I don't know where meat comes from?"

It was the most lucid I had seen her in days. I would have balked if not for the glare she gave me over her shoulder, which was a taste of the old Mabbot.

Knowing she needed proper nourishment, and as there was no other fresh meat, I dressed and went to the galley, holding Kerfuffle under my arm.

I thought I would take pleasure in skinning that watchful rabbit, but now that it was still, it engendered in me a tenderness for all fragile flesh. I sharpened a knife until it shone, then skinned and cleaned the rabbit, trying to make each cut a gesture of respect. Loath to waste any part of the animal, I set brains and hide aside for tanning.

As I progressed deeper into the body, I felt a mystery revealing itself to me and began to pray, not with words but with simple cooking, a prayer not for the soul of the rabbit exactly but for the generous blending of its life with Mabbot's. She had fed and loved it, and now its flesh would become hers and mine, and in this way I understood that all beings lived only to feed one another as even the lion lies down for the worm. In the striations of the rabbit's muscle, I saw eons of breath and death.

This was God's grace, without which all bodies would fall to ash. I had been cooking my entire life and had never understood the sanctity of my duties. For all of my kitchen philosophies were nothing compared to the truth that now opened me to the bone: that I was, myself, food.

This inspiration sent me looking for Asher, to join me in the galley. He had given up trying to emulate Bai's stoic mourning and succumbed to rum and wailing. I talked at him and fed him spoonfuls as I cooked. It is meager comfort, but it is the only kindness I have to offer and, over time, it is a good cure for many ills.

The bowl of rabbit broth I carried to Mabbot's cabin was a forgiveness and a plea for forgiveness, an acknowledgment that this blood is shared universally. With this meal I surrendered to the mystery of my days and vowed never to look askance at love of any kind, nor to defy it. For the world is a far more expansive and mystifying place than can be said.

Sunday, November 21
A ship makes its way on ruin and repair. Despite Mr. Apples's handling, the *Rose*

lost the fore topsail in the storm and cordage was generally fouled throughout the ship. All watches were on deck bracing and knotting, painting and sealing.

I feel though that the most important mending was happening in Mabbot's chambers. She was sitting up in bed and not quite herself, for she was being so gentle. "How could I have known when I took you aboard how much I would come to rely on our little meals, on your grumbling? In stubbornness you're almost a match for me," she said. "And now you've seduced me back to this world with your sips and nibbles."

I spent the night feeding her, massaging and kissing the constellations of freckles that decorate her warm back. She shared her returning strength.

Here, propriety censors me.

I may say, though, that I am happy. Once baked, the bread cannot return to flour.

24

GOLD FOR CORNMEAL

IN WHICH I DISCOVER THE SABOTEUR

Monday, November 22

Today Mabbot retook control of her ship. But not before she summoned Mr. Apples to her cabin. She was sitting in her stuffed chair smoking her ivory pipe while I was at the table, reading her copy of *The Inferno,* one of the few books she had saved.

When Mr. Apples arrived, Mabbot announced without preamble: "We've got to go back. We're going to blow the Pendleton warehouses to hell."

I was dumbfounded, but it was impossible to surprise Mr. Apples; he had already considered the idea. "Won't work — it's the Pearl River, packed arse to nuts with navy ships. And, may I say, Captain, that you still look about as healthy as a frog in a pickle barrel."

"Braga says the entrance to the caves is a few miles north of the mouth of the river," said Mabbot. "We'll dash in and be back out before they know we're there. Leighton primed and loaded it; we need only strike the fuse."

"There are ships of the line patrolling the entire coast," said Mr. Apples. "We may get in, but we'll never get out. Besides, there's not a shilling to be had in it."

"The Pendleton Company is a blight. Everything they touch rots from the inside."

I was used to hearing fire in her voice when she spoke about them, but now I heard only sadness. She was not commanding; she was pleading for Mr. Apples to understand.

"They ruined my son. Turned him into another baron wheedling for his cut of the profits. Fighting the Pendleton Company is the only good I do, Mr. Apples. It is the only good I've ever done."

Mr. Apples rubbed the back of his head as he considered it. "With the officers and records gone, with the warehouses wrecked, it could ruin their monopoly for a time. The jackals will come pick over the remains," he admitted. "Smugglers, the Fox's scattered army, hell, even the Portuguese will try to set up shop. Might even be enough to force the opium issue into the papers. Hard to say what China would do."

"If China did anything at all, it would be

an improvement," Mabbot said. "It could take Pendleton years to recover. How can we not try?"

"Captain, I know when you've fixed on a plan there's not a thing that will keep you from it. And you know where I stand, I'll never leave this deck. But we ain't the only ones on this ship. The boys have a right to know what we're sailing into."

"Do you think they'll do it?"

"They don't want to lose their silver again. Laroche haunts their dreams. Now Feng's gone and the men are sweaty . . . I can't say."

"Call for all hands, Mr. Apples," she said. "I'll ask them."

When the giant left, Mabbot rose from the chair with a groan.

"A terrible idea," I said. "Not that you've asked me."

I was ready for a fight, but her sad smile disarmed me. Her face was completely open, and I could see the ancient fatigue in her eyes as clearly as the strength behind it. She was donning the yoke of her life, as I had begged her to.

"Leighton's heart was upside down," Mabbot said as she tugged at her boots. "But maybe he was right about me setting my sights too low. What is genius but audacity?" She sighed when she looked at herself in the mirror. "Damn it, Wedge, you're a hell of a barber."

When every man had assembled on the tween deck, Mabbot stood above them on the poop. "I hope you'll excuse my absence," she shouted as she took off her hat and revealed her wound. "I've had a bit of a headache!" They laughed harder than the joke warranted, perhaps; the men were much relieved to see their queen alive.

When they had quieted, Mabbot's face had become somber. "There is not a man here who is conscripted, bound, or black-mailed. You have each chosen your place aboard this ship, free and brave. You have bled on this deck and you have danced on it. The sea is full of ships wealthier, ships faster, ships stouter than our *Rose,* yet you have each, for your own reason, stayed on. Think on that reason now. For we have dangerous waters ahead. An opportunity has arisen to strike at the heart of the company and we shan't have it again. But I must have you with me.

"History is a pageant of war machines plowing the earth to a powder, and the cruelest yet is the Pendleton Trading Company. There is a reason why China will not let them beyond the shores of the Pearl

River. There is a reason why the colonists in the New World sank their tea in the harbor rather than drink a single cup of Pendleton's brew. I need not tell you of the millions Pendleton has starved and murdered. I need not tell you how she mills slaves into poppy and poppy into sable-lined gloves for the mistresses of fat men.

"Now, there is nothing wrong with silver, and we have our shares below ready to be spent. I propose to you now that we spend them in Brazil. Brazil is full of dancing women, pinga rum, and chocolate. But not before we finish our work here. Lucky is the man who can right a wrong, and such a wrong this is. I question not your bravery, nor your skill. I ask only for your vote, for if you say 'nay,' we will turn today and head immediately for the New World. But if you give me 'aye,' we shall make a mark here that history shall not forget and sail on to Brazil with our sails full of victory. Now, who says to me 'nay'?"

The ship was silent.

"Who 'aye'?"

The ship exploded with cheers.

"I expected no less, you cougars, you falcons. Come round and jibe north as the wind wants us to, Mr. Apples, toward the Pearl River! Bosun! Paint the hull with something drab and cover the gilt with sacks. We'll have to go in mufti. Strike the colors and raise a blue flag. We are now a whaling ship."

Mabbot leaped into the crowd of men, slapping them on the back and pushing them toward their stations. "Aloft, men! Why are your hands empty, don't you hear the gong? We've an appointment with the Pendleton Company!"

I was tidying the cabin when she pulled Asher in with a stern yank and said to him, "I have a particular task for you. I need your help. When we pass the Pearl delta, you'll see endless fishing boats. You will take a few seamen of your choosing and silver enough to buy us two of those boats and enough black powder to fill them to the gills. Not the junks — get the dinghies that one man can maneuver."

Her trust in him made the man's chest fill. Though his eyes were still bleary, he stood straight for the first time since he'd lost Feng.

"I can send the bosun," Mabbot said. "But I'd rather —"

"Let me do it, Captain!"

What all of my soothing words and spoon- fuls of commiseration could not achieve, she managed simply by saying she needed him.

"I'll arrange it, and you'll have a longboat ready when the time is right," Mabbot said. "Remember, as much gunpowder as they can carry. Don't come back with so much as a shilling in your pocket."

When Asher ran below to prepare, Mr. Apples said, "The smugglers carry muskets, but those dinghies are just fishing craft, Captain. They're about as dangerous as tea cakes."

"We're taking a page from the Fox's book, Mr. Apples. We'll turn those tea cakes into hellburners."

"God's arse, I haven't had one in years. Spoons, can ye make tea cakes?"

"One thing at a time," Mabbot said. "If we get out of these waters alive, we'll find you some cakes."

All hands were busy setting sail or transforming the radiant *Rose* into a grey crone — all hands except Bai, who sat out of the way on the bowsprit near old Pete. Mabbot had just breathed life back into Asher, but she left Bai alone. Perhaps she could not bring herself to ask more of the man who had now lost the last of his family. I had heard that twins shared a soul, and seeing his vacant eyes stare at the horizon, I could believe that his had indeed floated away on the planks with his sister.

While the crew went to work, Mabbot walked proudly to her cabin where, once the door closed, she collapsed and slept through an entire watch.

Tuesday, November 23

It is not Sunday, but Mabbot's recovery has earned us both a meal. Taking advantage, perhaps, of her weakened state, I talked her into letting me snip a handful of the curling green sprouts from the base of her largest ferns and whisk them away to the galley.

The rabbit's bones and innards went to the broth, and now, with Mabbot awake and rallying, I took the time to check on the meat. It was still tough and in need of a little more aging. Instead I resorted to an ancient and knobby lobster that Kitzu had been keeping in a barrel since he caught it off the shores of Macau.

It is, admittedly, a base foodstuff, but lobster, well prepared, can nevertheless be made to satisfy the distinguished gourmand. I fried the moss-colored tomalley and glittering roe with chopped onion and a little flour, marveling as the heat turned the gravy a succulent orange. The meat I poached in sieved brine with a splash of vinegar, the tender shoots, and a drizzle of black soy liquor.

This meal of poached lobster and fiddle-head ferns with tomalley sauce we ate in Mabbot's bed, eschewing both table and attire. We left the warmth of the blankets only to refill our cups with wine from the *Trinity* barrel. For dessert we ate one of the pomelos that hung like promises from the branches of Mabbot's tree.

Citing modesty and a well-deserved hangover, I must edit the engagements that occupied us until daybreak, and offer instead a few notes:

1. Much has been written about the relationship between culinary and concupiscent appetites and their mutually amplifying properties; it is all true.

2. Before this adventure, Owen Wedgwood was a dour and prudish man, and poor Elizabeth was married to him. But Mabbot has kneaded, seasoned, and simmered me. Acts that before would have seemed wanton and carnal, now come naturally. The body is beyond reproach.

3. Since childhood, I have had trouble imagining heaven, for, I'll say it, the descriptions have always disappointed. All my life, I have secretly searched for a credible glimpse of eternal bliss, in fern-floored

groves, in echoing cathedrals, and in the iridescent surface of a perfect stock. Had anyone told me I would have found it upon a pirate ship, I would have struck them down with a ladle. To those imagined persons, I offer an apology.

Wednesday, November 24
I had risen from the luxury of Mabbot's sheets to make tea, remembering that the little silver pot lifted from the *Patience* had been stowed with the tea itself and therefore might have escaped the jettison. I had just found it and was on my way back toward the companionway when Mr. Apples appeared and pulled me rather roughly by the arm to the lower deck hatch. Though he was still limping from his gunshot wounds, we moved so quickly that the pot chimed on the bulkheads as we rounded them. He pushed me into the pit without the courtesy of a ladder, and I found myself in the bottom of the bilge where the cold blood of the sea chilled the wood. It was a part of the boat I rarely visited for the sense of drowning it invoked.

Here Mr. Apples gripped my shoulders and lifted me bodily into the air. Even in the dim taper light I could see that his eyes were red from sleeplessness, and the stress of the recent days twined the muscles of his neck into cords.

He shook me and whispered harshly, "I know what you've done in there with the captain! I haven't had a single moment to do anything about it until now."

I went limp, knowing it was folly to try to resist. I was going to die here in the bilge with a teapot in my hand. How had I not seen that Mr. Apples loved her? Of course he did. I closed my eyes, ready for the blow, but it didn't come.

Without setting me down, he hugged the breath out of me. "Thank you," he said into my ear. "I was sure she was doing the airy waltz."

"Say what?"

"I thought she'd ducked into the circus tent, gone to see the show. The bone jig. I thought sure she was shark food."

"She's . . . strong," I stammered.

"Well, your soups pulled her through. We're all indebted. And not just your soups, I gather." He winked and left me there, and I took a moment to consider my strange life. I was trying to pull myself up without dropping the pot when I smelled something familiar. The air down there was musty and dank, but the odor I had detected was an altogether different offense.

I followed it aft toward the rudder, passing through murky chambers filled with cannonballs and heaps of heavy line. The odor compelled me to squeeze past the massive barrels of wine that served as ballast, fearing they would roll and crush me. With every step, the smell grew stronger, and now water was running in rivulets over my boot. I heard a muffled hammering. I moved slowly, not trusting my step. Soon enough I was ankle-deep in the fluid. Wondering if the barrels had broken, I dipped my finger and tasted it: fresh brine, not wine and not the stale sludge of bilge water.

In the aft chamber of the boat, deep below Mabbot's cabin, I became aware of a figure in the shadows. Water flowed past me at an alarming rate.

"Conrad!" I shouted. "What is going on? What is this?"

He rushed out of the shadows, and only because my limbs were still tingling from the fright Mr. Apples had given me was I able to move quickly enough to evade his attack. We both slipped on the planks of the submerged deck, I upon my arse and he face-first. He scrambled upright holding a large cooper's chisel that he had been knocking holes in the hull with. I tried to regain my footing, but he was upon me again, plunging the chisel at my face and hissing, "Think I don't see through yer tricks?"

Only by frantic squirming did I avoid his thrusts. I rolled and, without thinking, swung the teapot for his head.

There is a reason I am a chef and not a fighter. Hoping to knock him senseless, I instead only flayed open his brow, which sent a torrent of blood over his cheek. He fell to the floor and I stood above him, much conflicted. By the smell of the rum that mingled with his customary odors, I could tell he had been lurking in the holds drinking for quite some time.

"You'll sink us! For what?" I demanded.

"Lubber loses a foot and thinks he's a sailor?" he croaked. "I give years to the *Rose,* but when I got shot, I lay in the berths with the rest, begging for a sip of water. Everyone knows you're cavortin' in her cabin! Why you and not me? Because you can talk French. Shove a fig into a bit of hardtack and call it 'Springtime Fancy Pudding.' Charlatans, the both of you. She pretends to be a real captain, but she's nothing more than a slattern hungry for a poke. I saw you dressed for an opera walking the deck like a panderer and his trollop. And the hunt for the precious Fox that whittled

480

our days to the marrowbone — what does it get us? Nothin' but the dead son of a whore."

Crawling toward the chisel, he said, "And now she wants to take us into the hornet's nest? For a grudge! We've already got our silver, but she'll sail us straight to the bottom before we can spend a shilling. I'll not die for that. Better to wait for Laroche to catch up. He'll show mercy to them what show sense and cooperation."

As he pulled himself to his feet, I kicked him hard in the chest with my peg. I heard his collarbone snap, and he fell back into the rising water. I took up the chisel and called for help. Just when I was trying to figure out how to carry Conrad to the upper decks myself, Mr. Apples stuck his head through the aft hatch and said, "What's the holler? Are ye being murdered down there?"

"Saboteur!" I screamed. "I've found him!"

Mr. Apples brought a lantern and stood over Conrad with disgust plain on his face — no doubt considering whether to kill him on the spot. While Kitzu surveyed the damage in the hull, Mr. Apples tied Conrad hand and foot and carried him over his shoulder like a side of pork to the officers' saloon. We listened to Conrad's painful wheezing while we waited for Mabbot to enter and take her seat as judge. When she did, Mr. Apples shut the door against the crew who had gathered in curiosity. I was explaining what happened, breathless myself, when Conrad wheezed, "Lies."

He spoke in short bursts, for his collarbone was now grinding with every breath. "The man lies," he said. "I found him chopping the holes. I tried to stop him, but he overcame me and broke my chest."

Mabbot gazed steadily at me and panic poured into my ears. I had not imagined having to defend my own innocence. My jaw went slack. Mabbot asked me, "Do you have proof, Owen Wedgwood, as I demanded? Proof, I said, or no accusations could be made."

Mr. Apples started to speak, but Mabbot cut him off. "Let them speak for themselves." I was aghast.

"Proof?" I held out the chisel lamely. "But I took this *from* him. No, I have no proof, save what is clear before you. There was no time — I did not think."

"You know, Wedge, the punishment for accusation without proof is loss of an ear."

"Captain," whispered Conrad. "Forgive me, I was too surprised to overcome him." He seemed to believe the fantasy, and I wondered then if syphilis or some other seaborne worm had nibbled his sense to tatters.

"The hull sprung, and two men emerge bloody from the bilge," Mabbot said loudly enough for the crew outside to hear. "But Conrad has been with us for so long, and now he's wounded, and Wedge holds the weapon. Who would want our demise more than our disgruntled captive?"

At this Conrad smiled like a baby. This Mabbot terrified me — this was the voice she used to order theater paint and floggings. With the crew listening at the shutters, Mabbot could give me no quarter. My relationship with her meant nothing — worse than nothing, as the crew would want to know for certain that she wasn't playing favorites.

"I saw him on the night of the steerage explosion," Conrad went on. "I saw him pour the pitch myself, but I had no proof, so I waited and watched him. It was only by this vigilance that I caught him tonight."

"The steerage fire?" Mabbot asked. "You saw him then?"

"I did, Captain. I swear by it," Conrad croaked.

She knelt beside the man and, while looking at him, spoke to me. "Here, Wedge, is your proof. His lies condemn him. The night of the steerage fire —"

"I was asleep," I blurted. "I dreamed . . . a woman came to me —" Her swift glare shut my mouth and told me that she remembered all too clearly the events of that evening.

"No one wants to hear your ridiculous dreams. Enough that you were locked in your chamber, weren't you?"

"Yes. Mr. Apples had locked me in."

"And now, Mr. Apples, you were saying?"

"Only that Spoons was with me below — he weren't the one making trouble there."

The crew outside murmured as they passed the verdict to those who couldn't hear.

Conrad opened his mouth to speak, but Mabbot drew a blade from her boot and placed the tip of it upon his tongue and held him there; his eyes became egg yolks rolling in a bowl. From his throat came the sounds of a cat.

"He said he merely wished to slow us, to surrender to Laroche." I was hoping to soften things for him somehow — to let them know that he didn't want to sink us outright, but at this the crew outside began to shout, pounding upon the door.

Mabbot nodded at Mr. Apples and he ducked out and roared, "Is this a ship or a

484

menagerie? All men to the foredeck."

As the crew dispersed, I begged Mabbot. "I want to claim my reward. Keep the gold. Only do not torture this man. I ask this favor. Do not mutilate . . . Oh, for God's sake. I beg you."

She crouched there for some time, and I thought she might gut him like a trout with that blade.

Mr. Apples returned with a satchel from Conrad's locker — inside was a cask of water, waxed bags of figs, hardtack, and two ingots of silver. I shuddered — except for the silver, it could have been my own escape provisions poured out onto the table.

"What was it, Conrad?" asked Mabbot. "Row for land in a longboat while we ran about bailing the water from the bilge? Or did you fancy Laroche would give you a cut of my bounty?"

Conrad was silent, though. His gaze was fixed on the middle distance; he had retreated to a place somewhere deep inside himself. Even his breathing seemed easier.

"I'm begging you, Captain. Show him mercy."

Mabbot told Mr. Apples to lock Conrad away.

When they had left, she gripped my throat, but instead of choking me, this time her hand was soft. "Wedge, what are you doing to me?" she growled.

Then she let me go and collapsed back into her chair with a sigh. "I'm afraid I might have contributed to this particular mess," she said, running her hand over her shorn scalp. "Before you inspired me to take on a personal chef, I got it into my head that all Conrad needed was inspiration. I tried to get him to make some of the dishes I remembered, spotted dick, mince pie, that sort of thing. Poor soul, he took it very seriously. It was demeaning for both of us. I tried to coach him but —"

"The man could curdle water."

"They were worse than his usual fare, and the crew came close to mutiny. Your arrival must have stung the chap."

"He loved you."

"Who doesn't love me?" Mabbot joked, but her smile was weary.

Wednesday, Later

This afternoon Mabbot made an announcement to the gathered crew. "The saboteur has surrendered himself. For this I grant him a certain clemency." The men hissed, but Mabbot continued. "Meanwhile, you are forbidden to molest him in any way."

The mob grumbled and one sailor, a

cooper named Peter, yelled, "You promised theater paint!" At this the mob erupted with calls for blood.

"Sentencing is a captain's prerogative!" Mabbot yelled as she jumped from the poop deck into the crowd to confront Peter. "But the cooper would like to be captain." Mabbot took off her coat and tossed it to Mr. Apples. "In order to be captain, you must wear the captain's hat." Mabbot walked directly to the man and looked up into his eyes, for he was a head taller than she. She drew her knife and handed it to Peter. She said, "Are you ready to take my hat, cooper?" When the man's eyes flitted to Mr. Apples, Mabbot called back, "Mr. Apples, go and check the bowsprit lines, will you?"

After a breath, Mr. Apples strolled away, leaving Mabbot alone before the mob.

"Now, then," said Mabbot, "I asked you a question."

Peter's lower lip was quivering. "No'm," he said, dropping the knife.

"Can't hear you over the wind."

"No, ma'am. I don't want your hat," shouted the cooper.

"Are you quite sure you like being cooper with your hoops and barrel wood?"

"Yes, ma'am."

"Well, good. Because you make a fine

keg," Mabbot said, and the crew laughed as the tension broke. "Back to work!"

When the crew had dispersed, I took Mabbot aside. "Wasn't that reckless, Captain? Sending Mr. Apples away?"

"If this crew wants my head, even Mr. Apples won't be able to protect me. In the end I am alone on a ship of pirates with nothing but their respect to shield me. But your weak stomach doesn't make it any easier, Wedge. I have gone back on my word and disappointed my crew all for your aversion to blood."

"I thank you, Hannah."

"Of course, the crew will be much mollified if they have a proper meal. After all, we've lost a cook."

"That's not fair —"

"I insist."

"I cannot cook for you and them."

"Don't be modest." Then her face softened. "If you do find a spare moment to sleep, come to my cabin."

Thursday, November 25
The crew is much disgruntled not to have Conrad to torture. Mr. Apples has stationed the bosun at the cell door to keep vigilantes from the poor wretch.

To appease them I set to the galley. With

the help of Joshua, I threw together a cauldron of spicy shark bisque built on a blond roux and the last of the cayenne pepper. Herrings were fried and served with cornmeal biscuits and pickled hominy. When the modest repast was presented, it triggered an impromptu celebration. Before long I was roped into dancing with the men, striking my peg against the boards along with the music from the fiddles and flutes.

Thursday, Later

Rat-belly Island is a craggy atoll of algae and coral no more than an acre in total, with stunted trees and a thin rocky beach curving around a lagoon on the northern side. It is distant from any proper trading route and not marked on most maps. Here, Conrad has been put to shore to perish as a castaway. His shoulder hasn't mended and his left arm hangs useless.

Mr. Apples and two others escorted him ashore in a longboat to leave him with a knife and a Bible and little else. Before they pushed off, I threw into the boat a sack of cornmeal tied to a tin cup. Mr. Apples, considering my deviation from custom, looked to Mabbot for guidance. Mabbot shrugged. "So it gives him a few more days of loneliness. Here," she said, retrieving a

489

gold piece from the sack that had been tied to the mizzen. "Let him buy more when that runs out!" She lobbed the coin and it hit the man where he sat like a discarded doll in the bottom of the boat. The crew loved this.

Mr. Apples and the others in the boat each spat into the cornmeal before handing it to Conrad.

When the transport was complete, the cook stood lamely upon the beach as we departed. I couldn't help but watch him shrink in the distance, and I believe that, just before he disappeared, I saw him wave.

Saturday, November 27
Today we passed the mouth of the Pearl River, the seat of the Pendleton Trading Company. A telescope was passed among us, and I saw the white slabs of the massive Pendleton compound set like a tiered cake on the shore, commanding a view of the kidney-shaped harbor crowded with junks, merchant ships, hulks, and, indeed, navy vessels. This was the fulcrum of the Eastern trade. Kingdoms could rise and fall on the wealth carried in those ships. Tea enough to darken the sea, porcelain enough to build another Buckingham Palace from saucers and cups, and silks to swath the moon

passed through this crowded port, jostled on all sides by smugglers with boxes of opium going in the other direction.

The Pendleton offices were still and glaring in the sun above the bustling wharf. The sheer number of ships in the harbor frightened me. It would be only a matter of time before our thin disguise provoked curiosity. Our crew was uncharacteristically quiet, as if we were tiptoeing past a sleeping giant. We tarried not, and on each of our lips was a prayer that our freshly painted hull and false colors would grant us passage.

Mabbot broke the spell by shouting, "The Chinese call it the Barbarian House. Take a good look, gentlemen! It won't be there when we come back."

My mind is with Conrad. Helping Joshua with the great vats of chowder for the men, I find myself measuring his portions and days. Is there water on Rat-belly Island? Are there lizards to eat? My guess is very little of either. He may eat on the cornmeal for a week at the most if he can find some clean water to slake his thirst.

No doubt Conrad's reasons were sufficient to him. If a pirate like Mabbot does not wake of a morning with malevolence on her mind, if she sees her actions as the pursuit of justice, can't I give Conrad the same measure of doubt? I can't help but notice in retrospect that each act of sabotage occurred after Mabbot and I were indiscreet about our lavish rendezvous. It was easy to picture him muttering about us in the darkness as he took secret drinks from the rum barrel to steel his courage. I had labored under the fantasy of escape myself, so I could imagine what Conrad hoped for: Laroche welcoming him with open arms and a bag of gold. The men call Conrad a coward, but isn't it bravery to lift your chisel against a world that despises you? And then to take his chances on the currents with little more than a week's worth of food?

A lifetime of sleeplessness will not relieve me of this guilt. The man's death is on my head as surely as if I had dropped the guillotine. No matter that he was a criminal. It is a tangled knot of blame, to be sure; he had tried to ruin us all and would have fled in his boat with our charred bodies in his wake. And yet I cannot escape the grim fact that draws my breath up short as if my own collarbone were broken, that if not for my testimony, if not for my teapot cudgel, the man would be alive. Nay, there is no escaping that I have killed him, whatever may be said for the circumstances — I killed him, and it is precisely because I cannot see or invent a path that would have taken me out of the dark wood to goodness, not even in retrospect can I imagine a better course of action, that I feel I have become at last a pirate myself.

25

THE BARBARIAN HOUSE

IN WHICH THE SEA BOILS

Tuesday, November 30

When we were only a few miles northwest of the Pearl River, we sheered off to open seas and spent the night circling over several miles of water, tacking for three hours in one direction, only to turn and run free for an hour in the other. Such are the antics of a ship that has found her location but fears being caught at anchor.

It was under the last of the stars that we finally jibed back to anchor a few hundred yards from a craggy coastline punctuated by short stretches of black sand and eddying colonies of killdeers and plovers. An old hulk lay beached and belly-up on a plateau of guano-encrusted rock.

Mabbot was preparing to board a long-boat with Braga and two other men. I climbed in. Before she could object, I said, "I'll not leave your side. Someone will have to carry you back when you get shot."

Mr. Apples had his own objection. "Why not just send Braga to set the charges? He knows the tunnels."

"Feels rather impersonal, doesn't it?" Mabbot said. "This is something I'd rather do myself. We'll just nip in and dash out; have her ready to run."

As we rowed toward the hulk, I saw that the rising sun was cloaked by a thick curtain of purple clouds. "I'll be giving you a full share, Braga," Mabbot said. "If we manage this, you'll have more than earned it."

"I've been itching to see that Barbarian House drop since we dug the tunnels," said Braga. "My father was a fisherman, Portuguese. Pendleton sank him for a spy when his boat went too far up the river. After that we dug ditches to buy our bread. That's how my father died, holding a spade in the mud. When the Fox told me he was going to beat Pendleton at their own game, I never looked back. I was still digging, but the Fox made it feel like we were winning a war. He took care of his people. He paid his smugglers twice what Pendleton pays."

It was rare for Mabbot to listen without interrupting, but Braga had her ear. "He wasn't a bad man," he said. "He was just . . . insatiable. He couldn't help it. *Adamastor,* my father would have called him, a hungry storm."

Mabbot said nothing for a moment; her face was hidden by the wide brim of her hat. Then, very quietly, she repeated, "A hungry storm." After that we listened to the sound of the paddles on the water.

We anchored our boat just beyond the breaking surf and Mabbot told the rowers, "We'll be making a hasty exit. Be ready for us."

The derelict was high on the rocks with her port hull bleached white by sun. Between swaths of bird filth, she was stove in and rotted to lace. In some bygone era she had been a Dutch *botter,* then, by her roof, a hulk before she was too old even for that and cast here by a storm.

"There are other entrances," said Braga, "but they're a hike inland. Better not risk being spotted by a patrol."

We entered the wreck through a hole where her forecastle might once have been. Boulders jutted through her starboard hull; though high tide might rock her, she was permanently pinned to the shore. Light came in through the gaps in her wales, and its angle only magnified the unsettling slope of her decks. Planks crumbled like cheese as we passed over them. The water we

496

trudged through was fouled by tangles of rusted rings that I guessed were barrel hoops.

Deep in her belly, a mass of blue that I thought was seaweed scattered into hundreds of tiny crabs that slipped into the water and were gone.

"No surprises this time, Captain?" I asked. "I shan't be leaping from the deck with my hair on fire?"

"I make no such promises," Mabbot muttered.

"In we go," Braga said, pointing to the dark water between two outcroppings of stone where the entrance to the caverns was hidden.

"In?" Mabbot's eyebrows rose.

"We swim down five yards or so, then up into the chamber."

"I employ a team of swimmers so that I don't have to," Mabbot said.

"I can swim," I offered. "Cleave to me."

Braga tied his beard into a knot and dove headfirst into the pool, disappearing boots and all.

Mabbot gave an unhappy sigh, removed her hat, and wrapped her arms around me from behind. In we went. My fingers touched sand soon enough, but there was no sign of Braga, and it seemed we had dived into a well, sealed on all sides. Then Mabbot tugged my hair; she had found the shaft. We wriggled into it, then followed the tunnel for a several disorienting yards. My lungs were burning by the time the tunnel widened and I saw light above us. We emerged in a shallow underground pool in the floor of a slick-walled cavern.

It was clear that our arrival had made a tense situation worse. The Fox's paramour, Kittur, and one of the lascars from the schooner were pointing pistols at Braga. They had backed him against a wall and were interrogating him so intensely that they did not immediately see us emerge from the water.

As we wiped the brine from our eyes, we surveyed the echoing chamber; its ceiling was blackened with soot and its sloping walls were hidden by shadow. A small corridor led from the cavern behind us, and at the other end, a monstrous tunnel led deep into the earth. The light from their lanterns reflected off the pool and cast a shifting web of gold upon the ceiling of the cave, where tongues of rock let milky droplets upon our heads. Clusters of what I assumed were bats rustled in the darker crevices.

When the lascar saw us, everyone began shouting at once, and for a moment I thought we had come this far only to be shot dead in the water. Mabbot and I raised our hands to show that we held no weapons, and managed to make our way out of the pool. We were herded toward Braga, who was trying to calm the situation in his broken Laskari while Kittur screamed, "Silence all!" The bats, disturbed by the noise, swooped and darted overhead, making monstrous shadows on the ceiling. Hindi, English, and Laskari echoed off the wet walls, and for a moment I could not even make out individual words. But all yelling ceased when a ghostly moan came from the dark throat of the largest cave.

Kittur went pale and shook her head as if to keep the sound from her ears. Her companion held his lantern toward the darkness and shouted, *"Aap kahan hain?"*

"I take it that isn't the wind," said Mabbot.

Kittur did not answer.

"One of your crew? Have you sent someone in after him?"

"Of course!" said Kittur. "Four of us — three have gone in after the first, and none have come out. The last went in two days ago."

The lascar yelled into the darkness again, but the moaning had stopped.

Then he turned on us and whispered something to Kittur.

"Where is the map?" Kittur asked Mabbot. "You must have a map, or you would not have come."

"In fact, we do," said Mabbot. Reaching into her satchel, she produced a waxed sack and from it pulled the vellum map Mr. Apples had copied from the rug. The lascar grabbed it and peered at it in the yellow light of the lantern.

"Won't help," said Braga. "The map shows the safe routes only. Nothing about the rest. For every safe turn, there are three that'll take you into the devil's gut. The walls carry sound — that voice could be miles away, probably at the bottom of a pit a hundred feet deep, his back broken. Those men you sent in, they're gone. They're calling you to join them in hell."

The lascar spat and rushed into the gullet of the cavern with the map. Kittur screamed for him to stay, but within moments the light from his lantern had been swallowed.

The woman was shaking. How long had she been in this hole, going mad with worry, losing one comrade at a time? Mabbot approached her and said, "You aren't going to shoot us all, are you? I think it's time you gave me that gun, pretty one."

Kittur handed the weapon to Mabbot and sat ungracefully on the floor, her head in her hands. Her luxuriant hair, I now saw, had been cut in mourning, leaving the back of her head ragged. Her hands and face were filthy.

"Now we've lost our map," said Braga.

Mabbot pulled the prayer rug from her satchel and tossed it to him; it was wet, but the flowers were clear and bright. Mabbot was more concerned with Kittur, though. She gazed at the exhausted woman for a moment and touched her cheek gently before saying, "When my son stopped stealing tiaras and began to smuggle opium, I thought to myself, he's gotten a pocketful of patience somehow. The impulsive child has learned to hold out for the right moment. Where did he learn it? It's something I could never teach him. But then Wedge told me about you, lovely thing with the charts and the knowing smile, teaching him to meditate. And then this grand scheme to win his father's shares of the Pendleton pie. I realized a pair of pretty lips was whispering into his ear — telling him to bide his time. So here you are, the demon on his shoulder who steered him toward calamity."

Kittur was looking into Mabbot's eyes with growing fear, but she was clearly too exhausted to try to fight back.

Mabbot placed the barrel of the gun softly on Kittur's breast, as if to rest it there.

"He made his own plans," said Kittur.

"Oh, no." Mabbot showed her anger now. "I know my child — his blemishes as well as his beauty. He would not have gotten this far without . . . shall we say *guidance*. Oh, no doubt you let him *think* they were his plans, you played the muse, the clever pet, but the grand scheme was yours. The man would still be snatching rubies from drunken sheikhs without someone marshaling his troops, steering his vessel, telling him to breathe."

"No."

"Wasn't it your idea to seize me like a stray cow? Sell me to Pendleton? How did you do it? Did you wait until he was almost asleep? Pour your body over him and whisper your poison in the darkness? Whispering, whispering, *'We can sell your mother!'* "

"I swear —"

"You lie!" Mabbot cocked the pistol. "Leighton wasn't only impatient, he was greedy and stubborn. He came by that last honestly, I'm afraid. So damn stubborn. Far too stubborn to listen to even the most gilded tongue . . . unless he managed to love you."

Kittur was crying now, tears running down her face and mixing with the ceaseless rain from the ceiling. She dropped her head, apparently ready to join the Fox in the afterlife.

For a moment, the sounds of her weeping filled the cavern.

"Why are you crying?"

"He's gone!" she moaned without looking up.

"So you're all that's left of Leighton's heart." Mabbot stood and, after a moment, pulled Kittur to her feet. "The only other person in the world who loved him."

"You look just like him," Kittur whispered, wiping her eyes.

"Quite the reverse," Mabbot said.

"I'm sorry. We convinced ourselves that we could do it," Kittur said. "We would own Pendleton or break it. He made me feel it was possible."

"Well, we still might be able to break it. The blackmail game is over," said Mabbot. "Ramsey's shares will be scattered to a thousand stockholders. But we still have this surprise for Pendleton, this little party Leighton organized. No more negotiations, no more schemes. Only deliver the blow . . . That's why you're here, isn't it? To knock them back to England?"

"Braga," Kittur said, "you must believe me, we were coming for you. We were on our way to the prison when we learned that Mabbot already had you."

Braga coughed. "Doesn't matter what I believe. My debt was to the Fox."

"It matters. He remembered you well," Kittur said. "Please remember him."

"Enough," said Mabbot. "Is there black powder in these caves or no?"

"Tons of it. This was our last resort," mumbled Kittur. "But the rest of it, the rebellion, without the Fox, what's the use?" Her eyes gleamed with tears.

"Plans be damned. If any are still loyal to the Fox, tell them it is happening now. We may be able to spread this fire beyond these shores yet. Who knows, it may even spur China to start a war against Pendleton. Other companies will rush in to try to cut their own piece of the pie while Pendleton rallies, but China might try to put a stop to the opium trade altogether." She offered her hand and Kittur took it. "You must know that Pendleton will send every ship of the English navy to these banks, and they will not stop until they've restored their empire. I'd offer asylum on my ship, but after this you'd be safer disappearing in the cities somewhere. Do you have any fight left in you, child?"

Kittur nodded.

"Then rally every man you can. Lie to them if you have to, tell them the Fox is still alive. Tell them the moment has come. It is time to strike."

"I'll try." With that Kittur turned and started down the narrow passageway. She turned back and said from the shadows, "I'm sorry, Hannah Mabbot."

"I believe you," sighed the captain. "Now hurry." Kittur disappeared.

We followed down the gaping maw that had swallowed the lascar, then quickly turned down a short sloping chute that gave way to a gritty channel carved by powder and shovel and reinforced with repurposed spars. Our course alternated between the sinuous channels of the natural cavern and these short stretches of rough-hewn rock where Braga had blasted shortcuts through the maze. The tunnels branched and branched again; we stopped every hundred feet or so to consult the rug.

As Braga held the only lantern, I walked in darkness, finding my way by occasionally reaching out and touching Mabbot's back — I may have done this more frequently than was necessary. Given the course of my life in recent months, I would not have been surprised if we wandered into Satan's own court to battle specters and serpents, but as long as I was within arm's reach of her, I was where I wanted to be.

Very deep in the earth, we entered a cavern with neither ceiling nor floor. We were forced to skirt across a narrow ledge on the very lip of an emptiness I had not seen since I floated alone on the waves. As we overlooked that bottomless grotto, I couldn't help but clasp her belt tightly. A wind pushed endlessly up through the cavern, the earth itself exhaling. I was much relieved when we found our way again into a man-made hole.

Given the intestinal course, I could not have said whether we walked miles or yards, sometimes passing through natural caves on our hands and knees, sometimes tiptoeing past sloping walls of algae-slicked stone. Not a word was spoken; we might have been on a religious pilgrimage.

Finally we came to large gallery whose walls were lined with kegs and chests. Braga lit more lanterns, and I saw that smaller tunnels branched from this main room, and each led to chambers filled with such containers.

"All of this is powder?" Mabbot asked.

"Some of it is salt to draw off the dampness, but between this and the other chambers up ahead, there is nearly two tons of powder here. The Fox has always accepted gunpowder in payment for opium from those who could not put their hands on silver."

"And the Pendleton compound —"

"Is right above us."

"Get to it, then, my feet are itching for deck."

After only a few minutes of sorting lengths of fuses on the dark floor, Braga began to curse under his breath. We watched him in silence for a long time before Mabbot said, "Mr. Braga, can't we be of use?"

"Hell . . . I'll have to take the tunnels to the surface. In the confusion, I'll have a chance enough."

"I don't catch your meaning."

"They weren't ready. The fuses aren't long enough to give us time to get back. You two will have to start ahead. I'll give you enough to get to the hulk, and then I'll light them and head up through the warehouses. Just follow this vine on the rug" — he pointed to a particularly large blossom and the main vine from which it was suspended — "and you'll find your way out."

"How do you plan to reach the ship?"

"I'm not a seaman. I've lived on the banks

of the Pearl River all my life. You've brought me home."

"Can I count on you?"

"I'm in your debt, Captain, for pulling me from the hole on the penal island. And I owe your son considerably more — he gave me a way to fight. Before I lose my nerve, let's end this."

Mabbot said, "Good luck, Mr. Braga," and with that, we made our way back to the first cavern, running when we could. It was all I could do to keep up with her. I was terrified that the explosion would collapse the tunnels around us.

Once we made it to the entrance, I waded immediately into the pool, but Mabbot was peering back into the tunnels.

"Captain," I begged, "he did say to hurry, let's not be caught."

"That coward," she whispered. "He's not going to —"

At that moment the earth shifted beneath us like a rug pulled stiffly. The water at my waist lunged toward the ceiling. A heartbeat later an eruption of hot dust blew Mabbot into the pool. I grabbed her and dove under, scraping our chins and elbows as we struggled through the course and back up into the hulk, which was quiet and dark. I wasn't sure how long we had been underground and thought for a moment that the sun had set, but emerging onto the beach, I saw a sky gravid with indigo clouds.

The men began to row before we had even seated ourselves, saying, " 'Phoon, Captain! Getting blunky since you left. A typhoon for sure."

"Couldn't have arranged it better." Mabbot smiled, tugging on her ears to get the water out.

From the longboat we could see smoke rising over the banks.

As we neared the *Rose,* the distant Barbarian House came into view, and through the drizzle, we saw wisps of grey streaming from her once clean lines. Then, as we watched, it collapsed into a maelstrom of soot. The smoke rose to a morbid column, and I tried to imagine the men who had been swept up in that explosion, hoping too that Braga had made it to a safe distance.

There was no sound but the grunts of the rowers, and the water parting for their oars. As we watched, the smoke and dust was smeared by the wind into a pennant that would be seen for miles in every direction — the Barbarian House gone, Pendleton unseated.

Mabbot was very still as she looked at it, almost prayerful, then I heard her humming a merry reel under her breath as our view was obliterated by swift brushstrokes of rain. Then the *whump* of another explosion reached us, followed by anguished alarm bells, and Mabbot's song picked up pace. She stood in the little boat and sang, "Row, boys, row, boys!"

Asher had made good on his mission: two wide-bottomed dinghies, their hulls gleaming with black lacquer, were tethered to the *Rose*.

As we came alongside, Mr. Apples called, "Jack ladder for the captain!" He was in a hurry to get us aboard, and I shared the sentiment. What greeted me as I gained the deck, though, was an unwelcome sight: even through the increasingly foul weather, I could see ships between us and the sea, massive, lined for battle and flying the Royal Navy flag.

"See there, Mr. Apples," Mabbot shouted over the gale. "A land breeze to carry us out, quite considerate."

"Wouldn't call a typhoon considerate, ma'am, this wind is slant at best and getting more and more peevish by the minute. And anyway, the door is locked." He pointed to the blockade. "That's two first-rate warships and a gunboat, Captain. Ships of the line, and it's quite a line."

"We do have the weather gauge," Mabbot said, "such as it is. And we have our little surprises, don't we?"

"Only have powder enough for one of the dinghies. The other we've doused with oil, but she'll do nothing more than smoke."

"It will have to be enough. And your gunmen, Mr. Apples, are they ready for chain shot?"

"You're not thinking of running them athwart?"

"Do we have a choice?"

Mabbot and Mr. Apples were looking disconsolately at the blockade through the downpour.

"I'll have to sail the dinghy myself, towing the other," Mabbot said.

"I forbid it," Mr. Apples said. "The gunship alone has seventy cannon on a side. They'll sink those boats soon as they're in range."

"In this weather those ships will be heeling and rolling. Hard enough to keep your feet, let alone aim the guns."

"It's suicide, Captain."

"Better lose the boats than the *Rose*. And you can't do it, Apples; we've no chance at all without you at the battery."

"You didn't hear me volunteering."

"With foul wind and cross seas, we can't

511

set them unmanned on the course and hope they drift to their mark," said the captain. "We need an able hand. After all I've put them through, I'm not about to ask one of the crew to martyr himself —"

"Captain," I interrupted.

"Wedge, this is no time for jokes, you couldn't sail a bathtub."

"No, Captain, look."

She followed my gaze to where Bai was freeing the stay lines of the first dingy and swinging the boom into position.

Mabbot shouted, "Tsang Ju-long Bai!"

When he looked up, though, she was silent. They regarded each other across the storm-tossed water for a moment, then Bai went back to hoisting the halyard of the mainmast until the dragon-wing filled with a pop. The boat lurched into motion as the storm winds caught it. It tugged on its towline, and the second boat swung in behind it like a swan after its mate.

As the dinghies came alongside and passed us, Mabbot whispered urgently, "Shouldn't we stop him, Apples?"

"The man hasn't moved since he lost Feng," Mr. Apples said quietly. "He's saved my life a dozen times. By my book, he can do what he pleases."

The winds picked up, and when the boats

slid quickly past the bowsprit, something in Mabbot caught fire. "Make sail and crack on after those boats! Cut the mudhook, we haven't time!"

"Captain," Mr. Apples objected. "Without anchor, the typhoon —"

"The anchor won't help us fly. Right now we need wings."

"But what course?"

"Crowd the sails and run, Mr. Apples, I want you to put this storm in her bonnet. Bai is going to make a door, and we're going through it."

"We'll be open to raking fire."

"I'm not going to trade broadsides with three ships of the line, Mr. Apples. Damn it, do you want me to set these sails myself?"

One of the dinghies had already begun to smoke.

"Cut anchor!" Mr. Apples bellowed. "Stations, aloft and set every inch! Ready guns! All hands!"

The gong thrummed and the deck swarmed into action. The fireboats had crossed half the distance between us and the blockade. The smoke from the first was terrible. It danced toward the navy ships, churning with the driven rain into an opaque fog that obscured the middle warship.

The *Rose* gathered way with alarming speed. I had never seen all of her sails drawing on a good day, let alone in the teeth of a storm, and by the look on the faces of the men handling the lines, they hadn't either. Even when fleeing from Laroche, the topsails had been reefed to keep us from pitching into the swells. Now the sails were as swollen and numerous as the clouds. The masts creaked and moaned. Swift contrary gusts swung around from the lee and drove the masts down toward the water, only to release them to thrash again toward heaven. Despite our careening, we sped toward the blockade. The surf, whipped to foam by our bow, sent a white fountain over the bulwarks and onto the deck.

One seaman held desperately to a royal buntline that had come loose, and the wind beat him against the mast like a dirty rug.

The sound of cannon fire brought all eyes to the boats. The rigging of the first dinghy was ruined at once, and soon the mast collapsed entirely. She sheered off course and drifted, still belching black smoke, wisps of flame occasionally licking across her deck.

Then the paneled sails of the trailing dinghy lifted and were seized by the wind. Bai had leaped from the smoldering boat into the second and was holding its lines like reins as it picked up speed. Only seconds later it was lost in the smoke, though the sounds of cannon fire doubled and trebled.

The guns stilled for a moment, and in the caesura I could hear the bow of the *Rose* scudding against the waves. Then the second dinghy exploded, her frame lit for the briefest moment like a lantern in the gloom.

The wind shifted and the smoke from the first boat parted to reveal a black smoking scar on the stern of the middle warship. Bai had found his target, but the warship was holding her line. The *Rose* was speeding toward a collision. We might as well have been facing a firing squad. Still we galloped toward them. The gunship was the first to fire on us, and I saw the "raking" that had so frightened Mr. Apples. A single cannonball made its way from our bow to our stern and left as much damage as an entire broadside. Ten of our crew were cut down like reeds, two of our cannon tumbled into the sea, and the aft longboat burst into kindling.

Another missile punched through the forecastle and lodged in the foremast with a thud that I could feel in my lungs. Still the winds increased, and the *Rose* was nearly lifted from the water with her speed, sails cracking and popping and the masts bowed. Before I threw myself to the deck for cover, I saw lightning crackling between the masts of the warships we were hurling toward.

Then we entered the furious region within all three ships' range, and the world was turned upside down.

It seemed we were taking fire from every direction. Mabbot had climbed to the first yardarm of the mizzenmast to bellow her orders, and they made an unholy choir: the wind, the guns, Mabbot, and the thunder.

The storm enveloped us so thoroughly that, despite the howling and biting rain, the world was a washed slate. For a moment I couldn't see our own deck. Only the cannon fire lit the haze in ghostly blooms. We were moving through the clouds themselves. Then the cannonballs danced across the deck, sending spars pirouetting out over the water. I felt the *Rose* would be taken apart plank by plank.

Then there was a pause in the calamity and Mabbot roared, "It's open! The gate is open!"

The haze cleared enough to show that the warships were indeed parting. My hope was short-lived, however; I saw that they were maneuvering not to avoid collision but to engage *La Colette,* which had come in behind them from open sea.

"Laroche has joined the fray!" Mabbot shouted, her voice almost jubilant.

Mr. Apples's erratic course may have baffled the Frenchman for a time, but he must have been trailing close since our last encounter, and our errands had allowed him to catch up at last. The dreaded corvette was indeed coming for us, but, in the confusion of the storm, the warships had already launched a volley against him.

At first I thought it was blind vengeance that prompted Laroche's reckless advance, but then I remembered his arrangement with Ramsey and the Pendleton coffers emptied into his experimental ship. He must know his sponsor is gone and how little time he has left to prove his worth: only bringing Mabbot to justice could keep the man from debtors' prison or worse. If another ship brought home the prize, Laroche would be ruined.

"He can't stand to let the navy have us!" Was it the wind lashing Mabbot's eyes or was she really laughing? "The *Rose* is the belle of the ball and everyone wants a dance!"

As the navy ships turned in the water, I saw three Chinese warships tacking in from the south to defend their coast from the enigmatic conflict that had already ruined the wharves of the Pearl River. The "gate" we had hoped to speed through had become a viper's nest, a blind brawl. The sea itself was boiling, and we were the dumpling in the pot. Unholy light lit the heavens. Bullied by the storm, the navy gunship and her wounded sister collided, and their masts became entangled. Still their batteries barked and snarled like dogs in a pit.

The greedy fists of the world were scrambling for dominance, each against all, the screams of the dying drowned by the brute grunts of grenades and close-quarter carronades.

I watched as fishing junks torn from the harbor by the storm broke their spars against the hulls of the approaching Chinese warships that swept into the fight at an angry list with their battle flags burning brightly. The years of kowtowing in their own ports while foreign interests bled their country dry had clearly made them eager to send a barbarian ship to the bottom; their decimated harbor and a convergence of British naval vessels was the excuse they needed. Mabbot was right — the relations here were so precarious that they needed but a nudge to come crashing down.

One English ship had been trapped between its tangled comrades and the crack of the Chinese cannon. Like the story of the man who lost his nose to a hungry crow, the bowsprit of the warship disappeared in the first volley, leaving a ghastly hole rimmed with guttering lines.

As the *Rose* raced past the furious navy ships, Mr. Apples, who had been waiting until he could send our shot through them lengthwise, finally gave the order to fire. Our guns roared, and, though it was horrible, I was compelled to watch as the navy decks were raked by the entire might of our close-quarter assault.

From Mabbot's perch came the call: "Bai is giving them hell!" Indeed, I could see a crowd of marines on the deck of the gun-ship converging toward his solitary figure. From a distance, his final fight on that canted deck looked like the culminating movements of a ballet. As I watched, the herd of marines closed around him, and he disappeared in the smoke that unfurled from their muskets.

"Heave to for Bai!" Mabbot screamed.

But Mr. Apples wouldn't allow it. "Cannot save him! Bai died with Feng; that is his ghost giving us a gift. We must take it, Captain!"

We were now receiving fire from *La Co-*

lette, which was maneuvering to intercept us just as we slipped past the navy ships.

Mr. Apples himself rushed to help reload the guns with chain shot.

As the caprice of the wind forced Laroche to come at us prow-first, it seemed that we would be spared the full brunt of his broadside guns. But as he swept in, we saw a battery of strange bundles fixed to the foredeck. I watched with horror as the sinuous tails of a dozen rockets snaked toward the *Rose* to deliver a cascade of bone-rattling concussions. Despite the hail of destruction that punched through our sails, despite the bodies that slid about the deck with every lurch, Mr. Apples did not respond. He was waiting for just the right angle.

I saw Laroche on the bow of his ship, his braid like a pennant in the wind. His cutlass was raised, and his mouth was open wide with commands I couldn't hear.

Just when Laroche's marines had reloaded the rockets, Mr. Apples finally gave the call and the chain shot was launched. This, then, was the perfect timing he had been training his men for: pairs of cannonballs linked by ten yards of heavy chain swung though the heavens. The first volley merely ruined the rigging of the mizzen. But the second cut the foremast of *La Colette* clean through. It plummeted like a tree, and Laroche dove for safety as the sails shrouded his forward batteries.

On we raced, giving *La Colette* every shot of our starboard guns as we passed. Only seconds later I heard the Twa Corbies growl and hoped they had delivered a deathblow.

My heart leaped up as I saw a clear path to a stormy but open sea. By the noise, the shells had cracked the firmament itself and brought it crashing down behind us. Through the rain, though, I could no longer tell which ship was which. The ghastly fulminations continued to light the gloom, but, it seemed, no more balls were making it to our ship.

The *Rose* rolled terribly as we sped on, and her sails looked like a beggar's rags, but the storm drove us away from the savage arena.

I am alive. The thought pealed like a carillon in my skull. Even as I leaped from the foredeck to find survivors, it echoed throughout my being: *Alive.*

Many of the merely wounded had crawled down the companionway to avoid the bursts of shot. The dead slid on the gore and made a grim pile against the port bulwark. With most of the remaining crew busy trying to keep the sails from tearing from their stays,

I was alone in trying to find the source of the moaning that came from that heap.

I told myself that the jumbled limbs were nothing but cuts of pork as I tried to sort through them. Then the ship rolled and the corpses moved as one, sweeping me off my feet. For a moment I was swimming among them, trying to keep my head above the wet tumble of bodies. Was it seawater or blood that had smeared itself across my lips? I wanted to scream but was afraid to open my mouth.

A scarlet hand came to life and tugged at my shirt. I found myself looking into Asher's eyes. His left arm and shoulder were simply gone, as if bitten off. He was trying to speak and fumbling at his belt with his remaining hand. There I found Feng's little book of sonnets tucked behind his hip. I put it on his chest and wrapped his hand around it, but he was already gone.

Behind me, Mabbot leaped to the deck and handed Mr. Apples the telescope. She pointed aft, to where the man-made thunder still rumbled. "What do you see?"

It took him a moment, then he said, "It's *La Colette.* She's making distance from the fight, but she's smoking like a cigar."

"It's only a matter of time before he rigs a

522

new mast. Put a sea between us, Mr.
Apples."

26
THE LAST SUPPER
IN WHICH I FIGHT FOR MABBOT

Monday, December 6

Am I now free? Is this the liberation I so ardently prayed for? We are through the Sunda Strait, and if the southeast trade winds remain faithful, we are mere weeks from the New World. There I may walk away from this damned ship forever. But I shall set down the facts as they occurred in the hopes of bringing some order to my torn spirit.

Only three days ago, but it feels so long ago already, I was cooking for the radiant Hannah Mabbot.

As Kitzu was not only occupied with the Herculean task of repairing the riddled *Rose* but had also suffered injuries from the rockets, I could not hope to have him fishing for me. Instead I turned to the men who clambered over the hull of the ship, lashed to monkey ropes, sealing, patching, and painting. I begged them to bring me anything remotely edible from below the water-line and ended up with a bucket of Oriental whelks.

The eating of terrestrial snails was the one French habit that I had never acquired. It had always seemed to me that the trouble it took to clean the slimy creatures wasn't worth it; the best thing about the chewy little nubs was the butter they were sautéed in. Sea snails, though, were a different matter, as they held up as well as clams or oysters in any sauce.

I saw that the men, having drained one of the massive Madeira wine casks to make their panch, were about to wash and repurpose it to stow rope. I stopped them just in time and scraped from the dregs a good quantity of wine lees, dark and heady. I could not help but think of Leighton's body, curled like a fetus in his wine casket in the bilge.

Those who had died during the battle had been solemnly sewn into sailcloth, the last stitch piercing their noses. The sound of the sail hook crunching through the septum made clear to me the reason behind the custom: it confirmed the dead, as any man who had yet a single ember of life in him would rise howling at that final offense. They sank into the water as a seaman played a mournful dirge on a viola. But Mabbot had decided that Leighton would be buried in soil. She intended to plant her pomelo tree over his head.

The men repairing the hull scraped the old planks down for repurposing, and I followed them, the gleaner in the field, gathering sea snails. The whelks were poached in the wine lees just long enough to curl their outer lips. As the lees lent a melancholy aubergine to the snails, I sprinkled them with pepper, glad for the simplicity. Brine being their element, they had no need of salt.

The rabbit, as tender as aging would make it, was cut into small chunks and browned with flour and lard. Having mastered the technique for our tart a few weeks earlier, Joshua and I chilled the crust shortening in the cold depths of the sea.

The filling for this savory pie consisted of a roux, caramelized onions, browned rabbit, diced apricots in brandy, roasted bone stock, and the last of the bay leaves.

For dessert I toasted walnuts in a skillet, adding cinnamon, black pepper, ginger, honey, rosemary, and a pinch of salt until they began to clump. Then I removed and separated them to cool.

That evening, cozy as ducklings, Hannah

and I dined on whelks in wine lees and brandied rabbit pie with apricots. We finished the meal with spiced candied walnuts.

What can be said about that pie? Some foods are so comforting, so nourishing of body and soul, that to eat them is to be home again after a long journey. To eat such a meal is to remember that, though the world is full of knives and storms, the body is built for kindness. The angels, who know no hunger, have never been as satisfied.

Mabbot wept a little as she ate the pie. Seeing her, I too fought the urge to cry as the taste began to assuage the anguish of the recent days.

Mabbot's cabin had been properly reorganized and cleaned after the mess the storm had made of it. We had finished our meal, and though Bai was not there to play for us, we held each other and danced a slow waltz, my peg tapping a hollow beat.

Though I tried, I couldn't suppress my anxiety. "If Laroche repairs his masts —"

"We are running as fast as we can, Wedge. But time is on our side. His men must know by now that Ramsey is dead. They've received their last pensions, and who knows how long their provisions will last. I need only wait him out." Then she whispered, "But if you stay here tonight, we may find ways to pass the time."

"Aye, you could lock me in my cell and I would still find a way to you, Captain," I said.

"What, free yourself with a flattened spoon?" she asked. I stopped dancing. "Close your mouth," she said, "you'll catch flies. Oh, for pity's sake, don't get in a huff. On this boat a rat does not piss but I know it. You described your escapes so well in your little diary."

"How long have you been reading . . . but I hide it!"

"Right. Who might have found it?"

"Joshua."

"Don't be angry at the boy, Wedge, I made him. He hated doing it. But you have taught him to read fairly well!"

I was chuckling a little, thinking of how all of my attempts to desert had been so artfully frustrated.

"Can you blame me, Wedge, for wanting you near?" Hannah leaned in, lifted my chin, and kissed me.

This was the moment when the world came apart; a burst of wood, glass, and sea mist hit me hard.

The cannonball shattered the windows and lodged itself in a rafter.

We were unscathed and had a fraction of

a second to stare at the thing: an ordinary cannonball save for a surface riddled with peculiar holes. I had time enough to remember the smell of pig shit on grass.

Laroche had taken his time aiming the shot, using our candlelight to send the missile home. It sat embedded in the wood above Mabbot's mirror as if it had always been there. It was the slimmest slice of time, two heartbeats at most, for the sound of the cannon had not reached us, and yet I had time enough to feel the chill from the sudden hole in the wall, to see flashes of light out there, to smell Hannah's skin, an aroma almost like bread, the yeast tang of her shorn scalp, the white tea of her cheeks, the caramel of her breath, time enough to regret that those perfumes were being overpowered by the sulfur coming from the cannonball. Wisps of white smoke issued from its pocked surface.

Mabbot shot from her seat, intending, I presume, to pry the missile from the wood and heave it out the window. It was then that the thing exploded, sending from its bores smaller shot throughout the room.

Mabbot's chest was sopped with blood and she fell back into my arms. She had, intentionally or not, shielded me. The wound was grave, and Mabbot, looking into my eyes, said with a smile, "A terrible misunderstanding, but I'm sure it's nothing."

Mr. Apples burst into the cabin, saying, "Captain — !" He stopped short, seeing Mabbot in my lap.

"It's bad in here, Apples," Mabbot wheezed.

"Very bad out there, Captain." Mr. Apples had to bend down to hear her whispers.

"Surrender. Have the boys put the lockpicks under their tongues. Chew your way out if you have to."

"Laroche won't take you alive."

"Let me handle that."

The sound of cannon fire, rent timber, and the desperate coughs of pistols sent Mr. Apples rushing out, and we were alone again.

I cannot say how long I held her in my arms and pushed upon the wound to stanch the flow.

She whispered, "You must tell them you're my captive, Wedge. Promise me. Or they'll kill you. I would not have you die."

Then she went limp, and despite my shaking and calling her name, the color drained from her face.

After some time I became aware again of the screams and gunfire. Outside, Laroche was conducting a massacre. He lobbed sticky masses of sulfur and phosphorus, which lit our deck with a stark glare and from which fire spread in all directions. Peering from Mabbot's cabin door, I saw that his ship was operating in complete darkness and was invisible in the moonless night except for the brief glimpses afforded when the weapons were launched.

Further, he seemed to have a deck gun capable of firing many bullets in quick succession, and with this he mowed down our crew as they emerged into the unearthly light.

Like an animal I went back and forth from Mabbot's body to the door, watching the calamity unfold in bursts.

Only when Mr. Apples threw his gun to the deck, tearing his shirt off to wave in surrender and ordering the others to do the same, did Laroche relent.

Within half an hour, the *Rose* was boarded and our crew bound in shackles and led to the bowels of *La Colette.*

I had locked myself into Mabbot's cabin.

When Laroche knocked the door down, accompanied by a Norwegian giant, I missed the twins acutely.

Even in my grief I noticed that Laroche seemed much older than the few years should have made him: his eyes seemed to bulge from their sockets, and tufts of hair hung loose from his queue. As he entered and saw Mabbot's body, he gasped with animal pleasure and his hand went to the locket around his neck.

I was seized by the goliath and would have joined the others in chains if I hadn't said it: "You know me, Laroche! I am Lord Ramsey's chef, taken captive."

Looking at the table and candles, Laroche asked, "You dine with her?"

"Je n'ai pas le choix," I said, finding it easier to lie in his language. "She forces me."

The foulest lie ever uttered. No matter that Mabbot had begged me to say it with her last breath. Laroche seemed not to notice my cheeks blooming with shame and rage.

"Very well, consider yourself rescued," he said. His brass buttons glittered in the candlelight against the black cotton. His uniform was unnaturally clean and still bore the faint symmetrical lines of a clothes brush; he had dressed for this moment. "Take her aboard *La Colette.*" His thug obeyed as Laroche muttered, *"Il m'a fallu deux semaines pour tuer les scorpions."* Just outside the door, though, in the bright light of his unnatural flares, he stopped his man, wanting to gloat over his prize. "Let me see her face."

The pale giant yanked back the sheet he had lifted her body in, and Laroche leaned down to have a closer look.

The blast made all of us jump. Laroche stumbled back, a great arc of blood leaping from the hole in his heart.

Mabbot, weakly holding the gun she had slipped from his belt, whispered, "You and I will have to agree to disagree, Laroche."

She dropped the gun and went limp before the giant, like a frightened child, flung her body into the sea. He immediately drew his chambered pistol and fired six rounds into the churning darkness where she had disappeared.

With a wail, I scrambled over the railing to leap after her, only to be caught at the last moment by the behemoth, who lifted me and flung me to the deck. I hurled myself against the man and loosed my hurt upon him, slamming my forehead into his nose and flaying my knuckles against his face until he fell back, ghastly and still.

Though I leaned far over the railing, I could see no trace of Mabbot — only foam and a stray barrel that the waves crushed against the hull.

Nearby, Laroche lay grey-skinned and

gasping. He had torn the locket from his neck and held it out to me. It opened to reveal the silhouette of a young maiden.

"Dites leur," he groaned. "You must tell them how close I came. I have given all."

I watched the locket drop from his shaking hand and said nothing. A dreadful stillness came over me as he breathed his last.

I readied myself for death, expecting to be shot by Laroche's soldiers, but when I looked up from the sea, I was surprised to see them firing upon *La Colette* instead.

The ships were side by side now, with both decks lit by the fires. Mr. Apples and the others, having picked their locks, had taken Laroche's ship from the inside and overwhelmed the guards. They had few weapons, though, and were pinned in their position behind the mainmast. In the torchlight, I perceived that the reloading rifle was mounted upon the bow of *La Colette* and had been turned against Mr. Apples's uprising. They hid behind the masts and crouched in the lee of the mizzen deck but could not move because of the crossfire they were receiving from the soldiers who had boarded the *Rose.*

Navigating the deck, which was black with blood, I made my way to the quarterdeck gun, the largest loose cannon on the *Rose.*

Leaning all of my weight into its locks, I freed it and watched as it rumbled across the deck, accelerating like a charging bull. I ran after it as it crushed Laroche's men. One leaped to safety, only to be knocked senseless by a jab from my peg. I became aware that I was bellowing. Another marine, to avoid being crushed, flung himself into the ocean.

I thus cleared the deck of enemies. Rather than burst through the railing as I expected, though, the cannon slowed as the sea shifted and reversed its direction. It chased me for fifteen feet before falling through a damaged hatch to the lower deck.

Seeing this from their shelter on *La Colette,* my comrades sent up a cheer. They were still pinned, however, by the reloading rifle, which operated by crank and was fed by a seemingly endless belt of bullets.

Joshua was with the rest and, reading Mr. Apples's lips, signed the message to me. The ship was pitching, and in the unnatural light I had to peer hard to see his fingers tracing the wisp of a fuse and the swift arc of his fist: "Fire the forecastle cannon."

I had to go below to get to that gun and, my mind blunted by catastrophe, did not plan my course well. I leaped with speed down the starboard companionway before I

535

remembered the loose cannon pacing there on the shifting deck. The phosphorus above had burned to a sputter and filled the air with a spectral smoke. I was inching carefully toward the door when I heard the cannon charging through the haze.

Only by diving headlong behind the windlass did I avoid being smeared onto the deck. The main anchor having been severed, the chains on the windlass were loose, and I swung several loops around the foot of the cannon before it could begin rolling again. I rushed then to the port forecastle gun. There, trying to remember all of the steps in order, I loaded the charge, then the ball, packed it home, pricked the charge and filled the vent with powder, and readied the flint. This may have taken two minutes, but with shaking hands and my heart in my throat, it felt like hours.

I opened the shutters easily, but pushing the cannon out took all my might. Finally, when the deck shifted with the sea, the gun rolled into place and I locked it home. I erred low, as I had been taught; for close range, it was better to hit the water than the air, for a ball would still skip into the target. Only a dozen yards separated the ships and I could clearly see the young, frightened soldier who operated the repeating gun on the bow of *La Colette.* The soldier quivered visibly, yet had not perceived my advantage. I wondered if he was perhaps the same soldier who had shattered my leg.

It was my moment — but with power enough to erase this young man, I hesitated. The blood rage that had fueled my murderous rampage across the ship had ebbed just enough for me to begin to feel the deep abyss of grief below it. Conrad, the invisible lords in the Barbarian House, the *Patience,* Feng and Asher, hundreds of men broken into kindling in a few short months. And now Mabbot: Could it be true — Mabbot too? Why not fire? Who was this thin whelp to me? Why not add one more body to the pile?

Perhaps I am not a pirate after all; I did not fire. Instead I rapped on the muzzle of my cannon with a marlin spike, ringing it like a bell to let him know I was there. He wheeled upon me and we faced off across the gap. With the cannon in place, he could see but a few inches of me. He was fully exposed to a twenty-pound cannonball while I was hidden by hull and steel. Seemingly relieved to be thus outmaneuvered, he released his gun and lifted his hands into the air. He was quickly stormed by my comrades and taken to join his colleagues in chains. As Mabbot had guessed, Laroche's men were weak with scurvy and lack of sleep; a good many of them were eager to surrender.

It was a gruesome night with blood on my hands and many on both sides feeding the sharks. The sun was high in the sky before the fires were fully extinguished.

Worse, though, far worse, Mabbot was gone. Not ill, not asleep, not hidden in her cabin waiting to mock me with her knowing smile, but gone.

Despite the desperate dives by the swimmers, her body could not be found. Though they seemed willing to swim until they too drowned, Mr. Apples finally called them back to the ship, and at that, our crew broke into a feral howl. I lent my voice to that ghastly chorus, screaming until my voice broke.

My servitude is over, my mistress defeated. I am free to leave the ship, free to find my way to any port in the world, free to take up a life of my choosing. Yet I have barely the will to scratch these letters onto the page.

Tuesday, December 7
After much debate and emergency repairs, the crew has split in twain, and thus one pirate vessel has become two. Many chose

to man *La Colette,* a bizarre craft with many deadly devices aboard. A terrible weapon it will be in their hands.

The smoke balloon was discovered folded tightly into a hold, and, last I saw, the men were teaching themselves to inflate it, tinkering with the wicker rudders. They have taken with them the prisoners whose fate is yet to be decided. Some argued for leaving them on Rat-belly Island with what is left of Conrad, who may yet provide one more unappetizing meal. Others called for immediate execution, while I added my voice to those calling for delivery to the nearest harbor. After all, Laroche was dead, and his crew were guilty of little but obedience.

Before going their separate ways, all of the men were awarded their share of the *Trinity* haul. I myself, had I been a proper pirate on contract, would have been awarded a share and a half due to my lost limb. As it was, I received a share, and that due only to the fairness of Mr. Apples.

Old Pete, the navigator, is gone without a trace. Lost, no doubt, in the battle. "It's fitting, I guess," Mr. Apples said. "Naught but Mabbot could understand him."

Mr. Apples, myself, and a skeleton crew have chosen to stay on the *Flying Rose.* He has assumed the rank of captain with an iron fist, and while he tolerates the men to show their grief with drink and song after the watch, he has excused none from their duties. His own sorrow is barely visible under the mask of discipline that serves to keep the crew and ship from falling into chaos, but the clues are there: No one has seen him eat or sleep in days. When the men erected a shrine upon Mabbot's stuffed chair, piling it with notes and gilded shells and tokens of their love, Mr. Apples broke his knitting needles in twain and laid them atop the heap.

After a day sitting still upon the water (I think Mr. Apples was secretly hoping, as I was, that Mabbot would crawl from the sea, crowned in glistening seaweed), we maintained course for the Americas, where it would be safe enough to set to port and recruit a full and proper crew. We've knocked the wasp's nest to the ground, and all agree that the New World is a decent distance from which to watch China and England duel for control of the trade.

Mr. Apples has agreed to go two weeks out of his way to deliver Joshua and myself ashore in Martha's Vineyard, Joshua's home.

EPILOGUE

Tuesday, July 15, 1823

I wear, about my neck, Kerfuffle's foot, and when not covered in flour, my hands inevitably find their way to worry its silken fur.

My share amounted to seven bolts of silk, nineteen ingots of silver, three hundred and fifty pounds of tea, and several cases of varied spices. With this wealth, Joshua and I have established our inn, the Rose, near the busy wharf on Martha's Vineyard, setting the tables with our own stolen china.

This community's hands are in the water, but its heart is nested on land. Following the sun, the fishermen return to their wives and sleep on beds that do not sway beneath them. Of a Sabbath, families picnic in the orchards, and the children feed the geese with bread fresh enough to make a pirate weep. A modest town, it has none of London's bustle, the endless clopping of hooves on cobblestone, or the hawkers selling their baubles beside the filthy gutters — here there is nothing louder than the distant jangle of the gulls at the docks. There are no towering buildings and the market is humble, yet I have everything I need. What goods I cannot get here, like the indispensable miso, the whalers or rum-runners bring me from distant shores, and I haven't set foot on a ship since my return.

Joshua is as excellent a host as he is a cook, leaving me at peace to invent new dishes and tinker endlessly upon an enormous custommade fourteen-square-foot stove of steel bound magnificently with brass. Our menu last night: grilled miso-glazed cod with fava beans; goose liver and sumac quiche; haunch of lamb with poached pears and fennel root; and roasted pecan ice cream.

Of an evening, Joshua regales the guests with stories of his adventures upon the sea. His dramatic flourishes draw a crowd, but the best seat is always reserved for his mother, who without fail wraps herself in the shimmering green silk shawl he placed around her shoulders the night he returned. So painterly is he, evoking the rocking of the ships and slowing a cannonball for every eye to see as it passes, that even visitors to the island who don't know the hand language are entertained by Joshua's tales. If there are many of them, I sometimes volunteer to translate. We draw a spate of tourists from the mainland who stay in our beds above the tavern's great room, where a fire always burns in the hearth to dry a sodden traveler. It has become a sign of high fashion to say one has eaten something unique at the Rose, such as Pilfered Blue cheese soup with fried plantains or anise-rum sorbet. We ship our Black Rabbit Ginger Ale to New York by the boatload.

Joshua spent his own share as only the young can, though at sixteen he considers himself a man. He has built his mother a two-story house and sails his handsome yawl to and from the mainland. Soon enough his culinary skill will surpass mine.

He has married a lovely young woman. Their first child, to their delight, is also quite deaf. The beauty babbles with her hands. Joshua calls me her grandfather. I will do everything I can to live up to the honor.

Almost daily we read stories of trouble brewing on the Pearl River. Our little commotion was enough, it seems, to give particularly conservative officials in Canton control of trade there. China has not allowed Pendleton to reestablish the Barbarian House on its shores and, further, has placed ever more strict embargoes and taxes on tea, silk, and spices to discourage opium smuggling. I know that I cannot fully trust the papers, but if it is true that England is planning to blockade Canton, then war is inevitable. Mabbot would have been thrilled. Of course, Mr. Apples, if he is still on this side of the waves, will do his best to make things hard on Pendleton. (I admit I miss the brute. One of the old salts who eats breakfast here is the Michelangelo of scrimshaw, and I have commissioned a pair of whalebone knitting needles that wait on the hearth in case Mr. Apples ducks through our door someday.)

But that is all so very distant now. I may wonder sometimes, while watching the sunset, whose blood has stained the skies, but except for the ever-soaring price of tea, life here is little affected by those dramas.

This near the sea, one cannot escape the sailors' tales: lies about giant squid and mermaids with their strangling locks. Once in a while I hear them talking about Mabbot, saying she is still out there, with a demon in her pocket and her red hair aflame. Some say she captains a phantom vessel that travels ten feet above the water, a vapor ship that cannonballs cannot touch. Many say they have personally seen her leading a pirate armada and that the sea is whipped into a bloody froth by her merciless assault against all that is "proper." I know it isn't true. At night, though, when my leg aches and my room becomes chilly, only dreams of Mabbot's sly grin can keep me warm, and I cannot help but consider the quiet, calloused whaler who seemed to truly know her. Not a braggart, he told his story to Joshua and me late one night after everyone else had retired. Mabbot rescued him, he said, not three months before he came to our tavern. His vessel had run aground and capsized and a red-haired woman risked her own sleek schooner to come alongside and throw lines to his crew. At the bow, he said, was a withered old man staring at the waves.

Who does it hurt if, sometimes, I let myself believe it?

I gave Leighton a service upon a green hill under some oaks, burying him barrel and all. I paid one hundred mourners to attend and fed them all rabbit pie. I worried much over the epitaph and finally decided upon something simple, lest his body be disturbed by those who bear grudges against his family. The headstone reads, simply, BE-LOVED OF HANNAH. It may seem a humble elegy, but I would be honored, when the time comes, to have the same written upon my own stone.

ACKNOWLEDGMENTS

I thank the following for their generous help with the book:

Melissa Michaud, Tonya Hersch, Anna Mantzaris, Sarah Steinberg, David Goldstone, Stephen Canright, Ben Steinberg, Julie's Tea Garden, Iva Ikeda, Ella Mae Lentz, Jenny Cantrell, Nova Brown.

Special thanks to my tireless champion, Laurie Fox, and to the wonder-worker Courtney Hodell, who edits like books still matter.

ABOUT THE AUTHOR

Eli Brown lives on an experimental urban farm in Alameda, California. His first novel, *The Great Days,* won the Fabri Literary Prize.